The Regnant

The World of Geoe, Volume 2

Shawn McGee

Published by Assetstor, 2022.

THE REGNANT

First edition. November 7, 2022.

Copyright © 2022 Shawn McGee.

ISBN: 979-8215545201

Written by Shawn McGee.

This book is dedicated to my wife who supported me, and listened to questions all year despite not liking fantasy.

Chapter 1

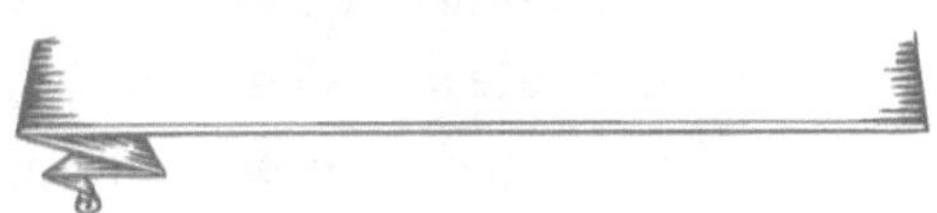

My head swirled and I fell backward into my chair in confusion. *Where am I?*

Home. I was in my new home in my new city of Sardyna on my new planet of Geoe. My living room wavered into focus and I ran my fingers over the blue cloth of my chair. I placed my chair here since it gave me views of both doors and both main rooms. Both front and back doors remained shut. My magical fires, cast from two *Fistful of Fire* spells, burned in the open hearth that separated this room from the kitchen.

Why did I stand?

Talindra called out from her office, "Honey?"

I made sure my voice sounded calm, then replied, "One sec. I got dizzy."

"Me, too."

I placed my hand on the wall, steadied myself to a standing position, and circled into the hallway. Two steps around the corner and I stepped into her office. She sat in her chair, a book laying open on the floor. Her plate armor sat displayed on its mannequin, but she still wore her sword on her side. I grabbed the book, *Religious Spells in Combat*, and placed it on the desk. "Are you okay now?"

She held her desk with both hands. "It's just..." She didn't finish, but her eyes focused on me and she released her desk.

I offered her my hand. "Let's go upstairs and check on Kitara."

Kitara had the upstairs of the house we rented from Innkeeper Braun. We followed the stringent requirements Sardyna enforced upon adventurers, Knights of Honor, and Sardyna University mages. The strangest rule dictated that Talindra and I had to spend a minimum of two hundred gold every month on living expenses inside the city.

Stepping outside, I noted that Naomi, my hawk cast with *Magical Friend*, sat in a tree across the street, watching our front door. Skirting the porch, we jogged up the wooden stairs, where I knocked on the door.

Talindra reached around me and entered, calling out, "Kitara? Are you okay?"

I followed her into the kitchen, where Scruffles, Kitara's owl, cast with *Mage's Ally*, watched us pass.

"I'm in here," he yelled from his living room. We followed his voice to find him picking up broken glass from the floor. Looking up as we entered, he sniffled with tears in his eyes. "These damn things," he placed his hands on his breasts, "I thought they'd be the best part about turning into a chick, but they get in the way."

Talindra put her hand on my shoulder and nodded gently. "You go downstairs, I'll help Kitara."

"Wow, neither of you brought a pad. Something is wrong." He wiped his eyes. Kitara had handled the surprising change into a woman's body well. Today looked like an exception to his normally stoic nature.

Although we looked the same age as Kitara in these new bodies, I had the benefit of thirty years of marriage to Talindra that taught me she could help him more than I could right now.

I did a quick check of my gear. My robe and staff were in my bedroom with that annoying sash. I picked up the bandolier and slipped it over my arm so that it snapped into place on top of my required noble silks and furs. My position as team leader for the Guardian Knights, a mage with the Master of Materials title, and a researcher at Sardyna University dictated my clothing. My bandolier held the squares for my keys, spell books, my game pad, and other holding slots.

As I finished positioning the sash, Daisidian and Marick entered the house with Gormesh. A year ago, having three friends—a halfling, a blue-tinted elf, and a half-orc—would have seemed preposterous.

"You can stop freaking out, OG," said Daisidian. He landed on the other side of the room in his favorite chair.

"We wanted to warn you," said Marick, "but they jumped the gun." He sauntered into the kitchen and grabbed two oranges, tossing one to Daisidian.

I inhaled deeply and collected myself. Talindra and the rest of the team were safe. A few even breaths later, my panic had subsided. "Who jumped what gun?"

"Where are Talindra and Kitara?" asked Gormesh. His half-orc tusks rose with the question. It's too bad they hid his smile. Gormesh had convinced me to invest in the Worlds Project back on Earth, which had played a key role in why Talindra and I were on Geoe instead of on a Vrelth slave ship.

"They're upstairs. Talindra is helping Kitara clean up some glass."

Gormesh rubbed his tusks and sat. He positioned his pad to project onto the wall. To test it, he projected the Guardian Knights' marketing photo. Talindra stood in the middle in her full paladin armor with her blue-flame sword in one hand and her shield with our heraldry in the other. Kitara stood on her left, holding magical green smoke and a longsword. Marick was on Talindra's right in his rust-orange lamellar armor, wielding a mace and boasting a golden glow in his other hand. I was pictured levitating behind Talindra, ice in one hand and fire in the other. Daisidian performed a split in front of the group, flashing daggers in his grip. Naomi, my hawk, and Scruffles, Kitara's owl, flew over my shoulders. *The Guardian Knights* appeared in bold letters in the blue and green of Earth.

Over-the-top marketing was used to get the propaganda to help Earth.

"OG, last month I agreed with you that healing potions were a better use of the money than paintings, furniture, and a friendly house. But I changed my mind." Daisidian's knife quartered his orange, and the knife disappeared.

"True," agreed Marick. "Coming here is like walking into my house. It's always warm, has food, and you two are always happy to see me."

"Don't get used to furniture. Braun and Talindra are redecorating," I said.

Talindra and Kitara strode in with blank faces, Talindra carrying two heavy steel chairs from the kitchen. When I had created my character, I hadn't realized they used my DNA to build this new body. I had gone from a normal-strength fifty-seven-year-old to a wimpy twenty-one-year-old. I couldn't lift either, never mind carry them.

"It's going to be lovely, and we won't need kitchen chairs when everyone is over," said Talindra.

Kitara waved at the others. It was obvious he had cried, but everyone pretended otherwise.

"Sorry for the short notice. You've all lost your memories of the last two weeks," said Gormesh.

I scanned through my memories from since we destroyed the signal blocker and killed Avaris. We'd ridden back, and I'd had Avaris' heart in my pouch. I never stopped touching it, with the wood skewering it. I had cut it out of his defeated body before I blew the cavern. The explosion had destroyed the remnants of the signal blocker and Avaris' crypt. Then... A pain shot through my head and down my spine.

"Please don't force the memories," said Gormesh. He tried to sigh, but from a half-orc, it sounded like water over gravel.

"Thanks for testing that for us, honey," said Talindra. She gave my arm a playful squeeze.

"You waited to see if it killed me?"

"OG, nothing can kill you with all of us here," said Daisidian. He put the last quarter of orange in his mouth and looked around the room with a huge orange peel smile to get a laugh.

I chuckled, not at the orange but at his comment, because, as fanciful as that sounded, it had proven accurate.

Gormesh grinned. "All your activities still happened. Kitara, all the business items you took care of are still done, and the presentation Argrenn helped you with on Salas Keep is complete."

"Thanks, Argrenn. That made me nervous," said Kitara.

He continued, "Marick healed quite a few refugees. Talindra, you studied with the Knights of Honor and remember the training. Daisidian, the young lady remembers the time you spent together and you keep the knowledge gained about the gnome airships."

"What?" exclaimed Kitara.

Daisidian held his hands in front of him. "It's not like that."

Marick waved both his hands. "I'm vouching for Daisidian. They're friends and talk about the airships when her ship is home for maintenance."

Kitara looked mollified, and we didn't have an explosive issue.

"Long story short—you exceeded everyone's expectations, and the game rules require you to be rewarded along with a game rebalance." Gormesh looked excited and pressed a button on his screen. "This is the advertisement sent to planetary broadcasters. Each broadcaster fills in pertinent information."

Meet the Guardian Knights, the newest Sword and Sorcery sensation from Geoe. Watch them live as they attempt their most difficult dungeon yet.

Gormesh played the ad shown to planets with humans and Earth refugees. Over-the-top fighting and sensationalized angles made us appear formidable.

"Gormesh, I can tell this is big news," I said, "but I don't have any basis for comparison."

"The Sardyna signal couldn't broadcast for the past three months. They advertised this live broadcast to trillions of Milky Way residents. This could boost your viewership higher than we hoped."

I could conceptualize a trillion atoms and a trillion stars, but a trillion sentient beings made no sense to me. The laws of large numbers helped me. Tell me a thousand people watched me and I'd be nervous. Conceptualizing a trillion views was impossible.

"So, no pressure," joked Kitara.

"Oh, no. Incredible pressure," said Gormesh. "If this falls flat, they cancel Sardyna."

"How can we make this a success?" I asked.

"Same thing as on Earth. Drama, sex, violence, visceral scenes, and humor."

I fought the urge to wink at Talindra and say something inappropriate. Instead, I said, "We will do our best. Any other changes?"

"Yes. As a personal reward, you will each receive a missive about family members. Also, adventurers may not buy explosives." He grinned, spreading his tusks and stretching the bottom of his mouth so the brown disappeared and his skin looked green. "The Vrelth lost unrecoverable equipment in that crypt."

Explosives guaranteed destruction of Vampire crypts. Since the Vrelth empowered the Vampires to break the rules of the game, we had to destroy their crypts.

"The Vrelth must have bargained for something else," said Kitara.

"Bet," said Marick.

"The major concession to the Vrelth, after the explosives ban, changed who decides the Battle of Champions participants. The city's leaders make the final decision."

"Sardyna supports us. That makes so little sense it bothers me," said Marick.

"Marick's paranoia is taking root. It's going to team up with OG's paranoia and grow to become a cryptid!"

"Wait, Marick is right. Sardyna gets over a quarter of its direct revenue from the game," said Talindra. "That's before a team makes it to the Battle of Champions."

"It's almost half, if you consider all the citizens employed by the game. But if we make it to the Battle of Champions, Sardyna's revenue would double," added Kitara.

Daisidian threw the remnants of his orange away and cartwheeled back into his chair. "That's what I meant. Marick had a reasonable concern."

Gormesh slid his tusks back and forth on his lip and packed his items. "It makes little sense to us as well. Keep your eyes open. But we have huge game news."

The energy in the room paused, and the team stopped relaxing and leaned forward. We had to play the game on Geoe, but we'd had zero game news since we landed.

"Worlds Project disqualified the team from New Connacht and New Connacht is no longer an allowed qualifying city." Gormesh leaned back as if that sentence meant anything to us.

"Team Renewal… they had the other mage from Earth, didn't they?" Kitara moved the bracelets up his arm and tapped on his pad.

"Yes. Liam Cassidy is a wildmage who specializes in magnetism and electricity. He has matched Argrenn level for level."

"We should meet," I said. "Two humans from Earth who master Geoe's magic must have common ground."

"Ummm," growled Gormesh.

"Bad idea Argrenn," said Kitara. He tapped his pad again. "The Vrelth brought that team here."

My head spun. The Vrelth attacked Earth and was systematically eliminating the last of the resistance and putting humans on slaving ships. We were here to drum up propaganda to get allies to help Earth.

"We should forget about them for now. All five spots to qualify for the Battle of Champions are still in play, and the Guardian Knights are in fifth place."

The Battle of Champions was critical to our strategy. Our few billions of views were a niche market in an area the size of the galaxy. However, trillions of beings watched the Battle of Champions. If we showed humans were noble and able to fight for ourselves, we could sway the other human-based planets and planets allied to humans to help defend Earth.

"We haven't even started trying to qualify," exclaimed Daisidian.

"Bet," said Marick. "When we kick this off, we'll be in first."

"Team," Gormesh turned off the projection and spoke with a slow, metered pace. "The Vrelth promised the other cities that Sardyna would not qualify a team while they ran the area. They still run the area, and troop transport ships are loading in Ardvente."

"Nice, play the game and fight a war," said Talindra.

"What I'm trying to say it that cities depend on the game money, and if you qualify for the Battle of Champions, cities that planned to win that money will not receive it. Expect some dirty play incoming."

We were up against the Vrelth, playing a game we barely understood, in a war zone of a city we needed to defend, and now other teams needed to cheat to beat us. Our situation became so ludicrous I couldn't contain my laughter.

"While my husband laughs, how close are the cheaters?"

Kitara tapped his pad. "In the game, the closest city is Lutetia. Oh look, they called out Argrenn."

"Let's ignore that," said Gormesh, but his sigh of water over gravel continued as I pulled out my pad.

I read the news, found the 'call-out,' and laughed harder. "This idiot could have called me out as a poor leader, even said I was a jerk or that I was lucky my entire team is strong enough to carry me. I agree with those statements. Instead, he calls me a fraud. He made fun of my magic, the only area I dominate Geoe. What a putz. I would love to meet this Witch Brencis and show him how a fraud could put him six feet under."

"That comment was ill-advised," said Marick.

Kitara held up his pad and his colorful bracelets slid to his elbow. "Wow, Argrenn, your response is already on the news."

Daisidian jumped up. "They even have a link to Earth terms to define putz."

I chuckled again. I forgot they filmed us twenty-four-seven, except in a few circumstances.

"Lutetia wasn't likely to be an ally. Don't make fun of other teams for the rest of the day." Gormesh packed up his pad and the papers in his satchel. "One more thing—enjoy Gaming Day. The holiday marks the day the war with the Vrelth ended on Geoe and this world became run with the current laws. And, also, do not read this." He dropped a packed on an end table. "It's a breakdown given to the other teams of your weaknesses and strengths made by professional game watchers."

Gormesh walked out in silence. Whether it was the folder or the upcoming battles to prepare for was a mystery.

Talindra stood up and clapped her hands. "Let's cook lunch and eat together. Argrenn, move your fires to the center of the hearth."

"Let me help cook," said Marick.

Nobody looked at the packet, though the temptation was strong. I wanted to burn that packet in my fires.

After I recast two larger *Fistful of Fire*, I walked into the backyard. We had a nice porch with a couple of old chairs. I had too much on my mind and needed the space to sort through it all. The war coming to Sardyna, new enemies, but worse, the memory wipe reminded me we'd almost lost to Avaris. To win, I had drunk a dangerous potion. Dean Jarlenteria told me, in no uncertain terms, that drinking a second potion removed the barrier between me and other planes. The barrier between myself and the plane of planar material thinned.

It wasn't just my life I played with. If I broke the barrier between me and the plane of planar material, an archmage would need to find me and close the portal. Dean Jarlenteria had said that in the time it would take her to find me and close it, Sardyna would no longer exist.

The main thought that bothered me was that my pompous title, "Master of Materials," didn't come with usable combat powers like everyone else's did. Talindra could throw her shield and block any shot on a teammate within line of sight. Since I *could* move rocks, it was possible I didn't understand my power, but now, we had a battle coming up and I needed to see if it was usable. I had to explore what little power there was that came with the title, see if I could refine it, weaponize it.

To test the power, I walked into the backyard and sent out my senses into the ground. I sensed loose organic matter that acted as one chunk, and scattered throughout this chunk were denser combinations of minerals. The power could control the whole chunk or only the dense items.

Focused on the dense items, I lifted the stones from the earth. Once free, I attempted to throw them, but they plopped a foot away. Trying again, I moved the rocks against the fence, lining them up.

Unimpressed, I left them there and refocused my attention, lifting the whole chunk.

"What are you doing?" cried Talindra.

I let the dirt drop. "Trying out my title power in case I've missed something." I didn't have time to finish my thought.

"We have a house in the noble district and want to fit in. You tore up our backyard!"

Oops.

The backyard now had dozens of rocks against the fence, and scattered dirt clumps littered the remaining snow.

Kitara walked into the yard. "This is the hard part. Let's be the first house to plant a garden."

"I can put it back."

"No. No more testing magic around the house."

I felt stupid. "What do you want me to do?"

Daisidian walked into the backyard. "Hey, that's a week's worth of work. You removed rock and dug up topsoil."

Now everyone had joined us in the backyard, judging my failure.

"Kitara has a good idea," said Talindra. "A garden would be lovely back here." She turned to Kitara. "Do you want to join me in the artisan district after lunch?"

"A fountain in the garden representing your religion would be tight," said Marick. "Unless it could start a religious battle."

"OG, let me show you something I learned," said Daisidian. "Do you have a better wall to where you can project your pad?"

I stepped into the house with Daisidian. "Let me blow your mind."

My office door opened to any extra-dimensional portal I associated with my office key, which was also used to open my university office. Once inside, I pointed to a blank wall. "If I pick out a library book, I can grab it up here," I said, "but this wall isn't only a projector, it's a second screen that is a touch screen, whiteboard, look-up device, input device, and has functions I haven't figured out yet. I tapped my pad and put the screen on my wallboard.

"Okay," said Daisidian, "check out the wall when I broadcast it. Skip all the normal stuff and tap the *News and Events* banner. Now tap the *Select by Location* banner."

I tapped on those.

"Ignore those and go to the search bar and type in *Atlanta*. This will be faster because it retains our home city."

They had grayed out the *News, Events,* and *Contact* banners.

"Tap on *Culture,* then *Music,* and then *Limit Search by Years*."

A pop-up appeared and asked if I wanted my preloaded suggestions. I tapped *yes*.

"You will see how much they know about you," said Daisidian.

Three selections appeared:

Lynyrd Skynyrd July 1976 Fox Theater
UFO and Ozzy Osbourne March 1982 Omni
Styx June 1983 Omni

"This is a joke, right?" I asked. "How did it pull up those three?"

Daisidian grinned. "My mom wasn't born for any of those, OG."

I selected Randy Rhoads's last concert, and the Omni projected onto the wall. My office lights dimmed to match the Omni's lighting.

"Whoa, check out your speaker system," said Daisidian, looking around for the speakers.

We stood in front of the wall as music filled the room and watched the actual concert.

I knew the Worlds Project had recruited the Groove Train, our hidden guardians, in the late sixties, but I didn't know someone had saved Earth's culture.

Daisidian touched the image of Randy, and information popped up next to the guitarist. Daisidian spun the concert around by dragging his hand on the projected stage.

"Is there a party in here? Gaming day hasn't started, has it?" asked Talindra over the music. She dried her hands on a kitchen towel.

I lowered the volume. "Did you know the pad had access to concerts?"

"Books, concerts, TV shows, movies, plays, important events, and classrooms of important teachers," said Kitara. "From every Country."

"Shelley showed me that a while back," said Talindra. "We watched a Depeche Mode concert in the Knights of Honor guild-hall."

"You made Paladins listen to Depeche Mode? Do the Knights of Honor hate Earth now?"

"Hey, hey, hey. No one disses Depeche Mode. Come on out, and we'll eat."

"OG, this was your answer to the question," said Daisidian.

"Which question?"

Instead of answering me directly, he turned and said, "Hey, Marick, do you remember when we asked OG why he worked so hard and he blew our minds with philosophy like 'I need my actions to be meaningful, even if this world exists as a simulation'?"

Marick laughed. "I stood watch alone in the dark for four hours and had to deal with it."

Kitara joined in the laughter. "I didn't get to sleep for a good hour."

"All he had to say is that they gave him an office with a wall that turns into an interactive screen with a killer sound system. If he'd given us that answer, we'd all sleep peacefully and say, 'Yeah, I'd work hard to get that.'"

"We wouldn't have believed it," said Kitara. "I bet he didn't know about watching movies and concerts or lectures until you showed him."

"Got me," I said, smiling wryly, and we all turned to leave.

We walked to the backyard to eat and faced the mess I'd made. I should have gone outside the city. I bet farmers needed my tilling powers.

"Did you all hear about the new players joining up in Sardyna?" asked Kitara. We shook our heads. Kitara's magical enhancement to research always put him ahead of us. "They're not from Earth, but the Worlds Project is betting ratings will recover."

If we died tomorrow, or worse—were boring, we had a zero chance of becoming a propaganda arm against the Vrelth and ruined our chance to gain allies to save Earth. But it was a good sign they'd made plans for our success.

"A rumor that another group from Earth will arrive soon is going around," said Daisidian.

"Where'd you hear that?" asked Marick.

"Um, around."

Another of Daisidian's secrets. Only he decided when to share them.

Kitara tapped on his pad. "Hey, Daisidian is right. They aren't in the game yet because they are in Caemlynn, but there is another mage. They aren't in the game yet, but a team from Earth is based out of Caemlynn."

"Possibility for a new mage friend," I joked.

"Nope. The mage got his team killed, took all the treasure for himself, looted his friends' bodies, and was surprised when they dropped from the team to reform without him."

"Well, there goes all my possibilities for new friends," I joked.

"We're going to ignore the folder, right?" asked Kitara as he closed his pad.

Everyone agreed. We knew it would only distract us. A tactic to get in our heads and question ourselves.

We joked around the table, finished eating, and I cleaned up when Talindra and Kitara left, casting Vern—my *Planar Butler*—to do the menial labor. He lasted an hour and performed tasks my limited strength did not let me.

With little else to do, Marick and Daisidian rode off to take care of a couple of items, and I walked into my office. I had an idea for a spell and wanted to note it. The concept contained four parts. The first part threw a chunk of iron, then the second cast my acid attack spell on it. This should make hydrogen gas. The third part needed to contain the gas, and the fourth ignited it. Then, *boom*.

I wrote it on a piece of paper on my desk and put it in the top drawer. The game didn't record what mages wrote in their offices, since we wrote deadly spells. Then I opened the lower right-hand drawer of my desk. Since we had a new rule that adventurers could no longer buy explosives, I wanted to make sure the one I'd hidden remained. The necromancer, who'd had orders to bury us in a cavern, had instead attacked us early, and I'd kept the device. The explosive had never appeared on camera. It stayed in a sealed glass decanter, hidden in a belt pouch and kept in this drawer.

Time to focus on the game. *Tomorrow, we fight.*

Chapter 2

The next morning, we left for our big show at the vampire lair of the dead Avaris. We didn't care about the video because it was life and death.

It felt good to wear my old jeans and t-shirt from Earth. I still wore my robe, bandolier, and Danaan-steel shirt, but those weren't a big deal. "Being out of the wardrobe feels good."

"Armor isn't wardrobe?" asked Marick.

"Out here, we can wear whatever we want. In Sardyna, I represent the university and Talindra represents the Knights of Honor. Silks and furs are not my first choice."

"I like to style wherever I go," said Daisidian. "I need invisible armor so everyone can see how I style."

"Nobles, professors, and leaders should dress to impress," said Talindra.

"That sounds like a paladin saying, and you added professors to tell me to dress better," I accused.

She stuck her tongue out at me.

Kitara and Daisidian rode in front, Marick and I behind them, and Talindra watched our backs. Naomi flew out in front, seeing nothing in our way. We ate lunch in our saddles, with a pause for Marick to pray. The melting snow allowed grass to poke up, and the horses had better footing. Steam rose from the soft ground and helped finish ridding the land of the last remnants of snow. We'd landed in Geoe two months ago and this felt like the first time my schedule was free. All I had in front of me was a quest to save Earth.

"Let's remember," called out Kitara, "Argrenn is the first mage in thirty-five years and only the second mage in fifty years to adventure at tier two. We will find things that have not been seen before."

"Come on, I enjoyed the freedom of being caught up at work and riding with you guys, and you bummed me out." The reminder that I exceeded the life expectancy of a mage on Geoe stung.

"Chill. It means more loot because of OG," said Daisidian.

The ride was pleasant and, thankfully, without incident. Using Naomi, I let everyone know when we were within a couple of miles, and we pulled over to the side. We ate a quick dinner while Marick prayed, and I sent Naomi toward the warren. Peering through her eyes, I viewed birds with long beaks darting toward me. I jumped to escape and landed on the ground, my last vision of a beak heading for my eyes. I stammered, "Guys, prepare for small birds. They killed Naomi." I landed on the ground with a thud and it jolted me to my senses.

Talindra pulled me to my feet. "They killed Naomi?"

I reminded myself that Naomi was a magical construct and that soothed the rush of loss I felt and her demise.

"You can bring her back later, right?" asked Marick.

"OG, how did you fall off of Starlight?" Daisidian asked as his eyes darted around, looking for an enemy.

My rear hurt, but I pretended it was nothing. "Naomi got attacked with my eyes in her. A beak came for my eye and I instinctively jumped out of the way."

"Hold up," said Kitara, and pulled out his pad, tapped, and showed me a picture. "Did it look like this?"

"It's close. The beak looked longer."

"Blood hunters," he said and put his pad away. "Vampires create them. They collect blood and fly back to thralls who drink the blood they collect."

"Thralls," I said. "Well, we expected sanguine creatures."

"These birds are easy to kill, but they can swarm," he warned.

We rode a hundred feet away from where Naomi had spotted the warrens and found a grove. Kitara tied off his horse to a tree and asked, "Argrenn, will you cast your dome thing to help hide the horses?"

The rest tied up their horses, and I dispelled Starlight, stepped away, and cast *Planar Protection* between the trees. Preparing for the winged blood suckers, we barely walked a hundred yards before we found two dozen birds flitting in circles. I stayed at the back of the party.

"Argrenn, see if you can get their attention on us," said Kitara.

Since I only had seven incantations and three formulas to use, glamors were all I'd need for these creatures, saving my larger firepower for bigger prey. I started my combat mode on my staff, put it in front of me between my arms, aimed at a blood hunter in the back, and threw *Fistful of Fire* at it.

Nailed it.

The bird fell to the ground on fire. A blood hunter investigated his dead friend, and I threw more fire. Hit. Another dead. They soared at us after that bird fell. I found one traveling in a straight line and threw another *Fistful of Fire*. Three dead.

Daisidian had two daggers out and killed them faster than anyone else could. Marick pulled one off his neck, threw it onto the ground, and stomped on it.

Talindra's armor kept her from getting hurt, but the swing of her longsword took too long to be effective against the darting birds.

Kitara and Marick were only effective after the birds sunk into them. They pulled them out and stepped on them. One targeted Kitara, and I threw a *Fistful of Fire* at it.

My aim with the fire glamor missed against darting fliers and I attempted again, still missing.

They were too fast when attacking.

Marick had two stuck in him, and one dove for his face. I lined up on its trajectory and threw fire—*hit*. It fell to the ground, its feathers blazing, and died. Another attacked Kitara and I once again threw fire. Missed.

Daisidian flashed a dagger, killed it swiftly, and soon Marick and Kitara pulled the last two out of their necks and crushed them underfoot.

Talindra stepped up to heal Marick and Kitara, but Marick held up his hand. "Save it." He pulled out a paste, which he filled his and Kitara's wounds with. "This paste will act like a healing for an hour, and I can re-apply it if necessary."

Gathering ourselves once again, Daisidian and I took up positions on either side of the entrance to the warren.

"Before we look in, be ready to give cover fire," I advised.

Daisidian made a dagger appear in his hand and we both peered around the entrance edge. There was nothing there.

Marick held out a torch to me. "Light this. I'll hold it."

Daisidian and I entered, moved ten feet to the left and right, and waved to the others. Kitara took the lead, Marick following him with the torch, Daisidian next, then I followed in front of Talindra.

Despite the sign of fresh digging further in, they had packed in the cave entrance long enough ago it had weathered. The earthy aroma from the excavation overwhelmed my nose, but I smelled no mildew or mold. Whoever had dug the tunnel had excavated the hallway six feet wide, and I had to extend to touch the ceiling. The workers had placed logs at odd intervals to shore up sections overhead.

Kitara held up a fist after we curved around a bend to the right. I did the same for Talindra's sake, and we stopped. Kitara motion me to the door with him on the left side of the hallway.

I spoke in low, clear tones, giving direction, "Marick goes left, Kitara goes right, Daisidian, you follow. Talindra and I will bring up the rear." We were unsure what lay beyond the door, but knew it would be a challenge. Quickly and quietly, the door was opened, and each fighter entered in order. When it came time for me to charge, I ducked viscous fluid spat at me and rolled to the left. From the ground, I cast *Planar Reflection* on the middle of three large scorpions. *Yep, knew it would be fun in here.*

The warren owners had trapped three giant scorpions, and Kitara and Talindra had limitations on their swings because of the low ceiling. They had to do without overhand swings. Talindra focused on bashing with her shield, and Kitara focused on casting magic.

Marick had one trapped, and I stayed out of its reach. I hit the scorpion square in the face with a *Fistful of Fire*, antagonizing the venomous creature, which promptly turned in my direction, wanting to kill me, but Marick prevented it.

Planar Reflection helped the others, so I spammed fire into the face of this scorpion. He ignored Marick to get to me. I hit the creature six times in a row, but it spewed something from its mouth that wet its face. Then its tail rose and it pointed its stinger at me. I stopped firing and leaned left just as the stinger shot its barb at me.

I'd successfully dodged, but my cloak pulled at my neck, yanking me off balance, as the barb grazed the edge of my cloak, and I plopped to the ground. As I congratulated myself for putting skill points into dodging, but I shook at being that close to death. The barb that almost passed through my body was implanted halfway through the wall. I took a breath, sidestepped my fear, and focused on the task at hand.

Blood poured out of its open stinger and the creature died with a thud. The middle scorpion bled black viscous fluid from its side and wobbled on a broken leg. I barely held my hand steady to cast a *Fistful of Fire*, and the scorpion hit the ground with a thud.

"Kill steal," yelled Daisidian.

I laughed and shook. The nervousness of dodging a death shot from the stinger had set me on edge, and the light-hearted jab from Daisidian helped me center myself, laughing through the edginess.

I repeatedly threw *Fistful of Fire* at the last scorpion, but all four shots missed.

Talindra had her blue-flame blade out and sliced off the creature's stinger. The last giant scorpion hit the ground with a thud.

As the adrenaline ebbed, my fear rose. I took a deep breath and tried to stop shaking.

"Talindra, can you cut the other stinger off too?" asked Kitara, pointing to the middle scorpion. "These go for good prices."

Talindra removed her helm. "Where's the third stinger?"

"The scorpion fired the barb at your husband and is impaled in the wall." Kitara pointed to the wall behind me.

"This got shot at you?" Talindra pointed at the wall behind me. The barb had sunk into the packed-dirt and through the wall. At its thickest point, it measured six inches. She pointed at the stinger. "This is instant death if it had passed through you." She looked at me with concern etched on her face, walked over, and hugged me. Me standing still and shaking seemed to calm her.

I made light of the situation. "Marick has a salve that fills in the hole and heals."

Marick shook his head at the joke.

She pushed me back and held me by the shoulders. "That isn't funny. If this goes through you, you die with no time to heal you."

There weren't a lot of excuses. "My dodge is pretty good."

"No, stop. I can use my shield and protect you from anywhere, but you have to let me know. This isn't the time for jokes or excuses."

"Sorry, I focused on my own powers and forgot about yours."

"My title power allows me to throw my shield and block an attack on any ally. Let me know if I'm not watching."

She hugged me again and let me go.

"I need to spend more time on the team's powers and stop focusing on my powers," I admitted.

Daisidian laughed and jumped up to pat my shoulder. "OG had it all figured out."

"Nope," said Marick. "We promised we would all help Argrenn, and Talindra is right. Argrenn, you have to know the team's abilities to call out strategy, and sometimes that strategy is to protect you."

They were correct. I grabbed Marick's hand and patted him on the shoulder. "Thank you."

"We're underway, guys. Let's get back into sneak mode," said Kitara.

Talindra whispered to me, "When you are in battle, it's easier to check on you." She pulled her hair back and placed her helm on carefully.

"I'll call you," I promised.

We continued down the warren's hallway, which ended in a T-junction, and we turned left.

"Wait a second," I said. "Kitara, when you make your pretend things, can you do floors and stuff?"

"Can I cast an illusion on the ground?" he asked.

His rhetorical tone let me know his answer. "Memorize the floor here." I reached out with my materials' power and grabbed ten inches of dirt at the junction and moved it toward the wall, creating a shallow pit across the hall. "Can you make it look like it's still flat?"

"Easy," he said. Then he did something, but it didn't change.

"Cool, when we hear someone break an ankle, someone snuck up behind us," said Daisidian.

"Does it look different?" I asked.

"Yes, Mister Tuatha," said Talindra. "To everyone but you, it looks the same as before you did your gardening power."

We continued on, and the hallway turned into a small rock cavern. Whoever made this warren combined it with natural caves. Kitara held up his hand, took a step back, and put his shoulder into something and charged forward.

Six sanguine hid in this room. The fight didn't take long. I only cast three *Fistful of Fires*. It didn't matter if I hit them. The team had this fight handled. Kitara did a quick search of the bodies.

"Kitara, let's keep disciplined even in simple areas. We want one person going left and another going right when we enter a room."

Kitara winced. "Yep, sorry. We need a signal, but I saw a chance to surprise a handful of weaker enemies."

I pulled up a *Fistful of Fire* and walked around the walls. This cavern ended abruptly without a taper, making me curious. One section appeared to have recent work done, and upon closer inspection, light dirt caught my attention. With my materials' power, I sensed a density difference in the discolored dirt and the lower area of missing rock.

"Back up," I said. I pulled the less dense dirt out into the room, revealing a two-foot-high tunnel.

With a shrug of his shoulders, Daisidian snuck through with the torch. I followed him since the other three wore armor that prevented crawling the ten-foot-long pathway. Spiderwebs spanned a room, wall to wall and ceiling to floor, and dark shapes darted throughout the web.

Spiders.

Daisidian backed up with me and I cast *Espuma Inflam* from the necromancer's book, filling the room with foam, then followed with a quick cast of fire. The foam ignited at once, followed by the webs, and the entire room ignited in a brief inferno. Daisidian and I covered our faces and backed away as high-pitched screams ripped through the air and spiders larger than dinner plates leaped toward us. I cast a *Fistful of Fire* and set it in the middle of the crawlspace floor to keep them back.

Daisidian stabbed any that entered the tunnel while I threw *Fistful of Fire* after *Fistful of Fire* at the enormous spiders. The poor beasts either died by fire in the web that had torched the room or by running into my fire in the hallway. The odor of burned spider permeated the air, gagging me. Holding back vomit, I doubled over in a sneezing fit and covered my mouth and nose with my cloak.

The warren's recent occupants had sealed off the spider's only exit. If a god of spiders existed, she had me on her short list after the massacre.

I dispelled my fire on the ground and crawled into the room.

"Are you okay?" Talindra's frantic tone seemed out of place as it echoed down the short tunnel. "We couldn't hear you over the fire roar."

"We're good," I called back. "Only a few spiders."

"We saw the fire from here. We heard hundreds of high-pitched screams."

"A few hundred enormous spiders," said Daisidian, "but Argrenn burned them in their web. Now we're walking into the world's worst barbeque."

With the spider room cleared of webs, it looked large—an eight-foot-diameter circle with a five-foot ceiling. Junk filled the space, surrounded by decades' worth of adventurer bones. We crawled in and pushed the burned spider corpses to the edge, grabbing items mixed in with bones.

I discovered a suit of chain armor and two uncorroded and unscorched swords. Daisidian crawled over a pile of loose coins and gems and found a chest and filled it with the loose stuff on the floor. I dragged the chain mail and swords out to the main room, sliding them through to Talindra. "It will take us time to get this treasure out."

Talindra handed me one of her torches. "I thought we discussed things like that."

"It's true, but if we'd backed out, hundreds of dinner-plate-sized spiders would have followed us. It was a judgment call."

"Go back to the room and I'll explain recon calls," said Marick.

With a handful of jewelry and a bunch of glowing liquids in stoppered vials, I wondered if it was worth taking them all, but Talindra had persuasion and charisma; she could find a seller. Next, I found a dagger and a quiver. None of the arrow shafts even had a scorch mark.

Looking around at the charred mess, a crown with three loose stones beckoned me. A vision flashed in my mind, and in it I wore the crown, the rocks floating above my head. When I attempted to envision Talindra wearing the crown, the first vision jumped back in my head.

With an armful of potions, dagger, quiver, and crown, the crawl through the tunnel was awkward. "Guys, check out this crown. My brain won't stop thinking about it, and the desire to put it on is consuming. Can you check if you have the same wish?" I handed the crown to Talindra. She took it and tugged, but I didn't let it go.

"Do I need to rip it out of your hand?" She tugged again and released it from me. The three standing there looked at me, but I shook off the feeling and crawled back into the room, helping Daisidian pick up scattered coins and gems.

When we were through, Daisidian dragged out the chest while I held both torches.

We called Talindra, and she pulled the footlocker-sized chest through with ease. It embarrassed me to see Daisidian and Talindra both move it when I couldn't make it budge.

The other three sat with two large stacks of items. "Nobody wants that tacky crown but you, Argrenn," said Talindra.

"But you're not getting it until Kitara checks it out," warned Marick. "We don't need you to be taken over by an ancient force."

They deposited everything into my handkerchief. I promised myself I would wear the crown once Kitara identified it, which allowed me to fight the urge to place it on my head now.

With the treasure stowed, we once again brushed ourselves off and readied to face whatever was thrown at us next, walking back to the hallway in our determined order.

Marick and I doused our torches when Kitara said he viewed light ahead. Our plan at the T-junction would come in handy for an ambush, so I told Kitara the plan, and he relayed it back.

Returning to the area stealthily, we watched as Yuennui slithered into the T-junction, then lurched into the wall.

I cast *Planar Winter* to pummel them with hail, then quickly threw up *Shards of Glass* in the hallway. The sharp attack ground up and made a bloody mess of the ambushers. They yelled in French—or, rather, in Formian, *"Atrrapez ces salauds,"* which I thought meant *catch those salads.*

They fought their way through the *Shards of Glass* and the hail, their scales flaking and tearing off as the creatures oozed black blood. Their forked tongues hissed, and in the face of the hail and glass, their uncovered eyes were scratched, blinding them.

"They'll be blind until their next molt!" yelled Marick.

I threw *Argrenn's Acid Attack* into the mix, and it sprayed everywhere. I spammed that spell into the kill zone while Talindra waited for the ones that made it through. Kitara and Daisidian shot arrows into them, and Marick shot bolts of golden energy.

More Yuennui struggled to glide through our trap, lurching and panicking, getting knocked to the ground with hail. If one enemy followed too close to the one in front of it, the two became tangled. This slaughter compared to the spider fight. Something must have driven the ambushers into the killing zone.

The *Planar Winter* died out after thirty seconds, but I was able to keep the *Shards of Glass* up as long as I focused on it. We made a snake stew with sulfuric acid, snake bodies, and glass, mixing it all together.

Talindra killed four that made it through the onslaught. They were easy kills for her, as damaged as the creatures were. Finally, the junction settled into the hole I'd created after the screaming of the creatures died out.

We crept closer to peer straight ahead and right to see if anyone survived. When nothing moved, Talindra picked up one of the dropped torches of the snake-men and crossed over to watch the other side while I walked into the exit hallway and kept watch.

The others searched and moved the bodies back toward the spider room, while I focused on my materials' power and flattened out the area.

"When did you learn the acid magic that makes them scream?" asked Kitara while he searched for belt pouches.

My nose itched. "I created the spell. The name is *Argrenn's Acid Attack*. It's like *Fistful of Fire* except its sulfuric acid. This is the first chance I've gotten to use it."

"The spell is cruel," said Talindra.

I raised my finger and spent the next minute in a sneezing fit. The sight of the dismembered Yuennui and the odors from burned spiders rushed through and overwhelmed my senses. With a roiling gurgle, vomit spewed on the ground.

After a minute I drank water, gargled and spit it out, then took a long swallow. Taking in a long breath, I covered and flattened out the T-junction to cover up my vomit and the remains that weren't big enough to drag away.

The others waited for me. "Even you can't take what that spell does to creatures," Talindra noted.

I gathered myself and shook my head. "The spiders had a lot to do with that, but the spell isn't cruel."

"Vouch for the spider smell," agreed Daisidian.

"What about the acid's construction benefits?" I argued.

"Construction benefits?" Marick chuckled.

Daisidian led the way since we could see a door ahead. "Argrenn's construction company. We promise nothing exists when we are done." We resumed our formation and moved forward until Daisidian held up his fist. "The door is skewed." Talindra and I held torches for him. He worked on it for a couple of minutes and said, "No good. They meant to break it."

"What's wrong?" I asked.

"This steel bar," he said. "You can barely see it. But this kicks off the trap, and they broke it. They never intended to return."

"Everyone back into the exit hallway, and give me room to join you," I said. "Argrenn's construction has accepted the contract."

Only Marick laughed.

They returned to the hallway as I studied the door. Setting my posture, I focused and cast *Argrenn's Acid Attack*, placing it on top of the steel bar, then ran back to them. Talindra caught me in her shield, and we waited. "How long do we wait?" I asked.

"As long as it takes to make me feel comfortable," said Talindra.

I waited a couple of minutes more and said, "Okay, I think we—"

A loud crash of metal on metal and splintering wood shattered the air as the walls shook and dirt rained on us. Splintered wood, wrenched metal, and six javelins flew by us, a loud *thwap* sounding as they sank into the wall at the far end. Talindra pulled me into her plate armor with her shield, and I struggled to catch a breath. Six more javelins followed and *thwapped* into the far wall. "Wait one more minute," I gasped out.

Talindra loosened her hold while Marick and Daisidian laughed.

Finally, she removed the shield, and I peered at the trapped door. Which no longer existed. Spikes shot out of the wall as a final deterrent, and I shook my head. "Good catch on seeing the trap, Daisidian," I said.

I stepped out, but Talindra grabbed my cloak and pulled me back, then strode to the room shield-first, followed by Kitara and then me.

After we maneuvered around the spears and spikes, we entered a room with painted wooden walls and a stone floor. A desk sat in one corner and a portrait of Avaris hung over it. A notebook and envelope lay on the desk and I put them in my belt pouch.

"Honey, thank you. In case I don't say it enough, having you nearby gives me the confidence to act boldly, and I should be more careful instead of counting on you to cover for me."

"Awwww" teased Marick, but I saw Talindra smile between the wings of her helm.

"Burn the desk and painting?" I asked. Everyone agreed, so while Marick loaded javelins into a sack, I started a fire on the desk and painting.

To prepare for an ambush from whoever forced the Yueenui into our trap, Kitara led the way, followed by Talindra, then Marick and Daisidian. I followed with my five incantations and one formula.

We reached the front of the warren, and I didn't need the warning, since Dragonforce's <u>Through the Fire and Flames</u> kicked off in my head, but Kitara and Talindra quickly charged out of the entrance, yelling, "Ambush!"

Three Yuennui with long bows aimed while I cast *Duplicate Me* that put me behind three archers near a handful of trees. Scanning the field and flanks, I deduced Talindra had the worst odds. With my additive extension *Planar Pull* and *Planar Escape,* I pulled one off Talindra and knocked all four near me onto the ground. *Four incantations and zero formulas left.*

Everyone fought against long odds. I had four *Ice Balls* and four Yuennui in front of me—three archers and the one I'd pulled from Talindra, who wore chain armor where the others left their scales uncovered.

Ice hit one and didn't stand back up. Nice—my new tier meant I cast three balls of ice now. I put up my armor with the staff and cast again. Another died to ice as it pulled its scimitar out.

The surrounding battle sounded phrenetic compared to our normal combat. Celestial light and green flashes were all over the place, and the cries of my teammates seemed unusual. The two enemies near me both attacked. One slashed through my armor, penetrating the Danaan-steel shirt and cutting into my left side. He fell to the ice attack as I hissed in pain, blood soaking into my clothes. The one I left for last was the enemy I'd pulled from Talindra, wearing chain armor. He slashed out and hit my left side through the armor, hissing, "*Tu es aussi faible que tout humain.*"

"Really?" I screamed, "The left side again?" Blood soaked into my cloak. Its weight dragging my left side. No spells left and his Yuennui still stood, but he wavered and his eyes lost focus. A globe of Earth surrounded the battlefield and Talindra yelled, "I bring judgment from Sol!"

The battlefield shook. Before my enemy recovered, I threw *Fistful of Fire* at him as blood pooled underneath me from my soaked clothes.

I moved my staff to block his scimitar as he sliced at me with a sloppy move around the staff. I stepped out of the way, but it caught in my armor. From the corner of my eye, I saw Talindra finish the Yuennui she fought against and ran to help Kitara.

Fistful of Fire. The one on me slashed and nicked my shoulder. Fire was all I had, so I cast it again. It slashed open the wound further on my shoulder. Two more casts of fire and he attacked upward, cutting through my thigh into my torso. I dropped to the ground to avoid some of the hit, but my vision became hazy. I struggled to reach out, to make a tunnel into the planar material, able to raise a shield. The barrier stood firm, but pain lanced through me and I lost the sense of the barrier.

Blackness filled my eyes and I gasped, assuming this was the end, until a golden glow surrounded me and Talindra lifted my face with her hands.

Blood, dead snake-men, and my teammates littered the ground. Only Marick and Talindra stood. The ambush had almost killed us.

Kitara, Daisidian, and I struggled to sit, and I caught sight of Marick covering Daisidian with a golden light, then announcing he was out of magical healing. Daisidian removed his leather armor and helped Marick bandage his chest before he searched through the Yuennui.

Talindra staggered over to Kitara and kneeled next to him, removed his breastplate, put Marick's paste on his wounds, and wrapped linen around his gut. Kitara said, "These were not regular Yuennui. They call these guys 'Garde.'"

Talindra laid him back. "Take it easy. You have parts you are not used to, and they will hurt."

Kitara cried out and Talindra teared up as she hugged him.

Daisidian winced at his old roommate's cry of pain and tried to pronounce the name. "Goo-Arday?"

Marick put his hand on Daisidian's shoulder and tightened the wrap. "Close enough. I don't think they care what we call them." Daisidian turned and hugged Marick, who held him.

Talindra helped Kitara onto his horse, handing him his breastplate, then helped me stand. "My big smite prevents me from casting prayers the rest of the day."

"We needed that," said Daisidian. "Good call."

"How do you feel?" she asked. Her helm lay on the ground, propped up by the wing on the side, and sweat plastered her blood-smattered hair to her face. But her concern centered on me. I put my hand on a slash through her armor, now tinged red.

My left side oozed blood, my shoulder ached, and my leg burned. Dizziness made me prop myself with my staff, but I wouldn't die. "I'm good for now. What about you? Is this wound healed?"

She let out a long breath. "I was in better shape than you are now, and Marick gave me a small heal to make sure we could both help the rest of you. Let's focus on you."

Daisidian unceremoniously dumped another ten belt pouches into my handkerchief.

"Let's get to the horses," Marick suggested. "We can't take another fight in our condition."

We got to the horses, where I summoned Starlight and dispelled the *Planar Protection*. Two of us needed help to mount, and blood covered each of us. Everyone's armor had slashes and dents.

"Kitara, don't ride straight to the city. Ride north for a while."

"I'm leading us out. Why north?" asked Talindra.

"Nagging thought. Outside the city, we get ambushed a lot. We're too predictable and move in straight lines. After the last ambush, I want to be more cautious."

"Caution from you? We ride north," she agreed.

Kitara rode next to me, slumped in his saddle and without his armor. His bandages covered his gut and chest. The paste and blood-stained wraps didn't exist for modesty. Kitara had wounds all along his torso.

We rode at a slow walk while grunts and occasional cries came from all of us until we stopped at dusk. Because of our pain, we didn't get as far as normal, and both Kitara and I stopped on the way to cough up blood.

We would not make it back today. I lit torches for everyone and Talindra and Daisidian took care of the horses, while my staff made the campsite. Marick heated a tincture with one of my fires and gave a dose to Kitara and one to me.

I took off my cloak and looked at my left side. A slice from the scimitar still seeped blood, struggling to close. I cast the *Planar Protection* over the campsite once everyone stepped inside.

"The side is getting infected. The shoulder is fine," said Marick. "Lie flat." He gave Daisidian packets and said, "Mix that," as he smeared a paste over my left side. "You and Kitara are having a race to see who takes more damage."

I laughed. "You know, when I hear music, I'm going to win."

"Cool, play it for the rest of us," called Marick from the tree stump.

Despite the snow, it felt warm without my cloak. They killed Naomi, the team nearly died, and everyone used our entire allotment of magic, but the sky looked beautiful. The universe could not care less. "Look at the stars. With no light pollution, we can see them all. They just gaze at us with indifference."

Marick rushed over to me and put his hand on my forehead. "You can recast Naomi tomorrow, and Talindra and I are in good enough shape to fix everyone. We will be fine unless they attack us, you know, out here in the open with no defenses."

"How many enemies are in the stars I need to kill?"

"Let's focus back on Geoe." He put another paste under my nose. "I don't know why you fought four creatures, but you did," he continued.

"They're easier when they lie on the ground," I replied. Was that a halo over Marick's head?

"Drink this." He handed me another cup. I drank and orange overwhelmed my tastebuds. "Go to sleep. Talindra can heal you in the morning."

I noticed him stumble over to Daisidian next, while Talindra checked out the abdomen of Kitara. But before I fell asleep, I swear I saw those decorative wings on the back of Talindra's armor glow.

The next morning, I shivered and watched my breath cloud the air. My blood-soaked cloak had dripped dry.

"Don't get dressed yet," said Talindra. "You and Kitara are splitting my big heal, and the rest of us are getting the smaller heals from Marick and I."

We were using our heals first thing in the morning. Not a good start.

Gold filled my vision and warmth emanated from my side, shoulder, and leg, where only a pink spot remained. I used planar magic to clean my clothes, mend them, and got dressed. After I mended the cloak, the blood pooled on the ground, and I draped it over my shoulders, grateful for its warmth. Then I used planar magic again to make myself presentable.

Casting *Fistful of Fire*, I put it on a rock, then, with a ritual spell, I brought Naomi back. "Welcome back, girl," I cooed with relief, looking around to make sure no one heard. Why did I welcome back a magical construct?

The rest of the camp was busy with their own repairs. It only took a short time to fix everyone's armor, Kitara's requiring the most work. The right side had been rent into three pieces. We needed to have everyone's best defense now that our heals were gone.

I put my hand on Talindra's face and hair, cleaned off the blood, and made sure she presented as a paladin. "Nobles, paladins, and leaders should dress to impress."

She smiled at me.

After I scouted with Naomi, I announced, "Nothing within a mile, and as far as I can tell, nothing within eight miles of us in any direction." Naomi flew back and landed on the perch on my shoulder. It was time to start the day.

We cleared camp and mounted up, each of us in our own minds, mulling over the battles behind us and those ahead. A whisp of my pearl white hair fell into my face. It contrasted with my brown beard to remind me every time I cast extensions with my magic, I became less human and more Tuathan. My exhaustion after battles was a reminder that mortal bodies weren't meant to pull the material of creation and pulling excessive amounts had penalties.

"Clean everyone up and fix our armor. That's a handy gardening power," said Marick, breaking the silence as we plodded north.

"That's not even his title power, just the benefit of being a specialist mage," said Kitara.

"What is your title power?" asked Daisidian, giving a burst to his halfling sized horse, Emcee Party.

"I'm a loremaster and can identify anything magical on Geoe," explained Kitara.

Daisidian rode over and checked out his old roommate. "That ain't bad, though I may have the best title power. I stay hidden in combat until I attack."

The journey was quiet, and no one rode high in the saddle. They had set the ambush to take us out, and everyone knew that this was a victory with an asterisk.

When we stopped to eat lunch, I addressed the group. "Guys, yesterday stunk, but we all worked together, and we're further along than a month ago. I want to say I'm happy you're my teammates, and I'm all in."

Daisidian jumped up from his perch on a rock and announced, putting his hand in, "I'm all in."

Kitara, Talindra, and Marick put their hands in as well, one on top of the other, agreeing solemnly, "I'm all in."

We traveled the rest of the day and soon rode back through the east gate where the familiar *Ding* of a completed quest sounded in all of our heads.

Chapter 3

"Argrenn, we're going to need cleaning," said Kitara. He opened the chest and pulled a clump of dirt off the coins.

I used planar magic and cleaned the outside of the chest, making it shine. The wood and iron looked sharp. After opening it, I cleaned the gems and coins, pulled the belt pouches off me, and poured each one into the chest. The gold and gems glowed, the copper shone, and the platinum looked nicer than the silver.

"Someone is keeping that chest," said Marick. "Elven forest-tree wood with dwarven metal hinges and wraps with titanium bolts."

"Argrenn, before we forget, can you translate the stuff off of Avaris' desk?" asked Kitara.

I glanced at the packet everyone pretended didn't exist on the table by the door and opened my office. It took me an hour to put the translated information together. Avaris had had had five prominent outposts before leaving Sardyna. He'd sold the Sardyna outpost to Feston. We blew up his second outpost when we killed him, but he had sold that outpost to someone named Urnovher.

We'd cleared the third outpost yesterday. The other hideouts were in the northern part of Twelve Towns and deep in the southern part of the Pyr Mountains. The Vrelth continued to scout more military sites.

I discovered the Vrelth Urnovher paid Avaris for the warrens and to create thralls of dead Yuennui to kill the "troublesome mage and his cadre of do-gooders."

Ooh, I hope he means me!

My pad vibrated. I checked it and had a missive. Archmage Kira had summoned me to the Planar Mage Guild.

"Huh."

I popped out to tell the team, "I got summoned to my guild."

"Look who jumps when summoned," teased Marick.

"OG has an OG?" said Daisidian to keep it going.

"When I met Archmage Kira, she, Dean Jarlenteria, Dean Mehli, and I were all within ten feet of one another, and I sensed the primal material of the area vibrating," I said. Not bragging, but still.

"We're going to go by the bank. Come back with the translation when you're done. No lollygagging," said Talindra.

The treasure engrossed them in calculating and identifying its contents.

I traversed to the Planar Mage Guild from my office, then walked through the main room to the shared room. Wallblamm greeted me. "The man holding out on us."

Dean Mehli, Bastion, and Archmage Kira were in the shared room with him. Dean Mehli appeared relaxed in his professor garb and wasn't wearing his elven mage combat gear. I saw that the few requests for help that were posted on the wall board a week ago were all cleared.

I looked at the two elves, the gnome, and the human in the room and smiled. "My cluelessness caused me to hold out."

They stood, except Archmage Kira, who was in the elven calming period. Wallblamm hugged me, Bastion gave me a fist bump, and Dean Mehli and I shook hands and patted the other's shoulder. Archmage Kira said, "It amazes me how fast humans move through life, but you have strong winds at your back, Master Argrenn."

I didn't know how to respond. "I see things that need doing, and I do them."

"Was creating a destructive acid spell that any mage can cast something that needed doing?" she asked, but a smile broke her stoic face. "My friend, Dean Jarlenteria, is in a difficult situation, but we will help her. Dean Mehli will present to you your promotion. This promotion will force upon you two guidelines. The first is that you may defend Sardyna with destructive magic." She paused and looked at me and added, "It is good you obtained Sardyna citizenship."

That was as close to a compliment as I'd received from the archmage. She continued, "The more important guideline, from my perspective, is you cannot release any spell you create to anyone at the college who is your junior."

"Everyone in this guild may see your spells," added Dean Mehli. "But no one else until it qualifies for release."

Despite my confusion, I knew I should share the spell. I opened my work square and pulled out the work around *Argrenn's Acid Attack*. "It's only a glamor," I said.

Dean Mehli chuckled. "Three beginning students can almost cast a glamor and want this spell after seeing your video yesterday."

"Let me guess. The construction portion where I disabled the trap?"

The gnome Wallblamm laughed so hard he fell out of his chair. With tears in his eyes, he said, "What's funnier, the word *safely* or that not less than ten gnomes have come to me since yesterday for help with cutting metal?"

"Check this out," said Bastion. "He put a slowdown to protect the tunnel and put a delay hook in the rune."

"If I didn't slow the spell, it destabilized. Of course, that reduces its value in combat," I said.

The four bent their heads to copy the spell, the archmage finishing in a couple of minutes. "It is customary for others to test your spells."

"I hope others use it," I said. "I finished it when no one was near and had half a day's notice to leave on yesterday's adventure or I would have found someone."

Bastion rolled an ivory scroll case over to me. "This is the only useful spell I've ever written. It's not combat, but please use it." I opened it and read the title—*Ingress Protection.*

I smiled. "You forgot to follow the naming rules. It should be *Bastion's Ingress Protection.*"

Bastion laughed. "Time to rename it."

Wallblamm rolled a scroll case over to me. "I followed the naming," he said and laughed. "It may not be useful to you, but this is my contribution to the gnome aerial ships."

He'd created an incantation called *Wallblamm's Friction Remover.*

"It's not as useful as it sounds. It's only good for fifteen feet. We use it for the engine parts on the flying machines. It's great because the components are all within ten feet."

Dean Mehli stood. "Because you translated Ancient Aossi to Aossi and created a spell, you have proven to be of more value to the University of Sardyna than a researcher. It is with my pleasure, on behalf of the head of the university, Dean Jarlenteria, that I present you with your new title and teacher's room key." He handed me a pile of pamphlets and squares. "The pamphlets will explain everything. But, besides teaching," he tapped his pad, and I felt my pad in my square vibrating, "I have chosen you to test and approve of my masterwork twenty years in the making."

"Whoa. I don't know if I can."

"You are the only one who could," said the archmage. "Consider your height and hair. You cast planar extensions with aplomb and are no longer human. You have resurrected the Tuatha race and are the sole mortal member of this race."

"The work is theoretical," said Dean Mehli, pointing to his book. "The potential in translating between power and magic is incredible."

"Translate. Oh, crud," I said. "Talindra told me to get back after I translated."

Everyone in the room laughed. "You better hurry," said Bastion. "That stinger in the wall perturbed Talindra. You don't want to make her angry."

They watched me live.

I said my goodbyes and walked into an empty living room—except for Daisidian. "Where is everyone?"

"They should be back soon. They rode to the bank to deposit their money. Oh, the crown is yours. Kitara left a note under Talindra's honey-do list."

I spotted the headpiece immediately, sitting on a side table, and the now familiar pull drew me to it. Picking up the note tucked beneath it, I read, *The tiara is called the* Scion of Hy Brasil *and can only be worn by a Tuathan wizard. It will conform to your style wishes. The tiara holds up to six stones. Talindra wants you to tone down the look. The current stones give physical protection, more intelligence, and spell protection.*

Taking the crown from the table, I thought of a subtle headband tiara with a thin titanium-looking band hidden by my hair. The tiara needed more input and jewels to meet a configuration acceptable to it. I imagined subtle blue sapphires and the heraldry symbol we were going to formalize when it had enough information. I conjured an image in my head and soon wore a thin band with two blue sapphires in the shape of a sword at my temples. They weren't subtle, but this looked fine to me. I placed the gold, silver, and bronze stones above my head and they floated above the tiara, just as I'd seen in the cave. It used Danaan steel for the base, the same metal as my chain shirt.

This information appeared in my head. I hadn't learned anything by it appearing in my head for a month and it bothered me this still happened. Geoe's ability to implant information in my mind vexed me.

I turned around and showed Daisidian. "How is this?"

"A lot freaking better. We worried you were going to walk around with a crown."

One vote of confidence. I peered at the pamphlet and put it out of my mind while I cast a *Fistful of Fire* into the hearth. I made leaf, poured myself a cup, and sat in the living room with Daisidian.

"Yesterday, you looked like you had it all going on. Today you look beat. Terrible news?"

"No, I got promoted at work. My workload increased from in-control to out-of-control."

"Yeah, adulting sucks," he said.

I agreed, since I didn't want to bring up the invasion in a record-ed location. "We finished one task and are supposed to jump on the next. It takes a while to get used to the new things."

"How do you get into the flow?"

"Well, I feel sorry for myself for a little while, do a couple of sim-ple tasks, and find myself in the new thing." I chuckled. "Feeling sor-ry for myself isn't a requirement."

Daisidian laughed. "I have my next job task, but I don't know where to begin."

"So, do you want to get past the feeling-sorry-for-yourself part and get to the minor tasks?"

He stood up, pulled a stick out of his pocket, and extended it. This small antenna-looking device hummed. "We have ten minutes where cameras and recording devices won't work."

I steeled my face at the surprise and hoped he would unload his secrets. "Okay, shoot. I have similar magic for writing in my office."

"The pad says I work for the Navarre Investigative Service. In reality, I work for the Coalition of Human Planets Investigative Service, CHIPS. I gather information, trade out documents, and report back."

That made sense. "Go on."

"Well, my next task is open-ended—to find out about a plan to break the gaming license of Geoe."

Things clicked together in my head. "Like the takeover of Sardyna by a Vrelth agent?"

His jaw dropped. "How did you know that?"

"I guessed," I answered. "Well, I took an educated guess. Gormesh mentioned it in our briefing. Plus, I translated information about an invasion."

"If I try to spy on Feston, it tips our team's hand and puts us in jeopardy."

"Well, we can't tell everyone in public, but Avaris sold one property to Feston and two others to someone named Urnovher. The Vrelth, through Urnovher, contracted Avaris and Feston to create an army of thralls to kill us."

"I have information on an Urnovher. How do I justify investigating him and not Feston?"

I showed him the note with Urnovher's name in it. "Tell them you got information from me in a team briefing and it's the best lead. It works because that's the truth."

Daisidian perked up. "OG, you are a lifesaver."

"We are friends, and a team," I said. "You helped me remember we're all doing tough things. Teaching a class and proofreading a doctoral thesis is nothing in the grand scheme of things."

We heard footsteps on the porch and Daisidian jumped up to put his device away. "Keep this on the down-low." He hurriedly folded and stowed it.

I jumped up to slow the team at the door as it hit me that I'd asked Daisidian to go into danger and spy on an unknown enemy.

He interrupted my thought. "By the way, I learned Innkeeper Braun is in good standing in the Coalition of Human Planets Military Service, CHIMPS. He's active reserve."

I staggered at the news, opened the door, and tried to steel my face while I stood in the doorway. "There you guys are."

"Can we enter?" teased Talindra.

"Oops." I moved after delaying long enough for Daisidian.

Talindra sat. "Did you get the papers translated?"

"For your information, he's translated it, gotten a promotion at work, and made the crown acceptable," said Daisidian, sitting in his normal chair.

"Oh, yeah, that looks much better," said Talindra. "By the way, I told Chaste and Cassiel you'd stop by the guildhall with me tomorrow for a couple of combat tests. They believe they can help you with gardening. No more testing around the house?"

"I'm a Knights of Honor student now?" I needed a hug and put my arms around Talindra.

She hugged me back.

"He's a teacher now," said Daisidian. "Gonna teach the world."

"Teacher? You?" Asked Talindra.

I shrugged.

"We changed how we distribute treasure and money," said Kitara. "Money and gems found are all divided equally. We calculate all the treasure values and divide it equally after ensuring the party gets the most benefit."

"Is it because of my crown's cost?"

"They listed it as priceless," said Talindra. "So, you and I gave up our treasure share, and now you're even for putting all the original money into my armor."

She must have known that wasn't necessary, but if it made her feel better, I wouldn't argue. "Did you deposit the gold from the trip to Schlobir Wap and the PvP?"

"Yes. We had plenty of money," said Talindra. "I dropped my Shield off along with Kitara and Marick's weapons for improvement. We have five hundred gold in the account, so we're still good. I ordered a custom item, plus, I bought a hammy!"

She showed me a mini statuette of a hamster, and when she spoke a word of inflection, it came alive.

"That's cool. What's the hamster's name?"

"Hammy." She looked at me as if I'd said something crazy.

"We're short on weapons and armor for a week," said Kitara. "Talindra has her sword, and I have a new dagger."

We heard a knock on the door, and Marick let Gormesh in.

"That's how you capture attention!" he exclaimed. "Drama with Talindra and Argrenn, exploding spiders, and gore galore. Bootleg copies of the uncensored fight are on the gray market because of the video restrictions."

"Gore?" asked Talindra.

"Your trap at the killing T, plus we dramatized the door trap's potential."

"I don't need to see that," I said.

Gormesh chuckled. "Well, cheers echo in the halls at the Worlds Project offices. You knocked this episode out of the park."

That felt good. We had a test, and we aced it.

"Billions of viewers know you're serious about helping Earth." He slowed his speaking. "Now, we want to grow slower. It's a marathon, not a sprint. We have two methods to accomplish this. We will release the same videos you are used to, but now we are going to build up the human interest in you as a team and as individuals." He stopped and asked, "Everyone following?" We nodded, and he opened his mouth to continue, when we heard another knock on the door.

Two royal guards and a palace courier stood on our porch. I invited them in, but they ignored me and announced to the room, "Congratulations to the Dawnstrikes. Armiger Argrenn Dawnstrike and Armiger Talindra Dawnstrike are now recognized as gentleman and gentlewoman."

He handed me a scroll with a wax seal upon it. "Queen Isabel accepted the Dawnstrike heraldry as part of the Sardyna families of honor. To commemorate this, Queen Isabel cordially invites you to dinner upon the anniversary of King Arag's day of birth at the palace with the queen, the king, and select nobles."

He handed us the invitations and departed.

I learned invitations from the crown did not require me to answer and that Lord Fergus had kept his promise to get us invited.

Talindra held my shoulders and guided me back to sit next to her. "Sit, honey. It won't be bad."

"This is wonderful, and excellent timing," said Gormesh.

"What was that about, OG?"

Kitara tapped on his pad. "That's about three weeks away and it's a big public event covered across all of Geoe."

I stared at Kitara and no words came to me. How was this good?

"It's a fancy dinner in the castle. Nothing for Argrenn to fret about," said Talindra. She patted my leg. "He even knew Lord Fergus had arranged for a dinner at the palace, so this isn't a surprise."

Gormesh tapped on his pad. "Let's get back to it. Now, we will release the new video to start your introductions. This is to make any tweaks, and you can focus on getting us video for these actions."

"So, we're changing how we do things?" asked Talindra.

"No, hopefully we haven't missed the mark, but in the future, if you see an opportunity to create a clip that emphasizes your story, go for it." He frowned through his tusks while watching us. "Let's watch the introductory video."

That made sense to me. I turned my chair to the wall.

A video showed a black screen with a formatted title, *Guardian Knights*. A bass voiceover said, "You know them as adventurers, but what makes them so good?"

We watched a five-minute video with slick production. It showed an exaggerated version of each of us. Talindra, Kitara, Daisidian, and Marick turned out well. The gore in mine was over the top.

The video ended with Talindra posed between Kitara and Marick, with me crouched in an attack position in front of Talindra, holding fire in one hand and acid in the other. Daisidian landed in a split position in front of me, picking his teeth with a knife. Naomi and Scruffles flew over the top.

"Don't you think the part about me seemed overdone?" I asked.

"Nope," said Gormesh.

A definite no.

He explained after watching my face. "That's the toned-down version."

"Mine looked gory. Plus, I'm more of a control mage," I said. "I'm not a killer."

The room laughed.

"What do you imagine the results of your magic looks like up close?" asked Talindra.

"So, Marick is the compassionate healer who fights against evil. Daisidian is the kindhearted assassin. Kitara is the mild-mannered team player, and Talindra is the loving wife who helps everyone on the team." I took a breath. "But I'm the nerdy professor who has an undiagnosed serial-killer instinct."

"Gentleman nerdy professor," corrected Gormesh. "Talindra, can you keep acting friendly and caring for others, protecting your friends and family?"

"Yes," she said.

"What if Argrenn can't keep up the nerdy professor thing?" joked Kitara.

"Really?" asked Talindra.

The team laughed.

"Did Argrenn tell you he and Talindra will dine at the palace?" asked Gormesh and joined the laughter. "We have a team who specializes in getting your name out. This is what you need to get enough viewers to bring attention to the Vrelth on Earth."

"Okay," I gave in, "to help save Earth, I'll act like a nerd who sidelines in killing and leaving a mess."

I don't want to be known as a killer.

"Great," said Gormesh. "One more thing. Kitara, you need to wear more skirts and dresses. We have triple the approval rate when you and Talindra wear traditional skirts and dresses when you're not on adventures."

Kitara's jaw dropped and the room fell silent.

Talindra patted me on the leg, and I got the message that she had this.

After we finished hanging out, I walked with Daisidian and Marick to grab their horses. They wanted to go back to their home in Schlobir Wap, and the circle in the Planar Mage Guild was the fast way to travel. I figured they wanted to experience the Gaming Day celebration with the gnomes. After the last party, I wanted to avoid free love parties with the gnomes.

The Groove Train brought sixties counter culture and free love to a gnome community and I loved spending time there, but free love parties were not something I wanted to be near.

There was no sense in beating around the bush with heavy topics, so I dove right in. "Guys, besides my becoming a leader, our team has blind spots where we need to take ownership."

"Let me guess. You want me to own the Yuennui and information from the continent of Ardvente, don't you?" interjected Marick.

"Yes. Thank you for knowing."

He popped his knuckles. "I got this. My title power gave me all the information about the Ardvente continent. This will be the thing that kills me, so I might as well get right to it."

Daisidian shook his head at Marick, then waved his hands and fingers. "I'm using magic to guess what Argrenn wants me to investigate, and I agree."

"Well, that was easier than the two I've got coming up."

"That's why we pretend you make the big bucks," joked Marick.

We crossed onto the street to head to the Inn of the Wayward, where the team kept their horses. As we approached, Daisidian pulled Marick and me off to the side and pointed to a tall fighter in red armor. "That's Noobkiller's roommate, TPKMaster," he whispered. "It looks like he's going to ambush the new teams."

"That's the one my wife crushed with a door?"

"Sure is, and I hear he's fixed on vengeance since you two killed his partner."

Avaris and Feston had hired and outfitted bullies to hold teams back. This made the new teams live like animals. "You wanna?" I whispered back.

Daisidian pulled daggers from somewhere. "Last bit of fun before the danger."

I put my hand on top of his. "I'm all in."

Daisidian and Marick put their hands on top. "I'm all in."

We snuck around the back neighborhood behind the adventurers' guild and found our secret abandoned sewer entrance. I had

found it during one of my early quests, and we had ambushed ambushers twice there.

Marick lifted the cover with a delicate touch and handed Daisidian an unlit torch. We had a practiced plan based on his ability to see
in the dark. I used my staff and summoned my smoky-gray armor. It
might be ugly, but it protected me.

We stood in darkness and Daisidian tapped me with the torch. I
lit it, and he threw it toward the fighter.

As soon as the red armor entered my sight, I cast *Planar Pull* on
him and brought him next to us. He slashed at me, but his sword got
stuck in the planar material of my armor.

Surprising us, he ran up the wall and onto the ceiling. Marick
and Daisidian didn't have time to swing.

Two actions before we got one?

"Got him." I cast *Increased Material*. The spell summoned primal
material through the planar material realm and built up his mass
until he hit the ground with a thud and struggled to stand. "Don't
climb or fly near me, sweetie," I taunted. *Six incantations and three
formulas left.*

"I'd feel sorry for him," said Daisidian, "but this guy cut the
heads off brand-new adventurers and displayed them on his door."
Daisidian removed his helm, and the guy laughed at us. Without
preamble, Daisidian slit his throat, but in a few seconds, the wound
healed.

I ran through my thoughts and remembered Avaris had funded
the bullies. "Guys, this is like Avaris. We need to damage him fast.
Marick, hit him with your mace and, Daisidian, slit his throat. I'll
cast an extended *Ice Ball*. The key will be to do it in seconds."

TPKMaster's face crinkled and his eyes widened. "Hey, we can
make a deal, right?"

"As soon as you see my *Ice Ball* come out, do the most damage
you can," I said, ignoring the killer's pleas. My fast spell followed.

To use *Tuatha Quickness*, I had to turn off gaining my powers from Geoe. That's why I practiced every night.

I cast my extended *Ice Ball* and the bully's high-pitched, piercing scream echoed around us. Before I cast *Fistful of Fire,* his scream cut off as Marick's mace crushed his face, then Daisidian's daggers slit his throat.

"Live by the ambush, die by the ambush." Daisidian pulled out a stuffed belt pouch. "Bingo. He wasn't a citizen. He carried all his money on him."

We stripped the body, left the sewers, and covered up our secret entrance.

"Let's parade this through the adventurers' district so the others know how much safer it's gotten," said Daisidian, patting the red armor.

We proceeded with the idea and drew a crowd. "The era of bullies is over," I announced too loudly. I wished I had said that less arrogantly, but the words kept coming out of my mouth. "If anyone has questions, check with the Guardian Knights, and we will explain it to you in a way you can understand."

Thralk ran up to us and gave me a high five. Grehn waved from her doorway. Brigham and his team jogged out and applauded. The other teams, those from other planets and those funded by the Vrelth, did not appreciate this.

At the stable, I put the armor and money in the handkerchief, dropped Marick and Daisidian in Schlobir Wap with their horses, and traversed home. I performed my nightly practice and looked forward to attacking Dean Mehli's work in the morning, since it had nothing to do with killing.

Talindra was lifting the bed in the bedroom one corner at a time when I finished. "What are you doing?"

"Apparently, the floors carry the banging from this room throughout Kitara's apartment upstairs. These are rubber feet and pads for the wall."

Oops.

Talindra finished with the last one. "There, we have a sound-proofed bed."

I grinned. "You know, we don't know for sure until we test it out."

Chapter 4

The next morning, Talindra and I rode to the Knights of Honor guildhall. Since she wore regular clothes, we rode double on Starlight to give her horse, Pearl, time without a saddle. Gaming Day crowds gathered and most held a drink despite the early hour.

Talindra leaned into me. "I talked to Grehn last night."

We knew Grehn and Thralk from before Geoe and they were grandparents as well, despite having young bodies like Talindra and I. "I regretted the words coming out of my mouth as I said them."

"Your heart is in the right place, as the city is already making repairs to the streets and the teams from Earth are helping fix the inns. Now all the bullies are gone."

"That's the first visible change we've made to Geoe."

She kissed the back of my neck. "You're so sexy when you make the world a better place."

"Hey, honey," I said, "later I need to talk to you and Kitara. Will you back me up with him?"

"Back you up? Is he going to attack you?" she teased.

"Kitara will need help, and you are the only one who can help him."

The area in front of the Knights of Honor Guild Hall was devoid of crowds. The white painted building, shining marble sculptures, and precious metal adornments shined. Talindra opened the heavy steel door for me, and we found the inside of the guild was just as clean and barren of colors, other than the required banners of Sardyna along one wall.

The back room had a row where the Knights and Paladins placed their helms, even though most still wore their armor. The members lounged in the back and greeted me with calls of "enemy in the midst."

I laughed. "This is the safest place to hide from the Gaming Day crowds."

Chaste guided me through the room and opened the door to their training yard. "You have that right. Let me give you background on what we want to accomplish."

Talindra had mentioned nothing to me except that I was to come.

"For over five centuries, the knights have had a set of rules, and the rule we are experimenting with today involves the smelting process for our armor. We only use steel with a certain amount of carbon and a secret mix of other additions. Our documents say that planar mages were our biggest concern. We don't know if it's true."

"Were they not married to paladins then?" I quipped.

He chuckled. "When Talindra told us of the gardening accident, we thought we should offer to help each other. We guessed you didn't know that we can train your title powers to be more powerful."

Wow. "No. That is a surprise."

Cassiel joined us as we walked into the training yard. "There are records of planar mages, power mages, and truth mages—all wearing white noble robes—joining the Knights back then. Planar mages wrote our doctrine."

Chaste emptied a box of items onto the ground. "Here is a collection of arrowheads and bullets. Can you move them?"

I reached out with my power and easily separated them out by types. "There are four types of metal here." With a flick of my materials' power, they moved across the room.

"Bronze and steel didn't move. Iron and copper are at least ten feet away," said Cassiel to someone taking notes. "Please stand next to the target with Chaste."

We walked the length of a football field. "He wants to see if you can stop these arrows."

Five paladins lined up and fired arrows in my direction. I grabbed for the iron and put them on the ground.

"Can we try that again?" I asked.

I prepared myself, and this time, I not only caught the arrows, but I also used the momentum to stack them in front of me. Chaste grabbed the arrows, and we walked back.

Knights filtered in from the back room and watched while Chaste and three other knights pulled four sets of armor on mannequins into the training yard.

"Our notes say you can crumple armor," said Chaste. "This claim reeks of hyperbole."

I reached out and discovered two iron sets. The unstable structure needed a sturdier state. I put the iron into a lasting state. Gasps sounded from the paladins and one man screamed. Mannequin heads rolled on the ground while two suits of iron lay crumpled in a ball. The notes in Cassiel's hand taught me more in an hour than I'd learned in weeks.

I focused on the bronze one. Its copper decorative belt and shoulder pauldrons melded together and ripped through parts of the mannequin and armor to go to a stronger state. I couldn't touch the bronze.

I focused on the last one and found iron strips inside the armor to manipulate. The inner iron bands in the steel armor ripped away from the steel and merged, which ripped the mannequin apart.

"Nope. No hyperbole."

When I examined the armor and mannequins, each destroyed mannequin showed that anyone wearing that armor would have died. Though the steel armor looked serviceable; the iron braces crumpled.

Cassiel walked in with a man wearing a thick apron. He carried a piece of metal and had black on his face from forge fires.

He checked out the inside of the steel armor. "Lookin' like armor be getting steel supports from now on."

Cassiel smiled. "Borak here is a genius with metals. He has excellent theories, but we have no records to support them. Will you move those as far as you can?"

Borak tossed a large box of different sizes and shapes of metals onto the ground.

My materials power detected a lot of confusing signatures. I grasped the metals I recognized and threw them. There was a bunch on the ground, so I grabbed the whole pile and tried to throw them all.

"Try the ones that didn't move again," said Chaste.

I attempted to sense everything left on the ground and move them, but some of them felt just out of reach, others I couldn't sense yet.

"He got a wiggle."

"He shouldna' been able to do that until he is next master. Hearin' 'bout magic and seein' it a few feet away is sure different."

"Looks like your theory is still pretty accurate," said the paladin with the clipboard.

"Aye, the full metals he has complete control over. Pure squishy metals—about half as much. With alloys, it's hit or miss, but the more nonmetal in the alloy, he loses control."

"This explains the Knights' bronze armor changes."

"This doesn't explain my movement of dirt, though," I said.

"We were testing part-two of your powers. Part-one deals with the natural order of things. We don't have those notes."

I wonder if Dean Mehli's master work had those notes.

"Aye, didya test the cold iron, too?"

"We'd like one more test," said Chaste. He looked hesitant.

"Chaste, this has enlightened me. Let's do it."

"Well, we need to slash your leg with a dagger three times." He added, "We will heal you after each one."

Nodding, I removed my belt, opened my cloak, lowered my silk pants, and steeled myself.

"It will hurt more without adrenaline," said Chaste. He slashed my left leg with a dagger. "Normal wound and reaction," he said after a few seconds, and Cassiel healed me with a golden glow.

It hurt, and I caught my breath, fighting the urge to react, my fight-or-flight response skewed toward the fight. That needed to change. The video wasn't who I wanted to be.

"Ready?" asked Castiel.

I took a deep breath and gave a nod.

He slashed me again. "Normal wound and reaction," he repeated after a few seconds, and Cassiel healed me with a golden glow again.

"Talindra, come over here, please. Hold on to Argrenn in case our notes are correct."

Chaste held another dagger. He slashed my left leg.

I screamed.

My leg burned with more pain that I'd ever experienced and dropped me to the ground. My leg needed to come off, ease the pain ripped through my body as my head jerked and banged on the ground.

Three golden glows from Chaste, Talindra, and Cassiel healed my leg.

The pain left, but the memory of the agony lingered. I struggled to catch my breath.

"Our records are correct," said Chaste. "Talindra will enlighten you at home, so it's not recorded."

I pulled up my pants. "Can I try something? Put that thing into the yard where the arrows were."

Chaste complied and threw the dagger, sinking it into a wooden target dummy fifty feet away.

I reached out to the dagger. This thing needed to be destroyed. Too much pain. It had to be evil. I hated that dagger. It needed to be gone.

"Honey, maybe you should calm down first."

But her words were like a buzzing in my ears as I focused. *I should extend this power.* Without a state, the metal never existed. If I removed the state variable from it... An explosion rocked the entire guildhall and thirty-foot hole appeared when the dust settled where the wooden dummy used to be.

Shields, magical and normal, surrounded me. All of us were on the ground. "That's impossible," said a woman's voice behind me. "We warded this entire area from magic."

"Huh. That was unexpected," I said.

Cassiel laughed nervously. He helped Talindra and me to our feet. "I sound like I dodged a scorpion stinger," he joked.

Talindra glared at me as if I'd said that.

Chaste hooked his shield on his armor. "We have a new entry to our base of material knowledge."

"I wish I knew more, but I believe I removed its state condition from it," I said.

A paladin next to Cassiel jotted something in a notebook. "Anyone who figures out how to hurt you with that weapon also knows what the penalty is."

"Argrenn, this is for you," said Cassiel. He handed me two books. Physical copies with paper and binding. "You lead one of our paladins and we would like you to help grow your leadership. Here are two Knights of Honor officer training manuals. The *Five Mandato-*

ry Rules of Close-Quarters Battle and *Ten More Guidelines to Close-Quarters Combat*. Remember, you are a friend to the Knights."

"Wow, thank you," I said.

"Thank you," he said. "We updated a six-hundred-year-old document, thanks to your help."

Talindra grabbed my arm and guided me into the packed streets. We didn't get time to summon Starlight before a gaggle of children ran near us. They screamed, waved wooden weapons, and pretended to fight monsters. They stopped when they ran into Talindra and I.

"It's you! The heroes!" Multiple children yelled toward us. "Can you fix our swords?" asked one boy.

"Are you the good guys or the bad guys?" I teased.

"We're the good guys," the children screamed.

"Bring all your weapons near me." I rolled up my sleeves and pulled the cloak over my head. I put on a show with the waving of my hands. A dozen wooded weapons appeared in front of me. I held the ends and used planar magic to set them to state zero. A quick peek and they looked like new.

"Cool! Wow!" The children yelled.

"You need to go vanquish evil," said Talindra.

The children ran off.

"That was sweet," she said.

The streets became too crowded to ride, so we walked and moved past posters of the Guardian Knights and action pictures of us posted all over the city. Adults filled taverns and the market square had enough noise to hear from two blocks away. "We will not get much done today," I said. "I'm going to spend the time reading these manuals in the office."

"Okay, party pooper. Kitara and I are going to go out and have fun."

"Will you two be okay?"

Talindra looked at me laughed. "Will a paladin in plate armor and a sword mage be safe around civilians?"

I laughed with her. "Habits."

While they were out, I did more than just read the pamphlets. Talindra's powers became part of my study, so I wouldn't make the same mistake I made in the dungeon.

She returned home tired, and we went to bed, despite the noise outside that went on until late.

After breakfast the next morning, Talindra reminded me that we had the furniture change out and the backyard work starting.

I opened the door to see deliverymen standing there. They took a step back when they saw me. Kitara took the space and walked into the house as Talindra gave me a small push and invited them in. Ordinary residents in Sardyna gave mages a wide berth. Talindra and Kitara killed things as fast, but the workers avoided me. If they viewed my actions in the Knights of Honor guild, they may run from the house.

Talindra put her hand on my shoulder. "Can you vamoose for the day while I get them started?"

"Argrenn and I have similar tier-two skill checks," said Kitara. "Plus, I don't need to be ogled by these guys." Kitara wore one of Talindra's long skirts, leather boots, and a normal shirt. It looked awkward, but Talindra was better than me in discussing clothing with him.

I grabbed the pamphlet Gormesh dropped off and put it and my book in my office, then Kitara and I left to do skill checks.

"Time for board quests," he said.

I groaned.

"They give mages and sword mages these quests for skill points—finish five in an hour, twenty in a day, one in ten minutes, and a few others."

"Well, let's do it. Skill points are worth their weight in gold."

"Okay," he said. "We'll ride double since you don't have to tie up Starlight. Where else can you get us?"

"From my house in the noble district, I can get to the planar mage building on the university campus or the guild district in the guild quarters. Then, from the Planar Mage Guild, I travel between Schlobir Wap with the circle."

"The creative mages use the word teleportation. Why don't you call it a teleportation circle?" asked Kitara.

"Because we don't teleport. It's why I use the word traverse when I use the circles and the office. We leave our current plane in the same way the office door works. We travel through the planar material, the material they make all matter from, in a pre-carved tunnel; think like a VPN. There is no movement through this prime material plane."

"That sounds safer than the creative mages."

"How do they move?"

"They alter the energy patterns around the person. Then they convert the matter to energy, move the energy at near the speed of light, and rebuild the patterns with the same energy, which they convert to matter."

"Well, safer than new energy or matter," I said.

"Right. That would be crazy."

We spent the day on the most mundane of tasks—delivery quests, escort quests with shell-shocked participants, fetch quests, and location quests.

"These are too easy with a Loremaster and Master of Materials," I said.

"We chose the easy ones because we don't do many of them." He tapped on his pad and shook his head. "You're already a level beyond the party. You will have two levels on us after we finish. The party needs to catch up to you."

Back at our furniture-less house, Talindra sat on the porch steps.

"We can't go to the Inn of the Wayward," said Talindra. "Braun changed furniture there, too."

"I'll set up my campsite on the back porch," I said. "A night under the stars won't hurt."

We circled the house to avoid dragging dust inside and walked into a further torn up back yard. I summoned my campsite with the infusion in my staff. A tent, three cots, and bedding appeared. Smoky-gray planar material without lines or other colors appeared. I made it large enough for the three of us.

The events from the Knights of Honor guildhall waited, and the three of us sat out on the porch and looked up at the sky.

"Daisidian got a missive with information about his brother," said Kitara.

Talindra looked at me and put her finger to her lips.

"His duty had him as an observer. But someone killed many pilots the night before the attack. The Vrelth hit his Hornet, and he lost power. He regained backup power in enough time to land the plane in a field near Dahlonega."

"Wow. Was he injured?"

"Broken bones, but he is flying again. All the governments and military on Earth have fallen, but ex-military continues the fight. Mercenaries from other planets joined the Earth resistance, and he flies an Umillon Atmospheric Combat Flyer."

"No video of that, I assume?" I asked.

"Right, need all the protection they can get. Aren't your grandkids on Umillon?"

"Yeah. It's the furthest planet out from Earth in space where the homo genus became dominant. It's about fifteen light years from Earth. They're terraforming the second planet in that system and have lots of room, which is why they're more active."

"Marick didn't get good news," said Talindra. "They lost his entire base in a ground attack."

"He seemed relieved they fought to the death and aren't on a slave ship," said Kitara. "I guess I'm lucky. I have no one back home. I won't get bad news."

"The best news we can receive is only good by comparison. Good news is someone is on a new planet with a brand-new reality, or they're on Earth in a war," I said.

"Yep, my aunt and uncle died and aren't on a slave ship," said Kitara. "That is good news too, in a way. So, what did you hear? I heard you've got good news."

Talindra looked at me. "Did you check your missives?"

"No, I do that right before bed."

Talindra scrunched her mouth at me, not taking the question. "You know Margaret took Ella and Ari on the field trip and landed on Umillon, where they live in a bubble while the planet finishes terraforming. We got one more piece of good news. Nick made it to the woods, and he's still alive."

Three months in the woods. He could survive out there.

"We got more news on the girls, but they didn't find anyone else."

"That doesn't mean much; they only looked for immediate family. If Nick made it to the woods, others did too," I said, but I knew it for a lie. Nick had a bug-out bag, plenty of camping gear, and enjoyed living in the woods for an extended period. Knowing about the immediate family felt good, but Talindra and I came from extended families. Our kids and grandkids were on Umillon, but we knew a hundred more relatives and had no information about them.

"Hey, I already hit up Daisidian and Marick, but we need to drop one unpleasant item on each of us."

"Kitara and I have talked," said Talindra.

"Good. Did you discuss how you need to step up and be an offensive force?"

"Uh."

"Honey. You have become a world-class defender. When the chips are down, you've shown you are a threat to evil as a stone-cold killer. The team needs you to step up and enter fights as a killer. We haven't read our weaknesses in there, but I guarantee that a strategy to fight us takes this into consideration."

Talindra didn't look convinced.

"I take vanguard for the party. I can help you like you're helping me," said Kitara.

"Are you sure I need to be offensive?"

"Yes, the threat has to be constant, that if you come within reach of Talindra, you will die."

She pulled out her hammy and let it crawl around in her hands. I let her dwell on it.

"Kitara, we have a blind spot in the camps of the nobles. Talindra is part of the Knights of Honor faction and has limited access. I represent the mage and university factions and have a limited ability to penetrate nobility further."

"Right, the four principal houses and seven minor houses have a lot happening."

"Well, you will only make headway in talking to them, explaining our position, and finding out how we can help them if you're someone they're comfortable with and dress the way they expect."

"You don't want me to be a spy. You want me to be a part of the noble discussions and represent us."

"We're the good guys." I paused. "Look, we all have work to do. We all know my leadership is the weak link in the party. Even Gormesh's video pointed it out. We need to have all the information and friends we can get."

Kitara played with his bracelets. "You're right. We all have to grow or we won't help Earth."

"Hammy agrees that I should attack more."

I felt sick to my stomach. I dropped a heavy load on my best friends, but we either wished for things to be different or we made things better. If we had any chance to help the Earthers, we couldn't sit around and mope.

"We shouldn't leave this heavy," said Kitara. "Everyone, tell us something silly about yourself."

Talindra and I stared at Kitara.

"Come on, you made us do the intense thing. You can act fun."

"Okay." I smiled. "It's weirder than fun, but when something big is happening to me, my head plays a soundtrack."

"What?" asked Kitara.

"So, like when I'm about to kick butt, I'll hear metal in my head."

"Nothing good?" teased Talindra.

"Like I know I'm about to cast my best magic when I hear a heavy, distorted G chord or a screaming vocal."

"Okay, I get it. That is fun. Talindra?"

"When I was younger, I had an MG Midget, and I did all the maintenance myself. I even replaced the brake master cylinder. Plus, I had a sailboat, and I did all of its maintenance, including all the barnacle cleaning."

"Whoa, that is so cool. Now I'm going to look lame."

I laughed. "Nope, you gotta do it now that you wrangled stuff from us."

"Okay. I began gaming because the high school's D&D group's computer broke. I opened the case and reseated a memory card and the computer worked perfectly. They invited me to join, and it was the first time I had friends in a long time."

Talindra clasped her hands together. "That's a sweet story."

"Yeah. we all scattered, and when my aunt and uncle kicked me out, I lost the ability to track them."

"I bet at least one of them is watching you now and saying, is that him?"

"If they saw me now, they'd stare while speechless."

Talindra and Kitara laughed together.

The next morning, Talindra worked with the workers and movers early. Braun brought breakfast. I couldn't shake a nightmare about Whizzburr. In my dream, I searched everywhere and couldn't find him.

I departed with Kitara after breakfast, since the workers avoided me and I slowed progress. Kitara and I got right to quests on the board of the adventurers' guild. We did three quick quests and ended up in the market district next to a magic shop. "Hey, Kitara, I hate to slow us down, but I need to shake a bad dream I had."

"A bad dream and you still remember it?"

I shrugged. "It's about Whizzburr, and we'll see him today." We walked into the magic shop, and after a quick perusal, I found a scepter that had three light functions. One was a beacon that went up twenty feet.

We rocked board quests the rest of the morning and ended up in Schlobir Wap for lunch, enjoying a pleasant meal since Daisidian and Marick joined us there. By horse, the gnome town took weeks to ride to, but with the circles, we visited each other whenever we wanted.

"Wallblamm said he thought you were in town," said Daisidian.

And just as I had predicted, Whizzburr joined us. "Most excellent, most excellent," he greeted as he approached the table.

"Whizzburr, great timing. Come join us."

The gnome mayor walked over with a big smile. "Most excellent, most excellent," he repeated. "A second lunch is most excellent."

I pulled the scepter out of my handkerchief. "Whizzburr, I had a dream I searched for you and I haven't stopped thinking about it. Here is a scepter that has three light functions. If you use this third one, it shoots a beam vertically."

"You are giving me a gift?"

"Yes. I want the peace of mind that if I look for you, I can find you."

The mayor's eyes teared. "You got me a gift so I wouldn't become lost to you?" He hugged the scepter.

"Yes."

The mayor hugged me too, and I hugged him back. He collected himself and joined us for his second lunch.

"Hey, guys," I said. "What have you been up to? We are power leveling with board quests because mages have weird skill checks for tier two."

"A bunch of refugees passed through here. It's like a parade north because they believe war is imminent," said Marick.

"Most unusual, most unusual are the stories the refugees tell," said Whizzburr.

"They may be right," I said. I watched Marick. He had received bad news but gave no signs that he thought about his old unit, and that worried me.

"Well, they have weird stories. I'll research more and get good info while I do the early season healing."

"Okay. Anything to research?"

Marick leaned in and lowered his voice. "Rumors say that the leaders from Ardvente can create vampire thralls when a soldier dies. Then, when the thrall dies, they can bring the soldier back to life."

Mayor Whizzburr shook his head. "Most unusual, most unusual."

I agreed. "Get as much info as you can, because if it's true, we have to do something."

"They also say troops are already inside Navarre."

"I need to get my mind off of this stuff. Mind if I join you?" said Daisidian.

"Do you mind sitting between Kitara and I on Starlight? We can fit, but when I say we move fast, I mean fast—regular horses are too slow."

Soon, Daisidian, Kitara, and I knocked off quests. We moved even faster since a halfling nimble assassin had opened a lot more quest possibilities.

Daisidian had us laughing during the afternoon, and the three of us joined Marick, Whizzburr, and Wallblamm for dinner before Kitara and I headed back. Kitara needed to level, and I had two levels. I needed to slow my experience gain.

"Thanks for hanging. Tonight, I leave on my job," said Daisidian. He looked at me, and I knew what he meant.

"Hey, Marick, got a minute?" I held the door open and he joined me.

We walked outside toward the airship port. It was quiet now that the workday had ended.

"What's up?"

"I wanted to make sure you are fine. I know you spend more time away from the group than anyone else, but you received bad news, and I'm just checking to make sure you're good."

"Well, I'm not good, but I'm not bad. I'm not ready to talk about it yet."

We were silent as we passed a couple of gnome guards and looked at an airship.

"You don't have to, but you can come hang out with me even if you don't want to talk."

He pulled something from under his armor. "Daisidian brought me dog tags. But, man, I appreciate you, and I may take you up on that sometime."

After dropping Marick back off, Kitara and I traversed back to my house, finding the new furniture set up inside. Kitara glanced around the space and then turned to me. "You and I have finished our skill checks for tier two."

"Wow, you two must have had a busy day," Talindra looked spent, and I felt guilty for how hard she worked during the day, but now I had to know what had happened at the Knights of Honor guildhall.

The three of us went into our bedroom and blocked out the lights. Besides, inside the "privacy"—what Geoe referred to as restrooms—only darkness assured the camera did not record conversations. Talindra started, "Guys, we've been lax in keeping each other up to date. Do we know anything new?"

I agreed. "Yeah, good idea. I have learned a few items."

I couldn't see Kitara's face, but heard him say, "Well, given the comments people make about the three of us in the comment sections having these meetings, we should be productive."

Talindra giggled.

I didn't want to know what that was about. "We know of the whole Groove Train except Jealder. We know the ages are because of Lighttouch absorbing years. None of that is new. Keep this on the down low, but Daisidian doesn't work for NIS, he works for CHIPs. The Coalition of Human Planets Investigative Service."

"Wow."

"Wow is right. I'm the one who threw him into mortal danger."

Kitara's bracelets clacked together. "I bet he volunteered."

"He did, but I stepped it up and have a pang of guilt over it. There are things I can do to help him, though."

"The knights heard that the team from Atlantia, the one led by a paladin and a warmage, are going to bow out of the Battle of Champions, leaving the field to eight," said Kitara.

"That is big news," I said. "But it sounds like a mixed blessing. A warmage and paladin led team could be allies to us."

"It's stronger than that," answered Kitara. "Atlantia and Sardyna have favored trade relation status with each other."

We were quiet for a minute, and I added. "One bit of unrelated news that's weird. The Coalition of Human Planets calls their military service CHiMPs."

"Funny, but not too relevant."

"Yes, but Braun served for decades and is still in active reserve."

"I told you he was more than a military geek," said Talindra.

"Right, we have CHiMPs support and the Groove Train. I can't wait any longer—how did they prepare the dagger that burned me? Special arcane magic? Demon-sourced?"

Talindra leaned over. "That wound on your leg opened so far and festered. Even though only one of us needed to, we all healed you. We were all shocked by how a cold-wrought dagger performed against you."

"Cold wrought with a spell, right? Cold wrought means unforged and hammered into place."

"That's what I mean," said Talindra. "We double-checked. That's why we were so shocked. It has something to do with your Tuatha race. A human put his strength, skill, and effort into a blade, and it changed the blade in a way we can't detect."

"That's a better theory than I have," I said. "I'll do research tomorrow."

"How did you make it explode? Explode in a magic free zone with an explosion large enough that our training yard is unusable."

"You blew up part of the Knights of Honor? How did they keep a university mage blowing up the Knights of Honor out of the news?" asked Kitara.

"I—I don't know yet, and I don't know if I can do it again. It happened after I lost control and got angry. I need to figure that out, too."

"The head of the guild, Cassiel, invited Argrenn for training," Talindra answered Kitara's question.

"That explains how they kept it quiet. If you two can bring the two strongest factions in Sardyna together, I understand why it's so important for me to become part of the noble court." Kitara's voice sounded resigned, but not happy.

The next morning, I grabbed water and a piece of nut bread and settled into my office. I left the door open to get rid of the claustrophobia I experienced in the small room. The back wall had fake windows with a live feed over the university quad. Today it didn't fool me. I'd dumped the heavy load on the team, but I had to accept my own heavy load. Unless I became a leader, I would be a killer, and our team needed the best leader they could get, not the leader I had been.

First off, I needed to reap the benefits of a day and a half of board quests.

Talindra strode out in her armor. "What's up?" I stood up and grabbed my staff.

"Sit," said Talindra. "Kitara said I needed to catch up in quests. We're going to do board quests today. Braun and Palmer are over to help the workers, so leave yourself available."

"Why the armor?"

"Knights of Honor cannot travel through the city for more than an hour without armor." She adjusted her Knights of Honor sash.

I walked over and gave her a kiss. "Okay. Be careful, and while you're out, can you sell any of this stuff from TPKMaster that Daisidian or Kitara doesn't want?" I pulled out a belt pouch of money. "Please make a run by the bank. I'll feel better if debt collectors don't come."

She gave me a kiss, grabbed the items, and walked out with the others.

Time to level.

At level two-point-four, I cast eight incantations and five formulas. I had five new spells, counting the ones from level two-point-three: *Trailing Pain, Planar Helper, Material Jump, Planar Destruction,* and *Jagula Segura.* The additive extension I made used two spells that required concentration: *Manos Planas* and *Jagula Segura.* I hoped it worked.

Selecting *Planar Helper* gave me relief. This is how I helped teammates, no matter where they were.

I chose *Two-Handed Casting* to work with *Tuatha Quickness.* It let me cast spells twice as fast with a bunch of restrictions. The two-handed nightly rune practice kept paying dividends.

I wrote these in my traveling and standard spell books. The formulas took a while to write in the books, but I finished up as Sardyna rang twelve bells.

I stretched my legs and sauntered into the kitchen, noticing workers milling around the backyard. "What's up?"

"The chain wraps around the pulley whenever we lower the fountain," said Braun.

A man I didn't recognize added, "They hooked the fountain up wrong, and if we undo it, it swings around and snaps anyone who climbs up there. If we raise it, we risk the fountain breaking."

Above me, I saw a chain wrapped a few times around the chains that had the fountain secured.

"You need the chain unwrapped and held out while you lower it?" I asked. I didn't ask why they'd lowered a fountain into my backyard or why we had so many hedges.

"That's the crux," said the man.

I cast *Body Projection* and created a projected hand.

Murmurs reached me from around the yard, but it wasn't loud.

I moved the hand up and untangled the chain. It snapped, but the hand caught the chain before it tangled again. "I got it. Go ahead and lower it."

Ten minutes later, the fountain landed. The statue of Archangel Michael on top of the fountain had thrown it off balance.

The workers applauded.

I dispelled the hand to ease any lingering concerns. "Need any more magic?"

The man laughed. "No, sir. I did not know that magic had uses other than killing."

"Thanks, Argrenn," said Braun. "I sent Palmer out for food. He should be back soon. Do you want us to bring you some?"

"That would be great," I said.

I grabbed a pear from the fruit bowl by the sink and walked back to my office. Maybe one glamor at a time was enough to start citizens liking mages in Sardyna.

But I had work to do, and researching my race seemed a good place to figure out yesterday's cold-iron events. I pulled up history and archeology for elves, gnomes, and humans.

I found a "tree of humanity" in a school textbook, which was perfect for my needs. I switched the words to Earth equivalents. Not all names had English translations, but I found *Homo erectus*, *Homo habilis*, and *Homo sapiens*. I asked my board to generate names to the unlabeled based on human naming conventions. It filled in *Homo eladrin* and spun *Homo habilis* and a *Homo orcus* off the *Paranthropus boisei*.

I learned half-elves originated before elves, and half-orcs before orcs. It did not create them only through procreation. Gnomes, dwarves, and halflings descended from *Homo floresiensis*.

Closing that screen stopped me before I wasted a day with interesting stuff that didn't help my goal.

Tuatha, Formians, Aossi, Vrelth, and Yuennui were what I searched next, but they hid that research from adventurers.

Huh. Another dead-end.

I pulled the note off my desk and added more detail to the spell I wanted to write. *~Sulfuric acid plus iron makes hydrogen. Contain the hydrogen and ignite it for an explosion. Use containment routing in* Jagula Segura *for hydrogen containment.*

With that done, I pulled open the book Cassiel had given me. Close-quarters combat techniques looked boring but necessary. The first page contained mandatory rules. Rule one looked basic. *Exposing yourself without cover fire is a good way to die.* They showed a picture of a person with only their head in a doorway.

Rule two stated to *only move at the speed you can think.* Easy enough, I had given a no-chase rule to the group.

Rule three discussed room entry. I knew the left-right clearance rule, and we'd followed it.

Rule four covered distance. We'd followed this rule too well. We kept each other within sight. While this gave us suitable cover, it opened us to an area of effect spells. Avaris had taken advantage of this with large balls of fire.

The last of the hard-and-fast rules covered weapon discipline. This had not affected us yet, but if others turned off Geoe's powers when I did, it might become an issue.

I took a break and walked out to check on the progress. A couple of workers had planted hedges, and someone had dropped off a load of bricks.

"I'm on my way to the inn," said Braun. "They'll wrap up soon, and I'll be back tomorrow."

"Thank you, Braun. Sorry for all this work."

"I should thank you. I had signed a contract stating I would make external property upgrades and had forgotten. Talindra's suggestions are beyond what I'd thought about, but they will make the leaders of the city happy."

He bid me farewell, and it wasn't too long before the sound of trudging feet clumped on the porch, signaling the return of my little family. I let the group come in to rest.

"It's a lot harder to do these without your mount and circle access," said Kitara.

"What do you think of the new living room furniture?" asked Talindra.

A quick look around got me up to speed. "This loveseat where you and I sit was a great idea to sit together and give more seating." The wall by the window had two chairs with more room. "I didn't even notice you got a halfling size chair until I looked right at it, and you put it in the spot where Daisidian normally sits." There was no reason to mention we had seven places to sit in the room. I passed the new furniture test.

I helped Talindra out of her armor, sat on the porch, and looked at the work that had been done.

"Wow, that statue is big," she said.

"All the hedges look awesome," said Kitara. "Almost like a maze."

"They needed the help of a mage to get this in, so I guess it's good I stayed."

We settled in for the night, allowing for a moment a feeling of peace to reign.

Chapter 5

The next morning, Talindra and Kitara rode off to the Knights of Honor for an errand and to do a couple of board quests before Kitara checked in on Lord Fergus' businesses.

Despite wanting to relax, I headed to my office. I put Dean Mehli's masterwork on the edge of my desk and organized my squares. There were eight on my bandolier now—the room key square, office key square, university pad square, a new camera square, a teaching room square, spell book squares, and two blank squares.

The pamphlets Dean Mehli gave me for my new position said I needed to teach two classes a year and write a spell for the college. My class was a new piece of stress that weighed on me, but I might as well get started on it. With my camera in hand, I walked to the kitchen to figure out a second location to film. The painting in the hallway captured my eye. *What if the painter captured the mage's movements like I plan to capture mine?*

I studied the mage lifting a wave of earth in the *Defense of the Defeated* painting. The artist captured the mage at the end of an extension rune. What was the mage doing to lift the ground where he used an extension?

I filed the thought away and sat at the table. This shot was a reasonable second location to record since it had the hearth in the background where I kept *Fistful of Fire* burning. Satisfied with a test shot, the next task was to program the teacher's room key. I quickly made one classroom for our team with comfortable seating.

Setting up the classroom for several students brought back the reminder that kids were prepared to take my class and, if I did not teach them correctly, they would go into the world and die. I certainly didn't want to hurt students who wanted to become mages, and determined to put thought and care into my instruction. I perused the list of classes and chose one on beginning hand runes. This class was a first year required course, but I knew this information inside and out. Since arriving on Geoe, my nightly ritual took an hour of practicing spells and hand runes with both hands.

I scheduled the class to start four weeks from now, which allowed me to put in notes and videos in preparation. Considering the instruction I was to give, I wondered, *What would I have taught if I relied on Geoe's control?*

Back in my office, I set up the camera and gave it commands: "Shot one is to capture me. The second shot is to capture my hand. In every shot, search for this symbol," I made the symbol for *Argrenn's Acid Attack*, "blur out my lips and hands during this symbol."

"Should this be a standard shot?"

"Yes."

It felt weird to have a camera talk with me, but snakes talked to me in French. It's not my job to tell Geoe what magic can and cannot do. I set up the camera to point at me, a green light lit, and I opened my standard spell book and practiced the hand runes and spells.

The recording lasted an hour. Perfect. I thought of the first assignment; four hour-long recordings practicing hand runes in different environments and conditions, which would show the dedication needed to master magic. I looked for a notebook to keep notes on my class and remaining tasks. Not finding anything, I put the classwork and pamphlets away and pulled out Dean Mehli's masterwork. As I prepped to make notes, I realized I needed supplies for this, too. No trained gobelyn traveled to the administration building for professors, so a trip to the university administration building came next.

In the planar magic college, I realized I should bring food back with me and my arms may not hold everything. A quick cast of *Planar Butler* and Vern followed me into the administration building, where the woman at the front desk pointed me to a checklist. I got the standard professor list and added a new traveling spell book, which appeared at the desk. To pay for it, a box appeared for me to agree to twenty gold per month for six months.

Vern picked up the book and supplies and followed me out toward the food trucks.

"Excuse me, Professor Dawnstrike?"

It took me a second to realize someone spoke to me and looked up to see two kids ambling toward me. *Kids—I should think of them differently.* My body looked their age.

"Yes?" I answered.

"Your course on hand runes—are you teaching that this year?" asked the one on the right.

That was fast.

"Yes, I've already filmed the first video and created the first assignment."

Their eyes were wide. "Would watching your videos now help?"

"I'd like to say yes, but no. When I teach a class, my interest will be in making sure I set the students who take the class on a path to make their own highlight videos. That means hard work and nothing flashy. This will be a difficult pass-fail course." *That should slow interest in it.*

Neither answered; both jaws dropped.

"I need to get lunch before my butler times out."

"Yes, thank you for your time, professor."

This was the first time people had come up to me and spoke about something that was not an immediate concern, and it felt weird. Maybe I made Sardyna more accepting to mages, and this was an early step. Vern added my lunch into his load and we ended up back at my office, where I had my lists of tasks. The first thing was learning Marick's powers.

Five hours later, the six bells of Sardyna rang and still little in Dean Mehli's work made sense. In the kitchen, I was preparing to film the next video for the assignment in the second location I'd scouted earlier when Talindra and Kitara strolled in, laughing, which made me smile. We didn't laugh enough.

"Hey, I'm going to film a video for class, but don't worry, it's my nightly ritual."

Kitara placed an armful of silk and fur clothes on a chair in the living room. He had bought feminine clothes to fit in, with Talindra's help. My focus on becoming a better leader needed to step up. I'd asked the team to take on difficult tasks, and they were coming through.

Talindra sauntered over and gave me a kiss. "Mister Professor. Retired from adventuring?"

I tasted... wine? Weird, she rarely drank back on Earth. Maybe she and Kitara had a glass of wine to make clothes shopping less awkward? "Nope, this is to allow me to keep adventuring. You can do whatever. It won't distract me."

I set up the camera, pointed it at myself, and instructed it to use earlier settings. I practiced each rune a hundred times with each hand and matched key parts of the hand location at spell points to make sure the spell worked.

If I created the rune at the same time I recited the spell, the spell fired, but I could not practice the two parts improperly. My solution was to add another round of practice where I matched key hand positions with the spell's proper time. My nightly ritual meant practicing with both hands, with the upshot being I practiced each spell four times.

Talindra dropped an apple near my hand. I caught it with my off-hand as a tomato flew by. She used to be a wonderful cook, but I guess becoming a paladin made it harder on her.

My filming location needed to be rethought when Kitara caught a dropped knife with a jerk that caused his bracelets to clack together, and my spell book almost got caught in a spill when Talindra knocked over a drink. After I finished the video and said, "End recording. Normal study routine two," Kitara and Talindra cracked up.

"How did you not break concentration?" Asked Talindra.

"Casting a spell and losing concentration with an open portal to the primal material of creation is bad. Part of my practice is to focus intently, so I never break concentration."

"Primal material bad. That sounds bad." Kitara laughed.

Great, Kitara had been drinking with Talindra.

"Chop up this meat so we can finish cooking dinner," Talindra instructed.

Kitara broke in and added, "Oh, Fergus figured out the ideas were yours on the Salas Keep project."

The meat needed to be unwrapped first, and I set to helping with the meal as we chatted. "Well, I can give you another once-over when you need it."

"He didn't mind. In fact, he seemed glad you knew about building out areas, keeps, budgets, and other requirements."

Talindra turned Kitara around to face the living room. "Go try on one outfit," Talindra urged. "Let Argrenn see one we picked out."

I chopped up the meat and was helping Talindra cook when Kitara walked out wearing a green and gold-trimmed dress.

"How do you do this belt again?" He held out a metal belt with flowers engraved on it.

"Line up the middle flower on your stomach. Nope, higher, you want to accentuate your waist, not hide it." Talindra guided Kitara through a strange loop and clip process.

I didn't know what to say. We knew Kitara played a lovely half elf woman even though he was a man, but I didn't want to hurt Kitara's feelings nor treat him any differently. "No fur on this outfit?"

"See, Argrenn notices more than he lets on." Talindra helped Kitara with his hair and pulled it out more towards his shoulders. "Kitara has the same issue with muscles and shoulders as I do, but where I need help upstairs, he doesn't."

Kitara turned red and my face got hot.

"So, we minimize this with thin layers of silk and drawn attention up and lower."

Our team wasn't a party team, and those two didn't handle wine well. "I think you have made excellent choices and I appreciate you stepping up to help the team."

Kitara went and changed back into a more relaxed skirt and top while we ate and hung out for the evening.

After Kitara went upstairs to her place, Talindra gave me a long kiss with wine breath, grabbed my hand, and led me to bed.

The next two weeks were similar. I prepared for class, studied Dean Mehli's work, reviewed the Knight of Honor training, Learned the powers of my teammates, and researched magic. Talindra took her class and picked up her shield. Kitara split his time with Talindra and Lord Fergus. Marick healed in Schlobir Wap at a timber camp. And Daisidian traveled on his errand that only he and I knew about.

The palace meal was hard to keep out of my mind as signs celebrating the king's birthday were all over the city, but I kept my focus on the important items. I finished the first section of Dean Mehli's work, studying the first few chapters, and I noticed something. Dean Mehli discussed the theory of parallel paths through the planar material. The next part caught my attention. It stated that when two parallel paths were stable, the first path did not need a rune if it passed through non-damaging material.

I traveled to the university to finish my work, pacing through the halls, forcing myself to sit when my legs hurt, trying to jump my brain into action.

Soon, I realized I needed to clear my head. After getting fresh air, I summoned Starlight and rode back to the house. The streets of the university, artisan district, guild district, adventurers' district, and noble district distracted my brain, but the ride didn't help me solve my problem.

The next day, Kitara and Talindra left early again. I took notes, researched, pulled out two more books, and still got nothing. Understanding the problem eluded me, but once I found the solution, I was sure the pieces would fall into place.

I sat at the table at the house, eating an apple and a piece of bread, when an exhausted Talindra and Kitara arrived home. "Where did you two spend today?"

"A class at the Knights of Honor. Is that all you ate for dinner?"

"Eh, my brain hurts from thinking for three days about a problem," I said.

Talindra slid by me over to the kitchen. "I'll cook for the three of us."

"You're not filming again, are you?" asked Kitara.

I felt my eye rolls remembering the last time I filmed with them in the kitchen. "I want one when we are in the field."

"That'll be fun," said Talindra. "Here, can you give me a flame in the hearth to speed up cooking?"

I walked over and tested my new extension on *Fistful of Fire* at formula strength and put a flame in the hearth over a foot in diameter. Then it hit me that while I studied Dean Mehli's work, my calculations only considered normal spells. This was the painting's epiphany. It wasn't one section of the work that referenced extensions; it was the entire work.

"Okay, I'll bite. Please put in a big flame and move out of the way so I can cook."

"Sorry," I said, stepping away. "I had an epiphany."

"Aarrgghh. Me caveman Argrenn. Me learn fire hot," teased Talindra.

"Ha, ha," I replied and laughed. "Argrenn, no space cadet."

We had a pleasant evening, sitting around and talking while Talindra played with her hammy.

"Argrenn," said Kitara. "I don't know if you've gone over your personal quest yet, but the two of us will travel to a mage-only area. Thirty-five years ago, the last planar mage who made it to this tier and tried this quest never returned."

Talindra opened the door in the backyard to let the heat out

"Whoa, slow down," I said. "Personal quest. Got it. What do you mean 'mage-only'?"

"Only mages who can cast incantations can enter through a certain door."

"Ugh. We have to take out Feston's group before we do this then. What about the last planar mage?"

"Finish the talk outside. It's nice out," said Talindra.

We had new chairs on the back porch. Healing potions might have made more sense for our money, but the backyard looked much nicer now.

Kitara fiddled with his necklace as he explained, "Fifty years ago, Timmeonne Mehli had a different personal quest. Nigel Queensman specialized in planar materials. He had this quest and never returned."

Kitara showed me the quest on his pad; *Recover Nigel Dreamstale's Body*. "You need to recover the body, too?"

"I have to recover a different body from the crypt."

"So, don't do the quest," said Talindra. "It's too dangerous."

"Not necessarily," I said. "I'll review the videos of this Nigel and see what spells he used. That will tell me whether it's dangerous and how to beat it."

"Talindra and Marick can quest together as well, since only a person who can heal can enter their dungeon."

"Oh, I don't like that," I said.

"Why not?" said Talindra. "You can go on a quest with Kitara, where everyone with your specific powers dies. A place where I cannot protect you."

"One person died."

"Where every person died," she continued. "But I cannot travel with Marick to heal others since you cannot go? Are you on a weird trip where you need to do everything?"

Okay, to turn into a leader I needed to delegate, know the strengths, weaknesses, and power of my party, perform my duties, but I also needed to trust them. "I don't like it, but that's not a no. We need to take out Feston's group, and you need to research the quest. In no way am I saying you cannot go. I want you to do the same amount of research I'm doing."

She looked at me and nodded. "Okay."

Leadership was hard when your wife was on the team. She and Marick together were a lethal and safe combination, but I still didn't relish the thought of not protecting her.

The sound of horses clopped nearby. The noble district stayed rather quiet along this road, and I looked up and watched as Lord Fergus and a dozen guards led a carriage toward our house. I stood and used planar material to clean myself.

Lord Fergus motioned us to stay put as he opened the door and the king and queen stepped out. The queen looked over our wall and said, "You are so right, Fergus. This is lovely. Such a good use of this space." They discussed our garden and fountain for a few minutes, got back in their carriage, and moved along.

"Weird. Or is it me?" I asked.

"Weird," said Talindra, "but we made improvements less than a mile from the castle."

"So, like an HOA on steroids?"

She laughed.

Kitara's bracelets clacked as he sat. "Oh, Daisidian accepted his personal quest and is out of touch with the pad again."

"No worries, there are spells for this situation." With a piece of paper, I wrote *if you need anything, write it, and I'll get it to you this way* and cast *Planar Helper*. A smoky-gray box with feet and wings appeared. I opened it, described *Daisidian Black*, put the pen and paper in the box, and sent it on its way.

"He's cute with his tiny feet. What is it?" asked Talindra.

"*Planar Helper*, I can transport that box to anyone. Once it's delivered, the box returns and disappears."

The box did not come back that night.

The next morning, while I examined the works of Dean Mehli within the context of extensions instead of as spells, my *Planar Helper* arrived.

I need food, water, and sense. Please check on me in a week. You're a lifesaver, OG.

Wow, glad I checked. I asked the elf at the front desk if the campus had a shop.

"Yes, professor," he said. "Next to the Immutable College, the pyramid, is a small, ancient brick house."

The store had a stranger selection of items than any student store I recalled. I walked over to the student behind the counter after I verified the money. "Hi, I need to send a care package to a friend in the mountains. Any suggestions?"

He seemed happy to help and pulled items off the shelf as he described them. "These cups generate three cups of water per day, regardless of the environment. These elven bars give a full day of nutrients for a human."

The prices for each were the same as a gourmet meal. I picked out a dozen bars and one cup. "Where are the potions?"

The student pointed to a shelf behind the counter, where I added a healing potion and a potion of invisibility. I paid five hundred and seventy-eight gold.

In the quad, I cast *Planar Helper* and put the bars, cup, and the two potions in the box. I described *Daisidian Black*, and the helper left, then I sent a note to Talindra to let her know I'd spent the money to send Daisidian a care package.

Back in my office, I made a breakthrough writing my new spell, but missed lunch because of my focus. To finish up the spell, I needed to move material while simultaneously creating another material without a rune.

I was deep in thought about the problem when two students stood in the doorway and knocked. One held a dummy made of straw. "Professor Dawnstrike?" the other asked.

"Yes?" I packed up my books and got ready to head home.

"I—I have a problem with my first glamor. I followed the process, but the spell fails."

"Which glamor?"

"*Planar Pull.* I see it's one of your favorites."

"Who are you testing it on? Are they a valid target?"

"It's a school dummy," he said.

"Put it over there, please." I cast *Planar Pull* at the dummy, and it landed next to me.

Someone had created a valid target to test. "We did not train on a school dummy. I cast my first spell at a gobelyn, trying to kill me with a crossbow."

They looked at me wide-eyed, like they'd never heard something so crazy.

His friend set up the dummy, and I suggested, "Let me watch you."

He cast the spell, and it fizzled.

"You didn't finish the rune before you finished the spell. My nightly ritual is practicing runes and saying the spell without opening the tunnel. I put my hand in the correct spot so the rune finishes a split second before the spell. This glamor finishes like this."

I rehearsed the spell and put my hand in the two places on the two syllables. "Match your hands at the lower left during the XOR syllable and your spell should work. Try it again."

He cast *Planar Pull* and pulled the dummy toward him.

"Oh, my. I did it! It works!" the kid exclaimed.

"You will never mess up a spell if you practice runes nightly." I walked to the door.

"Oh, I will, professor. Thank you."

Outside, to clear my head, I summoned Starlight and rode back toward the house to work on my problem. As I passed the library, I noticed Feston. He stepped out from the shadows near the building and pulled off his hood. His pale face stood out, glowing white against the black of the cloak. He smiled, waved to me, and mouthed, "Bye-bye."

I looked at both sides of the road as I crossed over. Shopkeepers had closed up shop for the evening. Then Starlight stepped off the bridge and disappeared from under me.

Chapter 6

"Getss the wissardss whilessss he'ss downsss!" The hiss startled my brain into action.

They made a mistake in attacking Starlight first, since I landed on my feet, ready to act. Two of the Yuennui with tentacles for hair and arms dodged shopkeepers as they charged me. I steadied myself by catching myself on the post of the wooden bridge, careful not to damage the tiny replica of Sardyna's five-hundred-foot statue that adorned the post.

I used the distraction of their phrenetic path to cast my panic move, the additive extension of *Duplicate Me* and *Body Projection*. It worked and gave me the time to hide behind a doorway and plan my attack. This was stupid of me. I lost focus and allowed myself to be ambushed with no support.

There were a few doors open and plants and other displays were still out on the side of the street. I made a determination to keep the fight centered in the street. My head kicked off with some Eerie music and the words "superstition, fear, and jealousy." My brain wanted to fight with Rob Zombie's <u>Dragula</u> as a backdrop. *Cool.*

Before they reached the false image of me, I used my projected hand to cast *Planar Winter* on them. Snow swirled around them, hail pummeled them, and ice made them slip. They were a good ten feet from the bridge. One made a beeline for the projected hand, so I cast ice at him with it. He died in place, bashed with hail and ice.

The other stood and ran toward my duplicate. *Six incantations and three formulas left.* I cast *Fistful of Fire* from my *Body Projection* hand to save spells. Missed.

They both stood now, and the first one swung and took out my duplicate. The other screamed in French—I mean Formian—at my *Body Projection* hand. I couldn't make out what he said, but I doubt it mattered. Another cast of ice and a hit. Blood poured from a gut wound where Ice broke through its scales. Wounds from the hail collected on his shoulders and back.

One Yuennui left the *Planar Winter,* attacked my *Body Projection* hand, and dispelled it.

"Now we will see where you are, pearl-haired Tuatha." The insult came out in perfect Navarre. There was something different about this Yuennui.

I threw an extended *Fistful of Fire* at the other one. It hit him and blasted through his chain armor. *Four incantations and three formulas left.*

They both charged at me. This song caused me to have some reckless ideas, but very few of my paths to victory allowed for me to hang back and hide. I charged back to throw off their timing and cast *Planar Escape.* A boom echoed through the street, ripping up stones and throwing the two Yuennui to the ground while stones and debris rained on them. I used my materials' power to dig up the ground under them, forcing them to dig themselves out, then ran behind some three-foot-tall planters in front of an artisan's store. I saw the half elf women hiding in the store and I nodded to them, hoping to calm them.

It suddenly hit me—I knew how to solve my problem with the masterwork. An extension could combine the methods to summon and move simultaneously. I would cast *Duplicate Me* without making a gesture or voice the spell. What a bad time to realize this.

The most gravely injured Yuennui staggered and fell to its knees. As it struggled to stand, I cast *Ice Ball* at it. It died, and his pummeled body bled onto the torn-up road, but the living one moved forward and slashed his scimitar into my thigh.

Why hadn't I put up my armor? Another hit would kill me.

Duplicate Me got me out of the way and away from the two artisans in the store while he recovered from a lurch that missed me. It staggered with its face smashed, bloodied, and covered in ice. Four of its tentacles lashed out toward me, and two of them stung me as I dove to my right. It ignored my duplicate and continued after me. The sting in my gut hurt more than the one in my arm.

This Yuennui ignored my duplicate each time, spoke perfect Navarre, and took more damage than his partner. My incantations were gone. The sting numbed my left arm, but I still had two formulas left. I cast a *Planar Winter* to slow him.

The Yuennui slipped, and the hail beat it to the ground, where it cast *Ice Ball* at me. My crown activated. The heraldry symbol caught the spell and sucked into the gold floating stone.

I threw a *Fistful of Fire* and missed.

Four tentacles lashed out toward me, two hit and sent a shock through my face and leg. My face felt like it was on fire and my left leg stopped working.

He closed on me and I cast *Planar Escape.* I landed prone fifteen feet away. The Yuennui lay on the ground, where rocks from the road rained on him.

I tried to get on all fours but fell, watching as it too tried to push himself up, but the tentacles failed and its face met the street.

I struggle to lift my good arm, but as I cast *Fistful of Fire,* the other lost feeling and planted me on my face.

With one last *Fistful of Fire* from a prone position to make sure it died, I took stock of my situation. There was a pool of blood underneath me. One arm no longer worked, and one leg wouldn't respond. Using my two useful limbs, I struggled to move to the side of the road. Failing to drag my body, I kept a wary eye on the two creatures. My face felt like it had been burned, and my gut screamed in pain. This was not how I had intended to spend my evening.

I heard galloping horses somewhere nearby, but failed to push myself into a sitting position to get a look in that direction. Twisting, my gut screaming at me for the motion, I was able to pick out white and brown horses heading toward me.

Blood spattered on the ground as I coughed violently, even as relief eased through me that help had arrived.

The blood puddle spun around me as I stared at the ground, then a golden glow sparked me to my senses. I felt better, but my gut and face still hurt. Talindra stood beside me. I wanted to hug her, but my left arm and right leg didn't budge. "Can't move, skin fire."

"Hold on," she said, her voice laced with worry.

Kitara was suddenly beside her and dragged the two bodies over, putting both of their belt pouches over me, tucking them behind my back.

"Shelley," cried Talindra. A woman in plate armor appeared over Talindra's shoulder. "Paralysis," she explained, clenching her necklace with the medallion of the Archangel Michael. She removed my hood and smoothed back my hair.

Shelley removed her helm and placed it next to me. She was my wife's friend and had heard things about me that might not have put me in the best of light. It's how friendship worked and how spouses dealt with each other for long periods of time. But Shelley was an elf who'd lived for hundreds of years, healed others for centuries, and exactly the person I needed now.

Her short-cropped brunette hair brushed against my face as a golden light filled her whole body. She grabbed my arm and leg. "Tuatha are so hard to heal," she said. "Can you move now?"

I moved my arm and leg, but the fire on my skin permeated through me. I felt myself jerk on the ground.

"Slow down, honey," said Talindra. Her whole body glowed, and she grabbed me by both shoulders. My body shuddered, and I vomited something black that Shelley burned with celestial power.

I was finally able to stand, and Shelley and Talindra guided me to a shop wall to lean against.

"They ambushed me." Too much had happened, and I craved sleep. The wall kept me standing. I pointed to my crown, in part to make sure my arm still worked. "The difference was the Scion."

"Professor Argrenn Dawnstrike of the University of Sardyna and the co-voice of the Armiger Dawnstrikes," said a male voice behind Talindra and Shelley.

"He is in his destructive phase," said Shelley. She pointed to the blown-up street, scorch marks, and piles of hailstones that had not yet melted. Still, she handed me a vial with a yellow fluid in it. "This will give you two more hours of alertness."

"They were Yuennui Teuer," said Chaste.

I drank the lemonade tasting fluid and gave her back the empty vial.

"Who helped him fight?" asked another male voice. I knew him from the Knights of Honor, but did not know his name. "The incursion alert sounded less than ten minutes ago and recommended a full squad with a healer."

These were the Knights of Honor. I needed to pretend I had it together.

"Who helped you, honey?" asked Talindra. "That's Chaste and Parisel. You remember them, right? Chaste is responsible for these assassins and has a ton of paperwork."

"No one. I rode alone." I stood up straight and looked over the situation. Eight riders in plate armor arrived besides Talindra and

Shelley, four provided crowd control. Two stayed mounted while the other two investigated the Yuennui.

"Thank you for the heal, Shelley."

"Impossible," said the Paladin I figured was Parisel.

"You should have seen him in the training ground the other day," said Chaste.

"They made two mistakes," I noted.

"Alone?" exclaimed Talindra. "We have a two-person rule for travel. Enemies want you dead, and you traveled alone?" She stopped holding onto her medallion and glared at me with clenched fists.

My eyes looked at the ground by her feet and struggled to meet her face. What a failure of leadership; I didn't follow my rule for the team. "Sorry, I got caught up in work and forgot about the game, and I—it doesn't matter. I screwed up."

Shelley put her hand on Talindra's shoulder. "Later."

Dean Jarlenteria rode up with four university guards. The time needed to sort out this situation grew, and now more than one person needed to be mollified. I felt sorry for the citizens in the artisan district trapped in their buildings.

Kitara handed Chaste a paper he'd taken from a dead Yuennui Teuer.

"Dean," said Chaste with a nod to the paper.

"We will assign guards from the university," said Dean Jarlenteria.

"He says no one helped him fight," said Chaste. "All evidence supports it."

"We counted two magical signatures, but the second originated from one of these two Yuennui Teuer, so it looks like we have a bigger problem."

"Indeed," said Chaste.

I saw a banner for the king's birthday and I realized I could not keep things out of my mind to focus on the most important. I should have prepared for it long ago.

They discussed a topic I was not privy to, so I kneeled and used planar magic to clean up my blood on the street. Next to the hole from *Planar Escape,* I scooped the dirt into the hole and placed as many rocks on top as I could find. It took five minutes, but with a few guards' help, I finished fixing the street with my materials' power by resetting it to an earlier state.

I waved at the woman who sold us the paintings in our house.

She responded with a weak-wristed wave.

An elven man jogged out to greet the dean. "Dean. I graduated the college last century. This mage kept the battle from the citizens and kept it in the street and never looked to retreat and leave the enemies there."

I looked up from kneeling on the street at the dean and paladin after a compliment which I wished was still unknown.

The paladins and dean stared at me as I stood up and brushed myself off by the repaired street.

"Okay, Talindra," Shelley said. "Maybe he is a keeper, regardless of the messes he makes."

The remnants of *Planar Winter* melted from the warm water flowing in the pipes under the streets of Sardyna, so other than an extra sixteen of us in the road, the area looked normal.

"Professor Dawnstrike," said Dean Jarlenteria.

I didn't appreciate the title. When someone used it, it meant I needed to do something for someone. Her tone didn't suggest I'd receive an award for effective street fighting. I steeled my face and turned.

"You will have an assigned university guard with you at all times. Do you have questions about the guard?"

I nodded and asked, "I will cast *Bastion's Ingress Protection* spell when we enter the house from now on. Should the guard be inside or outside the spell?"

She thought for a bit and answered. "Outside, but when you use your office, you bring them with you, and they'll stand guard in whichever location you work."

"I understand." Having a guard stunk, but it pacified Talindra, and this was an order from my boss's boss.

Jarlenteria waved me over and showed me the document. It had my picture on it and said *five thousand gold pieces.*

I pointed to the stronger of Yuennui. "This Yuennui—"

"That's enough, professor. You fought valiantly and with great skill, but you have not had time to reflect, and things you say out loud could cause unnecessary panic."

I'd been told to shut up before, and this time it was almost polite.

She turned to Chaste. "You should let Cassiel know Talindra will be at the palace for dinner tomorrow night. And remind him that Talindra is the wife of the mage who survived." She paused. "Won today's fight in front of an audience."

He chuckled. "After last week, no one in the Knights needs a reminder of who Argrenn is and who he is married to."

Shelley laughed and mounted her horse. The other knights loaded the Yuennui Teuer onto spare horses as Jarlenteria gave me a curious look.

I put two and two together. What would Jarlenteria know about that I witnessed? The Yuennui Teuer cast magic. They could not do that unless—unless they used Geoe's magic and that meant I had fought a Vrelth. No wonder she told me to shut up.

Chaste turned to Talindra and said, "Please escort the professor to his house. Expect a visit tomorrow for your successful completion of this week's course and preparation for your visit to the palace." Shelley patted Talindra on the shoulder and said something to her.

Jarlenteria handed one of the university guards with her something small and gave him orders.

One problem with adventuring is we become habituated to wearing armor and weapons and forget civilians do not think this way. I treated guards the same as professors when I should note guard factions and loyalties. I inspected the guards now to distinguish them later.

They wore black boots and navy-blue pants with gold greaves over the shins. They had thin chain mail that hung from their shoulders to their thighs. These differed from the green and bronze tabarded guards of the college. Gold vambraces over the forearms and a longsword at the hip completed the armor and weapons of the guards. They had a gold tabard with the university griffon in navy-blue embossed on the front. None of them had a helm.

Talindra and Kitara mounted. The guard Dean Jarlenteria had spoken to, threw something to the ground, and a warhorse with chain barding appeared at the spot.

Kitara headed to the Inn of the Wayward. "Hold up, Kitara. I need you nearby to cast this spell so you can get into the house," I called. He rejoined us, and Talindra gave me a look.

"We all traded spells in the Planar Mage Guild. We all have this spell because Bastion leaves his house in Mhenorian often and needed a protection spell for his windows and doors. When I cast this, only those designated in the spell's casting can enter through a window or door. You, me, and Kitara will come and go, but I will have to drop it for anyone else to enter."

"Can they dispel it?" asked Kitara.

"Nothing in the planar mage powers has dispelling magic as an option. We'll have to find an immutable mage and ask someday."

Once we reached our house, I stood outside and scoped out the three doors and four windows, with an emphasis on the large window in the living room. I designated Talindra, Kitara, and myself, and cast the spell, then turned to the guard and told him, "I won't be going anywhere tomorrow since clothiers will come to dress me."

"Acknowledged, professor."

Talindra followed me in while Kitara rode around the corner to the inn. "I'm too tired to cook," she said as she plopped onto the chair on the other side of the room and not on our loveseat.

An early relationship lesson I learned helped me now. Talindra looked upset and tired and told me she did not want to cook. That was code for I needed to cook while she collected her wits. If Shelley was right about that lemonade potion, I had enough time to make a meal.

"Let me see what we have." In the kitchen, I made sure the meat smelled good and moved the bowl of oranges and tangerines out of the way. On the hearth, I cast two *Fistful of Fires* twelve inches from each other. Since it warmed fast in here, I took off my cloak, sash, vest, and bandolier and hung them over a chair next to my staff.

With two *Body Projections* and *Planar Butler* to get Vern, I cut up and prepared the food. Vern worked the water pump outside to fill up our tank. I peeked through the hearth at Talindra, and she'd removed her helm, breastplate, vambraces, greaves, and boots. They lay on the floor next to her. I grabbed my staff and clothes and put them back in the bedroom.

When the water pump was full, Vern picked up the breastplate, plate skirt, and boots. I picked up the vambraces and greaves. We brought them to Talindra's office and placed them on her armor mannequin, and I set them to state zero. After heating a kettle, I plopped in my chair in the living room and kept the hands stirring the pot with the spoon.

Talindra had her hamster out, petting it with her finger. "Hammy wants to know why you used magic to cook and clean."

"We acted the same way back home."

"There is no magic on Earth," said Talindra. She let the hamster run over her hands.

The thin barrier to the planes didn't help as much as I'd like with extensions, and the lemonade vial was wearing down. "I read about and used new technology all the time. You adopted it slower. My job made me develop computer code to get results, while you used computers when you needed to for a specific task. Replace magic with technology, and our life is similar."

I stirred the pot with the spoon in my projected hand and moved the kettle away from the flame. "Talindra used to pal around with friends, go to lunch and dinner with them, and at work, she hung out with her work friends. "

She sat still for a minute before she asked, "Are we the same? Did we exchange technology for magic?"

"Some superficial changes—like you're muscular now and I'm weak. But, yeah, we're the same."

"I don't recall you acting like a hero."

"Heroic? How many in Sardyna would say I'm a hero? People would call this self-defense, since I'm a citizen. If we were back on Earth, saw a drug deal, and we shot two criminals who tried to kill us, would we be called heroes?"

"The elf said you did heroic things."

"I did the minimum to protect unarmed citizens, but this was an attack on me. They probably were in no danger."

She squirreled her mouth at me.

"I chose a wizard because it looked fun, but it turned out that I excel with magic. That makes others want to kill me. It's unfortunate, not heroic."

"I hoped we would be heroes," said Talindra. "Otherwise, what's all this for?"

"The team, and my part of the team, is heroic. The Guardian Knights are heroes. We're fighting extreme odds for a chance to save lives. We have no guarantee of success or guarantee that our success adds value, but we fight. That is heroic."

She dispelled the hamster and sat up straight. "That makes me feel better."

"Or we're stupid. Either way." I laughed.

"I'm glad you crack yourself up."

"Look, I spaced out by traveling alone. The problem I have is the city is part of the game, but we have to be functioning adults. That isn't a normal part of gaming. I focused on my job and forgot about the game."

"Kitara said the hard part of Geoe was 'adulting' plus gaming."

"You two have an advantage over me. Kitara has to learn to be an adult and to exist in a woman's body. That helps him keep his focus. You focus to learn how to game."

"That's an advantage?"

"I know how to adult, and I know how to game. Sometimes, this feels normal and I can lose my focus, like I did today."

"So, what do we do about enemies trying to kill you?"

I thought for a second and opened my mouth to speak, but had no ideas—well, no good ones. "Talk to the team, because I need help."

She stood and kissed me. "That answer is acceptable. Let's go see if your magic hand has finished cooking."

I stood. "You know, *I* cooked. The hands are a tool."

"Magic hand stew smells good."

After dinner, I had time to do my nightly practice before falling asleep. My last thought was my new number one worry. Feston had become more brazen.

Chapter 7

The bed rolled me over as Talindra got up. Despite the exhaustion from the extensions I cast yesterday, I needed to give out information. "Wait, honey. Block out the light."

She closed the blackout curtain again. "What's going on? Is this more of your leadership stuff?"

I sat up and rubbed my eyes. "I need to talk with you and Kitara about an idea to protect the Persevering guys and the Tree Huggers."

"Get dressed. He and I are going to the guildhall again."

Kitara joined us after we dressed and prepared for the day. We kept the bedroom dark so the game wouldn't record us.

"Is this about Daisidian?" asked Kitara.

"I have no more information about him. He asked for food, water, and common sense. I sent him a magical cup that makes three glasses of water per day, elven food bars, and a potion of healing and invisibility."

"Why invisibility?"

Kitara's bracelets clicked like when he gripped them. "I couldn't send common sense, so I sent the next best thing. A way to escape an awful choice."

Talindra giggled. "Sorry."

"I have a question. Your disguise—can you look like another person other than Kenton?"

"Yes, why?"

"I have an idea to trap the sales guys in PvP. Talindra meets with Grehn and Thralk's team. You meet with the Persevering team. We coordinate travel through PvP areas for them, and they mention it in the open. Talindra makes a point that she will escort them. I can alter my image for real—not an illusion. You disguise yourself so you and I can lie in wait to ambush the sales guys once we are in a PvP area."

Kitara took a while before he answered. "Right, your hawk is fast and can get Talindra back in a hurry. Plus, with your holds and my new area of effect spells to soften them up, we can pick them off one at a time, since we have a couple of levels on them now."

"Yes, you and I might kill them before Talindra and the party return. The two teams can focus on their quest after this."

"Okay. Over the next two days, Talindra and I will coordinate this. No one will pick up on the ruse if you stay out."

Three of Avaris' adventurers remained, and Feston still had his complete team. We need to remove those resources from Feston.

The three of us walked into the kitchen to grab some breakfast. I saw Talindra pull out two tinctures to dip into leaf. Then she mentioned which days they needed to drink tea with the addition.

I grabbed a piece of bread and fruit and move directly to my office. I knew why Talindra used that tincture. It wasn't my business why Kitara did. My feet moved even faster when I heard giggling behind me.

Alone in my office, I had the day to myself. After I learned Kitara's powers and finished writing the spell, I watched videos of Nigel. I gnawed on a pear, projected Nigel Queensman's party quest on my wall, and focused the picture on him.

Nigel had been an evoker planar mage. He liked to be in melee but didn't knock enemies to the ground. We called those casters *blappers*—a blaster with the mentality of a scrapper. His effectiveness as a combat mage mesmerized me, and I needed to rewatch the videos.

Three videos in, I picked up on his unconventional fighting style. He used wind spells for damage, relying a hundred percent on a shield he evoked at the last second. That's when it hit me—he had mastered non-metals. His control of air and water made me wish I could talk to him about combat.

This Nigel fought circles around his enemies in close quarters combat. His reflexes and ability to see the next move were beyond what I'd achieved, but that told me what I needed to know. If Nigel couldn't beat the dungeon by fighting, neither could we. Plus, Nigel was a stone-cold killer, and I didn't want to be a killer.

After I wrote my spell and matched up the party's powers with each other for lethal combinations, I configured settings for my classroom. The first configuration was for our team and contained a dozen comfortable chairs spread out in a large room. It wasn't a place to teach spell-casting, math, or anything important. Since I had a large class coming up, the next configuration held fifty students.

The student lab needed a practice room, and those I had to choose from got me excited. One room had casting dummies, protections from miscast spells, and monitoring from the administration building... a real practice room. No one told me I had access like this.

Now it was possible to test out my *Two-Handed* spell casting. I selected the practice room configuration, walked out of my office, closed the door, grabbed my teacher's key, and opened the practice room. The room needed to be tested, and I wanted to calculate my best damage combinations to work with my teammates.

Inside the room, after selecting it with my teacher's key, a two-person firing range appeared that measured one hundred and twenty feet long and sixty feet wide. Another thirty feet at the top remained for viewers, and each of the two firing portions measured thirty feet wide. The room was perfect and would make me better.

With a target dummy set up sixty feet away, I cast *Fistful of Fire* at it from each hand and watched the counter. My count per minute topped out at forty spells in one minute. Something didn't work correctly. The spells cast three seconds apart. *Tuatha Quickness* didn't work. I had forgotten to turn off Geoe's control of my powers. On the next test, fifty-one *Fistful of Fires* cast for over twenty-five percent more damage. The damage cast totaled three hundred and seven.

My next test cast at that speed for five minutes at multiple enemies. I calculated a better average damage per minute, what the counter called DPM. I removed my sash, bandolier, cloak, vest, and Danaan-steel shirt and hung them up behind me. The cloak only protected me from natural weather, and this was not natural. Then, with a counter reset and a five-minute timer focused on my skills, I recast at full speed.

Sweat poured from me and soaked my T-shirt. One thousand five hundred and thirty-eight fire damage made the room hot. My next test used my seven incantations for *Ice Ball* and filled out the minute with *Fistful of Fires*. I reset everything and began. One minute passed, and the ice balls helped cool the room. The heat made me sweat, but it felt good. I did one hundred and five damage in ice and two hundred and sixty with fire. My DPM totaled three hundred and sixty-five.

My *Planar Destruction* formula test closed out my testing. I had five formulas to cast. I reset and set up calculations based on the last tests. After the setup readied, I threw the five conjurations in rapid succession and finished the minute with *Fistful of Fires*. Before I got over ten seconds in, the room's alarm sounded.

Warning. Room environment at the limit.
Warning. Room environment at the limit.

"Hi, whose room is this?" said Dean Mehli's voice.

"Hi, Dean, It's Argrenn. I calculated my DPM with my new skills in a few different circumstances, and the room malfunctioned."

"That should be impossible. We can check it out if you swing by the university."

"Be right there. Let me get my guard."

The air outside the house was cold. My sweaty t-shirt clung to my skin, and the breeze reminded me how much I relied on my cloak. The guard and I traversed to the university and met Dean Mehli and Dean Jarlenteria. Thank goodness I'd brought the guard.

Dean Jarlenteria wore her full regal garb, and Dean Mehli wore his robe. They brought a handful of guards in full university guard regalia, who held back onlookers. My sweaty t-shirt and sweat coated silk pants were out of place.

Before anyone spoke, I told them what had happened. "I prepared for my class and discovered configurations for spell casting practice rooms. To kill two birds with one stone, I tested a configuration for the class and calculated my best DPMs."

Dean Jarlenteria walked past us into the room and looked at the board where I calculated items. She pulled a pad out and tapped on it while she scrolled through the screens I used. "How are you getting this damage?" she asked.

"I have *Tuatha Quickness* and *Two-Handed Casting* for major skills now. With the extended the *Ice Ball* spell... Oh, Dean, I tested your masterwork and could have gotten more damage if I'd used the double and split method attached to the *Ice Ball*."

"What I mean, Professor Argrenn, is Geoe has limits for damage. How did you exceed these limits?"

"Without Geoe magic. I practice hand runes with both hands for an hour a night. I focused on my skills and took full advantage of *Tuatha Quickness* and *Two-Handed Spell Casting*."

She laughed. "Professor Argrenn, the entire school can view these rooms. Killing a vampire one-on-one has made you a campus celebrity. Please let Dean Mehli know if you plan to practice in the lab again. You have broken no rules, but while lower dress codes work for most in the university, please stay dressed."

I pulled the sweat-soaked shirt from my chest and grimaced.

"Dean, I will have a team make a viewing screen in the quad. You present what professor Argrenn accomplished and we can clear out the quad before six bells." She whispered something to Dean Mehli that I overheard, "you were right."

Dean Jarlenteria stepped out and disappeared after two steps.

Dean Mehli watched the video of me. He shook his head after looking up and saying, "Cool. It's amazing to see theory work."

"It's nice to know it works before I put my life on the line."

"Enjoy your night. I'll give a quick talk to the students. You might be about to teach the most anticipated beginner's class in university history, and this will only increase the excitement."

Dismissed, I retrieved my garb from the practice room and threw on my Danaan-steel vest, silk shirt, other vest, cloak, and bandolier, fastening my sash around my waist, then waved my hand and set myself at state zero to look presentable. My guard and I went back to our house, and I walked through the door, exhausted. I couldn't continue at my current pace.

After a relaxing evening at home for the rest of the day and a leisurely morning with Talindra, I read the next class's material. I dared not ask Talindra about the plans she and Kitara were making to take out the group, so I focused on my class. Three-dimensional runes were the topic. The original class spent three sessions on different "trace holes," what the class notes called Ranura, the holes you made by leaving a space between the tip of your fingers. In fact, they recommended only teaching the easiest Ranura: the circle your thumb and index finger made when the tips touched, what we called the okay symbol.

The notes also suggested teaching two non-damaging glamor runes and *Body Projection* and *Light.* The book provided the glamors for both. While getting the light glamor for free was nice, in no way did I want to see students put parts of their bodies other than their hands around campus. Instead, I decided on *Planar Pull* and *Light* and crossed *Body Projection* off the class list. Now I felt grateful for the team taunting me during the swirl. Who knows what body parts they would subject the school to if the students learned that glamor.

I filmed my hand making each rune and broke them each into five core movements. My class storage let me store that in a different assignment area.

I answered a knock at the door. "Dean, it's a pleasure. Do you want to go to lunch?"

"No time." Dean Mehli's eyes darted everywhere, and he walked on the balls of his feet, ready for an attack despite his two guards with him. He wore his full elven adventuring gear, a magical robe, crystal sword, and round wire-rimmed glasses with a blue haze in them. His staff spun in front of him, ready for him to cast a spell. "Someone will deliver your clothes soon. After that, your carriage will bring you to dinner."

I had forgotten about the stupid dinner, even though it was exactly when I knew it would be and I still did not prepare.

"They have permitted me to ride with you in the carriage to and from the palace, though you will have to manage without me while you are inside," said the dean. "How much information can you learn now?"

I thought for a second. "Wait, what information? Things like protocols?"

The dean sat and grabbed his staff from battle position and relaxed. "Okay, Talindra got a rundown this morning. If you get confused, you can always follow Talindra's lead. Mages have allowances to be flighty."

He took a deep breath. "First thing to remember is that everyone knows you are not politically astute. They will use this against you to lower the esteem of the university or the Knights of Honor. The actionable item is that if they ask you about the role of the college, mention how much magic helped in the ambush inside the city."

That's easy—it's all I used.

"Second item," continued the dean, "is that the Duke of Rethel will be in attendance as well as the Count of Avesnes. Stay out of their fight, because they are feuding. Lord Fergus will be there. If you're worried, ask him a question that doesn't put him on the spot."

I swallowed a bit of cheese and cracker. "Okay."

"Number four, do not avoid the queen's questions, and you should ask her questions as you ask any other person."

"Makes sense."

"Number five, keep in mind the strengths of the voting houses. Queen Isabel is the highest authority, followed by her husband, King Arag. Lord Jeriche is not there, so in no way should you bring up laws, votes, or that he is not there."

The clothing artisans entered with armfuls of clothing. The dean nodded for me to carry on with dressing, and soon they washed me, scrubbed my hair, and powdered my body with god-awful scents. They dressed me in silver-colored pants with blue piping and draped a blue cloth belt from my waist to the floor.

Everything paused while I sneezed for a good minute.

Then they pulled out a frilly blue shirt with platinum piping and a patterned vest of diagonal platinum and blue stripes. They polished my bandolier, slung it over me, and slid a gold aiguillette on my right shoulder, linking it with the bandolier on my right shoulder. The male asked if I needed the floating rocks over the headpiece. The shocked look I gave him answered the question, because no one brought it up again.

Luckily, I got to wear my mage cloak, which covered much of the frilly garb. They put my cloak on me and tucked my hair into the cloak before they pulled the hood up, then made me practice taking my hood off without messing up my hair a few times before they let me walk out.

Talindra arrived during my dressing, and she looked as irritated as I felt. She had on a shiny breastplate with blue sleeves coming out and a platinum skirt with plates in it. Her boots formed into greaves and rose under her skirt. They had replaced her scabbard with a blue one decorated with pearls. Her hilt had a peace bond in blue attached to her blue scabbard belt. They had hung her Knight of Honor sash and a second sash layer on her, and she had a gold aiguillette on her right shoulder.

"What's the new sash?" I asked.

"Since you got a promotion, I took a class to meet the requirements for the royal guard," she said.

"You two look great," said Dean Mehli. "By the way, do you have cash? You will have a handler in the dinner room. After the night, it is customary to tip him ten to fifty gold for his service."

Talindra handed me a berry, two gems, and a handful of coins. "The quartz is worth ten gold, and the bloodstone is worth fifty," she said.

"Yes, I have the customary tip." The dean didn't laugh. He focused on everything he wanted to say.

"Eat the berry. It will negate one glass of wine," said Talindra.

"Also, you may get a mention of the aiguillette. It's for defense of Sardyna. The Yuennui attack inside the city is the signed-off reason for the award. Dean Jarlenteria pushed the award through. These have status at the palace."

Having digested the majority of the information dump the dean had clipped out in quick succession, I swallowed the bitter berry, and the dean opened the front door, peered left and right, and climbed inside the carriage. There was a replacement guard in formal guard attire waiting outside for me. Following the dean and my guard in, I reclined in the seat across from him, giving the interior a raised brow as I looked around. The carriage had red velvet walls, doors, and seats, boasting glass on the doors.

Living as close as we did, the trip was brief, and we soon pulled up. I took deep breaths and settled my mind and stomach, focusing on the task ahead. In games, nobles could make or break an adventuring party. One false step tonight and we would fight delays on everything we needed to do. The best-case scenario would be nothing changed in our lives.

I made a couple of runes with my left hand to calm myself.

The dean put his hand on my arm. "Don't even pretend to cast magic inside the palace." The carriage rolled to a stop. "I want you to have fun, but be careful, because it won't be fun." He handed me the invitations. "Keep these in your right hand. You get out first. Talindra takes your arm as she gets out. Hand the invitations to the doorman. He will open the door, announce you, and you walk past him." He opened the upholstered door to let us out. "Sending good vibes."

My guard got out of the carriage, made a show to scan the area, stood out, and held the door open. I got out and held my arm out for Talindra. She took it, and we proceeded between the red velvet ropes along the red carpeted walkway they spread on top of the white marble step to the doorman. We walked past a couple dozen well-dressed onlookers outside the palace with many pointing pads at us. The doorman took our invitations and announced us as Master of Materials Argrenn Dawnstrike and Defender of Light Talindra Dawnstrike. He opened his arm to let us in.

Now I'd run out of instructions, so we walked forward over a carpet with well-dressed citizens and noblemen holding drinks on either side of us. The ceiling was at least thirty feet above us and had painted frescos. Alcoves throughout the space had carved marble statues. I whispered to Talindra, "Did anyone tell you what any-one looked like?"

"Nope," she whispered back.

"Lord Mage and Lady Paladin, right this way, please," said a man in a sharp black suit with a black cape. He held out his arms to guide us. My guard stayed outside the room with other guards dressed similarly.

A man at the end of the carpet guided us to another room. He could've been a serial killer for all I could tell. My fight-or-flight response kicked in and flight was out of the question. I took a defensive stance and kept a wary eye to keep from getting overwhelmed.

I put on my spell-casting face and strut into the main room. When weak, appear strong, right?

"The queen and the king have not entered. The Duke of Rethel is on the right side with his wife. You can keep them straight, knowing Rethel and his red gloves. Lord Fergus is the man over there," the man in black added, pointing to the other side.

"I know him," I said.

"Yes, well," he said, "the other man is the Count of Avesnes. You can remember him by that gaudy 'A' he wears on his jacket. Go to the wall on your right. You will want to finish a glass of sparkling wine from the queen's vintage. You can lower your hood as you walk there."

"I can't keep thinking of you as the man in black," I said. "Who are you?"

"I am your personal assistant for the night. My name is Barrister Kaliber, if it pleases you to know."

"Thank you, it does."

Talindra and I walked over to the sparkling wine. They'd placed it on a table against the wall, covered in a thick black table cloth. Two dozen extra crystal glasses filled with wine stood ready. I lowered my hood as I'd practiced and grabbed two glasses, handing one to Talindra.

I needed to fight the urge to dump out the wine, but Talindra would not have given me the berry if it did not work. The wine tasted fine and had no hint of orange in it.

"It's warm in here. You're lucky you wore your cloak," whispered Talindra.

"Are you going to be okay with all your extra accouterment?"

She adjusted her cape to uncover her shoulders. "Yep."

Barrister Kaliber crept behind us. "Go stand next to your chairs. Lord mage, you stand behind the one with the black cloth and Lady Paladin, the one with the white cloth."

We did as instructed, and I counted seats from the front of the table; there were six on each side, and we were in seats four and five. He took the glasses out of our hands and placed them in front of our settings. Everyone had a handler and a server. One person sat between me and Count Avesnes. His seat clearly caught the poor man between his fear of the count and his fear of a mage. I gave him space and didn't make him any more uncomfortable.

After a few moments of standing ready behind our chairs, the king entered, followed by the queen. The myriad of servants held their chairs to seat them, and they asked us to sit. The king's eyes were clearly red, and he had a bit of a stagger to him.

My entire goal for the meal consisted of smile, listen, eat an enjoyable meal, and go home to bed. I did not understand why they'd invited me, but the less I said, the better. The dinner kicked off fine, and the man next to me was the diplomat to Lutetia. In a lull in the conversation, I spoke one sentence to act social, "An envoy to a city that is one of the game cities. Your work is very important."

He smiled at me and I felt the tension leave Barrister Kaliber behind me when I said nothing further.

Nods across the table near the king and queen acted like I'd said something profound. The fact people listened to me when I spoke meant I did not want to speak the rest of the night.

Lord Fergus looked our way. "Lady Dawnstrike, it honors me to be at the table with a Knight of Honor, but I must ask—your husband has the eyes of a mercenary, but you do not. You have a metered stare."

"Lord Fergus, I apologize. I do not fully grasp the reference," said Talindra.

I felt sorry for Talindra, but she could handle herself. The king's eyes focused and looked at me during this talk between Lord Fergus and Talindra.

Lord Fergus gave one of those bard smiles, where he realized he should not be saying this, but he said it anyway. His natural charm helped his delivery. "Your husband has the eyes of someone who has gone to war and will not allow these things to affect the world as much as he can help it. For instance, if we found the Yuennui responsible for sending the attack on the city that attacked him, you would approach it methodically. You would only take action if the situation dictated you should. On the other hand, your husband would use his Tuatha magical powers to make sure that the creature would not act against anyone again and would make a new set of boots from his scaled skin."

Talindra smiled and replied, "That is why we make a good pair. He gives damage and I absorb damage. He gets hurt and I heal, and as I take a methodical approach, he will save the world, even if he has to extract every bit of revenge himself."

King Arag spoke with a slight drunken slur. "Tuatha Argrenn, what do you think of Lord Fergus' suggestion you would make boots of the Yuennui?"

My brain forced me to stop and not react. To delay, I placed my fork on my plate. My limited knowledge of the court knew this was a loaded question. I chose self-deprecating humor to diffuse the situation. "King Arag, I have thought about a new set of boots. My cloak, clothes, and staff are new, but my shoes are old. Lord Fergus has described a set of boots that are more fashionable than I can imagine."

Laughter erupted at the table after the king laughed, and I breathed an internal sigh of relief. I swear I saw the Queen did as well.

Duke Avesnes turned to us. "Lord Mage, as a game participant, are you aiming to make the Battle of Champions or even make noise in the battle?"

"Duke, with all respect, I don't play a game for second place. If I did not believe my team could win it all, I would not be playing."

The table went silent with my statement. Talindra placed her foot on top of mine.

Queen Isabel spoke next. "This is such a breach of decorum, but since we brought up your capabilities, I must ask. How did one mage take on two of these assassins when ambushed? My guards requested a squad to deal with them."

That was a loaded question where I had to be careful and avoid throwing the guards under the bus.

I focused on the queen's forehead to fight the distractions. "Much of combat comes down to mistakes and how big the mistakes are. The Yuennui ambushed me because of my inattention. They made a mistake in the way they initiated combat, and by the time they realized it, I had turned the combat in my favor. That is what I do. I turn the battlefield favorable for my allies."

"Very good," replied the queen. She leaned forward toward me. "However, I do not wish for a political answer. I would like to understand exactly how you defeated them."

A drink from my glass of water gave me a second to prepare. "My first mistake, where I did not realize they'd spied on me and had an ambush spot picked out, almost got me killed. Their lack of preparation evened the fight out. My horse is a created mount based on a stable north of the East Gate with beautiful white Andalusians, and this saved my life. They wasted their first attack on killing my mount, which I can re-summon whenever I wish."

Murmuring to my right caught my attention.

"So, instead of falling on the ground with a dead horse, I took co—" The murmurs grew loud enough to interrupt me.

"Please continue," said the queen. She glared at the others. The room became silent again.

The interruption had given me a second to find a way out of this discussion, but Dean Mehli's fourth rule overrode everything. "I have a panic move, to use one of my magical extensions to cast two spells at once. I cast a duplicate of myself and a magical hand I cast spells through. They charged my duplicate, and I hid. The battle went from an ambush to me having an advantage. I threw *Planar Winter* in front of my duplicate from my hand." I took a breath and every-one listened. "By the time they got to my duplicate and discovered the deception, they lost me. The hail pummeled both of them, and I mixed in fire blasts in case they protected themselves from ice."

I stopped and took a drink of water. The faces around the table implored me to continue. Realizing I must at least conclude what I had begun, and wary of needing to be honest to the queen's question, I forged ahead.

"My glamors were inaccurate because of the creature's armor, so I attempted a different spell. Once they located me, I ran forward and cast *Planar Escape*. This ripped up the road, but the spell killed one of them with the blast and raining rock, though the other slashed through my defenses with his curved blade."

I thought I heard something, but the queen nodded to continue. "The two of us poured blood on the ground and he cast a spell at me first." I pointed to my Scion of Hy Brasil. "I absorbed his kill shot and pummeled him to death with *Ice Balls*."

"So, you advocate wearing armor?" asked the queen.

I looked into her eyes so she knew this came from me. "I believe that weapons, armor, and magic all working together are the best method when fighting. Talindra and I together might not have taken any damage from that ambush."

"Thank you for your full description. I rarely hear someone talk about their mistakes and their successes."

"You make me wish to be twenty years younger and adventuring," said Lord Fergus.

Barrister Kaliber brought another glass of sparkling wine. He whispered, "Excellent. You two don't have to talk the rest of the dinner if you do not want to."

Neither Talindra nor I wanted to, and we listened to excruciating discussions of families, shipping licenses, and property deeds. I pretended to drink the second glass but consumed little of it. The only useful item we learned was that two game participants from Atlantia had arrived by boat and would meet nobles tomorrow—Viscount Renaudin, a paladin, and Dame Teffin, a warmage.

Soon, the king and queen excused themselves from the table. The Count, Duke, and Lord Fergus stood. I noticed we had staff ready to pull our chairs out, so I stood and finished when Talindra stood. Duke Rethel and his wife and the Count of Avesnes, without his wife, left through a door across the room.

The man to my right said, "Lord Mage, I return by the end of the week and wondered if you had a message for the team from Lutetia?"

My focus prevented me from acting immature and I kept my leadership stance. Leaders did not do that. "I wish them well and would like to let them know that my earlier gamesmanship does not mean I do not respect their team."

Lord Fergus walked by us on the way out the main door through the onlookers. He said out loud to Talindra and me, "You did fab. Peace out."

He took the arm of the envoy to Lutetia and guided him away.

If I'd nailed it, Barrister Kaliber kept me grounded. Well, this man earned the fifty-gold tip, so I slipped the bloodstone into his hand and said, "Barrister Kaliber, whoever assigned you to us, did us a great favor."

With that, he escorted us to the carpet and said, "Congratulations on a successful dinner. I will pass on your thanks to Lord Fergus." *Lord Fergus provided the best handler for us.*

My guard took a quick step in front of us and led us out the door. I pulled up my hood and offered Talindra my arm. She took it, and we walked to the carriage with Dean Mehli inside. We sat, and they shut the door behind us after my guard sat with us.

"Well," said Dean Mehli, "the night is over. How did it go?"

"The only clue I have," I said, "is that Lord Fergus said I did fab."

"Which is surprising," said Talindra, "since he told everyone he intended for us to win the Battle of Champions and regaled the table with a magical fight with descriptions of a sword slicing through his thigh, pummeling the face of Yuennui with *Ice Balls*, and he and his opponent pouring blood on the ground in one desperate chance to survive. At that point, one wife needed to leave."

The brief look of shock on my guard's face let me know he was a real person. "Did Duke Avesnes' wife leave because of me?" I asked.

"You locked your eyes onto the queen since she asked you to keep going. But yes, she swallowed vomit and had to be escorted out."

"Well," said the dean, "if the queen said to keep going, you did well. What else happened?"

Talindra relayed the night with things I missed, but both she and the dean thought things had gone well. The carriage let the three of us off at our house and the dean informed us, "I'm going to the university. It's a relief to give Jarlenteria a stellar report."

He created a circle in the street with a spell, stepped into it, and left. A new guard in regular armor replaced our current guard.

Once we stepped inside, I took off my coat and immediately heard a knock on the door. The clothiers were back to undress us.

Having been freed of the pomp and lace, soon we were alone and going to bed.

In the dark room, Talindra told me we rode to ambush Death and Deceit tomorrow morning. Something much safer than dinner at the palace.

At least this did not catch me off guard. They had worked on this after asking me to stay out and I kept it near the forefront of my mind. My delegation of tasks to everyone on the team had taken hold, and though I had mixed feelings about it, I had to admit it was working.

Chapter 8

The next morning, Kitara and I left before six bells and walked to the stables. Naomi flew to Relic Grounds ahead of time, since enemies might use her presence to identify me. At the stables, I asked my guard to become invisible while we rode out of the farmer's gate.

"There's been no word from Marick, and he keeps in contact with me," said Kitara.

"Yep, we should check on him." Inside the stable, I cast *Planar Helper,* wrote a quick note, and put it with a piece of vellum in the box. A quick description of Marick, and the box left.

Kitara put on farmhand clothes. I used *Manipulate Own Material* and made myself a farmhand. We took a horse we hadn't sold yet and rode double toward Relic Grounds.

We left the protected area of Sardyna after riding the well-traveled dirt road for a couple of hours. It had been cleared of snow due to horse and foot traffic even this far out from the farmers and guard traffic. Kitara tied up his horse behind an abandoned wooden structure with a handful of hay and a bucket of water. I cleared out a small area to hide in and used my materials power to bring up dry dirt to lie upon behind a small mound of snow just off the road.

"This way," said Kitara. He covered us with a white sheet, like he had on the horse, and cast a spell. "There. I have a snow illusion covering us and our horse. The sheets make it so much easier."

"Okay, we wait. When they pass us, I'll hold them with *Manos Planas* and *Jagula Segura,* and when they're stuck, we pick them off."

"Let's hope they come soon. I have dinner tonight with the Viscount and Dame from Atlantia."

"I'd like to meet Dame Teffin, since warmages have similar powers to mine, and to meet one friendly spell caster in the game would help me keep a grip on my magical decisions."

After more waiting than I desired, Talindra rode by joking with Grehn and followed by the rest of the two teams. Soon after, Deceit and Deception rolled up—Ryanair, Dahleen, and the other three—passing within thirty feet of us and stopped within hearing distance. With one thought, Naomi took off from Relic Grounds to find our party on the road and buzz them.

"We are out of Sardyna proper," said one voice.

"Yeah, let's cast this to go after Talindra, find her jerk of a husband, and rub it in," said Dahleen.

Ryanair pulled out a scroll and read it out loud.

I'd heard enough and cast my latest additive extension, *Manos Planas and Jagula Segura.*

To focus on this extension was excruciating. It worked as an extension, but even with the thin barrier between me and the planes, the tunnel threatened to collapse and my focus caused a pain in my temples. I kept the concentration going and picked the trapped enemies off with *Fistful of Fire.* It wasn't possible to summon enough power to cast an incantation. My temples thumped with pain when I cast a glamor or arrows whizzed by me while I maintained the extension.

Jagula Segura dissolved flesh and ripped apart organic material. Breathing it meant it ate away at the lungs.

Two, then three of them died. Ryanair finished the scroll, and a circle formed on the ground, but Dahleen was the fourth to fall dead and erased part of the circle. I hit one with two more *Fistful of*

Fire; that and an arrow from Kitara killed the second to last, leaving Ryanair.

My vision blurred and the spells almost slipped, but I held the tunnel open.

Suddenly, I fell back as fire erupted and the ground shook. A demon appeared, stood to its full thirty feet in height, and attacked Ryanair. Fire burned from its eyes and it howled with hatred.

The extension dropped, and I breathed a giant gulp of air. My head pounded, but there was a larger problem in front of me.

The demon grabbed Ryanair, sucked something out of his mouth, and dropped a lifeless body to finish the last of the Death and Deceit team.

Every demon we faced came from Feston. Were the Vrelth or Feston aligned with demons?

I dove to the right and tried to get behind another mound covered with snow as the demon raised his hand toward me. A bolt of lightning scorched the ground next to me, and ozone filled my nostrils. My easier extension of *Duplicate Me* and *Body Projection* allowed me to cast *Planar Winter* on the new enemy from my projected hand.

Seven incantations and one formula left.

I invoked planar armor from my staff and used my materials' power to rip up the ground underneath the demon. It staggered, stomped its foot, and sharp rocks ripped from the ground outward from him in a circle. One hit me right in the gut. The Danaan steel saved my life. Another took out my duplicate.

It was time to unload. "Keep moving," I yelled to Kitara and focused to cast *Planar Destruction* and an extended *Ice Ball. Six incantations and zero formulas left.*

The demon bellowed, held out its arm, and projected an orange beam into the ground in front of me. My tiara only caught spells that targeted me, and the demon was smart enough to hit me with an area of effect spell. The ground exploded under my feet, and my body shuddered as I hit the ground with a thud.

I rolled over to catch my breath. He used my move. I panicked at the thought of staying in one place and rolled to my left twice.

The demon held a brimstone javelin that smoked and dripped magma. The weapon pointed at me and the demon heaved it with full arm extension.

Why did acoustic music start?

Just now standing, I stood flat on my feet and could not dodge. A shield of silver and blue flew in front of me and blocked the javelin.

An image of an angel on horseback overshadowed its howl of rage. The angel leaned over, scooped up the shield, turned her white mount around, and pulled a sword of blue flame. Talindra! The team had arrived.

"You're in trouble now," I shouted.

The song was Skid Row's <u>I Remember You</u>!

Grehn and Thralk charged at the demon. Two punches from it, and the two of them were flying back twenty feet as it swung its tail at the Persevering group. Talindra charged and sliced at it with the blue flame of her sword. She yelled, leaped from Pearl, and surrounded the melee with the globe of earth. It crushed around him.

That allowed Kitara to spring up thirty feet to its head with a green blast of energy and slash the demon across its face before catching himself with a dagger and stabbing it in the thigh to slow his fall.

The demon only cared for Talindra. He roared at her and slammed her with his fists as I cast *Ice Ball*.

Talindra raised her shield. The fists and shield met, and neither moved. The boom sent out massive reverberations, knocking the junior teams to the ground.

Brigham jumped up and swung his mace, turning it to celestial energy, bashing with the power of that energy. The demon backhanded him, and Brigham flew at least twenty feet, then it roared fire as Talindra raised her shield and deflected the flame. She followed up with a jab at its leg, but he danced away.

I cast *Ice Ball*. Reminding myself, *Watch the battle, the team needs a leader.*

The demon took its eyes off Talindra, backhanded Grehn and Thralk, and they flew away like minor nuisances instead of large barbarians. Talindra stepped inside its arms, jabbed up at his thigh, and drew a green ichor that hissed when it hit the ground.

I cast another *Ice Ball,* and the demon faked a fist-slam, kicking Talindra's feet from under her. She fell but had her shield up to stop his fire breath from scorching her.

Kitara stood underneath the huge enemy now and shot a magical green beam into the wound. Howling, the demon raised its foot to stomp Talindra, but Thralk bashed up at it with his giant hammer and was stomped instead.

I cast *Ice Ball* again as Talindra jumped to position and feigned at the thigh, but spun and slashed at the Achilles of the leg that stood on Thralk. As the demon roared again, lifting his weight from pinning the paladin, Grehn dragged Thralk away from immediate danger.

I cast *Ice Ball* once more and ran around the side to get a better view of everyone's position. "Distance, people!" I called out. "Keep spread out to avoid the area of effect and aim high. Brigham, have your team stay out of melee range and use distance attacks unless we can topple it."

Brigham guided his team behind various rocks and tree stumps off of the road to have cover out of immediate range. I pulled Kitara back behind Talindra to use distance attacks and prepare for a combination.

Kitara cast a green ball of flame at the same Achilles tendon Talindra had slashed. An arrow landed, piercing the red skin. Then someone landed a javelin.

The demon roared fire at Talindra again, and again Talindra's shield deflected it away harmlessly. She jabbed at its leg, but he danced away, though now with a noticeable limp.

Another arrow, another javelin, and I cast *Ice Ball* as my last spell while Thralk bashed a knee, staggering it.

I maneuvered around the battlefield and placed people appropriately. This fight was too hard to rely on chance. I had to lead.

Off to the side and out of close range, Grehn healed Brigham as the demon raged and crashed both fists onto Talindra. She had both hands on her shield and the fists bounced off. The area was filled with the sounds of battle, clanging metal, battle cries, and roars resounded, creating a cacophony in the morning air.

Talindra slashed with her blue flame sword and followed it up with celestial power. A golden glow pierced the demon's head and exited through the wound in his thigh.

The wounded demon cried out and tried to step on her, but she held the foot up with her shield. The attacks from all sides continued as she held her shield against him, arrows and javelins flying.

There, an opening! I screamed at the top of my lungs through the chaos, "Talindra, use *Judgment of the Shield,* and Kitara, use that to use *Magical Assisted Attack*!"

Talindra screamed. "I find no redemption for you!" She pushed the shield with its blue glow, and the demon toppled. Kitara ran and jumped off of Talindra's shield, absorbed the blue energy from it, and swung his sword, burying it up to its hilt inside the chest of the beast. He rode it to the ground while blasting the demon with a green burst of magic from his hand. A puff of dirt rose as it hit the dirt of the road.

"Now, Brigham, have your team charge! Everyone, surround it evenly."

No one stood near the head. I threw *Argrenn's Acid Attack* there. The sizzle burned, and the demon clawed at its face. "Keep spread out. He has focused-area attacks."

The team spread out and surrounded the massive beast. I threw another *Argrenn's Acid Attack* in its face and it howled while earth rose around me. It blew me ten feet back, and I landed on the ground face first.

The rest of the team positioned to attack the top of it now. Talindra planted her sword in its gut, calling more celestial power from the sky. Kitara dug into the kidney with his sword and blasted his green jets into the wound.

Thralk crushed the knee, and bone chips flew out. Grehn sliced its neck with her ax and demon ichor spewed to the ground. I threw another *Argrenn's Acid Attack* in its face. The rest of the team attacked again, and finally, the demon stopped moving. We jumped off and watched it, wary, with weapons raised. After it caught fire, we retreated.

"Talindra, they had a scroll and summoned that to go after you," said Kitara.

They were coming to kill Talindra. I lost control of my temper and screamed at the sky.

They put a bounty on us? The game allowed that. A pair of assassins going after one of us? The game allowed for that too. No one summoned a demon of that power without extra items. This wasn't Feston acting brazen. He flaunted his cheating, and he did it to kill Talindra.

I focused on the blackened earth and ripped the ground into the sky as the body disappeared, then screamed at the sky as the head flew up without the body.

Kitara ran to me with his hands in the air. "Gardening is an enjoyable hobby, but this isn't our land, and it's not the time."

Everyone, including the villagers of Relic Grounds and a contingent of guards that had ridden out, stared at me. I didn't care and ran to Talindra to hug her. "They had no access to that power. That is one hundred percent cheating."

"We're all fine," said Talindra. "Let's be calm. They've cheated since the beginning."

I hugged Talindra tighter. "They were coming after you with an overpowered demon."

When did I become taller than her?

A thud followed by the rattle of bouncing stones interrupted us.

"Heads back," said Thralk.

"Are you okay?" I asked Talindra.

"The question is, are you okay?"

"Someone needs to tell Feston to send enemies with treasure. We've got expenses," said someone I didn't recognize.

"Why don't you sit there? You can practice your spells," said Talindra. "We've got a lot of stuff to do and you shouldn't handle this right now."

Kitara suggested, "You said you wanted to get a video of yourself while hurt, practicing for your class." They walked me over to a stump and Kitara took my camera, set it up, and told it to use the standard setup.

They had a good idea; my emotions had the better of me. I pulled out my two traveling spell books and began my practice, where I demonstrated my full nightly ritual in a sedate classroom setting.

After saving the recording to the class, I stood up with control over my emotions. Covered in blood and hurting everywhere, I stumbled and had to brace myself with the staff. Without the adrenaline, I needed support and had trouble focusing my eyes.

"Whoa, your wounds are worse than they look. Can you summon Starlight?" asked Talindra. "It's okay if you can't. You can ride with me."

I lifted my staff to summon Starlight, but saw the ground come towards me as the weight of using extensions caught up to me.

Talindra and Kitara's laughter woke me up in time for a late dinner. They were watching videos in the entertainment section of the pad and reading comments.

Talindra noticed me first. "Shelley said you were exhausted and though she is the one abbess in all of Evros that can heal that level of exhaustion, she said it's better for you to sleep."

My face felt weird, and I put my hand up under my beard. My chin was thinner, I was sure of it. A dozen or so hairs came away with my hand. Everything they had warned me about was coming true because I needed to keep unloading as much magic as I could.

"Did you research Nigel?" asked Kitara. He sat in the red chair and wore his green dress.

Before I answered, my *Planar Helper* arrived. I checked inside the box from Marick.

> *Sorry for the lack of contact. There are injuries during timber season. But a wave of refugees passed through. Could you research firearms? I know explosives work now, but I swear these guys are describing guns.*

I sat next to Talindra on or loveseat. "Marick is fine, and I researched Nigel. He chose damage spells and knew how to use them. A pure damage guy who loved confronting enemies up close, like a papier mâché cannon."

"How good?" asked Kitara.

"He would beat me one-on-one."

"So, you aren't going?" asked Talindra.

"Oh, we're going. We won't fight in the dungeon unless we see no other possibility. We will still think twice."

"So, it's a brainiac kind of mission?" asked Kitara.

"Out-of-the-box solutions may be more likely."

A knock signaled a visitor, and Talindra answered the door.

After a muffled conversation. She handed something to the man on the other side of the door and strolled back, carrying a box. "Honey, you got a present. Wait. We got a card, and you got a present."

She read the card:

Argrenn and Talindra Dawnstrike,

Thank you for your attendance at the palace. The two of you were pleasurable dinner guests. Please accept this gift on behalf of the royal court. We know it's not made of Yuennui scales, but they made the boots from the skin of the most poisonous snake in the deserts of their homeland.

The king and the queen had signed it. I opened the box. It contained a set of snakeskin boots.

"Let me check," said Kitara. "Wow, the wearer takes half damage from Yuennui and the Yuennui masters."

"Oh, wow, I don't know how to thank them other than to wear them."

"I'll ask Braun in the morning," said Talindra. "Try them on."

They fit as if I'd broken them in. I stood and reset my state to zero to include the boots and walked in them. "What do you think?" I asked.

"We can put your old dad-shoes away."

"Oh, man, the gnome children who copied the style will be upset," I joked.

"You're saving them from a long-term fashion faux pas," said Kitara.

"Kitara and I should do our personal quest before my class starts. This is the right time. The Knights will protect you during duty. Though I may need to send you a note to ask you to buy something Daisidian needs."

"I don't know," said Talindra. "You showed today the team is better with you as a leader, and now you're going after power where a person you couldn't beat died on this mission."

"Maybe Nigel rescuing another person named Nigel confused the universe," I joked. Not seeing anyone laugh. "We must level to make the Battle of Champions. Leveling is required in the game and as a leader. I need to set the example."

"Let's go the day after tomorrow," said Kitara. "I have items to take care of in person. I'll also pick up body bags."

"If you need anything, I better see that little box with feet."

Not ready to go back to bed yet, I added notes for the spell I wanted to write. First, I threw a chunk of iron with an exposed surface area. Instead of my acid attack spell, *Planar Destruction* gave more hydrogen gas. The gas needed to be contained and ignited. The *Jagula Segura* spell used a containment sub-routine that fit this idea.

The last item for the night was a review of Dean Mehli's masterwork. But the spell he'd written remained too complicated for me, which was good, because Talindra stood in my office doorway and didn't say a word. I jumped up and joined her in the bedroom.

I spent the next day studying the first and third chapters of his masterwork. He'd written an additive extension without mentioning it. He'd needed to make sure only a few read this work. It made more sense when I reviewed my actions from the previous day. When angry, my powers lost control. I'd have bet that in my anger the power extended without a control around it.

In chapter three, I picked up that title powers, class powers, and spells all needed to be treated separately. Then things started falling into place when I focused on title powers. The third chapter discussed a way to boost the title powers—specifically, my mastery of common materials with incantations, formulas, and conjurations. Though I wasn't sure how to do it yet.

Because Marick had brought up firearms, I wanted to jump on that before the day ended. They locked explosive research out to adventurers, but neither of the two methods of firing weapons in Geoe relied on gunpowder.

The rarest method of firing a gun required an infused bullet that propelled with an aiming spell while another method used explosive-infused sheets of paper cut up into slips. The wielder loaded a bullet and a slip of this paper into the weapon with each shot. A hammer hit the imbued paper and cause a confined explosion that projected the lead ball out. Both required magical preparation and didn't sound cost effective. Unless you brought an army experienced with guns. I hoped Marick got more information.

On the last day before I left, we chatted with the lights out.

"Do you have to go tomorrow?"

"Things are crazy. I have to be back to teach my class, level for the game to keep our protections, and get to tier three so we can fight Feston. And I need to finish Dean Mehli's masterwork."

"Can you put some of this off?"

"I'm putting off writing the spells that could make us safer, and we have a need for me to dive further into Cassiel's tactics class. This has to get done before the invasion starts, and I've had no time to research more on the upcoming invasion."

"How did this get so crazy?" she asked.

"I don't know, but let's make it through this week before my class starts and new problems start."

Chapter 9

The next morning, Kitara and I rode out the Farmer's gate. Anyone who watched would have viewed Kenton and a dwarf ride out. We rode double on Mahogany, but Kitara assured me it appeared as a draft horse. I had trouble staying in the saddle with my short legs. The horse clomped through the remaining snow and mud, and I held on to Kitara to keep from falling off.

Once we were a couple of hours outside the site, at the site of the blackened earth from the demon fight, I altered my material back to my personal state zero, summoned Naomi and Starlight, and Kitara dropped his illusions. I needed Naomi since we were going through horker and gobelyns infested areas. While harmless at our level, we did not need delays.

The sky clouded over and wind whipped Kitara's cloak. With only a few patches of snow left on the ground, the warm weather caused mud, which made Mahogany a mess.

After a long day in the saddle, we finally agreed to call it a day when it was too dark to ride. We found a pleasant area between some trees and dismounted, stretching and twisting out kinks. "You don't need to set up your campsite. Just put up your dome protection," said Kitara.

He cast a spell and created a small house and stable. We walked inside and had food, a couple of beds, and a fire going. "Nice. How did you get this spell?" I asked.

"Sword mages don't follow strict rules about magic schools. The invocation is from the Creative realm."

I cast a ritual of *Planar Butler*, and Vern took care of Mahogany, Kitara's horse.

This was a good place to grab the third video and upload it to the first assignment. I'd been lucky to have gotten the fourth one done with the demon. I setup in the stable with the house behind me for a bit of scenery for the students to reference and repeated the video. After setting up the camera and going through the motions, my first lesson plan was done.

While Kitara handled missives for business at the table in front of the hearth, I read over chapter three while I laid in a bed, and it wasn't long before I felt my eyes close and weariness take me.

The next morning, we dispelled everything, and Kitara summoned Scruffles. Two riders with aerial surveillance avoided most any encounter. Twice we hid behind illusions of Kitara. Starlight did not leave footprints, so the one set of prints from Mahogany were the lone animal prints. That should throw off anyone tracking us.

We rode for five days through the hectares of Salas Keep, avoiding villages and hamlets to not give landmarks to anyone watching us. Scattered rocks and scrub lined the coast, but a few miles out, it had farmable land. We needed to cross a river in these lands. I stopped and tested the ground nearby. "Kitara, this isn't as good as the red Georgia clay back home, but you could establish clay making around here."

"I'm glad we learned this going into the dungeon," joked Kitara.

"Random subroutine in the back of my head just fired." I still did not understand why the game wanted us to be responsible for people or even for defending the landing site close to Sardyna.

A couple of days later, we neared the entrance to our dungeon. Before we walked in, I sent another *Planar Helper* to check on Daisidian.

Kitara tied up Mahogany behind a small group of trees and left her a bucket of water and food. I left Naomi with Scruffles in a tree above her, and Kitara and I climbed a slope covered with thick bushes and trees to get to the edge of the sea.

Kitara pointed to a rock, and I moved it with my materials power, revealing a cave beyond. I fit, but I moved it a second time for Kitara and his armor. Once inside, I moved it back so nothing large followed us.

"Do you have any night vision? You look more Tuatha than human."

Kitara's body outlined with his heat image. "Wow, I can see body heat when it's dark." That proved the point of how I was becoming Tuathan because of the magic I cast. But I was a mage. What choice did I have other than cast magic? I needed to talk to Talindra about becoming Tuathan, but I needed to make sure I was okay with it—well, it didn't matter. I better be okay becoming Tuathan.

"Okay, we'll creep along without light. I can see for a little way."

Kitara's orange outline led the way, and I did my best to stay upright when his body heat was all I saw.

"Okay, there's a large stone door that doesn't open. Let me cast light on a stick here."

We were in a large stone cavern with salt stains right at my head level. If anyone had died here, they had washed out to sea long ago.

At the top of the door, it said "*Noncomposite*" followed by a dash, then between two vertical lines it said *Natural*. Below, a column of six numbers appeared to turn. My brain tried to put the words together.

"Maybe we missed a clue," said Kitara.

"I got it," I said. "The lines and dashes are mathematical operators." I scribbled on the salt with my finger to make sure I understood the combination. "Top to bottom: zero, zero, zero, one, two, five."

Kitara looked at me as if I'd grown a new head. He moved the numbers, and the door slid open.

"It's just..."

"I'd rather not know."

An alcove head-high in the wall opened, and glowing mold formed the words, *Congratulations, mathematician.*

"I bet the door lets adventurers through on any answer, but only the right answer keeps you alive," said Kitara.

Ten more steps in, a blue light scanned us as we passed. It turned green as it touched each of us. The smooth stone continued and felt like modern machinery cut it. *Or magic.*

Kitara doused the light, and we walked on. "T-junction," he said.

"Left." I always turned left.

We walked along the stone floor for a while. I dared not touch a wall without light.

"The path turns right, and I can hear something ahead."

With *Body Projection* cast on my ear, I sent it into the room.

"I'm so lonely. There are two mages, but they don't want to talk to me."

"Turn on the light. He's made us," I said.

Kitara lit the stick and walked around the stone through an arch into a chamber.

"Hello," I said to a skeleton on a large, comfortable chair. They'd carved the vast chamber out of one chunk of solid stone with no cracks. They set the chair up on a stone platform a foot off the ground.

"It was wise not to attack me, for my knowledge is the only way out of this room," it said.

"Why is that?" said Kitara.

"The information I hold regards the two doors in front, but I either will either lie about the doors or only tell the truth, and I will answer only one question. Choose the correct door or take my place."

A quick search around the room showed a top door and a bottom door with wooden constructed stairs and a platform for the top door.

"I got this."

"Hold up, there should be two guards." Kitara kept looking for the second skeleton.

"I didn't get a master's in philosophy for nothing." My chuckle at the ridiculousness of virtue ethics and moral luck studies paying dividends caused me to laugh until tears ran from my eyes.

"I'm glad this is funny," said Kitara.

The skeleton even cocked his head at me.

"Okay, okay. I'm sorry." I paused to get this correct. "Here are three statements about the bottom door. First, you are lying about the door. The second is you respond the door is safe. The third is that the door is safe. My question is, is there an odd number of correct statements?"

I knew this would work regardless of whether he lied or told the truth, since I put the condition that led to a logical inconsistency if I chose an unsafe door.

"No." The skeleton's shoulder bones drooped.

"It's the bottom door," I said.

Kitara fiddled with his bracelets. "Wait, how do you know? I mean, other than the poor skeleton showing he knows we trapped him for decades more."

"He couldn't have answered the question if that door ended in death. He'd have a paradox."

"What does that mean? What would have happened?"

I opened the bottom door, and we walked through into a torchlight lit stone hallway.

"Not my problem. They should have made a better puzzle," I said.

Kitara walked up in front of me. "But that's cheating."

"Our lives are on the line. It's logic. The game did not plan through all the possibilities."

"I'm so glad we're friends. Lord Fergus was right about you being mercenary."

"He called me that at the palace in front of the nobles."

"Fergus meant it as a compliment. He says you are a mercenary and will take no prisoners. The Vrelth will regret the day they attacked Earth. I always believed it, but you outsmarted the game."

"How do you know I'm not just good at outsmarting doors?"

Kitara snickered. "You are good with doors."

We walked under the portcullis until the door left our view. Inside, a scale sat in the middle of the room on a pedestal. They scattered rocks of all sizes on the floor.

"I got this one," said Kitara.

He picked up the rocks and put them on the scale. Once the scale balanced, the original portcullis closed, and the other opened.

"Nice job."

"Kitara move rocks after Argrenn confuses game. *Grrrr*, Kitara smart too," he said.

I laughed.

We came across another of these annoying doors. The next room had light throughout from a magical source in the ceiling. It had black walls, floor, and ceiling.

The walls had chalk drawings of gobelyns, weapons, and other creatures. There was a piece of chalk on the floor.

"Whoa, this one is dangerous." I examined the different creatures and weapons drawn. One drawing of a skeleton looked faded.

"Hilarious." Kitara picked up a piece of chalk and drew a doorway with a doorknob, then opened the door he drew.

"What the...?" I exclaimed.

"While you were doing things like getting degrees in math and philosophy, I watched cartoons."

"I guess if I bet our lives on a logical inconsistency, you can bet our lives on a Roadrunner cartoon."

We walked further into a cavern. A cauldron hung from the ceiling and boulders were scattered the floor, along with bloodstains.

"Others died here."

We read writing on the wall: *Light what's above me, bring me downward. Hide me, heat me, then leave coastward.*

"Can you cast light inside the cauldron?" I asked.

Kitara cast a *Thieves' Hand* and cast *Light* into the cauldron. The ceiling lit up.

I cast *Aumentor Masa* on the cauldron and watched it lower until the rope tightened.

Kitara cast a spell on it.

"What did you cast?"

"I made it as invisible as my hand," he replied.

Part of me wanted to point out I could not see it, but leadership meant trusting your team. "Cool beans." I cast a *Fistful of Fire,* put it in the cauldron, and held another *Fistful of Fire* underneath it.

"Cool... beans?"

"Sorry, saying from back in the day."

A piece of the wall moved, and we hustled over and through the opening, finding ourselves in an underground crypt at least fifty feet squared and thirty feet high. Three bodies lay on marble tables in peaceful repose, wearing white robes that stated how each of them had died. Items lined the dais around them as if someone had placed them there for display.

"These are some sick people." I rolled the bodies to make sure nothing hid underneath them and read the robes more carefully.

Nigel Dreamtale had drawn a skeleton in the chalk room. Nigel Queensman had attacked the door room skeleton and chosen the wrong door. Tordil Aastar had put a boulder in the cauldron, and the cauldron tossed it out and crushed him.

Nigels' face was peaceful and wore a smile. It had none of the focus in his eyes from the videos I'd watched of him. "Thank you, Nigel. If you were worse at combat, we may have made the same mistake. Watching you gave us our strategy."

Kitara stood back on the crypt floor with his hand covering his mouth. "This is horrifying."

"Are you okay? These bodies are pretty well preserved for how long they've been dead."

"No. It's… they summarized these three mages' entire lives to how they died. Nothing of who they were, what they dreamed of, or even loved ones remembering them."

Kitara was so clutch and useful to the team; it was easy for me to forget that he was still barely an adult. He hadn't experienced salespeople, investors, or hedge fund managers. I stopped to give Kitara my full attention and looked him in the eye. "When you call me mercenary, this is why. This is what our enemies think of us. They don't care that I'm a husband, father, grandfather—only how I die."

"That sinks in deeper every day, but this is another level."

I jumped down to talk to Kitara face to face. "As a kid, I went through the religious rites of passage. Not everything about religion is bad. I learned the golden rule—treat others as you want to be treated. Well, that also means others treat you in a way they want you to treat them. If my enemies only care about wanting me dead. I only care about wanting them dead. It's what they want, and it's the golden rule. My friends care about me as a person, so I'm going to care about my friends the same way."

Kitara jangled his bracelets, gripping them as he looked me in the eye. "Were we this evil? You know, on Earth?"

I took in and let out a breath. "There is a street in, err, was a street in New York City? Anyway, it was called Water Street. It acted like an arm that controlled all the evil fingers in the US. Hedge funds who took joy in stealing from people, politicians willing to sell out their constituents for fun, drug companies who.... Well, you get the idea, there was a lot of true evil."

"But life was worse in other places on Earth, right?"

I nodded. "Yes. Earth has a poor track record, but that's not what I focus on when I want to save Earth."

Kitara looked up to his right, lost in thought; his eyes had a far-away look to them. "All the good people, the ones that are hurt no matter who is in charge."

I scooped up the spell books, staffs, swords, darts, robes, and other items on the ground. The piles of items contained more stuff than three adventurers carried.

Kitara jumped up to help me. "These enemies, they don't care about my gender. I'm someone in their way of taking what they want." We arranged the bottom of the handkerchief so the bodies could lie in a dignified position, and Kitara looked me in the eye. "Is becoming a leader changing who you are?"

We carefully put the body bags and the items in my handkerchief. "I don't think so, but that's why I listen to concerts to relax. I may grow as a person, but at the core of who I am, everything past the superficial parts needs to stay me."

We both sat on top of the table and said nothing for a long time. Kitara patted me on the shoulder. "Thank you. Let's get to somewhere less depressing." We lumbered to the top of the marble staircase where the door had a face.

The mouth of the door moved. "Congratulations on your test of intelligence and magic. Choose magical items as a gift from us."

"I would like the most powerful of stones that go into my Scion of Hy Brasil," I said.

A stone appeared in my hands.

Kitara looked up from the ground and knocked on his breastplate. "I take the lead and withstand initial damage, so armor that gives me better survivability would help me the most."

A breastplate with a brushed-titanium finish appeared. It had forest-green marks tracing from the shoulder pauldrons to the stomach fauld. The door opened, and we were out a few hundred feet from the entrance. We closed the entrance and walked to the trees where Kitara had tied up Mahogany.

My *Planar Helper* arrived from Daisidian before Kitara changed. *Hey, OG, please send lock picks?*

"Do you have lock picks on you?" I asked Kitara.

"Do you know how to use them?" he asked. He fished a small black case from his pack.

"They're for Daisidian."

"Take the big set." He pulled out a larger black case and tossed them to me.

Planar Helper took the set and left. "Now I'm worried for him," I said.

Kitara put his hand on my reward. "Wow," he said. "My armor is good, but that rock lets you cast the two incantations you've cast the most an extra three times per day each. Let's see what those spells are."

I put the stone in my tiara and it floated there.

"An extra three castings of *Duplicate Me* and *Ice Ball*."

"I asked for more power, and it gave me an extra six incantations a day," I said. "What about you?"

"Breastplate of the Vanguard," said Kitara. "I don't take damage in the first round of any combat and it gives me extra defense."

"Exactly what you asked for. Plus, I gotta say, the armor looks sharp."

"Yep, the first round is where I get slaughtered, and it changes all our strategies."

"I have much less reservation about Talindra going on her quest if she gets an armor upgrade," I said.

"Are you going to tell her to take armor?" Kitara gave me an evil smile.

"No, I'm going to trust her judgment." I stuck my tongue out.

We rode back the same way we arrived and avoided anyone who might slow us.

"Argrenn, I'm going to have to put back on the girl clothes Talindra helped me buy."

"Yep. I have to get into wardrobe, too."

He looked at me. "Isn't it more than wardrobe? I'm dressing like a girl even though I'm a guy, and Talindra says I'll start walking and standing differently, too."

"You have a bigger issue, but I feel like I'm dressing like a pompous English lord." I made a falsetto voice, saying, "Call me Sir Fruity Wigglebottom."

Kitara laughed. "I'm missing part of what I'm trying to say. Let me say it this way — do you remember your Earth name?"

I thought for a moment and realized I couldn't recall mine or Talindra's real name.

"Me, neither," he said.

"Do you think of yourself as a Tuatha Extension Mage or a human IT guy saving up for retirement?"

"Wow."

"Well, it's becoming that way for me with the body of a half elf woman who is a sword mage. I'm trying to hold on to who I am. It's not superficial."

I stared at Kitara and wished I'd known that it was more than dressing up. "You're choosing between playing a role to help Earth and holding onto your identity."

"What happens if I become a woman?"

"You're still Kitara. With me, nothing changes," I assured him. "You're changing more from the amount of success you're having in Geoe than anything else."

"Am I changing?"

"We all are. The saying 'you can never go home again' is true, because everyone else stays the same while you change." I paused and added, "Imagine this new you at your old company. You walk in, take charge of sales and logistics, and handle the projects."

Kitara cackled before he caught his mouth with his hand.

I continued. "You step first into a room filled with creatures ready to kill you. You make changes for the chance to help the Earth without a guarantee of success. This is who you are becoming. It's who we all are becoming."

"I understand why you said the whole life portion of Geoe would be the hard part. Gaming and adulting are easy; it's hard to grow into a complete person in a gaming world."

I agreed, and we turned to ride home. This was not the time to really talk about me moving from human to Tuathan. Kitara needed the support, and I didn't know what I needed.

A week later, we arrived, grateful to have the quest behind us. We went straight into town and dropped off the bodies in the appropriate guildhalls.

Archmage Kira took the bodies of the Nigels.

"We will dress them without their last failure on their clothing," she said, "but the censure upon our guild by the primal forces is less. You did well."

Ding. Ding. It had been a long time since Geoe rung the completed quest bells in my head.

Kitara and I traveled back to our house to go through the loot. I emptied the handkerchief in the living room and we stared at the pile.

"This trip has been a lot. I want to make sure the rest of the team is fine and lie down for a while." But first, I would tackle the task at hand. We moved staffs and wands to one side; armor, and weapons to another. Kitara moved the other items and stacked up the spell books.

Something scratched at the back of my head, so I sent a missive to Talindra to check on her. "Something is wrong. After this, I want to ride out and look for Talindra. Could you check on Marick? I'm going to send Daisidian another box."

The *Planar Helper* returned fast, bearing a note, which I read out loud:

Dear Argrenn,

I hope this finds you able to gather everyone, and once you have the entire team, come save me. Though I am safe for the time being, it may not last another day. Follow these symbols in the circle where enemies hold me against my will.

Yours,

Daisidian.

"We have to go," said Kitara.

This is my fault. "I have the duty as a leader and have to go. Stay here, hold on to the note, gather Talindra, and prepare to assist when I have more information."

"But it's a trap."

"It's a trap after we collect the full party. It's not a trap for one person traversing immediately."

Chapter 10

I grabbed my staff and traversed to the circle coordinates via the Planar Mage Guild.

The new circle's room had sand on the light wood floor. The walls were white stone cast into bricks where they didn't have the same light wood. Two Yuennui Garde stood between a door to the hallway and a door outside.

Planar Destruction came to mind first, but there was no path to the barrier of planar material. The laughter of the two Yuennui didn't make it through the surrounding silence, but the pointing and head movements gave it away. After I tried to run, I discovered a second magical power held me. Held and silenced, which was death to a wizard.

Think.

A third Yuennui ran out the door and the laughing lizard men gathered themselves, approaching me with scimitars. The long tongue of the one in front reached out and licked the curved blade and stared directly at me in what is what I could only imagine was the smile his face made.

Then I knew my brain was a step ahead of me because some original Van Halen, <u>Running with the Devil</u> playing in my head.

My mind worked fast to figure out a solution, and I quickly formulated a plan. With my new master extension from Dean Mehli's work, I cast *Duplicate Me* using only thought. Once free, they sliced at my duplicate and I threw *Planar Destruction,* which blasted them with a thick coating of sulfuric acid. It engulfed them and burned the wood floor near the exit, eating at their scales. Where the walls got splashed, the rock dissolved like they were made of salt. The two Yuennui screamed and ran out of the building. *Eight incantations, four formulas, and five of my six extra spells left.*

Move fast, reinforcements coming.

The hallway had windows along the left wall that showed nothing but sand stretching to the horizon. Ten feet before the stairs, a doorway led into an office with a scared Yuennui sitting behind a desk. They made the desk of the same white sandstone with a glass top. He stood with his hands up, but he was part of a kidnapping crew. I hit him with an extended *Ice Ball* and his chest caved in, killing him.

I scooped up the desk into one pile and spied another wooden door in the office, which I found opened into a closet that held weapons and armor. Daisidian's leather armor leaned against a wall with his pack and weapons. Everything got stuffed into my handkerchief. Back in the office, I scraped the pile on the desk on top into the cloth. Mess be damned.

Returning to the door, I peered down the stairs and saw tentacles on the right and left. Yuennui Teuers. Payback time with the new stronger me. *Planar Destruction* led my charge to the bottom of the stairs, and sulfuric acid blasted, coating nearly the entire stairwell.

One turned around, and I threw an extended *Ice Ball* at his face from point blank. The floor now had a hole, and the white walls were not holding up well in the spells area. *Eight incantations, three formulas, and three of my six extra spells left.*

The other lizardman took two steps by me up the stairs before his foot disappeared into a hole in a stair eaten by acid. Acid covered his body and melted the flesh. It couldn't scream because his face and neck had disintegrated.

I turned off Geoe's control of the magic and cast two successive *Fistful of Fire* at him from inches away. The heat reflected at me before it died. The other fell in the acid and screamed. I hit him with four more blasts of fire, and he died with the third bit of fire, setting his innards ablaze through the open acid wounds.

I ran to the bottom of the stairs where a thin layer of sand covered normal rock and jumped over the remaining acid, finding a thick wooden door with an iron lock stood between me and the rest of the jail. I cast *Argrenn's Acid Attack* and placed it on the door lock and waited. It took forever, but the lock fell to the ground, and I pushed the door open.

Two more Teuers were in front of a cell where all the stones were standard gray stone and not sandstone. Daisidian lay motionless behind them on the sand in the cell, and anger rose in me.

Control your anger and exact retribution. No Mistakes.

The Teuers pulled out a long scepter that ended with a curved scimitar with a slot in the middle to plug in a tentacle from their head. They attached one tentacle from their right shoulder into the other end and wrapped another around the entire length.

Humans couldn't use these weapons to level the playing field.

I cast *Shards of Glass* in front of me and used my staff to put on my armor. Time for my second extension from Dean Mehli's masterwork. I cast an extended *Ice Ball*, but I doubled and split it to hit both. Six thunks pounded into them.

One charged into the *Shards of Glass*, slashing at me and nicking me through my armor and Danaan-steel shirt.

A viscous black liquid dripped off the blade to the floor and the familiar sting of Vrelth poison hit me in the chest.

I cast *Duplicate Me* and put myself in the cell with Daisidian. Even my limited strength lifted a halfling.

One Teuer slashed through my duplicate, and it disappeared. I hit him in the back with an extended *Ice Ball*. The burn in my chest from the black fluid increased dramatically, which meant my timer to escape got shorter. The locked cell door stopped the newest pursuers as the one in front had to fumble for keys.

I hit the guy who put the key in the lock with another extended *Ice Ball*. He screamed, fell to the ground, and his tentacles grabbed at his crushed face.

With only my left hand available, I cast two *Fistful of Fires*.

The other Teuer tried to run through the *Shards of Glass* for help edging along the gray stone wall to minimize damage, so I cast three more fire glamors. The first missed, but the second and third hit. He died in swirling glass and fire.

I sensed the cell bars, finding they were iron, and crushed the door into a ball with my materials' power and tossed it behind me. "Sorry, buddy," I said. I put Daisidian in the handkerchief. If I had it right, he had a couple of hours of air.

Three doors opened further down the hall, and handfuls of Yuennui ran toward me. I cast another *Planar Destruction* at them, right in the middle. They screamed and hissed at me as I ran up the stairs.

The screaming continued after I cast one more *Planar Destruction* into the midst. Two daggers zipped by me, but a third lodged in my thigh. The screams from the direct hit of the acid were ear-splitting, as they avoided none of the splash and stayed in the acid. Four *Fistful of Fires* finished those eight.

I jumped over the acid and landed on the other side of the circle. Targeting the door, I cast *Espuma Inflam* and ignited it with a *Fistful of Fire*.

Two spells shot at me. One a red line of liquid fire and one dark green blob that rotated as it flew toward me. My tiara absorbed them both. I jumped into the circle and two more daggers plunged into my leg and side before the symbols of my guild formed in my mind.

Two more daggers whizzed by my head, then an alert with a red light assaulted my senses. My transport had worked. I was in the Planar Mage Guild. We weren't safe yet, though. With a frantic shake, I emptied Daisidian's body from my handkerchief onto the floor by the wall. After groping his neck, I found there was a weak pulse on his left side near his shoulder.

The alert blared, and lights flashed. Two Teuers followed me, so I cast *Jagula Segura* in the circle.

Dean Mehli showed up through an office door.

Another of Dean Mehli's master spells, an extended *Ice Ball* that I doubled and split, gave six more thunks. *Four incantations, one formula, and one of my six extra spells left.*

Dean Mehli threw a lightning bolt that zapped both of them. They died doing the sixty-cycle shuffle. The cloud and two dead Teuers disappeared, but four wounded Garde and four healthy Garde appeared.

Dean Mehli threw lightning that hit the eight of them while I cast another *Jagula Segura.*

The four Garde fired arrows, hitting me with one. With a thick trail of blood from me on the floor, I struggled to cast another masters' extension, but the planar barrier opened far enough for regular spells. I pulled up both hands and cast four successive extended *Ice Balls,* one at each.

Zap shot Dean Mehli's lightning bolt.

Two died. *Zero incantations and zero formulas left and one of my six extra spells.*

"Go get healed," said Dean Mehli. "Come back."

I quickly dragged Daisidian into my office and heard Kitara talking to someone in the living room. I yelled, "We need healing. Kitara, come back with me. Where is Talindra?"

"What the flip?" Shouted Shelley from the doorway.

Shelley healed me, and the three daggers clattered to the floor. I threw open my robes and pulled up my shirts to show her my chest. She cast another spell, and the burn intensified for a second, then something black fell onto the floor that Kitara stabbed.

Shelley scooped up Daisidian while Kitara ran into my office with me. "I promise to explain," I yelled before I traversed to the Planar Mage Guild.

The alert blared, and the red light flashed. Dean Mehli bled from a slash on his thigh, but the room appeared empty.

Everything stopped as Archmage Kira arrived.

With blood on the floor, scorch marks, over a dozen melting balls of ice, and arrows in the wall, the guild looked like a war zone.

"It seems that Argrenn is back from his trip," said Archmage Kira. Her deadpan delivery made me unsure if she'd made a joke.

Kitara handed the Archmage the note from Daisidian. "Daisidian doesn't talk like this."

"So, if I understand you. Master Argrenn discovered an obvious trap for a group and gambled on arriving before they completed setting up this trap." The archmage glanced up from the note to me. "You succeeded, but they followed your traversal signature."

I thought it through for a minute. "That's correct."

"The amount of primal material on you is excessive," she said. "Your body shows signs of passing through the fourth physical dimension."

"Cleaning." Dean Mehli touched the room and set the entire room to state zero.

The archmage handed the dean a scroll. "Here, Timeonne. Will you lock out this other circle?"

Dean Mehli took the scroll, read it, and the circle glowed with brilliant white. Soon he stood up and said, "Done."

"I unloaded all my spells," I said to Archmage Kira. "I don't... dimension?" The archmage confused me, though I doubted it was her intention.

"Here. Pull it out." She ignored my confusion and handed me a garbage can and Daisidian's note, motioning at my beard.

I scraped my beard, and it fell off in clumps into the garbage. The entire beard rubbed right off.

She took the trash can from me and handed it to Dean Mehli.

He cast a spell, and the can's contents disintegrated.

"We don't want that falling into other hands. I'm going to nap since you all have this under control." The archmage handed me a book, *Circles, Protections, and Associated Magicks*. "Learn this for all of our safety." Then Archmage Kira left.

Perfect, I needed more on my plate. Plus, the brand new question was awesome.

"I hope to be as active when I'm in the calming," said Dean Mehli.

"To get the story straight for the students who will ask me. You walked into an obvious trap in an unknown area to rescue a teammate, and the Yuennui chased you."

"Yes, but use a term like 'guns blazing' to give it a bit of a flare," I joked.

"I don't think the students watched westerns as a kid, but I loved them," he said. "But you should consider how much magic you are throwing around, since casting magic has a cost."

"I cast two of your extensions," I said. "In fact, the first one saved me. They'd cast silence and hold spells in the circle."

"Plus, you have those extra spells," said Kitara. "What did she mean by the fourth dimension?"

"Oh, yeah. I used five extra spells. I need to unload to keep up with the game."

"This amount of magic will change you as you become more Tuathan than human. The hair and beard are just the beginning."

"Yep, Talindra will not be happy about my beard." Then it hit me—Talindra wasn't at home. "Kitara, I didn't see Talindra at home?"

"Shelley arrived, and I didn't get to hear her story, other than she said not to worry."

Now I worried.

"My work has something to do with dimensions, but I cannot explain it. But Talindra is fine and, well, good luck with that. I will let her tell her story since I gotta skitty." Dean Mehli walked to his office and left.

"Let's check on Daisidian."

We traversed back to the house, and Daisidian sat in his halfling sized chair with a glowing bright light sending a golden beam of light onto him.

"It's just me," said Shelley's voice. "This is one of my forms."

The ball of bright light vanished and Shelley stood in its spot. "That's all I am risking giving you for now."

Daisidian waved to us. "I really thought I was a goner."

Shelley glared at me. "I've already watched your wife's decision that required me to heal her. Let's watch yours to see who was the more foolish."

Hearing Shelley had already healed Talindra and that was enough to relax me. Shelley would not have left Talindra in any danger. I plopped in the loveseat and Kitara took a seat next to Shelley.

While we were watching the rescue, Daisidian chimed in "OG, you are the man." He continued sitting and his face was pale.

"What do you call this style of entrance? Argrenn has become judge, jury, and executioner?" Shelley shook her head.

"I told the Dean it was called guns blazing, but you could call it American Cowboy."

"Since the Vrelth destroyed Geneva, I don't think OG needs to worry about war crimes against the Vrelth."

Shelley almost retorted, but Talindra walked through the door, bloody, her sweaty hair matted to her face, and carrying her winged helm and dented armor.

"I thought you were going to have a day where Talindra acted more impulsively than you, but I'm calling this a tie." Shelley pointed at Talindra and I. "You two sit next to each other." I helped Talindra sit, and Shelley finished healing us.

She pointed at Daisidian. "We don't want to heal his weakness. No one can eat elven bars for weeks."

"I hoped he wouldn't need to." I helped Talindra take off her pauldrons and unhook her breastplate. She dropped them on the floor next to her.

"He needs to eat proper food and rest for a few days."

Kitara sat next to Daisidian and gave him a hug. "You look rough."

"I pointed him at Urnovher. I'm the one who'd gotten him captured. This is my failure as a leader."

"Of all your mistakes, don't go making things up," said Shelley. "You were impulsive, reckless, used excessive force, and barely put together a backup plan. But sending Daisidian out on a mission was the correct call as a leader. It's called delegation."

"I can't wait to sleep in my bed," said Daisidian.

"Oh, no," said Talindra and Shelley together.

"I have the halfling trundle bed installed now," said Kitara.

"It's right upstairs," said Talindra.

"My bed at my sister's house," said Daisidian with a grin. He added, "Can I see what you scraped off the desk? I want to know if I failed or not before we file my report."

Shelley stood. "I will be back tomorrow morning with tinctures. Your stomach will appreciate it if you eat a big breakfast," she told

Daisidian. Before she left, she looked at Talindra and I. "I know the game requires too much of people and I know your hearts are in the right place. But Sardyna needs you alive." Then she pointed at me. "Sardyna needs the real you, not the American cowboy."

After she left, I let that sink in and then shifted to the floor where I pulled out Daisidian's armor, daggers, shattered pad, and belt pouch.

"Did you two know Shelley can turn into a mini sun?" asked Daisidian.

"Shelley is a High Priestess and Abbess of Sentient Beings," said Talindra. "At tier four, most classes get a form they can take that gives specific abilities."

I knew Shelley was powerful, but wow. "So, we'll have a form at tier four?"

"Tier five gives a second form," added Kitara.

Talindra looked at me with sad eyes and nodded.

"Let's see what we saved of Daisidian's stuff," I said to change the topics from one that made Talindra sad.

"Hold on," he said, pulling out his rod and expanding it to three feet long until a green glow made a shape like a satellite dish.

"Can we talk now?" I asked.

Daisidian sat next to his broken pad, an armful of papers, and his blocking device. "Yep."

"Man, I'm sorry for suggesting you go look into Urnovher."

"What?" asked Talindra. "What's going on?"

"No, OG, you were right about everything. It only blew up because Feston showed up and saw me. If you hadn't sent that little magical box, I would have died in the desert. Then, of course, the rescue."

I pulled out papers, notepads, and other items from the desk and handed them to Daisidian.

"Meh," he muttered as he read them one at a time. He placed them into two piles and said, "Gotcha. You grabbed it, OG. Everything we need."

"I only grabbed your stuff and everything near your stuff."

Daisidian stood up between Talindra and me and pointed to a section of a document and summarized it. "Feston will become ruler of Sardyna once the Yuennui conquer it."

"What?" exclaimed Talindra.

"I knew that the new rule had something weird about it," added Kitara.

"Yep. Urnovher is the Vrelth emissary on Geoe, and Feston will be king of Navarre and leader of all cities, with the castle in Sardyna as his capital."

"What are these points?" I indicated a dot in Schlobir Wap, a dot in the lower Pyr mountains, and a dot well north of Sardyna along the ocean coast.

"That location is brand new and we know nothing about it. I have to turn this info in, and you didn't hear any of this."

"I heard nothing," said Kitara.

"Wait," said Talindra. She looked at me. "How much do you know others don't?"

"At least one other person knows everything I do." Daisidian paused at Talindra's frown. "I'm allowed to confer with Argrenn since Argrenn gathered so much information, but I have requirements for data security."

"So, we're going to ignore a map point?" asked Kitara.

I shook my head. "It's a data point. We can't take action yet."

He folded his device and put it and the papers into his pack.

"So, what's all this treasure on the floor?" Daisidian pointed at the pile of loot Kitara and I had spread out.

"Argrenn and I have a lot to divvy up," said Kitara. "We finished our personal quest."

"Thank goodness you had a boring quest," said Talindra.

"Whoa, you did a personal quest and jumped right in to rescue me?" Daisidian asked.

"You should have seen him beating doors with mathematics and philosophy."

"Five pass-fail tests where it's live or die," I said. "I'd rather fight a demon."

"Pass through the door without a mage or getting the code wrong—dead. Go through the wrong door in the skeleton room—dead. Draw anything but a door—dead. Mess up the cauldron—dead. Don't balance the scale and open the portcullis—dead. Easy."

"We had the right mix of mathematicians and cartoon watchers," said Kitara. "We should put off the divvy until tomorrow. At level two-point-four, I become an infuser, and we will know a lot more about how to combine all this stuff. You can level to two-point-five and know how to balance yourself out."

"You had me at tomorrow." I thought for a second. "Wait, don't you mean level three-point-one?"

"No, go to two-point-five first. After you level, meet the tier three requirements and go to three-point-one. It's a neat way to pick up extra spells."

Talindra picked her armor up off the floor to put away. "There's blood all over Argrenn and confusion in levels, so let's skip my video."

"I'll watch both videos, wait—all three!" exclaimed Daisidian. "I want to see Argrenn and Kitara outsmart doors!"

"All three videos it is," said Kitara.

Talindra lumbered back in regular clothes and sat next to me. She left her breast plate next to me for cleaning.

Kitara played my rescue first.

"Leaving by yourself. Interesting choice," said Talindra.

"Only I could escape the circle. I made the right call."

"Which you did not know. Oh, wait. Look there. He didn't check left and right when he walked into the office."

"Watch the cell door," said Daisidian.

Kitara looked at me and said, "Wow."

Talindra laughed and caught it with her hand before trying to put on her disapproving glare. "You should watch him showing off at the Knights of Honor. He blew up our training yard."

"I'm missing cool stuff while I'm working?" asked Daisidian.

"Only if you call the Knights of Honor having a crater in their guild made by a university mage, and both factions keeping it out of the news as cool," teased Kitara.

Talindra pointed to the wall with the projected video. "Dean Mehli to the rescue."

Kitara tapped his pad. "Now, Talindra."

"Talindra has kept quiet about her day," said Daisidian.

"In my defense, the Knights of Honor called it a duel for honor and justice."

"In my defense, my friends said I rocked, kicked butt, and they are happy I did it," I said, then laughed along with Daisidian and Kitara.

Talindra stuck her tongue out at me.

When the team's safe, it's fun to joke.

I focused on the video. Talindra rode Pearl next to Chaste. They rode and talked. Avaris' three remaining team members—an anti-paladin, a dark rogue, and a dark cleric in jet black armor—cut them off. The anti-paladin challenged Talindra to a duel.

"That's foolish," I said. "I can tell by equipment you outclass him."

Talindra dismounted Pearl, handed the reins to Chaste, and announced, "By my faith and the honorable dueling laws of Sardyna, I accept your challenge."

"Wow, Talindra can be as pompous as Argrenn," said Daisidian.

"After thirty years of marriage, they're going to sound alike sometimes," said Kitara. "But her keywords invoked the dueling laws of Sardyna. Very smart."

"What are the dueling laws of Sardyna? Plus, I've never acted as pompous as Talindra just did."

The laughter of the room didn't comfort me.

A blue cube of light appeared around the two. The words *formal duel by the powers of Geoe* appeared at the top of the barrier. Citizens gathered around to get a first-hand view of the fight. Talindra charged and knocked the anti-paladin to the ground.

He got up and took a phrenetic swing at her head. That's when the rogue and cleric that had ridden up with the anti-paladin tried to enter the blue light of the declared duel and became stuck mid-stride.

"I accepted three successive duels here," said Talindra.

I bit my tongue and patted her on the leg. She patted my leg back and chuckled.

Kitara pointed to the screen. "In an accepted duel by the laws of Sardyna, you do not need to be in a PvP area and they enforce the duel's rules with the city's magic."

Talindra had three successive duels with wild, swinging opponents. She took her share of hits but sat back, waited for openings, and killed each opponent in succession. "If Avaris were alive, he would have stopped them. They thought they'd ambushed me inside of a duel," said Talindra.

Kitara spun up mine and his dungeon, but it wouldn't compare to the first two videos. "You have five skill checks related to duels, Talindra. They did you a huge favor."

"Well, I need to report to Cassiel tomorrow. We'll see."

I hoped this was a sign Talindra turned the corner and become more offensive minded, but we know these rejects came from a Vrelth sponsored team and threatened her kids and grandkids.

The door swung open and Marick burst in with another blue tinted elf. "Guys, we have information."

Daisidian extended his signal blocker again.

"Is it that Urnovher leads the Yuennui and works with Feston?"

It did not phase Marick that we had that information. "That's half of it, but check this out." He handed me a bag.

Looking inside, I discovered the bag held shells and bullets.

"Wow. This is new. Did you collect pieces of paper with these?"

The second blue elf pulled strips of paper out. I pointed to Kitara.

"Kitara, do those have an explosive enchantment on them that invoke upon a bludgeon?"

Kitara focused on the paper for a few seconds. "Yes, how did you know?"

"Marick told me to research this before we left for our quest."

The other blue tinted elf looked at Marick. "You weren't bragging about your team; you told the truth."

Marick continued. "Yes. Plus, we verified the dead Yuennui soldier's rebirth as a thrall anywhere on Evros, and the rumor that they resurrected dead thralls into a Yuennui soldier is a fact."

"Oh, no."

"Anything about how they supply the power for resurrections?"

"Not yet." He stopped and looked at the four of us. "Why does it look like everyone fought for their lives today?" He looked at the elf beside him. "Come on in, ignore the battle-hardened warriors covered in blood. This is how they relax." He looked at us. "Guys, this is Kelgolor. He is one of the last two Qalpa."

Chapter 11

The next morning, we all gathered for breakfast. The team had not been together in a long time. The team and Kelgolor sat in the new furniture or on the floor depending on how much food was on their plate. Everyone got caught up on everything caught on camera. Kelgolor looked at us wide eyed the entire time.

Marick downed a spoonful of eggs. "Argrenn, I know you're trying to protect us, but enemies attack us whenever we leave the city. We need to study the strengths and weaknesses report."

I walked to my office, grabbed the report, and held it up. "Are there any weaknesses you have that you aren't ready to confront?"

"Dude. Why are you worried? We know we're not the best fighters."

I glanced at Marick. "Okay. But are you ready to confront harsh views about your insecurities? For instance, you realize that your pessimism and worry about new information is part of your PTSD from your medical discharge?"

Marick's jaw dropped, and he grabbed his dog tags.

"Do me next," said Daisidian.

"Daisidian never had validation and craves it from those he respects."

"Ouch."

There was no sense in stopping now. "Kitara has abandonment issues and Talindra has a co-dependent need to help others."

Kitara's eyes widened as he had shrunk into his chair and Marick plopped into a chair next to Kelgolor.

"I hope you're doing this because you'd rather a loved one say this first." Talindra walked into the room and sat next to me and winked. "I'll co-dependently support you if that's the case."

"Look, I come off bad as well. The reason I know all this about you is because I have abandonment issues, I need validation, and I believe doom is around the corner. This is why I have always relied on myself."

"Is that why marrying a co-dependent person was such a good match?" teased Talindra.

"Sure, Talindra can take she's not aggressive enough, Daisidian can take 'he takes too many chances,' Kitara knows he has issues adapting to his new body, and Marick isn't comfortable with his new body, but those are small compared to the things we keep hidden in ourselves."

"So, what's the way to attack us?" asked Kitara.

"Separate us. Each of us was not worthy of rescue from Earth for different reasons. As good as each of has become, we stink as individuals. My big mouth would have had me dead long ago. Talindra didn't know about games. Daisidian would have taken on too much and brought Kitara with him, and Marick would freeze with fear. But together, we are unstoppable."

"Man, if the report says this, I'm going to shut up and realize you've been the best leader for us. I'll even work on my negativity," Marick promised.

I handed Marick the packet, and he pulled out the different sections, handing them out. We sat, read our sections, and the team passed around the team breakdown.

"Marick, looks like you owe OG an apology."

"No doubt, and I'm glad you broke the news ahead of time. It hurt a lot less hearing it from you, because this is brutal."

"This is why you learned to traverse with circles and learned *Planar Helper*," said Kitara. "You knew you had to keep us linked without this silly report."

"For a group of professionals, they use unprofessional verbiage," said Talindra. "Misfits, immature, emotionally wounded, weak, unpredictable, and rudderless."

"That should be our new team's name," said Kitara, and laughed through tears in his eyes.

"Read the last paragraph out loud," said Daisidian. "That makes me feel a tiny bit better."

Talindra read the paragraph to the gathered team.

This group of misfits could not qualify to make any other team. Not one of them can stand on his own. Each of them picked a class that does not fit the needs of the game. That is why they must be separated. Together, they have formed into an unstoppable force where each of their broken personalities has merged into a completed person. They have become so strong as a single team that they are favorites to defeat the Vrelth, qualify for the Battle of Champions, and if they make it, the smart money is on them to win it.

Talindra teared up at the end. Kitara rocked back and forth. Marick stood up and paced. Daisidian juggled some daggers.

I still stood, so I sat to ease the tension from the room. "What's scarier? The fact they know how to beat us or the fact that together we are odds-on favorite and can save Earth?"

Kitara wiped tears from his eyes. "I'm glad we know, but wow. This was a lot for one sitting."

"Okay, let's make a list of our next steps."

Talindra stood up. "Plus, a catch-up for our traveling members. Everyone to the bedroom where we can say this in private."

"Daisidian stays for Shelley's healing. Talindra, Kitara, and I have this pile of stuff to go through. Marick, I cannot keep up with Ardvente and need you to run lead on it—but keep up with us. I need to teach class, track Feston, track Urnovher, find Feston's crypt, talk to the other groups, go through the magic items, level up, save Earth from the Vrelth, and step up in helping the team."

Kitara also caught up everyone on the Groove Train and I gave the basics of what we knew about the incoming troops, which wasn't much but involved Yuennui, guns, possible resurrected troops, and suspicious locations.

"Dude, we are a team," said Marick, while he clasped my shoulder. He winked and added, "maybe doom isn't so close anymore."

There was a quick knock on the door before it opened and Shelley walked in, handed Talindra a flyer, then walked over to Daisidian. She smiled at the empty plate of food next to him and gave him two vials to drink.

Marick and Kelgolor rose to leave to perform library research for the next task in the quests from Ardvente. "You get better," said Marick with a point toward Daisidian, "and the rest of you keep it real."

Talindra leaned back in her seat and read, *Come learn proper runic form with the Guardian Knight leader, Master of Materials Argrenn Dawnstrike.* She put the flyer on the end table by the door.

"That's not funny," I said. "We need to burn that before others see it."

Kitara picked up the flyer on the table. "These are all over town."

I sank into my chair. "I told students it wouldn't be flashy and they would learn basics the right way."

"Here, I sent you a missive with instructor notes and lesson plans from earlier classes," said Kitara. "Work from these notes and don't start from scratch."

"The students didn't take me seriously when I said I planned to teach the basics and nothing flashy," I said.

"OG, really? Did you really say that? Do you remember college?" asked Daisidian finishing his first vial.

That made my stomach come up into my mouth. "Go on."

Kitara helped out while Daisidian's face contorted. "You told a bunch of idealistic students that you were going to teach them to be a great spell caster in a mandatory class and followed it up with you wouldn't waste time with fluff."

"I will keep the students who want to attend. Those students are fun to teach. Like the students who asked for help."

"Wait, you helped students who weren't in your class to give them proof you were serious? You thought students would drop out?" Talindra chuckled.

"When you say it like that, it makes me sound silly."

Shelley laughed as she made Daisidian drink something that turned his nose. "It's fun. We've found an area where he is nervous." She put the to vials away, cast a spell on him, and pulled out a third vial.

Talindra grabbed the flyer and put them in the trash. "Let's circle back at lunch. Daisidian will need to sleep and Kitara and I need to meet the knights at the guildhall."

"Good idea. A ride will help me clear my head," said Kitara.

Shelley handed Daisidian the third vial. "I'll join you as soon as our friend drinks this last one."

Daisidian held his nose and drank his medicine, then he leaned back in the chair and fell asleep.

Once in my office, I leveled to two-point-five and read the last spell in the vampire spell book, *Caja Fuerte.* My three new spells—*Create Circle, Material Abundance,* and *Planar Swords*—were a collection of useful spells for out of combat and combat. Conjurations were now part of my repertoire. My daily spells were eight incantations, six formulas, one conjuration, plus the six free spells from the stone in my tiara.

I took the scrolls and put them in my standard spell book. The *Planar Swords* got placed in my damage spell book and the other two in my other traveling spell book. The standard and vampire spell books fit back up on the bookshelf with the book of Aossi poetry and the Necromancer spell book, and I put the two traveling spell books back into the square.

Dean Mehli's masterwork spell in chapter four eluded me. That meant he'd written a tier-three conjuration. I practiced my hand runes, wrote the new symbol into my traveling spell book, and wrote *Urnovher* next to it, memorizing them with my spells as normal.

A knock sounded at the front door and I jogged from my office to answer it. On the way, I used planar magic and set my clothes to state zero. Outside, the same guy who invited me to dinner at the palace stood next to Kitara. "Argrenn Dawnstrike, Talindra Dawnstrike, and Kitara Black. The noble court summons the three of you to be on the palace steps at six bells today. That is all."

"Talindra is at the Knights of Honor Guild Hall," I said.

"We accounted for all probable locations." He turned around and walked away with his contingent.

Kitara looked pale. He wore a new dress, with his sword strapped to his side. Talindra had done a good job helping him dress better, but I figured I'd keep my mouth shut since he looked so pale.

"Well, come on in, today is the day of the firing squad," I said.

Daisidian snorted himself awake.

I laughed. "You aren't pale anymore, but you better eat more before you see Shelley again."

"You two haven't read the proclamation, I'm guessing," said Kitara.

Daisidian ate an orange and worked on a new pad. "I'm glad to see you're styling now, Kitara. The clothes are sharp." He looked so much better than he did yesterday and his energy looked almost like the Daisidian I knew.

Kitara seemed unphased. "We are to be awarded by the noble court."

I waited for the rest.

Daisidian stabbed at a sausage. "That's it? Is it good news?"

"Nope. The noble court isn't good news. But it's not dreadful news, so let's enjoy the morning and go through magic items. This afternoon is supposed to be fun."

"You know what? You're right," I said, and searched on the pad for some music, projecting a Music Midtown concert from 2004 above the hearth.

"We're going to listen to music from the nineteen hundreds and go through magic items?" called Kitara from the kitchen.

"Nineteen hundreds? This concert happened in 2004."

"Oh, 2004," said Daisidian. "That makes all the difference. I was two years old."

Kitara grabbed a peach and joined us in the living room. "Check out those robes, because I can put your weather infusion into them."

I lifted the gray robes. The material felt thick and I couldn't make out any seams, but it looked a little dingy. "What do they...?" I didn't finish before Kitara showed me the description. "Mother of God."

"I'm putting your weather infusion from your current robe into this new robe?" He laughed and took both garments. Less than a minute later, I took off my vest and slipped it on over my silk shirt.

"I'll take this sword and scabbard. These should be an even trade," said Kitara. He belted the new scabbard belt on around his dress.

Talindra walked in with Shelley. "Do you all know what's going on? Ooh, it's a fashion show."

"Kitara is getting honored," I said.

"The three of us are," said Kitara. "Ooh, I thought that would happen."

The robe evened out and changed from gray with red piping to bright white with blue piping.

"Now you look like the old-time mages in the Knights of Honor legend's room," said Talindra.

"Exactly," said Kitara. "Noble-aligned wizards will turn this robe white."

"You sure kill a lot to be noble," joked Daisidian.

"I would wear pink with this kind of power."

Shelley gave a last tincture dunked in leaf to Daisidian. "Nice robe, Argrenn. You're going to surprise many people today. Let Talindra help you wear it correctly and you'll fit in anywhere."

"Thank you, Shelley."

"What does your staff do?" asked Kitara.

"It summons Starlight, my armor, and the campsite."

"You can't use armor with the robe." Kitara pointed at two staffs and said, "Only the one on the right could take the spell for Starlight."

"They're both great, but I need to keep Starlight, so it's the one on the right," I said.

Kitara infused Starlight into a new staff with a blue orb at the top held by a Danaan-steel claw.

"I'm taking this necklace and matching earrings as a trade."

"Nice, I like those," said Talindra. "They aren't flashy like a crown, with stones floating over your head."

Kitara didn't let me retort as he tossed two sets of bracers to me. "Now, here is a choice. Which bracers do you like?"

"Okay, better defense that works with the robe or—wow, I gotta do some math."

"Bracers that make you want to do math. I hope you share," joked Daisidian as he gulped his last bit of medicine down.

"Talindra thinks you should wear these, but I realize the ones you hold are part of your build, and you'd want to see them before deciding on higher defense."

I had the bracers on. "This is why they nerfed *Tuatha Quickness*," I said. "For this exact build. I'll get two glamors off per second and an incantation off per second. I bet I set off the alarms in the improved testing chamber."

"Plus, with these robes, I can get rid of the shirt, vest, and belt."

Talindra walked over and undid the top button. "Wear a shirt." She bent over both lapels to expose my shirt, then grabbed my old belt and draped it over my neck, letting it hang to below my waist on both sides. "Yes, that breaks up the white nicely. Plus, show your cuffs." She yanked my shirt sleeves, so they popped out.

"OG, that's more stylish."

"Yes, listen to Talindra. I have to say, you come across as a noble," said Shelley.

"Oh, well, I got rid of wearing a vest."

"I'm going to use these vambraces and rings," said Kitara.

"Any dangerous stuff we don't want to sell?"

"We haven't gone through the spell books yet."

"Do you mind if I take an extra item?" asked Kitara. "These boots are an improvement."

"Go for it. For the spells, we should both sit in my office and copy spells so we both get everything we can cast," I said.

"Let's put all this stuff in Argrenn's office," said Talindra. "We can stop by the Tanned and Sewn and get the new clothes fitted and matched."

We must have both frowned.

"Oh, get the looks off your faces. You have time to be presentable on the palace steps."

Once we stored our items and moved the rest to my office, we set out, striding to the Tanned and Sewn. They sewed a larger Dawnstrike heraldry on the front of the robe and did some other changes to our garb that made sense to Talindra.

Even with the delay, we made it in time to the palace steps.

Crowds gathered at the bottom of the steps and packed the streets. They'd cleaned the marble steps, the walls of the palace, and the statues. Dozens of nobles and merchants wore fine clothes, standing either on the lower part of the stairs or along the side.

Daisidian stayed at the bottom of the steps and talked to a person I had not met. He swung his arms around like when he'd described his capture. Marick and Kelgolor stood next to them, reading a couple of scrolls and reading them.

Dean Jarlenteria stood on the steps across from us with Dean Mehli. Cassiel and Chaste were there as well. My new robes caused a stir with that group.

"They're talking about me," I whispered so only Kitara and Talindra heard.

"Nigel Queensman wore the robes last, and they were gray when he wore them. For over a century, no one has seen the robes of the noble wizard."

"I can tell Cassiel and Chaste like them," said Talindra.

Lord Fergus stood behind us next to my guard. "Way to put your detractors in their place, Argrenn. Plus, to do it on the palace steps in front of an audience—your timing is impeccable if a little arrogant."

"It's accidental. We divvied up the treasure this morning."

"You might have destroyed that Yuennui base had you worn the new robe," he added. "Though you burned and melted that building to the ground."

Well, the circle coordinates were useless. The circle had burned away.

The king and queen stepped out to a fanfare of trumpets. They released birds behind them, which flew into a clear blue sky.

A thousand citizens gathered in front of the steps to watch the festivities.

The queen stepped forward. "For too long, we have had a noble house without an heir. Today, Lord Fergus has nominated, and we have accepted, the newest lady to the kingdom. By my word, I present to you, Lady Kitara of the House of Fergus, heir apparent."

"Step forward, wave for three seconds and step back," whispered Lord Fergus.

Kitara followed the directions. His jaw hung open, and he looked panicked.

I whispered to him, "Remain stoic. You have friends to help you."

He calmed his facial features.

"There exist fallow lands," said the queen, "and the nobles agreed they needed a new noble to help defend our coast and build up these lands."

"Same thing," whispered Lord Fergus. "Count to three. It helps."

"By my word, I promote the accepted heraldry of the Dawnstrikes from armiger to noble and promote Lord Argrenn Dawnstrike and Lady Talindra Dawnstrike as Barons of Salas Keep and surrounding lands."

Lord Fergus gave us a gentle push. I waved my hand and counted to three, then stepped back with Talindra.

Kitara whispered to me, "Remain stoic. You have friends to help you."

I bit my lip to not laugh, but I pulled it together.

The rest of the ceremony was a blur. I knew it must have gone on long because my legs cramped, but I remember nothing after the shock. The game had upped the difficulty on us again. But lands? Barony? How did this help us? It only added complications.

"Thank you for coming out. Today and tomorrow are official holidays to celebrate new nobles in Sardyna and Navarre."

The king and queen turned back around and walked inside with their retinue.

Daisidian jogged up and patted me on the back. "We'll meet you back at the house."

"No," said Lord Fergus. "It will be a long wait. Come to my mansion."

Chaste and Cassiel walked up, as did Dean Mehli and Dean Jarlenteria.

"Those robes are remarkable in white," said Dean Jarlenteria. "It's much more fitting than the black you've been wearing." She looked at Dean Mehli. "Timeonne, you were right all along."

"Congratulations, Lord Argrenn," said Dean Mehli. He smiled and added. "Once it all calms down, come by and we'll talk."

Chaste and Cassiel shook my hand next.

"I knew you were the right choice. Wearing the robes as a white mage is the best thing that has happened to Sardyna in a long time. Congratulations, and do not become strangers," said Cassiel.

Chaste shook my hand next. "You won't become strangers. And congratulations." He winked, and they left.

"We're out," said Marick. "I'll send you an update missive soon, this shouldn't take too long."

Lord Fergus helped us navigate the throngs of well-wishers, though the mage stigma slowed many from approaching me. My guard let no one get close. Within an hour, we were at Lord Fergus' mansion.

"Hey, OG," said Daisidian. "Do I call you Lord OG now? Anyway, I'm allowed to brief you." He spoke a mile a minute. "Guess what your new lands are, according to information I've discovered? The primary landing spot for the Yuennui invasion of Sardyna."

Chapter 12

The small house party had a couple dozen nobles in attendance. They were congratulating the three of us on an honor that surprised us. Despite the size of the mansion, I felt cramped.

A tall woman with deep red hair surrounded with floating gems wearing a long white cloak and carrying a staff that I sensed planar material upon walked up to me. "Baron Dawnstrike. Your friend Kitara said you wished to speak to me."

My mind raced for a link, but I came up empty. "I'm sorry. Today caught me off guard and my memory is gone."

She laughed and offered her hand. "I'm the warmage from Atlantia."

I shook her hand. "Dame Teffin. I wanted to meet you. Although I hoped for a quiet library where we could discuss the use of metals and metalloids as two mages with similar powers and not a party."

She laughed harder. "I understand. I became overwhelmed when they promoted me to Dame and gave me lands to run. Especially since I was still tier one."

Talindra, Kitara, and another paladin walked up to us. The male paladin greeted me with a handshake that crushed my hand. "Lord Argrenn, it is a pleasure to meet you. After reading your team's strengths and weakness report, I know I have much to learn from you."

"Learn how to be the team's weakness?" I nodded to Kitara and Talindra. "Without Kitara and my wife carrying the bulk of the hard work, we'd be nowhere."

"Yes, I had Dame Teffin in the same role, yet, I dare say, my team would have fared better with you in charge than me."

"Don't let his sadness of our predicament affect your opinion of him. We had an extraneous circumstance that proved our undoing," said Dame Teffin.

Lord Fergus sauntered up to us. "I apologize for my interruption, but I must take the Guardian Knights into a meeting, and if two teams in the game get talking, they'll forget they have additional responsibilities."

Dame Teffin shook my hand again. "We will talk at some point."

The rest of us said our goodbyes and Lord Fergus led us through a door hidden behind an offset wall. We entered the alleyway, where Fergus cast what he called an umbrella spell to hide us, and arrived at the stables for the Inn of the Wayward through back alleys.

Squint had Pearl and Mahogany ready to go. I summoned Starlight and breathed a sigh of relief that my new staff worked. I cast *Alter Own Material* and Kitara and Fergus cast other spells that they said disguised them, and we rode toward the coast.

We didn't stop when it became too dark to ride. Instead, surprisingly, Talindra lit up the top of her wings.

"What's with the lights?"

"It's dark out, and I have human eyes, not Tuatha."

"No, when did you get lights?"

"I told you. Remember when I dropped off my shield with Heitour and bought a couple of extra items?"

"Silly me," I said.

"You better not be judging me. I haven't heard your new spells in a while, and I know you've leveled."

"Yeah, Argrenn," said Daisidian. He rode on the back of his sister's horse. "I watched the video of you rescuing me, and you were throwing a huge thing of acid around that made your little acid attack look pitiful."

"Okay, as all the spells have been on camera now, I have *Material Jump* now. I can move in a line of sight, like three football fields, with whatever I hold. You've seen my cloud spells, which make enemies stop attacking. The big acid attack is called *Planar Destruction*. My escape spell now lets me run through the area and tear up the ground under the enemy's feet. It's called *Trailing Pain*."

"They sound like they're more powerful versions of your old spells."

"Yep, I can create my own circles with *Create Circle*, and from the vampire spell book, I have *Caja Fuerte*, which I can use to put a cage around an area and protect whoever is inside from damage. But the rest are essentially upgrades."

"I like the protective-cage spell. That protects innocents, unlike your acid," Talindra noted.

I had a captive audience for my pet peeve. "We will talk about that."

"Sorry, gang," she apologized. "I crossed his line and put him on a soapbox."

I took a deep breath. This topic made me passionate. Those who were evil used excuses and waited for someone else to take action. The unredeemable slowed or stopped those who acted nobly.

"Destructive magic isn't related to good or bad. It has everything to do with intent. A person who ignores evil is evil. A good and noble person will fight evil with all tools at their disposal. Anyone who allows evil to perpetuate to avoid violence is not noble or good."

"You're saying that protecting children from attack isn't good?"

"No. Protecting children is taking action. You use your best ability to stop evil. It just so happens that my best abilities melt the flesh from enemies."

"I like that," said Lord Fergus. "When you say it in court, restate the 'melt the flesh' part."

Dusk turned to full dark during our debate, and Talindra, with her lit wings, rode up front. I had gotten used to seeing red blobs around me, so I had forgotten Lord Fergus rode with us.

"Are we going to get an explanation?" I asked.

"Yes," agreed Talindra. "We should know what's happening."

Lord Fergus rode into the middle of us. "The chief argument against Argrenn as a noble had two principal points. He wore black and invented an acid attack. Also, they argued you were leaching nobility off of Talindra. The Knights of Honor stood up for you, and that swayed the court."

"Did they stand up for Argrenn because he blew up their practice yard?" Teased Kitara.

Lord Fergus snickered. "I doubt it, but when Argrenn wore the robes of the noble wizard, he put all those arguments to rest in front of everyone."

"Did everyone know the robes show the alignment of the wearer?"

"Yes, the Isilrings and Avesnes protested your inclusion because they feared you were evil. They lost sway in the court and didn't show up for the ceremony," said Fergus.

"Was Lady Avesnes the one who had to leave during the dinner when Argrenn regaled the table with his story that was more fit for a sailor's bar?" Talindra giggled and finished her sentence before laughing.

Lord Fergus laughed. "She held vomit in her mouth until she got to the side room."

We didn't need to discuss my inability to fit in with the nobles. We needed to get to the bottom of the purpose behind our new station. "We are nobles in charge of lands, and I want to know why. The keep is on the coast and a landing is imminent."

"Ah," said Fergus. "I cannot give you a satisfactory answer. But I can say that the ideas you gave Kitara for Salas Keep were excellent. The Knights supported your and Talindra's defensive knowledge. Plus, with your standing in the university and Talindra's standing in the Knights of Honor, you have two powerful factions behind you."

That explanation would have to suffice. We rode on in silence, chewing on what had been shared and what still needed to be said. We were all drooping in our saddles after a long day.

Fergus pointed to a clearing. "Pull up here. We can get four to five hours before first light. That will get us to Salas Keep by six bells."

Kitara cast a larger version of his stable and house, and I put *Planar Protection* over it.

Fergus cast a spell with magic I didn't recognize. After all the ambushes, nothing seemed like overkill anymore.

I dispelled Starlight.

"You should get used to not dispelling your horse," said Fergus. "You copied a horse from the king's private breeding stable. The king takes great pride in his breeding program and you complimented his results in a formal dinner at court. You need to remind citizens that the king approves of you riding one of his horses."

I didn't bother to argue that I rode a copy because the big takeaway was my life had become more complicated. But politics needed to be acknowledged, and, as baron, I needed to add it to my list of 'self-improvements.' Besides, the nobility of Sardyna acknowledged we were the best line of defense against an initial landing of troops.

Kitara hung one of his bracelets on the door handle while I helped Talindra out of her armor. After I had practiced runes, I collapsed onto my cot and fell right to sleep.

After a full day of riding through the lands of Salas Keep, we arrived at a gate in front of a bridge. Lord Fergus dismounted and asked Talindra and me to join him.

I dismounted, but didn't dispel Starlight.

In front of two city guards at the gate, he said, "I hereby hand over Salas Keep to Lord Argrenn Dawnstrike and his wife, Lady Talindra Dawnstrike." He tapped his pad.

"Your room key isn't fancy like your university office key or your classroom key, but it is two sided. Test it on the gate."

I motioned for Talindra to test hers first. She put it up to the piece of black on a post by the gate that Fergus pointed to, and the gate unlocked. The guards swung it open.

We mounted and rode until we made it to the bridge at Salas Keep. A thirty-foot-wide flowing body of water in front of us put Salas Keep on the closest of three islands off the mainland.

The stone bridge that crossed from our mainland to the island with the keep had fallen blocks in the water below and cracks throughout. It looked solid, but it needed maintenance. The bridge crossed over onto a wide stone road, flanked on the west by a two-foot wall, which sloped into the water.

A series of walls connected a circular one-level tower in front of the main house and three two-story houses. A mansion sized main house had three towers taller than the rest of the buildings. The aged stone contained clumps of green patches over its original gray and black.

We rode around the one-story circular tower with a stable. With no one to take care of the horses, we stripped the tack from our mounts and set them in a crumbling coral to relax, eat, and drink.

"How long would it take you to fix the outside walls?" asked Daisidian.

"There is a bunch of stone to get to state zero. Wow, months, even when I upgrade to tier three."

"That's right—you're coming up on tier three. The first mage in fifty years," said Fergus.

"Don't congratulate me. I have many people saving my life. In fact, they need imaginary numbers to calculate all the times they saved my life." I used the joke Daisidian told me our first day in Geoe.

"OG, you're awesome. When I said that, I didn't know how often you'd be saving my life."

"Things were so simple back then. I'm teaching my first class in thirty-six hours and haven't prepared for it yet. We need to create a circle here before we even begin discussing preparing this for an invasion."

Lord Fergus walked up behind us. "You'll be fine. Tomorrow, you'll create a circle here, teach class, and will come back."

"It looks dreary," Talindra commented.

"It's a fixer-upper. The outside doesn't show all the neglect. Wait until you see the inside," said Lord Fergus.

We walked to the door of the main building, and I tested my room key. It opened the house and led into a grand hall. Lord Fergus walked in and showed us the area with broad sweeps of his arms. "Your grand hall is over nine hundred feet. Current living space of all buildings and towers is four thousand square feet, and this island is over twenty-five thousand square feet."

The empty hall had rotted wood and nothing else. None of the windows had glass; though they had frames. The shutters were long gone.

"Lift those faces," said Lord Fergus. "Let me show you the crown jewel." He pointed to the left tower. "The bottom floor is a suitable location for your circle." He led us up the stairs of the right tower.

An empty bottom floor had broken windows and the barren second floor had arrow slits and broken windows. The third floor had a ladder that led to a hatch in the ceiling besides the arrow slits and broken windows. Lord Fergus opened the hatch, and we followed him to the tower top.

Both three story towers butted against the roof on either side of the house. A taller four-story tower stood between the towers twenty feet to the south and were connected with stone walkways, which were too broken to use. That tower had an unimpeded view of the ocean.

"This view is lovely," said Talindra.

The ground below sloped down to the sea's edge and ended in a rocky area devoid of plants. "How deep is that inlet?" I asked.

"Ten feet from the shore, it drops to twenty feet and keeps getting deeper," said Lord Fergus.

"That's why this keep is here," I said. "It's the ultimate spot for landing craft."

"What's with the bigger tower?" Talindra pointed to a forty-foot-tall tower behind the main house halfway between the two thirty-foot towers.

"The walkways haven't been safe for decades, so I don't know."

The paths connecting the tallest points of our keep had been solid stone at one point but had since collapsed, stone littering the ground below. One walkway between the towers appeared over half complete, even with the rocks on the ground, but I couldn't tell which stones supported weight. I cast *Duplicate Me* and put myself over to the larger tower, peering out over the sea. For a forty-foot tower, the visibility calculated to eight miles in every direction. Priority-one needed to be to get this tower operational.

Weather had rotted away the wooden hatch and ladder. With my new staff, I levitated and lowered myself to the fourth level, pushing the door to the walkway open. The rotted wood broke in my hands. I waved at the others, even though they were looking at me like I was a psycho and not a lord facing imminent attack and needing to understand his defenses.

Mold covered everything, and nothing in the lower level remained usable. The ground floor didn't have a door to the outside. The builder planned this tower well, with its only entrance at the top. This keyed my defensive strategy.

I levitated back to the top and used my staff to push myself onto a solid part of the tower, casting *Duplicate Me* on myself to land on the original tower. I had a sneezing fit, and my body expelled the mold.

"That tower is the key to the defenses here. We're going to need workers, stone masons, scaffolding, and others. We'll need to set up a town to live close by. Guards and rapid response troops are required. What are our options?"

"There you go, Lady Kitara. Lord Argrenn has some legitimate questions, and you have all the variables to consider," said Lord Fergus.

"We don't have this kind of money," Talindra argued. "We became comfortable with finances in the noble district and the game changed it on us."

"You guys hit the super-adulting level," said Daisidian.

"Lady Kitara has all this information, but he only now received it. He will need some time," Lord Fergus explained. "Now, Argrenn has a class to teach in thirty-six hours. Daisidian has a debriefing tomorrow morning, and I'd like to sleep in my bed tonight. Let's go get our horses ready and Argrenn can make a circle and take us home."

Unless we were going to beat up Kitara, we had no more information available. We may as well return, regroup, and begin planning.

Within an hour, Fergus had gone to a different circle, Daisidian had traveled to Schlobir Wap, and we were back home with the mounts back at the Inn of the Wayward stables with the guard in front of our door. I cast *Bastion's Ingress Protection* on the house and stood in the living room, considering a snack.

"I've got so much to do. No sleep for me," said Kitara.

"No, Kitara. You can't rush this or do it without sleep. I'd rather wait a week for answers. Even though this is the newest priority, it has to fit in with the others."

"Speaking of that, you two have out-leveled us, Argrenn especially," said Talindra. "We need to deal with that."

"When Marick is back, you all are going to have to adventure without me," I said. "We'll need to figure out how that will work. At least you have the personal quest to help."

After we were alone, I sent a note to Dean Mehli about his availability tomorrow during lunch. Then Talindra slowly straddled me on my chair, closed my pad, placed her hands on my head, and gave me a long kiss.

I wrapped my hands around her waist and said, "Why don't we go back to the bedroom where there are no cameras?"

The next day, the three new spell books beckoned me. Sometimes, you needed to make time for things that finish quickly, even if they aren't the most important tasks on your list.

The spell books contained duplicates, but I added an incantation, *Planar Stair Case. Material Abundance* cast at formula strength and used runes similar to the ones for *Aumentor Masa,* but it doubled smaller items and didn't use as much material. Where these books shined were in rituals. *Bring It Back* let me put a mark upon an object and bring it back to me. *Create Room* created a room with a choice of pre-configured options. *Create Presence* added primal material to me, not planar material. I wasn't sure of the difference, except the description said I'd turn big and booming.

Nigel had a page similar to mine with a list of circles. The Planar Mage Guild kicked off the list with Schlobir Wap. He listed five more in Mhenorian, Connacht, Aridhol, Caemlynn, and the Half Men Inn.

I finished around lunchtime, left the books out for Kitara, and traversed to the university.

"Groovy. Argrenn, you're here."

Dean Mehli walked up behind me with his arms full of books.

"Hi, dean."

"Awesome. Go on in. How were your first days as Lord Argrenn?"

"Not as dreadful as I'd thought, even though I got caught by surprise. By the way, I have made significant progress on your work. The introduction and the conclusion make sense and chapter two is already in my spell books."

"Well, you know how to blow my mind."

"I learned a regular extension, an additive extension, and master extension I read in chapter two."

"Hang loose on extensions for a while, as you'll find chapter two works with chapter four."

That must mean I missed something in chapter two and have to look and see what I'd missed. "Thanks, will check it out."

"Also, the response to your class has been unreal."

Wait, wasn't unreal a good thing? I wracked my brain to see where I messed up my seventies slang.

"Yeah, ninety students signed up before we closed the class."

"Ninety?"

"Oh, it sat at fifteen students, then word got out about how you put no fluff in the class, only hard-core basics, and forty students signed up that day, including twenty never enrolled in the college."

This sounded like my fault.

"Word got out to the villages around Navarre about your first assignment, how you showed yourself doing all the runes a hundred times with each hand no matter the distraction, location, or wounded. We had a dozen meetings about new student enrollment and your class."

"Ninety?"

"Yes, so I reconfigured your lecture hall for you, and Deans Jarlenteria and Szianszerra reconfigured your practice area to have five lanes of practice, and, of course, they upped the safety measures."

"Ninety?"

"You look weirded out. Are you cool?"

"I expected far fewer students than ninety."

"We talked about it and figured, for you, this would be no sweat. You impressed Dean Jarlentieria with your practice videos, since you had to have come up with them yourself. You practiced nightly in Geoe since your first week, and it shows."

"Yeah, the months of practice were to make sure I would be the best I could."

"Also, relax if students call you by your new title. The university advertised the class as taught by Master of Material Argrenn Dawnstrike, but everyone knows you are Lord Argrenn now."

"They can call me Argrenn," I said.

He laughed. "Hope for professor. Also, I know you met Dame Teffin. A noble in Caemlynn is leading a university initiative to have knowledge shared between all the cities. No worries now, but soon your wish to talk to other mages without politics in the way may become reality."

I meandered back into my office and prepared for the first class, my head swimming.

In the auditorium, I went through my opening walk and introduction in my mind ahead of time, trying to get ahold of the intimidation that tried to rattle me. With a cast of *Body Projection*, I held my camera with the projected hand. The camera aimed itself, and I gave it a voice command to project my actual hand to show runes.

I had keyed up three portions of the homework videos in case I got stuck. A second *Body Projection* held my tablet with the notes. That left my hands free for any runes I needed to show. I cast two

Body Projections and pointed my camera at the screen in the auditorium. Comfortable with my setup, I got a good night's sleep.

I paced in my house before starting the class. I reviewed my setups, the first few sentences I would say, and logistics. The students had a class key, and they entered through student doors. My key would open to the professor's door from my office door in my house.

Deep breaths. They want to be here.

Right on time, I walked into the classroom. "Greetings, class. I am Professor Dawnstrike, and this class is for hand runes," I said.

Murmurings spread through the class.

"Okay, I hear mutterings. Can you hear me? In the back?" I pointed to the back.

"We can hear you fine, professor."

"Okay, most of the class is going to be based in the labs. If I don't get to your question, save it for the next day. The labs have fewer students. Questions?"

"Some hands raised, and I already found a problem. The students in front had an advantage to catch my eyes."

I pointed to someone.

"Are we going to cast a spell?"

"I have too much energy. I'm going to walk around the room, so don't freak out," I said. "Answering two questions. The class is a pass-fail. Either you can create the rune or you cannot. As I told some students, I did not use dummies. I cast my first spell against a gobelyn with a crossbow and did not have a safe place to practice until I hit tier two. I will not accept, 'I can usually get it right' or 'I only mess up sometimes.' You will not receive my approval to go out and die."

That was a lot to give out, so I waited for a rebuttal. Seeing none, I continued. "To answer the question you asked, once I have seen you cast ten of the same run ten times in a row, I will allow you to cast one of the two spells in the lab."

I walked up and pointed to another hand.

"What if we are not mages who adventure?"

"You are still a mage," I answered. "You either know how to open a portal to the plane of primal material or you will soon enough. Most of your initial control comes from this rune." I cast a quick *Fistful of Fire* and held it. "Would you be happy with someone who opened a portal to an ignitable portion of primal material and did not control it? What if it spilled all over you?"

I dispelled the *Fistful of Fire*.

I pointed to someone else.

"How are you holding two *Body Projections* and still casting a fire spell?"

"Practice. There isn't anything else. Please save your questions for tomorrow's labs, and let's get into the lesson. Tell me what you noticed between the four videos..."

I escaped the first class without falling on my face and collapsed on my bed.

Chapter 13

I ambled into the living room and plopped into my chair. I just wanted an hour to stare into nothing and clear my brain. Gormesh should have plenty of video for his promotions. I'd prefer a fight in the wilderness than to teach in a classroom. Tomorrow's schedule had me leading seven labs with a dozen students in each.

Once my eyes opened, I trudged into my office and sank myself into chapter three of Dean Mehli's work to forget about teaching. The chapter length in Dean Mehli's work was my main critique. He should have broken the sections into smaller chapters. I didn't understand chapter one until I broke it into its three parts. Chapter two broke into a dozen parts.

Now that I understood he used extensions with a power, his theories and conclusions made more sense. Chapter three and chapter two needed more organization from me. If I broke the chapter into parts; I comprehended the material, but too much interlinked and did not separate.

In my last attempt to break the work apart, there were nine portions with two materials sections, two planar sections, and two additional planar sections joined with sections on types of spells, infusions, and innate powers.

Dean Mehli's advice to look at my materials' power for influence struck me as this morning's focus. The problem centered on the interlinking of the innate power. The two materials sections made sense because my two innate powers came from my title, master of materials.

On a hunch, I asked the pad to look up extension mages and grabbed a book written by mages who had studied the same magic as me. A quick search of future titles and accompanying powers granted to planar mages showed that Master of the Inner Planes and Master of the Outer Planes were the next two most common titles for my skill set. Though there were interesting choices for dimensional powers. I wanted to read up on dimensions even though I intended to take the planar path.

With the information about planes critical to me in the future, I'd found my key to unlock the work. I made a mental note and let it circle through my brain. Then, with context switching, I took up the need to understand *Create Presence* and prepared to work with it to make a new spell.

"Get your butt out of that book and come have dinner with me," Talindra ordered, standing in the doorway in her armor. She didn't say that often, so I responded, "Two minutes," which appeased her. I took out a piece of paper and wrote my thoughts of how the linkage worked, then closed everything up, put my pad in my square on my bandolier, walked into the house, shut the office door, and helped her finish getting out of her gear.

New dents covered her armor, so I hung the pieces on the mannequin and brought them to their state zero. "What's going on? You armor looks like you've fought today."

"I have stupid muscle memory. Good friends helped me. I'm in a stupid game, where I'm supposed to be, and, apparently, I'm good at this."

The tone of her voice needed answering more than the content. "We can get dressed and go out to dinner once we relax."

"Oh, you had your first class today. I'm sorry for my bad mood."

"I worked through my bad mood. We can change and leave once we rest."

When we sat, I pretended to look up restaurants and instead looked up our bank account. We had enough to give us breathing room.

"So, the palace has a section where they expect Royal Guards on duty to practice without the magic of Geoe, since the Royal Guard is supposed to give protection in any circumstance."

"Okay, you've practiced with Enmeline and Chaste, right?"

"Yes, well, the muscles you get with Geoe giving you skills do not go away, and all the moves I have used work the correct muscles."

"Yep, I follow you."

"Well, I learned the eight basic lines of attack and defense. Thrusts, parry, and shield use for blocking, pushing, and balance. I performed fine with the other guards until Cassiel, the head of the Royal Guards, stepped in against me. He said I coasted and relied on muscle memory."

"He used deceptive tactic after deceptive tactic. We worked for an hour, where I blocked none of his follow up attacks. I got maybe three hits on him the entire hour."

"Ugh. He sounds like he's a master."

"He's Sardyna's grandmaster of bladed weapons."

I did my best to stifle a laugh. "Oh, well, that shouldn't hurt your position, should it?"

"No. At the end, he apologized for saying I coasted and that it would honor him to spar with me when I had court duty."

I covered my mouth, as I couldn't contain my laugh.

"What are you snickering at? Every day!"

"Now that you're a noble, he knows he is the only one who can challenge you, and he wants you to be your best."

"Really?"

"Yes. Paladins don't beat up junior paladins for fun."

"Well, it still stinks."

"Well, let me tell you, I agree with you. It will not be fun, and when I teach for eight straight hours tomorrow, you and I will have full empathy toward each other."

She smiled at me. "Let's go eat."

"Let me change first." I grabbed a basin and filled it.

"Oh, have Vern pump up the water again."

I cast the ritual for Vern and had him go fill up the water.

"Do you mind my beard gone?" I asked.

"Once your hair turned pearl white, Kitara said it would happen."

I pulled my hair from my back to the front, holding a lock of white hair with a pearl luster. I felt my ears, discovering they had changed. "When did my ears do this?"

"After the demon fight. You've become four inches taller over the past two months."

I had stood taller than Talindra for decades. I had not realized I had gotten taller than her again.

"The hair is fine. It suits your complexion, and your ears don't stick out, they suit your new look. I traded your clean-shaven face for a taller husband again."

"I'm going to miss my beard," I said.

"Me, too."

On the back porch, I checked on Vern. The water read full, so I dispelled him. Looking around, I noticed the workers had finished the wall, hedge, and flowers. "Backyard looks nice."

"Yep, workers will finish a mage's house fast to get away."

We lumbered to Dwarven Meats for dinner. Talindra ate more at that meal than I had ever seen her eat. I knew how much she had worked out. Her body must have craved the food.

I took a quick opportunity to send a missive to Braun to up the protein this month since Talindra worked out more.

"I can't believe I ate so much," said Talindra. "But I never felt full."

"I told Braun you were working out more and to up the protein for you. When I worked out in the navy, I ate like that, too." We finished our meal, and relaxed in silence as we both digested our day, refueling body and mind to do it again.

The next morning, I got up early, opened my classroom, and entered the pre-configured class. I had seven labs today. Each morning lab had twelve students, and fourteen in each of the afternoon labs. A quick check of the rolls showed no one had dropped out.

I didn't have to see what student showed up to a 7:00 am class. That student was me. I'd enrolled in college as a non-trad after the navy and loved to take early morning classes before work.

I walked in to find students milling around. Everyone had shown up early. "This is a lot more comfortable for me," I said. "Far fewer students and a place to cast spells. Questions before we start?"

"You said if we can learn the rune, we can cast a spell in class. If we can cast a spell, can we do a second one if class time permits?" asked one student.

There it was. My punishment for being an eager go-getter student in my youth. "Yes. *Light* and *Planar Pull* are the two glamors we are doing in class. So, it is possible you can come out of this class knowing two glamors. But please do not shoot for that. Mastering the hand rune is important. This gives you control over the material you are pulling. I practice for an hour every night. You should do that as well."

We reviewed the hand shapes. The smaller classroom gave me time to adjust each person's hands. "Keep in mind, this is drawing a letter in the air. Only it's three-dimensional, and to make the required turns, you need to start the rune with weird twists of your arm and wrist. You cannot practice this enough," I said. "It may sound silly, but you are building up muscle memory. It is obvious to anyone who travels in the wild, but imagine you are walking home. You have an upset stomach from old oxtail stew. You aren't sure how you are going to pay the bills, and your wife or husband is mad at you—when a thief grabs your belt pouch." I paused for a second to let the image sink in. "Do you want to have to think how to hold your hand, or do you want to cast *Planar Pull* and bring him back to wait for a guard?"

Nods around the room reassured me I preached to the choir.

The first lab had one goal—to achieve the correct starting position of rest for the two mandatory runes, which made the first lab nice and easy. The first lab in the afternoon had one lab with only elves, and they already knew how to cast *Light* and *Planar Pull*. Unfortunately, they learned a shortcut to cast the glamors.

"Who taught you how to cast like this?" I asked. They gave me an elven name from an elven village, Osahil.

"Can he cast *Manos Planas*?"

They shook their heads.

"This is the problem. You took a shortcut that is going to prevent you from casting higher level spells."

All of them frowned, squirreled their mouths, or squinted their eyes. A couple even took a step back, like I affronted them.

"Here is *Body Projection*. Who else can cast this?" Two hands rose. "Show me the rune."

They both used the same shortcut. "Watch this rune." I showed the rune for *Manos Planas*. "Watch this spot." I slowed the rune. "See how three quarters of the rune are the same, but you need to go up and forward with a snake motion at this point? Slow your rune down, and show me how you make that move."

Neither of them could.

"Decide for yourselves. All of you use shortcuts that prevent progressing to a complete spell caster. You can't be in this class if you're happy with what you've learned. I will not pass someone who uses a shortcut."

The shocked faces did nothing to temper their foul moods for the rest of the class. To their credit, they did not complain, and achieved the correct starting position for the rune.

The afternoon classes were more depressing. Many of these students looked exhausted, had zero magical preparation, and were not ready. It was a chore to get each student to master the correct hand position, but at least all of them had that bit of success.

Dean Mehli had joined in the last class and invited me to his office afterward. "You look fried," he said.

"I am. The morning's labs went fine, but the afternoon labs were a challenge."

"I have good news for you. Liluth Ararieth is an elven mage who checks up on the elves at the university. She had high praise for the reality check you gave the elves. She also made them break into different labs."

"I didn't give them a full reality check. I told them they had learned a shortcut that limited them and would not be able to pass my class."

"You were honest with the class without compromise. These students had heard nothing in their decades of elven life except they were exceptional and their elvish blood made them natural spellcasters. You took the first step in making sure they can survive in the harshness of Geoe."

"What's worse is, I counted three dozen students who may not pass the class."

"Nobody is going to call you out. Give your best to everyone, like you did today, and let them work it out." He smiled. "So, relax. You're doing great, and university administration is noticing you for something other than your adventuring. But let's blow this taco stand. You need to get home and rest after a day like today."

I trudged home and plopped on the chair next to Talindra.

"You look how I feel," she said, still in her armor. New dents covered her gear again.

I stood up and looked in the kitchen. Braun had dropped off bread, eggs, and sausage. "Tell you what—you change, and I'll cook us breakfast for dinner."

"Deal." She sauntered to the bedroom. "I cannot wait for Marick to finish his research thing, and we can go on an adventure. It's safer."

I put an extended *Fistful of Fire* to heat the hearth. "My schedule is good since there are no more classes until the middle of next week."

An enormous slab of butter landed in a pan heated on the hearth, away from direct fire. Once the butter melted, I dispelled the larger fire, put two smaller ones on the hearth, and put the pan between them. The sausages got placed first and followed with the eggs. I pulled out a couple of peaches, an apple, and a loaf of bread.

Once it finished cooking, I scraped most of the eggs on Talindra's plate with three sausages and the peaches. We both ate, chewing in silence as the energy from the meal seeped into us, then retired to the living room. Talindra fell asleep at once, while I tabbed through my pad and made cards for the next lecture.

The next day, I cooked breakfast, fixed Talindra's armor, and performed what became my daily morning ritual for the next thirty days. I grabbed my guard, traversed to the Planar Mage Guild, traveled to Salas Keep, cast Vern, cast my *Planar Platform*, picked up stones off the ground, brought them up to the thirty-foot tower, fixed the bridge and tower tops, and cast my new *Create Room* ritual in each of the eight sections of the main area and towers. My last act made a new circle to last another twenty-four hours. Did I cheat by casting magic to make Salas Keep habitable? Maybe. But I had a lot on my plate, and this got stuff done.

I got back at twelve bells, walked upstairs, and knocked on Kitara's door.

"How's it going?" I asked.

Kitara's hair fell over his face and looked unwashed. He wore wrinkled clothing and his face looked frantic. "I'm over halfway to things you need," he said. "What do you need first?"

"Wow, I'm glad I checked up on you. Come on downstairs after you get ready. Let's go visit the other teams and have lunch. We can synchronize our schedules."

"There's so much to do," he protested.

"We'll talk about that. But we have to balance everything. Right now, you need a friend more than you need two more hours of work."

He went back to clean up, and soon we were off to the adventurers' district to visit with the other teams.

The change in the district was clear. First, the streets smelled so much better. Buildings had fresh coats of paint and shutters, and doors were being fixed. The city had a crew fixing the road edges as well.

Kitara and I walked into the adventurers' guild, expecting to see cheerful faces. However, The Persevering team sat with Grehn and Thralk and they looked sullen. They were the only table filled in the giant hall.

"Lord Argrenn deigns to socialize with the lowlifes," said Thralk. He got up and hugged me and the table turned to smiles.

"I don't need to be called lord, professor, or baron. Those who call me those titles want something from me." I shook hands with everyone except Grehn, who got up and hugged me.

Kitara hugged Carzummin and Bright Blade and shook hands with everyone else.

"I'm glad you joined us. We weren't sure if Lady Kitara would associate with us," joked Carzummin.

"First, has everyone eaten? I've cast rituals all morning, and I'm hungry."

"We don't eat here," said Brigham. "We have to watch our costs. We're saving up for the horses."

An idea percolated in my head, one which eluded focus. "Lunch is on me, but no alcohol. Talindra only gives me so much leeway."

Thralk and Grehn laughed. I thought the Persevering group should have laughed too; they didn't drink. "Why is everyone so sullen?"

"The Tree Huggers are disbanding," said Grehn.

"Why?"

Thralk shook his head. "Elyon, Rhys, and Sudrih died in the last encounter. They all got a free resurrection, but they're going to retire."

The idea gelled in my head. But first, I had to warn them: "Whoa, Rhys is a mage, right? He needs to research every mage who has retired in the past fifty years and how long they survived afterward."

"What's going on?" asked Brigham.

"This is something everyone should do. Get on your pads when you have time and research survivability in the game and outside the game of certain classes."

"If it's too much work and you want a summary, I have one," said Kitara.

That took the suspense out.

Grehn looked at Kitara's pad. "There are only three mages who have adventured who are still alive?"

"One guy in Connacht, my boss who has left the Sardyna campus a handful of times in fifty years, and me. If you take out the tier ones who are still adventuring."

"This—what does this mean?" asked someone in the Persevering group.

"If you have questions, please research it," I said. I gave a sideways glance to Kitara. "You will find related information—this is important."

We ate, and I swore the other teams gobbled their food.

"What about you all?" asked Kitara, looking at Brigham.

"We've conquered the sewers, but we still need a defense of Sardyna to become citizens, and don't want to leave the city until we're citizens," said Brigham. "We're going to move at the pace all of us are comfortable with."

"Grehn and Thralk, do you have plans now?" I asked.

They shook their heads.

"You can stay active and be ready for hire. Barbarians at level one-point-four have options."

All the ideas came together and formed a coherent thought and lit up in my head. "Are you all up for helping Kitara and I out?"

Even Kitara stopped eating and looked at me.

"Look at Kitara," I said. "Tell me he looks normal."

"His eyes look worse than yours," said Brigham. "And you have the look of someone working on forced energy."

I thought I hid it better than that. "Right. We're both burning ourselves out and need help in two areas. Grehn and Thralk, since Kitara and I can't adventure with the party, and they have to adventure to catch up to us, could you accompany them?"

"Are we strong enough to keep up?" asked Thralk.

"Talindra said she and Marick can do it on their own, but it may be too much of a risk without Kitara and I. While it's not that they're weak—they're undervaluing the flexibility magic gives."

Grehn and Thralk smiled.

"Brigham and the Persevering team."

"Persevering through Adversity," said Brigham.

"The Persevering through Adversity team." I nodded and went on, "I have a keep, and the lands need work. It's safe land, but horkers and gobelyns patrol still. I cannot give quest experience, but I can give the safety to retreat to a keep and..." I turned to Kitara for help.

Kitara pulled up his pad and continued my thought. "Room and board at the keep, use of horses, a minimum kill count to earn the horses, and upgraded armor."

"Plus, I cast about ten rituals a morning every morning for the next thirty days, so if you find something you cannot handle, I can be told within a day," I added.

"Do you have jobs for the other three from our group, even though they're retired?"

"Oh, he does," said Kitara. He smirked and added, "In his defense, I haven't told him of all the positions he needs to hire."

My stomach sank.

"You in, honey?" asked Thralk.

Grehn agreed, and I sent missives to Talindra, Daisidian, and Marick about the change.

We discussed logistics, and it wasn't too long before Talindra rode by with paladins I didn't recognize. The three of them walked into the adventurers' guild and joined us.

I stood up and gave Talindra a quick kiss.

A dozen or so citizens and adventurers filtered into the adventurers' guild and the hall still wasn't half full.

"Enmeline," said Brigham, "you know our situation. Argrenn has offered us an opportunity to base out of his keep for free. He'll provide us with horses and food and a place to retreat if we clear out the horkers and gobelyns from the surrounding area. What do you think?"

The female paladin with Talindra answered, "This is something well within your abilities. Defending Salas Keep at his request meets the citizenship requirement, and as his robes are white, the tasks he gives out are for the greater good."

"I'll agree," said a woman in the Persevering group who I had not heard talk until now.

"How do we begin?" asked Brigham.

Kitara said, "I will come by in the morning. We'll pick up the horses and Argrenn on the way, and he'll will use the circle to get us there."

Talindra grabbed a bite off of my plate. "Grehn and Thralk, we were planning to leave after breakfast the day after tomorrow. Will you be ready for a long ride? I mean long. We're going to pack a month of food and buy more on the way."

"I'm excited again," said Thralk.

We hung out for a while, and Kitara and I rode back.

"Do you need to go to Schlobir Wap?" I asked him.

He sighed. "Yeah, I'll never get this all done."

"You and I will go after lunch tomorrow."

"How are you keeping all this together?"

"I made a list. Teach my class, level to tier three, write a spell, go through books, finish Dean Mehli's masterwork, prepare for an invasion, find Feston's crypt, and prepare the first keep of my area. Each item has sub-tasks with due dates. I don't have time to plan more."

"That's crazy."

"I schedule regular tasks at a certain time and practice spells and runes before bed. For the next thirty days, I cast rituals in the morning and try not to freak out."

He laughed, and the honest smile on his face relaxed my shoulders.

Chapter 14

Back at the office in my house, despite being overwhelmed with tasks, I relaxed, reading my notes for myself on Dean Mehli's work. It was apparent I had organized his work backward. Once my organizations had no infusion references, innate powers tied the entire section together.

To test my hypothesis, I ran a sub-item in every chapter with innate powers as the core topic.

I had it.

The core of the work had two sections—one for infusions and one for innate powers. The other seven sections enhanced two others. Why did Dean write this way?

I put the book on the bookshelf and found a piece of paper stuck to the bottom. It had not stuck long; I'd moved this book every time I entered my office. I unfolded the paper on my desk enough to read it:

My man, my man,
Do me a solid and confab when Flower Child needs to truck
to Hip town.
Catch you on the flip side,
The man

I folded it back up and put it in my desk drawer; not because I understood it, but I knew the implications. I guessed someone wanted to know when Zyronk needed to go to Schlobir Wap.

Who left that note was a new mystery. Though the vernacular meant someone from the Groove Train had penned it, none of them had access to my house.

Marick sent me a missive to let me know Kelgolor had some stuff to do and Marick was hanging back at his and Daisidian's place.

After stopping work early to spend time with Talindra, I prepared oxtail and a plethora of vegetables in a stew. We were lucky that Braun had brought these over pre-cooked. Without knowing how to cook, I heated Braun's food and threw it into the pot, and we had a proper meal.

"Look at you, outside, acting all social and stuff." Talindra tossed her helm into our loveseat, where the wings kept it from tipping over.

I walked out of the kitchen to welcome her home. "As social as I can be. My mind was all over the place and I figured everyone else must be too, so I checked up on everyone."

"Well, I'm proud of you." She gave me a kiss and ambled back to get out of her armor. I carrier her helm back and put it on her armor mannequin and we cane out and ate the stew.

Afterwards, I put the dishes in the sink and winked at her. "We don't get a lot of time alone and I have plenty of time for dishes." I held out my hand and when she took it, I led her back to the bedroom.

I got up early and cooked us breakfast, after which, she left for her last day of duty and I took the Persevering group and Kitara to Salas Keep. Before they dropped off the horses in the stables, I configured the gate entrance for them and gave them the nickel tour.

"I have done nothing with this small entranceway yet, but this is a throne room, and behind it is a war room. If I don't recast the ritual every day for the next thirty days, this all goes away and becomes barren." I pointed to the left tower. "The arcanist study has the circle. There is a workshop, and an armory is above it. Let's go up this tower."

We climbed in while everyone followed with open mouths.

"This is another workshop. Here is a guard's room, and another armory." We climbed to the top of that tower. "This is where I focus on my repairs. That tower," I said, and pointed to the large tower, "is only accessible from the top, but from there we have an eight-mile line of sight out to sea."

"I'll give them the tour while you do your magic stuff," said Kitara.

Huh. I guessed Kitara thought they needed more than a nickel tour.

Three hours later, they were riding out to see the lands. I had done my morning tasks, and Kitara, my guard, and I were on our way to Schlobir Wap.

When we arrived, I said, "Take your time. We need to pick up Daisidian and Marick to be back by six bells."

He left to go attend to Lord Fergus' business items. I walked across the town to Marick and Daisidian's place.

I ran across a few gnomes painting a house and smiled. Spring gave the perfect weather to paint. They had bright pink shutters drying on the ground and were painting the trim neon green. The vivid green of the main sections looked normal. Their townhouse neighbors placed shutters on saw-horses, and cans of vibrant paint labeled neon blue, orange, and a candy-apple red lined alongside their work area. This house fits its new colors.

I sauntered to the buildings where Daisidian and Marick lived. They had a red building with white trim, white shutters, and a white door. Tame by comparison. My guard set up watch outside the building.

"OG, you're early," said Daisidian.

"Kitara had a bunch of stuff to do, so I wanted to hang out with you guys and check out your place."

I had dreaded seeing the level of disarray of a bachelor pad. I'd expected old pizza boxes, empty beer cans, and a couple of rats, or the gnome equivalent. Instead, I walked into a clean apartment with a feminine touch; items such as curtains and a table setting.

"Come in, we're still packing." I walked into their large room, noting the colors were subdued compared to the orgy of bright colors outside. Marick sat with his pack and armor, listening to a concert. I didn't recognize the band or rappers, but that was fine with me.

He fiddled with his dog tags and smiled almost wistfully. "The concert I went to was on this tour. My buddies and I went right before I left for jump school."

What a relief that Marick confronted his feelings.

He pointed to a singer. "Beantop loved this guy, but he got so drunk he passed out before they played."

I chuckled along with him.

We listened for a while and Marick told us stories of his old unit. After the concert ended, he turned it off. "Thanks for listening."

"Thanks for sharing."

He tucked his dog tags in his orange lamellar armor. "So, are we getting ready?"

"Talindra waited for you to come back. She's itching to get out of duty and go adventuring," I said.

Marick talked with a hint of a smile. "I'm ready for the simplicity of traveling on an adventure. But let me tell you what I learned."

"Go for it."

"Get this. Thousands of years ago, the Aossi drove the Formians out of Connacht. A bunch of Formians joined villages on the way south, but the militant Formians crossed the sea to Ardvente. They found a bunch of loosely aligned villages—my villages—humans and elves, all with blue skin tinted from the way the two moons interact with the desert."

"Got it so far. My race, Tuatha, were allies who taught the Aossi during that period."

Marick slipped his finger underneath his dog chain on his neck. "So, the humans and elves banded together under the Qalpa leadership and drove the Formians back. The Formians were desperate and about to lose their second battle for land."

"You're into all new stuff now."

"Well, they tell of an ancient legend of a fish-god. The refugee histories tell that this fish-god raised a pyramid in the desert and blew sand over all of Ardvente and its farmland."

"Jerk move," said Daisidian.

"Yep. The Formians who traveled to the pyramid became part snake and grew powerful enough to stand on their own."

"This happened thousands of years ago."

"Well, the Qalpa fashioned three magic items. They ended up at a draw with the Formians living in the desert and my ancestors living along the coast."

"So, something changed."

"From eyewitness accounts, a ship from space landed on the pyramid. Some days later, the Yuennui multiplied overnight and took all the land."

"Vrelth."

"They hunted the Qalpa family, but two descendants remain, and at least one of them hunts for the artifacts to protect the people of Ardvente again."

"Cool story, bro," joked Daisidian. "How does this affect us?"

"The Yuennui army is coming for two reasons. One, to take Sardyna for the Vrelth, and two, to stop the Qalpa from recovering the artifacts. We have to turn back the army."

"Well, that aligns with us. Anything else?"

"I've taken it on as a holy quest to make sure they find the artifacts."

"Wow, are you still going on tomorrow's quest?"

"Kelgolor has a lot to do, so that quest is on hold. Especially since you and Kitara can't go out with us."

"Do you know these two Talindra said are joining us?" asked Daisidian.

"Yes. Grehn and Thralk are good people. I played the test game with them back on Earth. Talindra and I ate dinner out with them twice after their last child moved out and they became grandparents."

"Wait. I met them. Thralk worked out with other gym rats, and he met his wife in the air force."

"The barbarians who were nurses on Earth?"

I smiled. "They both were."

Marick looked at Daisidian. "We're good. They can hang."

"Let's go put our stuff in the extension house and say goodbye to everyone," said Daisidian, carrying his stuff.

We caught Mayor Whizzburr on the way back. He waved the scepter toward me. "Most excellent, most excellent. My friends will always find me."

I ran up and gave him a hug. He beamed around us and the smile infected me.

"Most excellent. Most excellent," said the mayor. "The new lord of Sardyna."

We all chatted for a minute, then walked around and found Wallblamm.

"Argrenn," he called out. "Oh, wait, I mean Lord Argrenn."

"Come on, Wallblamm. We're friends."

We spent the afternoon with the gnomes, enjoying catching up and visiting, and when Kitara finished, we journeyed back to our house. I got back in time to cook dinner for everyone.

The next morning made me want to ball up in bed and hug myself. Talindra and the team were going out adventuring without me.

Even though Kitara and I saw them off, I needed to work through my anxiety or become a basket case.

"You need to be careful," I'd told Talindra.

"I'll be more careful than you ever were," she'd said.

"That's a low bar."

"Watch our videos when you get a chance. We're cleaning Grehn and Thralk's leftover quest, then Marick and I will complete our prayer quests."

Before they'd left, Daisidian put out his hand. "This is my first-time adventuring outside the city without you guys. I want to remind you I'm all in."

My hand went in. "I'm all in."

Kitara put his hand on top of mine. "I'm all in."

Marick and Talindra dismounted, put their hands in, and said, "I'm all in."

With that, they'd rode off.

Kitara looked much more relaxed this morning now that he had before we traveled to meet friends. "Kitara, if you get lonely, come work with me. I can spin up my classroom, and we can work together in there."

"I may take you up on that."

Despite a genuine desire to lie in bed and mope, I took off for my morning tasks.

Traversing to Salas Keep showed me the Persevering group had adventured in the area. So, I performed the rituals for the whole keep without an audience. My guard and I ended up at the top of the tower, where he watched me fix the walkway with my materials' power. The walkway was usable even if only half of the parapets were and the walkway wasn't completely finished. The signs of progress helped my mood immensely.

During a break, I leaned against a parapet and a reflection in the sea caught my eye.

Ships sailed near the shore on the way to Sardyna's port. We were only a day or two from Sardyna's harbor and docks. Ships passed by often, but this time, they looked moored. The waters in this are stayed fairly calm unless one of the rare storms blew through. I heard when swirls came through the tide could rise ten to twenty feet. Today, the water was as calm as bath water.

I re-summoned Naomi and flew her to check it out, careful to keep her a mile up to stay invisible to those on the water. She spotted four smaller boats rowing toward shore with multiple predators in each boat. Judging the distance, the boats needed an hour to make it to shore, so I waited and resumed work on the walkway.

Using planar material to fix objects with lots of mass took time. At half an inch thick, the road with the rocks had little mass but still took ten minutes. The tower thickness measured three to four feet and twenty feet long. I needed the tops of the towers finished before the stone masons arrived.

An hour later, the boats rowed into view. I put Naomi back on the tower and walked to the shore to see where they were aiming. From behind a large rock, six armored Yuennui rode in each boat. *Twenty-four Yuennui wearing armor.* I might need to grab the guards and retreat to safety. For now, I stayed, since if I had to retake the keep, I'd need to know how many guards to bring.

I reached out with my material sense to figure out what armor they wore. *No way.* The Yuennui wore iron armor. My new assignment surprised them.

The boats maneuvered to circle the keep. There was enough rock to approach them and stay out of their line of sight. Once I verified the information and gave my guard the plan, I sprinted around the keep and told the guards to stay hidden, that I had the upcoming incursion handled, then returned and took a position behind an enormous pile of rubble.

The four boats were in the inlet that circled the island. My strategy began in the back of the fourth boat to avoid alerting the invaders for as long as possible. My materials' power grabbed as much iron as I sensed and crumpled it like in the Knights of Honor guildhall.

Three suits crushed into balls in one attempt. The fourth boat had three more that were crushed without me straining. It now drifted without oarsmen. My gardening power fired faster than they reacted as the crumple sounds threw them off. These were easy kills.

By the time the first two boats pulled near the short to disembark, they were all that remained and died in their crumpled armor before reaching me. There were four messy boats on my beach, and I pulled with the lead ropes, tying them to the bridge.

The boats were gross. Crushing armor did not make a neat kill. But there was still the matter of the ship, and my soaring confidence in these gardening powers made me feel invincible.

The ship had raised anchor and sailed closer now. It entered near the shore and took a broad arc. Did they believe Salas Keep abandoned? With Feston out of the city, I wondered who fed them the information now.

I reached out to it with my materials' power, but it was too far away. The ship came around and I saw an open window on the side, catching movement in there. The ship wanted to bring its cannon to bear.

I need a cannon.

If I took out their best twenty-four warriors, how many more were onboard? The ship hoisted a single sail and had a length of fifty feet. I searched my memory for the word: not a bireme or trireme... a cog. A cog could transport around fifty warriors. For the first time, there was relief in information popping into my head. If it carried twenty-four armored warriors, the rest needed to be sailors. Especially since the cog needed room to carry the raiding boats, which were now my property.

A quick review of my spells, and only *Material Jump*, could reach the ship.

"We should head back and warn the others," said my guard.

"Let me gather a little more info." I winked and cast *Material Jump*, putting myself on the deck of the boat. The guard would write something unpleasant about me in his report for that move, but the sailors were not ready for me. The twelve on deck had their hands full with the rudder, rope, and sails. Some of them sat with their legs under the railing while they scraped the edge and were in no position to respond quickly. I felt sad for them, but they aimed a cannon at my new home, and I hadn't even finished fixing it yet.

The aft had seven of the sailors, so I cast a cloud of *Jagula Segura* on that section. I turned off Geoe's powers and threw five successive extended *Ice Balls* at the five who were coming at me with belaying pins. *Six incantations, four formulas, one conjuration, and three of the six extra spells left.*

I ran forward on the ship, and the screams brought the Yuennui from below decks. I threw two extended *Ice Balls* that doubled and split. Seventeen sailors were dead that fast.

I cast regular extended *Ice Ball*. Eighteen dead. These guys should not have fought me. What were the Yuennui thinking?

Feston floated forward from the aft section down the handful of steps between the handrails. Now the suicidal attack of the sailors made sense. He would send his own family to their death. "Now you will die, mage, or will you run?" he taunted. His cloak didn't move, but his smooth float had a jerking motion as he descended the stairs.

His gloved hands shook, shoulders slumped, and he wore his hood far over his face.

No music played, did this mean no battle?

I took a step closer to look at his wardrobe changes. He wore long, heavy gloves and had a face covering on inside his cloak.

"Even though you locked out knowledge of your current form, I bet you've fed me enough information to act upon. You cannot traverse the ocean without a boat. That means your crypt is on Evros and the closest port to your crypt is my keep."

"Your intelligence is your greatest strength, mage, but remember how often these strengths show to be weaknesses."

"I know from your coverings you aren't immune to the sun now. So, I have a boat." I never learned how to sail one or what I should do with it, but only Feston defended this boat, and rules prevented his direct attacks on me. Well, unless he wanted to make himself susceptible to tier-two powered attackers.

"Then die," he said, and held up his hand.

I hoped I had not overplayed my hand. But my *Jagula Segura* had not hurt him.

"I feel confident that you will not attack me at tier two," I said. "That would open you to attack."

"It was worth a try, but this is one boat." He shrugged. "This minor battle does nothing but ensure the Yuennui come back stronger next time."

"I'll be smarter next time, too," I rebutted. I did my best to keep my mouth in control, but it appeared I had already burned any bridge between me and the Vrelth agent.

"Don't let those brains go to your head," he said. "Or let it. Your abrasive personality will be your downfall." He turned to leave, but stopped. "Let me give you more information. Though the Vrelth trust me, my flaws prevent further promotions. It is my nature that I cannot let slights go and will focus on them. The reason I have risen so high is that I succeed with revenge. Sleep on that."

Feston turned to mist, which floated inland, and I stood alone on a fifty-foot cog with no sailors or soldiers.

That was the easiest naval battle I'd been a part of. It was the only one, but still.

A quick search and I found the lever to release the anchor in the back. I summoned Vern, since I couldn't budge it.

A quick message from me on my pad to Kitara, and Fergus informed everyone who needed to know that I had fought off the first raid of the attack. The message also told them I had a cog with no crew and needed help, and gave them my circle's coordinates.

While on my pad, I hunted through unfamiliar screens and found the boat. I couldn't pronounce the name. Then, with a little research, checked if I could claim the ship under maritime law.

By the Sardyna version of maritime law, battle victors could not take possession of a ship. Agents of Sardyna could seize an invading ship, so I put in to seize the ship. On the screens, the ship needed a new name, so I rechristened it after my first car, *Sixty-Five Stang*. I put in a request to be a trader in Sardyna's merchant fleet, because that option popped up.

Geez, this paperwork stunk. It made life easier when someone filled out forms for me and I only had to say yes. Finally, I put away my pad and lowered the flag on the mast after trial and error for the right rope, then cast *Material Jump* back.

Three incantations, three formulas, one conjuration, and three of the six extra spells left.

"Let's recast the circle," I told my guard. "I sent a request for help now that the cog is mine. He dropped his stoic demeanor, curled his mouth, and glared at me. *I should leave threatening Feston off the update.*

I left Feston's eerie promise off of my update to the guard. Giving a report where I judged staying on a boat and facing a superior foe because I didn't hear music inside my head was not a good way to let people trust me.

"They had no troops left, only a few civilians who were under compulsion to attack me," I said. "Once I dispatched them, I filled out the paperwork to take possession of the ship." I yawned and fell backward until he caught me.

His face didn't give away his thoughts. But I knew that drawing duty to guard me was the worse duty he could have pulled. I spent six years in the US Navy and since he wasn't chipping bilge paint while wearing a forced air rubber mask next to cold North Atlantic water kept my sympathy to a minimum.

I traipsed over to the bridge, re-summoned Vern, and cleaned out the boats. Well, Vern cleaned out the boats and pulled the wreck of armor and bodies out. The weapons were iron as well and had not fared well in my attack. The only items of value that had survived were their personal items and a pittance of coins.

During Vern's work, I fell asleep on the bank.

I woke up, and it was past noon. My guard had a lemon-based tincture to give me. "This will give you more alertness back. The few hours of sleep helped you recover."

After drinking the tincture, and fighting from making a face at the bitterness, I used my materials' power to lift the crushed iron armor, placing it into the flowing inlet. I recast Vern to clean the gore out of the boats and drag them up on the grass. We now had four ten-foot boats to work with in the future.

My pad vibrated that there was a reply to my missive, but reading it told me they needed a couple of days to gather resources to help. One boat attacking Salas Keep didn't raise many hackles in Sardyna.

So, I settled in. Stuck at Salas Keep—other than going to teach my class tomorrow.

"Well, crud. Looks like I'm going to get plenty of stone fixed until we can do something with the ship."

I climbed to the top of the tower and zoned out while working on the bridge. With only a brief break to eat, I worked into dusk until my guard yelled from the smaller tower, "Incoming! By air."

Looking up into the darkening sky, I spotted two dark shapes with huge wingspans. I jumped up on the large tower and took cover behind a parapet. Well, they weren't dragons, but they had long leather faces, huge, scaled wingspans, and scorpion tails that curled up over their bodies. I didn't know what to call them. So, I called them scordrons.

They lined up for two successive attacks, ignoring my guard. Drum lead in and dual guitars. What song played in my head?

Huh. Intelligent or guided?

The glowing red eyes of these scordrons gave away Feston's involvement. As soon as he recovered energy, he must have sent these. *Scordron Thralls or Vampire scordrons? Does it matter?*

The first one flew close. Its wings spanned a hundred feet. I hit the deck and cast *Aumentor Masa* on it. It nose-dived past the tower. The second raked me with its claw.

I'd have to be careful. We had no healer or healing potions. I had paintings and new furniture in my house instead of healing potions.

I stood up to get a good view. It was definitely Iron Maiden.

Before the scordron turned, I cast *Duplicate Me* to the other tower and hid behind a parapet there. *Three incantations, four formulas, zero conjurations, and two of the six extra spells left.*

Most of my spells were useless while he flew. Especially at that speed.

Both claws, a bite, and a sting hit the duplicate, and it disappeared. The scordron turned as it realized it had missed, and I cast *Aumentor Masa* on it. It tumbled with a clumsy roll in mid-air and crashed to the ground with a thud that shook the tower.

The first one stood on legs that wobbled. It crawled out of the broken trees and dug up earth.

"Let me know if the second one can fly!" I called to my guard, then ran over to my bridge under repair and through the open door. Once up the ladder and onto the large tower, I cast *Argrenn's Acid*

Attack on the one that crawled toward my bastion. Even though I missed, the splash still damaged it. I saved my remaining incantations and formulas. Four acid throws later, everything but the skeleton flopped to the ground.

The boned beast leaped into the air and flew toward me. This was not the best way to verify Feston was involved in resurrecting dead troops. I cast *Fistful of Fire* as a formula as it tried to grab me as it flew by me. The claws raked my chest, but my robe and the Danaan-steel shirt kept the claws from penetrating far, though my robes turned red with blood and I hissed in pain.

I grabbed the cold stone of a nearby parapet to steady myself and hit it with an extended *Ice Ball*, while my guard cast an *Ice Ball* as well. The scordron didn't even consider my guard, and I didn't think it was because my spell was stronger.

I cast a second *Fistful of Fire* as a formula and the creature crashed to the ground. My guard took a position next to me and set to take on the last one as it tried in vain to crawl up the tower.

My acid attacks worked as I intended, but I needed to be careful not to splash my tower. I'd have to fix it if I dissolved any of the stone. My guard supplemented with fire spells at the creature, and it soon died.

While I finished new calculations to check on my improved accuracy with my staff, ten more creatures flew into view. They looked different at this distance. "More incoming!" A quick *Duplicate Me* and I put myself on the large tower.

The second the skeleton charged, I hit it with two formula, *Fistful of Fire*.s It made a beeline for me, and I got a second formula-sized fire on it before I ducked and rolled as its claw raked my leg. *Two incantations, one formula, zero conjurations, and one of the six extra spells left.* I threw two *Fistful of Fires* at it. My guard cast two more, and the fire combined to kill it. Just in time to get a grasp of the second wave of new enemies, which resembled super-sized bats.

My guard threw a ball of fire the size Avaris had thrown, and the blast hit four of the creatures. I cast an extended *Ice Ball,* doubled and split, at a different two. The six thunks sounded, but I couldn't focus on that now.

It was the <u>Flight of Icarus</u>! I knew I knew that song!

I wanted to test the theory of obtaining my highest DPM through accurate quick glamors in the practice room, but there was no time. With my new bracers, improved accuracy from the staff, *Tuatha Quickness,* and *Two-handed Casting* working together, I ripped out *Fistful of Fires.*

Fire filled the sky with the bats and the six wounded died in the fire before they got to me. The other four tried to bite me, but my robes and Danaan-steel shirt held.

I killed two more with my barrage as they circled back. My guard had hit the other two with fire as well.

I stood up and kept casting as they assaulted me. The last two died right before they hit me.

My guard and I searched at the sky. It was too dark to see far, and I dropped to the third level of the large tower and walked over to my repaired walkway to the smaller tower.

"Let's keep an eye open." I took off my bandolier, sash, robes, Danaan-steel shirt, and undershirt, revealing a nice claw mark across my chest.

"You watch, I'll bind," my guard suggested.

Seemed reasonable to me. I sent Naomi to fly in increasingly larger concentric circles around the keep where she discovered we were clear for many miles.

My guard put a paste on me and bound my chest and my leg wound.

"We're clear for about eight miles. Thank you. Let's head to the main house." I wanted to make camp, but my create-a-campsite power had stayed in my old staff. The throne had the only cushion to rest on in the entire house. Since I had not planned to be at the keep overnight, I'd brought no food, no clothes, no blankets, and no healing supplies.

"You should cut the items out of the wyverns before it gets too late," said the guard.

Wyverns. Huh. I liked scordons better. To cut the items out of the wyvern, I needed a dagger from the armory. I trudged up the stairs, pulled out my pad, and looked up the items Kitara normally told to me.

I took two steps and exhaustion claimed me and I dropped to my knees, then to the floor.

Back in the main house, an unfamiliar voice said, "Shift change." Dean Mehli and two guards strode into view. My current guard had a look of relief in his eyes as he watched me sit up. He must have found me and carried me here. The two guards took up positions outside the door.

"Argrenn, before anything else, the armorer at the university wants the wyvern and bat hides. Do you mind if he comes and butchers them to get the best use of all materials?"

I agreed and breathed a sigh of relief, plopping on the throne, hoping no one else had caught me reclining on a king's chair. I couldn't keep throwing extensions with aplomb. The price could be deadly if I couldn't summon enough energy to escape. But how else could I survive?

Fergus, Kitara, and a dozen others arrived in my circle and I jerked awake; there were way too many people for me to only recognize three.

"Drop those over there," said Fergus. "Stay sleeping, your lordship."

I hoped he joked.

Weathered men dropped three ten-foot bags on the other side of the entranceway and joined Kitara. "We're going to go check out your ship. Anything you needed done before it goes to Sardyna for a refit?"

I reached into my belt pouch and grabbed the handkerchief, handing it to him. "Please roll the cannon and cannonballs into the handkerchief. I want to put them on the large tower here."

"The skinny. I've got four ships leaving for Atlantia in two weeks," said Fergus. "The quickest way to get a turnaround on this new ship is to load it with two hundred tons of shale after removing the cannon and round tripping with my boats."

I gave him the thumbs up.

"Be back in a little," said Kitara.

The university staff with Dean Mehli stood outside, and the dean handed me a sandwich, orange, and a covered mug of water. He wore his magic cloak, glasses, and carried his staff while wearing a crystal sword.

Feeling famished, I drank and ate as fast as I unwrapped.

"Save room for this," said the dean. He handed me a red potion, which I drank straight away. "It's not super powerful, but it'll keep you from getting weaker or bleeding out."

"Thank you, dean."

"Don't thank me yet. Here is a book of circle protections you'll need to add to your circles."

I opened the book and read the opening, but my eyes kept closing.

"It's special spell infusions to only allow arrivals from certain areas or certain people. The first two infusions are minimum requirements to cast on every circle. But put it away for now so you don't drop it."

Tucking it into an empty square, I asked, "Dean, in Nigel's book, I found a handful more circle addresses. What's the decorum for traveling to new circles?"

"Do you have Mhenorian and Aridhol?" he asked.

"Yes." I didn't want to waste any more time since he didn't leave the campus often.

"Those two are fine. Aridhol isn't part of Navarre, but we get along with them. Who else?"

"Connacht, Caemlynn, and the Half Men Inn."

"Connacht and Caemlynn are invitation-only. We aren't at war with Connacht. If you need to use one, contact the universities first to ask. I've never heard of the Half Men Inn."

We chatted for a while until the leather workers returned and dropped gems in my hand. It was hard to focus, as I almost fell asleep, but I kept jerking awake, thinking Feston was about to come attack our separated team.

"One of them ate someone with gems," he said. "Wyverns can't digest or pass them."

Kitara grabbed them, tossed them into the handkerchief, and put the handkerchief in my belt pouch. "One cannon with twenty-one cannon balls." He picked up the two stingers. "I know who wants to buy these, but I don't know about the teeth." He stopped and then pulled my hood and hair back. "I need to check out your ears. We have a human, half-elf, elf, halfling, and Tuatha in our group. My books have nothing written or pictures of Tuatha ears."

"Don't bother hanging the banners and such until after your rooms are permanent," said Fergus, pointing at the large packages his men had dropped off on the other wall.

I wasn't sure if everyone was talking over each other, or if I was drifting off to sleep in front of everyone.

"You get to spend the night in your bed tonight," said Dean Mehli. He helped me to my feet, got the guards for me, and walked me over to the portal. "I'll drive."

With that, I traveled to the Planar Mage Guild. My guard and I then traversed to my house through my office.

In the morning, I got the water basin. After filling it and heating the water, I stripped off everything and changed my bandages. I felt better, but not enough to go without bandages. The chest wound hurt when I cleared out the medical goop in it. But I didn't go to the temple. I wanted to learn how fast one healed in Geoe.

I got dressed, used Planar Magic on my full setup, retrieved my guard, and traveled back to Salas Keep. After casting rituals for the eight rooms, I recast the circle, cast the two protection spells, and traveled home.

The last instructor's notes got me ready for the second week of class, which taught how to make different circles with the hand. Fourteen low-level hand runes before the students learned to combine the runes with other movements.

I made it to the class on time and after demonstrating the fourteen runes twice, I showed the two runes they needed to pass the class, demonstrating a dozen times each. To pass the class, they needed those two to be perfect.

A quick lunch and a closed-door office session helped my mood, despite feeling overwhelmed, as I had an epiphany on how to fix my explosive spell. If I used a services section of the verbal portion of the spell, I could make the calls to it as a reference. I doubt other mages used the terminology of a services section; this was the vernacular I used from writing code.

The first two calls were easy. In stage one of the spell, I called them upon initialization. I used a crumpled piece of iron for more surface area, tossed it to my target, and threw heated sulfuric acid on top of the crumpled iron. I closed those two calls since I only had two openings into the planar material at once. Once both were closed, I summoned a covering of planar material to trap the hydrogen gas and closed it. It needed a three-second delay into the spell, which made the hand runes tricky. In the final stage of the spell, *Fistful of Fire* cast into the contained hydrogen ignited it.

Argrenn's Explosive Cloud was in the books. Other than my testing it and getting someone else to test it.

The next day, I had labs all day. The labs had changed up, and the elves had spread out, so I had two in every lab. They paid attention now and worked to improve. I noticed the classes had two standouts—an elf named Nylien and a fifteen-year-old human boy named Elovar. Still, a third of the class coasted, but each person made the two required runes at least once.

That night I did my nightly practice early, grabbed a snack, sent a missive to Talindra, and slept.

The next day, I resumed my normal morning ritual with the protection spells, worked on Dean Mehli's masterwork, and fought the urge to level up to tier three. I compared a tradeoff of more power compared to my exposure to Feston. When he fought at full strength, I couldn't fight him one-on-one.

The wound had not changed. Healing with just Geoe's regular healing seemed to move at the same speed as healing back on Earth.

The exchanged missives with Talindra were uneventful. They were traveling and having minor battles on the way to the quests. That alleviated my stress about the team traveling without me.

The next five days transpired identical to one another—I used Vern to set up the cannon and finished the pathway from the two towers to the large tower. I went to the temple after the fifth day when I saw my chest would take weeks of not months to heal.

The information Kitara put together on the basics of the Salas Keep Barony needed my review. It measured a contiguous thousand square miles. The list showed fifteen villages of one hundred to five hundred residents each, totaling over four thousand. I needed to turn Salas Keep into a manor house with three yeomen in it. Cowling and Oceanacre were both villages that had the population to support one in each as well, and I needed to hire three knights to maintain them. To make a village and grow it into a town, I either had to own the land and bring in vassals or build out a village and partition land with a purchase program. If I followed that plan, I needed to build a fourth manor in Eanverness. So, the knights got paid with lands to work.

What a pain.

I spent a full day calculating the town's revenues and expenditures. Money at these levels made no sense. My rule of thumb of fifteen dollars per gold comparison no longer worked.

The five thousand gold in our bank account covered nothing for the Barony. However, the Barony ran at a small profit, but we needed to improve the income of each village.

Common sense then snuck up and hit me that while I had a good long-term plan, there was no defense plan for the imminent invasion.

Chapter 15

In my class, I separated the students into four groups. The highflyers cast spells in the lab. Then I delineated the above average students and would cast a spell before the end of class. The multitude of students had its share of try-hards, as well as those with no actual skill but who worked hard and would also cast a spell by the end of class. That left the rest.

The two standouts in the class, Elovar and Nylien, were casting a second spell. They wanted to petition the dean for more work, so I wrote them a letter of introduction.

After class preparations, the progress I made on Dean Mehli's work moved fast. The third chapter made sense. He laid out how a magic strengthened materials powers with extensions, planar material, and spells. Once the materials power connected to the planar material plane, I could logically connect spells, extensions, and planar material.

After that, I made progress understanding my *Remove Presence* spell. Primal material manipulation and poking holes in an unfamiliar area of the universe had consequences I had not considered.

The last morning of the third week, the Persevering group returned. They looked better. They had success behind them, and it showed.

"Argrenn," yelled Brigham. He jogged over and waved.

"Brigham, how's it going?"

"We're coming together. We've achieved almost everything we can, but I have one item you might want to know about."

"Okay, shoot."

"A tribe of large gobelyns holds the quarry in Oceanacre. We counted over thirty in the quarry. Oceanacre cannot stop them from raiding now."

"What do you think of your team's chances?"

"I have an idea. We have one more run until we will be tier two. Can I come back to you?"

"Yes." I had little choice. I'd be fighting soon with them to make sure I kept my promise.

To keep from feeling lonely, I kept myself busy. I watched a few videos of Talindra and the team, took a few breaks with some concerts, but spent the bulk of my time working and sleeping. I met Cassiel at the end of the third week. He took his whole duty team out to dinner and invited me. I was always down for a free meal.

We met at Dwarven Meats, which I learned was a favorite of the Knights of Honor. We sat at three combined tables to fit everyone and I stood out as the only one not in plate armor. I did have to say, my white robes fit in and gave me a level of comfort among the paladins and knights. I'm glad I liked this restaurant too, since Talindra enjoyed the portion sizes.

Next to me, an elf wearing plate armor with a plate containing a giant tomahawk steak said, "Nylien is my cousin. He said you threatened to fail all of them. When he and his buddies complained, Liluth laid into him, but now he raves about your class." He laughed. "No one had ever told him anything except his greatness. You gave him a great life lesson."

"Nylien is going to be as successful as he wants. He is one of the best in the class."

"Good to hear. We were wondering why elven mages were look-ing second tier. That's why we sent a contingent of our best young elves here. The timing to join your class was fortuitous."

Cassiel got everyone's attention after the group finished eating. "There are changes at Salas Keep and the threat of another invasion." He turned to me and his hand motion suggested he'd like me to say something.

"Cassiel, I'd like to say that I'm in good shape, but I'm not. I've worked my tail off and I'll have a manor house and a few towers in a couple of weeks. I'll have a transport circle and one cannon. Unless the Yuennui show up with one ship again, I don't believe this is good enough and I feel like I'm spinning my wheels."

He laughed. "Now you sound like a real Knight of Honor."

The rest of the table laughed along.

"Well, we would like to station two permanent guards on a two-week rotating schedule in your guard room and send a ballista to mount on the tower where you have the guards' room. What do you say?"

That doubled my defenses. "Well, yes, of course I accept."

One thing about the Knights of Honor—their celebration might be geeky to others, but I fit in fine.

That night, I wrote another missive to Talindra to let her know the Knights were going to be full time at Salas Keep.

I missed her, so I watched a video of the last fight they had. The team had a normal campsite. No protective dome and no secret house. Thralk stood guard and didn't see a group of large gobelyns sneaking up—a dozen of them, with one big hairy gobelyn in charge. Before they attacked, Thralk finally noticed and woke the whole campsite.

The large gobelyns charged and Marick's bell appeared. Daisid-ian walked right through them to behind the big hairy guy while

Thralk swung his huge hammer and Grehn had an aura of a globe of Earth.

Talindra called celestial light, and everyone but Daisidian glowed.

Grehn's giant ax cleaved through two at a time, leaving a mess and lowering the numbers of gobelyns swiftly. Thralk's giant hammer pummeled one as Marick struck one with a bolt of celestial energy and another with his mace. Daisidian took out the big hairy guy with one attack, which was entertaining to see the large ugly beast fall to the smallest in the group. Talindra hit one with her shield to knock it to the ground, carving into another.

The battle didn't last long. The two-to-one advantage disappeared in fifteen seconds, and the battle finished in thirty.

I closed the pad and drifted into a peaceful sleep.

Back at Salas Keep, I made it to the last day of ritual spell casting, celebrating by unrolling Lord Fergus' packages. Banners filled the bag, along with pictures detailing where each should go: Sardyna's banner, Narvarre's banner, the Dawnstrike banner, the Fergus banner, and Queen Isabel's banner.

I cast *Cloud Staircase* in the throne room to the banner tops and summoned Vern, putting him to work. While he hung the Dawnstrike banner, I got a visit from Dean Jarlenteria and a handful of the guards with the griffon tabard.

"Argrenn, we would like to station two permanent mages on a two-week rotating schedule in your arcanist study and establish a defense cauldron in the magical tower. What do you say?"

"You mean this tower? Is there room for mages to stay?"

"We will create an extra dimensional room off the side for safety."

"Well, yes, that is a great help."

"Excellent. Take the Knights of Honor banner to go over the entrance to that tower and the university banner to go over this tower.

Despite the forces lined up against you, you are a boon to the university and should be proud of all you have accomplished."

"Thank you." I didn't know what else to say. The assistance from both the paladins and the knights turned the tide in preparation for any planned attack while we readied for the invasion. A couple of quick casts had Vern and a *Cloud Staircase* for him to hang the banners.

She smiled at me, turned and went back to her duties.

I felt things were under control and that's when I missed Talindra the most. I had missed her and kept up with missives, but I kept myself busy and focused. But now half of my hand-rune classes were in the books. I had the experience to level to tier three and my idea for a spell based on the primal material spell took shape. The work on the keep progressed, and our friends were doing well, and the invasion had not started.

I had to focus even though I was in a bad mood. My brain needed a rest, but too much work piled up to stop, and I was afraid of losing momentum. We hadn't found where Feston hid his crypt, the invasion target dates, or my availability to adventure with my team.

I sat on the throne and pulled up a live view of the team. *We needed to put other chairs here.* They were in the mountains and leading their horses. They slouched in their saddles and had dented armor. No one smiled and my mood became fouler. The team needed their leader with them.

It was time to care for myself and my team, regardless of what else I was doing. I traveled back to Sardyna with my guards to the university and bought a few handfuls of those elven bars, then rode to the Inn of the Wayward where I bought a bunch of jerky and hardtack. After a cast of *Planar Helper*, the box appeared, and I told it to find Talindra and bring her the box with the food. Then I grabbed lunch at the Inn of the Wayward, and ate it while I gave my brain a break with a concert from Daytona Beach in 1989 with the Cult,

Queensryche, and Metallica while I waited for the return. I left a few of those bars in my belt pouch. They were too handy to ignore.

After the concert, which I slept through part of, I got the box back filled with coins and gems from Talindra. The letter said to deposit it in the bank accounts for the team. They were tired of carrying the weight.

Palmer sat next to me and had watched the concert with me. "This is cool. I like oldies too."

Oldies? The 80's were only... I stopped counting the years. These weren't oldies.

"Where is Braun?" I asked.

"He is looking for a property in Schlobir Wap. He said he'd be with the gnomes for a while."

Weird. "Thanks, Palmer."

Feeling better, I rode back to the bank, made the deposit for the team, rode to the house, and knocked on Kitara's door.

He answered. "Once I saw you sent food to the others, I figured you felt better about your workload."

"Why didn't they ask me for help? I would have dropped things for them."

"They watched us like we watched them and realized you burned the candle at both ends. By the way, Salas Keep looks good. Are you ready for the deliveries and the workers to arrive?"

"Yep. Marketplace and docks are the first two items."

"I've got an optimal project plan from other build outs, but, yeah, a road, marketplace, and fishery are first. You also need to do a walkthrough with me and find out what else you want to do with the keep," he said.

"Let's do a walkthrough after my class tomorrow."

The time spent working in my classroom had eased. The next topic prepared the students for future runes. They needed to complete the rune on time and prepare for the next rune. Since so few students needed full lab time, I changed and scheduled three labs.

Forty students received a passing grade from me to sign up for new classes. I sensed thirty-five more students were going to pull this off. I didn't know how to get through the last fifteen.

"Professor," said a familiar voice.

Elovar and Nylien had stayed after class.

"We got permission." They handed me approval notes from Dean Mehli to learn destructive spells.

"You understand this is actual fire, right?"

"Yes, professor. We are required to have a burn salve with us," said Elovar.

"I'm heading to the keep now. The keep has safe places to practice."

I brought them into my office and picked up Kitara.

The two stood away from Kitara and diverted their eyes from him. There were no words to explain to teenage boys that Kitara was male, while their hormones told them otherwise.

The four of us traveled to the Planar Mage Guild. We passed through and traveled to the keep. We stayed on track because the guild had too much to show.

"I can't believe this is real," said Nylien.

"Let's go outside, and I'll get you started, and then track down Brigham."

Near the bridge, a huge rock underneath the bridge rose above the water. "Throwing the *Fistful of Fire* is the easiest spell for avoiding burns. Remember, you close the rune with your thumb before you let it go." I threw one and hit the rock. "If you burn yourself, stick your hand in the running water. Clean it off and apply the salve."

They put the salve to the side. We watched a couple of attempts before Kitara and I searched for Brigham. He talked with the Knights of Honor on top of the Knights Tower, as they called it.

Two persevering guys were experimenting with the cannon.

"Hi, Brigham. What's the plan?"

He laid his plan at the top of the Knight tower in front of the paladins, Kitara, and I. No one saw any flaws and we decided to make it happen.

We made plans to leave tomorrow, to help the Persevering group fight after Kitara and I got back from my labs. Both students had salves on their hands when we picked them up.

"Are the burns bad?"

"Hilarious, Lord Argrenn," said Kitara. "Show me your hands."

They both had minor burns on them, but they each had a smidge of second-degree burns. Kitara shook his head. "Nope. Who is your medical person at the school?"

"Shaerra Vagwyn," answered them both.

"Those second-degree areas can get infected. You go to her when we get back."

"Yes, Lady Kitara."

Once Kitara and I made it back home, we sat and relaxed, hoping to watch the team. As soon as my brain relaxed for a good minute, a thought came together and I blurted, "We can figure it out. Plus, we get to do math!"

"Wait, before you make that sentence make sense, I forwarded you an application to hire those two nerds as student assistants."

"Nerds? They're both outstanding students—courteous, hard-working, driven to learn magic, and..." I didn't finish. They were exceptional students who would make excellent mages.

We walked into my office and I filled out the paperwork to get two student positions opened. I pulled out a blank sheet of paper. "Let's not say this out loud."

On a map, I drew a circle around Sardyna, Schlobir Wap, Salas Keep, and Mhenorian. For distances, I put four hundred and twenty miles from Sardyna to Schlobir Wap, sixty miles from Salas Keep to

Sardyna, and three hundred and eighty miles from Schlobir Wap to Mhenorian. I calculated the distance from Salas Keep to Schlobir Wap and Mhenorian as four hundred and twenty-four and five hundred and sixty-six. "All good?"

"So far."

I wrote, *A vampire can move twice as fast as the fastest mage without special powers.*

He rolled his hands for me to move along.

I can cast Material Jump *for five hundred feet every six seconds.* I wrote *I can move sixty miles an hour in short bursts, so we know Feston can move at 120 miles per hour. We know wyverns can travel at eighty miles per hour.*

Kitara chuckled. "Okay, but the bus driver's eyes are blue."

I wrote *Feston had no power when he landed. He had to go to his crypt. Therefore, those attacks originated from his crypt. So, if a vampire travels at one hundred and twenty miles per hour from point A to point B, then a wyvern flies from point B to A at eighty miles an hour, and we know the total time is seven hours, where is point B in relation to point A?*

"Talindra said you were like this in math," said Kitara. "You're going to have to do it and realize I believe your answer."

The crypt location has a high probability of existing near a population center. Agree?

His eyes widened. He understood where this was heading.

With the calculation, we drew an eight-hour arc from Salas Keep and a six-hour arc from Salas Keep. One large population center existed in the arc.

Kitara put his hand up to his mouth, shocked.

"It's not definitive, but if we had a second corroborating piece of evidence, it would give us actionable information." I pulled out the folded piece of paper from my drawer, slid it across my desk, and unfolded it.

We both read it:

My man, my man,
Do me a solid and confab when Flower Child needs to truck
to Hip town.
Catch you on the flip side,
The man

I folded it up and put it away. Kitara stared at me wide-eyed. *Fistful of Fire* burned the map from the top without lifting it.

We walked out to the living room to watch the team in the dungeon. Kitara looked dumbfounded, but relief poured over me. We learned where Feston's hideout was. More importantly, I knew the Groove Train had the exact location.

Chapter 16

"What level are they after these weeks of adventuring?" I asked.

Kitara had cut up some early harvest vegetables, pulled the end table over in front of the love seat and sat next to me while we munched on these. "Daisidian has almost caught you. Talindra and Marick have caught me. Don't you and Talindra talk about that?"

"No. When we talk, we keep each other up on our lives and how we feel and what we are doing with our time. I mean, sometimes the game comes up, but rarely."

"Huh."

The battle to enter the dungeon didn't go well. Yuennui thralls outnumbered them four to one. The team played tactically and reduced the enemies for the next fight. Both sides retreated.

"Well, Marick removed dozens of them," said Kitara.

"They unloaded on them, whittled down the numbers, and made a strategic retreat before taking casualties. The team made the right call." I hated it because I wanted to be there.

Kitara patted my shoulder. "They'll be at full strength tomorrow. We can watch again."

My pad vibrated, and I read the approval for my two positions.

"I need to offer the positions to Elovar and Nylien, because we'll be fighting tomorrow with the Persevering group."

Kitara sent me a missive. *Here's what you can tell them.*

I read it and went into my office to traverse to the university, finding the two of them together in the Planar Mage College.

"Hey, guys."

"Professor Argrenn, how are you?"

The two stood up, and I motioned for them to keep sitting. "Hey, I'd like to offer you two positions as my student assistants."

"Really?"

"It comes with access to my classrooms, practice areas, and higher library privileges, as well as experience in incantation writing."

"It's great for us," said Nylien. "Why do you want assistants? You do everything yourself."

"That's the answer. I can't do it all myself. In fact, the class has fifteen students in danger of failing the class, and I can't give them every opportunity to succeed."

"We will help students," Elovar offered eagerly.

"Plus, there's a lot coming up soon and need backup plans."

They both agreed, and I sent them a list of the fifteen students.

Sleep eluded me since my mind raced, reviewing the team's performance. They needed to have either Kitara or me with them for magical support. The team had missed an opportunity, and it made me wish I'd been there.

I needed to do something to get my emotions in check so I reviewed my toughest decisions. Even though Daisidian was captured, I'd made the correct decision to send him after Urnovher. It was also the right call when I sent Marick to research Ardvente. I wished that making the right call would feel better instead of making me toss and turn in bed for hours until sleep arrived.

The next morning, I worked on my spell *Remove Presence* for an hour and leveled to tier three, because I realized the risk of running into Feston had to be taken. My pompous new title had changed to Master of the Prime Material. I cast nine incantations, six formulas, and two conjurations per day now. *Bring it Back, Create Spring,* and

Create air were my new spells. I saved a couple of extensions since Dean Mehli advised me to.

More exciting, I read the spell in the fourth section of Dean Mehli's book, *Timeonne's Spirit Entrapment*. It captured the spirit of a soulless creature, such as a vampire, if it got near death. The spirit stayed in the small cage forever without a release for death. *Good old Timeonne.*

Because we did a good job with skill checks, I gained sixty-bonus skill-check with my normal twenty-five points to spend,

> *Your title, class, and actions have locked in the following items: comeliness (class), confidence (title), discernment (actions), and judgment (actions).*

> *There are statistics with minimum values because of your class and title: mental capacity (class), understanding (class), constitution (class), and fortitude (title).*

> *You have received the following alterations to your statistics and skills because of your actions: Guts, plus five; Magic Theory, plus five; Research, plus ten; Judgment, plus three; and Dodging, plus seven.*

I knew what I wanted to improve. Mental Capacity and Understanding got the bulk of new points, and I maxed them out at forty. Tier three had a maximum of forty. Guts, Dexterity, Agility, and Dodge hit thirty. I boosted Chance and Fate so they caught up to Constitution. Magic Theory and Research were higher than them.

The next morning, I didn't have tasks. I traversed to the university store and bought six hundred gold worth of potions. I cast *Planar Helper* and sent the potions to Talindra. The box returned with another belt pouch full of coins and gems.

After the bank trip, we arrived at the Planar Mage Guild and knew it was time to gather the second-to-last piece of information. With a quick warning to the guard, I put the symbol for the Half Men Inn inside my head and brought myself and my guard there.

The circle landed us in the common room of an inn. A twenty foot bar with stools took up the wall next to the circle and eight tables sized from four to eight chairs were scattered to the opposite wall where stairs went up to another level.

"Breakfast will be—whoa, we have a celebrity." A half orc wearing a dirty apron lifted chairs onto the tables to mop the floor underneath.

"I'm sorry. I had to know this location."

"It's five silver pieces for a circle trip per person," he said as he leaned his mp against a table. "I suppose we will waive it for you."

Relief washed over me and I walked over to the bar where a green glass container partially filled with coins displayed prominently. "Coming and going—three gold. Here is five for me and my guard arriving and departing outside of normal business hours." I put five gold on the bar next to the green jar.

He leaned over the bar and grabbed a pamphlet which contained a map of the Southern Pyr Mountains.

"Here is where we are, in the mountains, at the halfway spot between Caemlynn and Mhenorian. It's an important trade route, which is why you'll find a few towns and us on this road."

I let him return to work after thanking him. Why wasn't everything that easy?

After leaving, we picked up Kitara and met Brigham in the keep. We left the guards at the keep and rode out with Brigham.

"These gobelyns are smarter than the normal guys. They'll recognize you."

"Me?" That made little sense.

Brigham adjusted his helm. "The Persevering-through-Adversity team attacks at the secret entrance we will lead you to. The large goblins will recognize us and come out to engage. We will retreat into the two of you, and our team will leave you and ride out to the main entrance."

"Wait, how smart are these large goblins?"

Kitara tapped his pad. "They have access to adventurer feeds through stolen items from villages."

Brigham waited until Kitara finished. "That will allow us to engage the front defenses without fear of reinforcements. You two either continue through the secret entrance or support us on the main entrance, whichever is easier."

I understood. "The secret entrance is our first plan. If we come around, it's because something unexpected happened."

We finished the ride by talking tactics and what happened in the Salas Keep Barony. He had more knowledge of the lands around Salas Keep than I did.

Kitara spent most of the ride catching up with Carzummin and Bright Blade.

We got to the quarry before dinner, and Brigham showed us the secret entrance. They'd hid it well between two hills, but trees and rocks prevented anyone from seeing a pathway.

The Persevering group walked into the entrance. Kitara hid behind a large rock. I tucked into a small alcove formed in the entrance's side and drew an imaginary line three feet from us on the ground in front of the entrance. The rock walls weren't sheer but a mix of shale and another rock I didn't bother to use a power to identify. Sunlight didn't make it to the ground, though it did around midday.

Soon, the Persevering team ran through the entranceway, past us, followed by more than a dozen five-foot-tall goblins chasing them. They carried maces and swords, not cudgels.

I cast *Manos Planas* and laid out a stream of black hands on the ground. The line I'd estimated worked. Only one got through. Kitara ran it through with a sword. While he held it with the sword impaled through its chest. He shot a stream of green magic into the gobelyn's face until it died.

I cast a *Jagula Segura* over the hands area. *Nine incantations, four formulas, two conjurations, and my six extra spells left.*

Kitara and I picked them off one at a time with *Fistful of Fire*, and streams of green magic. It took a dozen casts, but soon we had fifteen dead in front of us. I grabbed the pouches and put them into my handkerchief. Kitara took two weapons that looked good, and we jogged into the quarry.

We had significant cover when we arrived. Persevering's battle echoed through the large quarry. Its deepest part was fifty feet down, and it was at least two football fields in diameter.

The large gobelyns didn't expect anyone to come this way. We caught them gearing up to stop the Persevering team at a choke point.

"The games call these dire gobelyns. They sure use the word dire a lot to mean something bigger or meaner," said Kitara.

"One of those led the gobelyns ambush against the rest of the team the other night." I realized that the information hadn't popped into my head. *What does that mean?*

We snuck into range, and I cast *Planar Winter* at their choke point. I wanted to trap them, but I also wanted a visible spell, so the Persevering team knew they had support.

While the dire gobelyns struggled to stand amid the ice and hail, Kitara threw in a giant ball of fire, similar to the one Avaris had thrown. No gobelyns stood after that.

The dust we kicked up sent me into a sneezing fit and my nose kept running after that. That was embarrassing.

We hunted for lone survivors. The cleanup of the rest happened fast. We were standing on the quarry's edge talking to the Persevering team when we heard hissing behind us.

I grabbed Kitara and dove behind a rock. Luckily, he didn't resist and fell with me. Arrows flew over our heads. "Go take the lead. I'll cover you," I told Kitara. "Brigham, stay near the front with a healer. Send the rest back for distance attacking. Cover is most important."

I stood and grabbed the earth under the feet of the Yuennui and threw it up with an extension. The materials power had improved. I tossed two dozen of them to the ground.

With a focus on my materials' power, I reached for any iron armor. None. I had more control over other materials, but these soldiers wore leather or hides.

I cast two extended *Ice Balls,* both doubled and split, and heard eight thunks hit the enemy. Attackers attempted to flank us. "Brigham, have your team take the flank. Kitara and I have the main under control."

"Got it," he yelled back.

I ran to my left, took cover behind a tree, and cast *Planar Swords* into the midst. Sharp pieces of ground flew up and into the attackers, and their strength halved.

Kitara had taken out their leader, and the Yuennui were in disarray. I charged and cast *Trailing Pain* as I ran through them. Six of them hit the deck. Before returning, I ran into the middle of them and cast *Planar Escape.*

Carzummin healed Kitara, who bled from a few places. His armor had slashes, scorches, and dents. The enemy tried to fill in gaps but failed due to insufficient numbers. They called to retreat.

"Back up," yelled Kitara.

I backed up to him and threw an extended *Ice Ball* at the only attacker not wounded.

Kitara threw that enormous ball of fire again, and none of the enemy stood.

Brigham hiked over and shook my hand. "I see how you did well. You have good battle tactics and react quickly."

"Being weak, I learned how to avoid damage." I leaned against the dirt cliff to catch myself. My face felt flushed and I needed to catch my breath.

Carzummin walked up to me. "Did you get sick? You didn't get hit." She crossed yellow patterns on my chest, then it turned gold and I felt fine.

"Thank you, fever?"

"Yep."

Brigham and his team stayed because they wanted to follow up on a couple of leads and had a quest in the same location. We left the treasure of the dire gobelyns inside the quarry for the Persevering team.

"How can we know where these things are going to pop up?"

I leaned against the wall next to Kitara. "We just have no intel from them and almost losing Daisidian to gain more information was too high of a price to pay."

"Information is so valuable," he said, "but you are right, not that valuable."

Kitara and I traveled back to Sardyna. Over the next few days, Kitara leveled to tier three, and I finished the spell *Remove Presence*. I hadn't learned what removing the primal material accomplished. I knew primal material bonded planar material, which formed into the material of the plane; in this case, the prime-material plane.

I needed to test it.

I visited with Dean Mehli, taught my class, introduced Elovar and Nylien as student assistants, and visited Wallblamm and Whizzburr in Schlobir Wap. When Kitara finished up, we took two construction managers to Salas Keep.

I gave them a tour and told them the ideas of the road extension and a marketplace for housing to set up around. Inside the gate, we walked around the south side of the inlet, and I told them my ideas of fishing docks and a harbor.

I brought them inside and into the completed interior of the throne room, and the towers blew them away. We walked up the Knights of Honor tower to the top, where I pointed to the two islands and explained I wasn't sure what to do with them, but wanted a wall around the towers in the back.

I showed them the stables and the other two buildings: a barracks and a yeoman house. They got to work with samples and measurements, site lines, and whatever people worked with when they didn't have access to magic.

Back in Sardyna, I did two things. The team received another care package, this time with better food, using *Planar Helper*. I marked the package I'd hidden in my desk drawer with the explosive in the decanter with *Bring It Back*. Then I responded to the mysterious paper.

> *My man, my man,*
> *Do me a solid and confab when Flower Child needs to truck*
> *to Hip town.*
> *Catch you on the flip side,*
> *The man*

I wrote on the bottom of it:

> *Cool Beans, Narc, I'm jonesing to have the primo posse motor most directly to Chill town.*

If enemies didn't grasp early seventies counter culture lingo, they wouldn't pick up on eighties lingo either. I changed clothes and cleaned.

"There you are," called Kitara as he walked into the kitchen, where I sat eating an apple. "Brigham has something to show you."

I tossed the pit, wiped my hands, and we stepped outside, where I summoned Starlight. Kitara jumped on the back with me, and we rode to catch up to the Persevering team.

Brigham greeted us. "We found two anomalies on the coast. One a half hour south and one a half hour north of Salas Keep. We noticed dirt piles while looking for landing spots and found tunnels."

The seven of us rode to the northern tunnel entrance and discovered an eight-foot-tall, five-foot-wide hole cut above the shoreline. We hiked up the slope and my new prime material master power searched through the ground to look for the tunnel.

"Back up from the cliff." Once everyone cleared, I grabbed the excavated dirt and threw it as far into the tunnel as possible. After grabbing dirt from under the sea to pack in the tunnel, I walked along the top and collapsed it along the way. Even if I needed to rip up land further from the cliff to help even out the ground.

It took me most of the morning to collapse this northern tunnel. They hadn't gotten within a half mile of Salas Keep.

Kitara mentioned Yuennui in the tunnel might dig out, so I grabbed more dirt to put on top and crushed the earth into a higher density to kill anything that hid within.

We rode to the southern tunnel and followed the same steps. This one ended up closer to Salas Keep, but again, nowhere near enough for explosives to matter.

"Good job, Brigham. Hidden explosions from the tunnels would devastate Salas Keep."

"We knew you wanted to see them."

"I don't know if I can repay you for that."

"Yes, you do," said Kitara. He tapped his pad while he rode.

I pulled my pad off the square and read that he had me hiring the groups, assigning them an address, and paying for their citizenship. He even had a banner on the missive that said *Make It Happen*.

"Let me get Talindra's input."

"Already have it." He tapped his pad again and showed me a few missives between them, discussing it.

I clicked the *Make It Happen* banner. "Do you need me involved in the keep at all?"

"Sure. You had the plan. When things get too big and are going to blow up, we'll need you again."

They kept me in reserve for the worst of issues. No sense in fretting. I turned to Brigham and informed him, "I have two student assistants, Elovar and Nylien. You may see them at the keep. They're allowed to be there and may look like they're doing weird stuff. It's okay."

"It's not okay," said Kitara. "They're young and trying to learn everything at once and learned caution from Argrenn. If you see them, make sure they don't hurt themselves."

"Movement ahead," called Joseph.

I put the pad away. "Let's move to a point where we can engage." We galloped forward.

"Yuennui chasing two riders," called out Brigham.

"Engaging," I yelled and pushed my mount to its full speed. The others were in my dust quickly.

In under a minute, I pulled close to the four Yuennui chasing two elves on horseback. I reached out and sensed two of them were wearing iron armor. They were out of the battle with one quick thought of my materials' power. The gore-covered horses panicked, reared, and ran in circles.

The other two Yuennui turned toward me. These were Teuer and had tentacles instead of arms and hair.

I cast one of my newer spells, *Planar Swords*, following it with a master extended *Ice Ball*, doubled and split.

A flurry of swords made of stone flew up from the ground and impaled themselves into the Teuer. Next came my *Ice Balls* and the eight thunks.

The Yuennui Teuers were on the ground, their horses running. The Teuers turned to flee, but I caught them and cast *Planar Destruction*. They quickly died in the bubbling acid.

I pulled up to see who ran from them, and Marick's friend Kelgolor waved.

The others raced past me and quickly caught the riderless horses and brought them all back to us.

"Man, you are quite the killer," said Bright Blade.

My habits took over, and I had made a mistake; I was a leader, not a killer. My instinct to protect someone running had to be balanced with those working for me.

"Sorry, guys," I said to the Persevering team. "I wanted to talk to the two who were running from our enemy and didn't want to risk them dying."

"Let's get inside and get the story from Kelgolor here," said Kitara.

"Marick said this keep protected us better than Sardyna if we got caught," said Kelgolor through labored breaths.

Blood surrounded the tentacle wounds on him, but he cradled a package in his arms.

"Does anyone have healing for these two? They are allies fighting the Yuennui."

Carzummin stepped up and healed both elves.

We returned to the keep, put the horses in the stable, and walked to the main house.

"We need to get a message to Salas Keep and find a place to hide," said Kelgolor. "There is a naval raid imminent."

I opened the doors to the main house. "Welcome to Salas Keep."

Chapter 17

"Those job titles are official," ordered Kitara, tapping his pad. The Persevering group ran to both towers.

I walked with Kitara and the two elves to the war room, which was really the area behind the throne, projected a map from my pad onto the table, and waited for Kitara to project his pad onto the wall.

The entire continent of Evros appeared on the table, and for anchor points I put in Sardyna, Salas Keep, Half Man Inn, Aridhol, and Harmstead.

That gave me the whole peninsula, from the ocean to the mountains and the southern sea to the northern ocean. The map took up too much room. I removed Aridhol and Harmstead and put in Schlobir Wap and Mhenorian. That gave me the southern third of the peninsula.

I viewed Kitara's projection. Talindra led the team on horseback. I knew they rode southwest by the angle of the shadows. Too fast.

"Kitara, can you zoom out? They're riding too fast for this to be normal."

Kitara pulled out to where there were a handful of dots on the wall an inch behind them. He zoomed in on the pursuers and found a full company of Yuennui cavalry.

"I can mark the two groups, share them with you, and you can put them on the map."

Brigham joined us as both maps populated. "Nothing is close enough to hit Salas Keep today."

My fingers touched Talindra's horse, Pearl's image on the wall. "What's the chance their horses hold out?"

"Brigham stared at a few of their horses and then scrolled back over the past days. The way they are treating the horses is pushing the horses to the limits, even with Grehn's magic. They canter for a few hours, dismount and walk for six, canter for three and then water, feed and rest the horses for six hours. All the horses except for Talindra's have three days max before they collapse."

"They are seven to eight days out."

On Salas Keep, I created a blue dot and gave it a speed of two hundred percent of a warhorse's speed, assigned it to me, made the party green, and the Yuennui cavalry red.

Kitara walked with me to the door. "I can message them. What should I say?"

"Two days. Hold on, help is on the way."

"You can't go alone," said Brigham.

I walked out. "No, everyone has a duty to hold Salas Keep. It is my duty as a leader to make sure I leave no one for the enemy. You're the Knight's regent at Salas Keep now, right?"

"Yes."

"Hold the keep for ten days. Oh, and welcome to the team."

"I'll send a note to Elovar and Nylien to teach your class," said Kitara.

He got a thumbs up.

Outside, I ducked my head into my hood, sent Naomi northeast at full speed, summoned Starlight, and didn't hold back any of the mount's ability. I didn't need to look back to know my guard, who stayed at the tower without instructions, burned daggers from his eyes.

The ground blurred below me, and when I closed my eyes, it was like back in my car on I-20, going west to Alabama on an early Sunday morning with the sun behind me. A power shift into fourth got the RPMs up to forty-five hundred and allowed me to caress it into fifth gear. When there was no more accelerator, I slid the gearshift into sixth gear with a gentle slide. Now the car would maintain its highest speed. In this reality, I rode a magical mount that kept me safe, and no laws existed for speed limits. The snow had all melted and the ground had begun to green, but nothing grew large yet.

Truckers call it white-line fever. I don't recall when my sash tied my staff to me or when I ate two of those bars, because sleep took me off and on until Kitara spoke in my head.

Turn north. You're an hour from them. Scouts are chasing them and closing.

That brought me to the here and now. The days had gone by fast, but my eyes and thoughts didn't focus right away. Within a few minutes, I had enough wits about me to take action and sent Naomi to buzz the team. When they entered my view, I picked the largest hill and rode to the top.

Six riders charged and closed on my team. *Not today*. With the pursuers in my view, my materials' power ripped up the ground in front and landed the riders on the ground. Their horses were untrained and fled, so I grabbed the ground in front of the thrown riders and threw the earth on top of them.

I projected my voice toward my team. "To me!"

The team rode up, and I cast *Torre Mirador*. "Get inside."

"We can't stop. We've got maybe two hours," said Grehn.

The team had ridden for days with insufficient sleep. They had circles under their eyes and had passed exhaustion.

"I got this." I gave them my best smile, given my condition.

Talindra looked at me. She had dark circles under her eyes, they were moist, and she shuffled instead of stepped.

"I promise, I have this. You're looking at a tier three Master of the Prime Material."

Talindra didn't look impressed. "We're almost out of food. I can't conjure enough food and water for the horses."

Her safety calmed me and I needed to be empathic now. I hugged her. "Believe in me. I'll make it work if you create what you can."

She gave me a look, then used her magical feed bag and set out the food and water. They had a few gallons of water and horse feed after Talindra poured out what her item made. I cast the *Material Abundance* ritual and doubled it.

"Is that enough?"

She sniffled and rubbed her eyes.

"OG, can you do that with people food?"

"Lay it all out."

One pile had open water skins, and another had jerky and hardtack. I unwrapped the last two elven bars and cast the ritual once each to double it all.

Then, with another ritual, *Create Room,* we had a barracks with bunk beds on the second floor and it was time to climb to the top of my tower and scout.

Everyone followed me.

"Guys, you have been through more than you should have. I got this. Care for the horses, eat, and rest."

"Argrenn, the rest of the team is out of action. Barbarians can go without sleep. Grehn and I will nap up top for an hour, and we'll keep watch all night."

I gave Thralk a hug, too.

"Okay, plan to keep the tower tonight, tomorrow, and tomorrow night. We will traverse your horses back."

"If we do that, I can save the horses," said Grehn.

The distance gave a little time, so I doubled ours and the horses' food and water, then I hugged Talindra again. This time, she hugged me back.

"Even if you're crazy, and this is where we die, I'm glad to see you."

That made me laugh. "Aren't you a pessimistic sleepy-noggin? I may look rough, but you are about to see what a Master of the Prime Material can do when they have understood Dean Mehli's work. I'm the man in the painting."

"OG, you aren't being a one-man band and not a leader again, are you?"

"Your hallway painting, the man who can bury an army?" asked Marick.

I smiled at Marick and answered Daisidian. "I appreciate you looking out for me, but I'm also a team member and the only one here that isn't spent." We fist-bumped.

"They're within sight. Should I block the door?" asked Marick.

I grabbed his shoulder. "Guys, have I bragged about my powers since we landed yet? They won't get within bow distance of here."

They followed me to the top of the tower, I used my staff to cast levitation and project my voice.

"Company of Yuennui. It is too late to save yourselves. Realize that I, Argrenn Dawnstrike, bring your destruction."

A Yuennui leader, at least by his size, slithered to the front of his lines and raised a flag. I reached out and grabbed the ground near them with my materials' power, extended and powered it with five incantations' worth of power, then the throw, powered with two extended conjuration-spells' worth of power, sent a wave of ground twenty feet high on the flank of the horses and cascaded over the mounted troops.

Not all the enemies died. The ones that struggled to get out got crushed by my second wave from the front that used three formulas to raise and three to throw the second wave from the flank. There was no trying to save horses. This was life and death on my attack.

I'd accepted I'd turn Tuathan, accepted I'd collapse after this, and accepted I would do all of this to save my friends.

I watched for a minute for movement, but tons of earth buried them. No one could have survived that. After lowering myself to the tower, I stopped projecting my voice and turned to my shocked team with mouths agape. "Do you believe me now?"

On the second floor, it took maybe five minutes before I collapsed asleep.

Everyone woke before me. Talindra and Marick were healing in the morning, and everyone had removed their armor. They looked sluggish, but laughter bounced off the walls of the tower.

"Good morning, team," I called out to them.

"OG, if anyone ever says you're too over-the-top, this halfling has your back."

Talindra laughed. "Did you mean pompous?"

Marick raised his arms and mimicked me. "Know I bring your destruction."

"It's not pompous if I pull it off, right?"

Grehn gave me a hug. "We love you, but now Thralk is going to talk like that."

Talindra hugged me and gave me a kiss. "A cute, pompous bringer of destruction. But that power you used drained you."

"I rode for two straight days; it was a low bar to take me out."

They placed bags of stuff into my handkerchief. Grehn took care of the horses, and I refreshed the tower and barracks, doubled the food and water, and got to sit with Talindra and the team.

Marick, Grehn, Daisidian, and Thralk searched the remains of the army while Talindra and I watched from the tower. Naomi assured us that nothing had moved within eight miles of us.

We were eating dinner, and I finally needed to tell the team about my change of race. "Guys, all the extensions I cast has turned me from a human to a Tuathan. I knew it would happen if I kept throwing magic like that, but it's not just the exhaustion that gets me, I'm now a different race."

Daisidian popped out of the chair and walked over to me and stood on his toes next to me while I sat to look me in the eye. "You know I've been a halfling since we landed."

Marick chuckled. "Dude, I'm not only an elf, I'm a blue tinted elf from another continent."

Talindra giggled, "and Kitara is a half elf. Have you really been stressing about this?"

"Um, well, I mean, it seemed important."

"Good thing there were no signs like your hair turning white," added Daisidian, who sat back down.

"Or growing eight inches in height without putting on any weight," said Marick.

"Or losing your beard," said Talindra as she rubbed my chin. "However, this exhaustion thing scares me."

"Yeh man. You fling power like nobody's business, but then sometimes you can't even stay awake for an hour before you go down."

"Yeh OG, I'm the risk taker. You can't take that away from me."

A second night of rest allowed us to ride to Salas Keep. We were bound to a walking speed to protect the horses. Only Talindra's horse had recovered, but Geoe had given Pearl to Talindra as a power. The mare's durability exceeded every other horse. Well, except my magically created mount.

"Argrenn, I've been thinking. If Kelgolor made it to Salas Keep, he has the second piece of the staff. If we get him the third piece of the staff, he can take control of the pyramid and make this the shortest war possible since the Yuennui will lose reinforcements."

"That'd be big," I admitted.

"Is he really a Qalpa?" asked Daisidian.

"I think so, but there is no way to know."

"Let me create a circle in the morning and we can get everyone to Salas Keep, take care of the horses, and gather the information."

The next morning, everyone looked rested, and I created a circle large enough for the horses and team. We stepped in and I brought us Salas Keep.

The keep shook as a cannon fired. "Take care of your horses, I—"

Talindra cut me off. "Take care of your horses and you." She pointed at me. "Do not outpace me."

Talindra and I ran to the back, around the Knight's tower, where a handful of guards fought Yuennui. I turned off the power from Geoe, used my bracers, and threw *Fistful of Fire* at the attackers as we moved toward the water's edge.

My guard ran from the tower to me now that we returned to protected lands. Being assigned guard duty to me must go to the guard who drew the shortest straw.

The extra damage helped enough to give our defenders the edge. The invaders quickly died.

"Has that ship sent its landing party?" I pointed to the cog nearest the shore.

The guy panicked and grabbed someone next to him.

"Has that ship sent its landing party?" I pointed to the cog nearest the shore again.

"Yes, Lord."

"You are not going alone," said Talindra.

I grabbed her and cast *Material Jump*, and we landed on the deck. I'm sure my guard loved me, leaving him behind on the shore.

The cog rocked gently, as any ship I'd been on, and the deck had mops and buckets with soapy water in them, which did not spill. A handful of sailors charged us with belaying pins. I threw *Fistful of Fires* with my fastest castings, and they died as fast as the last group of sailors.

These ships were ready for me, though. I had to be more careful and quit repeating strategies. But my brain was one step ahead of me and in my head Savatage kicked off with a beautiful piano into. That lead into <u>Gutter Ballet</u> and these guys didn't stand a chance. A second ship grappled onto ours, and Yuennui swarmed at Talindra and me. Most of my best spells and powers involved ripping up the ground, acid, or fire. Small blasts of fire were helpful even if they missed since the sailors instantly grabbed buckets of sand or rolled on the fires to keep them from spreading.

Talindra met the first two, and I cast *Manos Planas* along the length of the ship in front of Talindra to hold them in place.

A frigate a hundred yards off our aft fired four cannonballs at the keep.

My keep.

I reached out and grabbed those lead balls and made them take a delicate curve to keep their momentum, and threw them at the frigate. Metalloids had fallen into my domain; however, I was so much more effective with metals.

After a cast of *Rotten Material* to help Talindra, our cannon sounded a boom at a second frigate a couple hundred yards past its starboard side. They'd aimed too high. I guided that lead ball through a hole with a cannon with more umph to penetrate the below decks.

I threw two master extended *Ice Balls* at Yuennui in the hands of the *Manos Planas,* doubled and split. There was no way I could count the sixteen thunks, but four Yuennui died with chests caved in by ice.

Talindra killed another three of the boarders. "Drop the hands," she yelled.

I dropped the spell. *Eight incantations, five formulas, one conjuration, and four of my six extra spells left.*

With *Duplicate Me,* I put myself on the ship that had grappled the first one. A few casts of *Fistful of Fire* at the sailors made many jump ship. The captain and first mate charged Talindra from her rear flank. They had a frosty glow around them. They'd planned this ambush from my last encounter. If Talindra hadn't come with me, I'd already be dead—more proof of how well I'd married.

A couple of formula-powered casts using fire hit each of them without igniting the ship.

I cast two more master extended *Ice Balls,* doubled and split, at the boarders. Between Talindra and me, we'd killed a dozen boarders, and she now focused on the two with rapiers.

Two daggers pierced my back. One tip stopped at the Danaansteel shirt, but the other dug deeper and drew blood. I tripped and barely recovered enough to cast *Duplicate Me* put me on the other side of the ship where I turned to see a Yuennui with daggers coming at me. I cast two extended *Ice Balls* at him.

His confident slither stopped and staggered and covered himself with frost. *Why did I think of this guy as a him and not as an it?* After a few more castings of fire at him, I had started a new fire and burned the arm of the attacker. It yelled, "my brother hunts your family!"

I spammed six glamor strength *Fistful of Fires* at him. Five hit and the one that missed added to the flames. The Yuennui writhed in pain as scales burned off his body and he never once cared that the ship burned.

A mage slithered up from below deck, looking menacing and every bit the snake he was. It poured water on the fire and hissed, "Usesss the spellsss, Sargrennssss?" He covered himself in a frost and a thin coat of fire. His scaled arms raised from his snake torso and shot a bolt of lightning at me. Now it was obvious, multiple Vrelth in Yuennui form. I wished I wasn't blocked from knowing of other types of magic and how he became protected from fire and ice.

Okay, maybe they did have a chance and my music was overconfident.

The rock on my tiara absorbed his lightning. "No, but I will give you an 'A' for effort on the ambush."

His bulging eyes popped out, and he contorted his body to slither to the right and threw a dagger at me.

I ducked it easily and cast *Planar Destruction* and coated him in burning acid, then cast *Shards of Glass* in front of me, then one of my old favorite combos, *Planar Pull* and *Planar Escape*.

He screamed and twisted in agony at the acid and cast a giant ball of fire at me. The bow of the ship caught fire, but so did I. My flesh sizzled and robes caught fire. The heat passed through the cloak, since this had nothing to do with the weather.

"Youss don't blocks big spellsssssss." With my cast of *Increased Material*, he plopped onto the deck and allowed me to cast *Duplicate Me,* then *Planar Winter* on him as he lay on the deck and tried to recover his stance.

He shot at my duplicate, and it gave me the chance I needed. I raced toward the winter storm that kept him in the *Shards of Glass*. He screamed as his body tore apart and then received a pummeling of ice.

I ignored the sizzling of the fire on my burning body and swung my staff at the creature connecting with his jaw. I screamed in pain from the burns as I couldn't ignore them any longer as I used the staff to send a jolt of electricity through him through my staff. His two protections faded away with his life.

I rolled on the ship to put out the fire on my robes, but the adrenaline left me and I couldn't contain the pain of the burns and the sickening smell of my burned flesh.

Talindra had problems with the captain of the other ship, but still jumped over to me and cast a heal upon me. She took a wicked shot in the back, but after her golden glow calmed my burns, I kneeled and cast two extended *Ice Balls* at him. He staggered until she planted her sword into his chest and laid his body on top of the first mate.

I grabbed a bunch of earth up from under the water and put it on the fire of the bow, then did it again on the fire amidships. After a cast of *Duplicate Me* to get back to Talindra, I had zero incantations, zero formulas, zero conjurations, and zero of my six extra spells left.

She helped me to the deck and prayed to heal us both. A golden beam surrounded us for a few minutes while we healed.

Soon, we stood, taking in the damage and carnage around us.

"Bring us back now?"

I held my hand as <u>Gutter Ballet</u> was just finishing, and I screamed along with the Oliva brothers.

"Are you done being crazy and will bring us back?"

"I used my return spell to kill the mage."

She shook her head but smiled. "Were you singing the end of a song you liked?"

I chuckled but then it hit me. Geoe could lose access to giving me information. The music never stopped. As long as the music played, I knew I was still me.

The battle had ended. The ships that were not sinking sailed away from the keep. They didn't organize the withdrawal and took wind from each other in the attempt to escape.

We'd defended the keep.

On the other ship, I stripped the mage of everything, took whatever armor and weapons were in good shape from the others, summoned Vern, and dropped the anchor on this ship. Talindra had dropped anchor on the first cog.

She knew how to sail, if we took one cog instead of two, so Vern and could sail it under her direction to Sardyna. But with two ships, we were stuck until crews arrived.

I pulled everything out of the captain's room and strode to the first ship again to empty the second captain's cabin into my handkerchief. Having no more to do, I sat next to Talindra.

I filled out the same paperwork much faster than the first time. "What do you want to name this boat we seized?"

"*Joyous Breeze.*"

The second one I named *Cleansing Fire* before sending a missive to Lord Fergus, letting him know we had seized two more boats from invaders and one to Kitara, letting him know we were out of spells and needed a lift back to shore.

My guilt stopped me from relaxing. Talindra needed to know the truth. "Honey, Feston has something planned. We are going to need to go through his trap he planned for months before we can take him out."

She patted the deck next to her.

I put the pad away, Talindra put her head on my shoulder, and we held each other, thankful to be alive for another day, together.

Chapter 18

The next day, inside my smaller classroom, the whole extended team gathered for briefings. The door opened, and Nylien poked his head around the student door.

"Come in. Is Elovar with you?" Talindra guided them to a couch to sit against the far wall.

They needed to listen to this, given how fast events moved. "Brigham is the knight steward of Salas Keep. I've told him you will be there occasionally, so it's good he sees you. Have a seat, but realize this information is confidential within the game, so avoid talking about this."

I sat at the instructor's desk and looked around. My two assistants sat on a couch against the wall to my right and my guard stood just inside the doorway at parade rest. Kelgolor and Marick sat in chairs behind my students. Talindra and Kitara sat in the middle, and Daisidian sat in the back. I stood up first. "Guys, if this is not a protected area. If you are going to say something about our next steps, hold it to the end, where we can protect the information."

Brigham began his briefing. "Six boats sank. Two boats were seized and are in refit. Two dozen raiders were killed, and another dozen captured. We have two more cannons. Twenty-two ships turned to run. Argrenn's fleet is now three cogs."

Kelgolor shook his head. "I counted one hundred Yuennui ships a month ago. This was not the fleet."

"We found no more ships," said Brigham.

I put the map on the projector wall. "Is anyone aware of any landing spots that handled that many ships?"

The room stayed silent.

"You don't have to raise your hand." Talindra's voice jolted me.

"I'm from Osahil, part of Lord Isilring's lands," said Nylien. "Well, Lord Feston has a port about fifty miles southeast of us that is huge, but he doesn't let anyone land there."

I groaned. It was a failure of information, but we had no way to have collected this before now. "I'm pulling it up." We turned to the map and drew a hundred-mile circle around Osahil. There was little searching needed as a fleet of a hundred plus ships showed up. The screen centered on the fleet and drilled in.

This wasn't a couple of companies. I counted two full armies.

"Kitara."

"Already filing a report."

"Well, we know they will sacrifice a full company and up to thirty ships to make sure we won't stop them."

"Darn. They outplayed us," said Marick.

"Not yet," said Kelgolor.

"OG, you need to hear him out. We've validated his story."

"Did you complete part one?" asked Marick.

"Yes," said Kelgolor.

"Backup," I said. They were moving too fast for me to keep up.

"Just the facts," said Talindra. "The background is good, but I'm at the point where I need to be actionable and figure out the whys later."

Kelgolor adjusted his lamellar armor. "Urnovher the Usurper has control of the pyramid of the ancient god who walked out of the sea."

"The fish god?" I asked.

Talindra glared at me.

"Yes. Well, the pyramid allowed him to resurrect the troops he created at the pyramid from the undead."

"That's why he has so many troops," said Marick.

"Right. Feston turned them into thralls. They threw the thralls into battle, the thralls died, and Feston converted the dead thralls back to living troops."

"The upshot being Urnovher has infinite troops," said Marick.

Kelgolor continued the explanation. "But I have the first two parts of my ancestor's staff. If I get the third piece, I gain authority over all my citizens and the ability to shut down the pyramid."

Something was missing from this explanation. "The pyramid is too far away to have that kind of power."

"Not without an amplifier," said Kitara.

An amplifier, that idea took root in my mind, but shutting down the pyramid was a straightforward decision. "Get the staff, and rock it."

"I don't know where the third piece is."

We sank into our chairs. Except for Daisidian, who walked over to Kelgolor. "Will you give me a drop of your blood?" He looked at the floor. "Sorry, my bosses make me do this."

Kelgolor pricked his finger and a drop of blood dripped into a finger-sized vial Daisidian held. He shook the vial, and the liquid turned green.

My mind raced. "Daisidian, that map with the..." I shut up and Daisidian put up his blocking device.

"OG, you're on the right track. Put these coordinates on the board." He handed me two folded sheets of paper. One said *Private*. I opened the other one and put in the coordinates, stuffed both pieces of paper into my pocket.

Daisidian handed another piece of paper to Kelgolor. "The last piece is there."

The Southern Pyr Mountains popped up first. I turned off the map before Half Men Inn showed up.

"We have a plan." Energy powered through me. I had the entire plan now, and it made sense.

"Wait. I didn't see it," said Talindra.

"Trust OG. He figured it out."

"Time is tight. Here are everyone's orders—Nylien and Elovar; after the final tomorrow, I need you to be on standby to purchase items and put them in a *Planar Helper* box. Do not leave the university grounds."

They both agreed.

"Everyone else, we are leaving tomorrow at twelve bells. Thralk and Grehn, we are dropping you off at Schlobir Wap. Protecting Schlobir Wap is of the utmost importance, and I cannot stress that enough. Talindra, convince the Knights of Honor that Schlobir Wap is about to be targeted and its protection is crucial for the survival of Sardyna. Brigham, stay at Salas Keep and defend it, but if Wallblamm shows up and says Schlobir Wap is under attack, take that as your priority."

"What if Salas Keep falls?"

"My skills give the ability to retake Salas Keep but not Schlobir Wap. Schlobir Wap is too big and has too many points to defend. I cannot emphasize enough that Schlobir Wap is the priority. Everyone else, we leave to take Kelgolor at twelve bells. Expect a fight as soon as we arrive."

"Be ready at eleven bells," said Kitara. "We have one task before we leave."

Daisidian pulled down his signal blocker and everyone packed up.

There wasn't any time for me to worry about what Kitara needed. I sent missives to Wallblamm and Mayor Whizzburr and got the rest of the stakeholders up to date. Things were moving fast, but too much was at stake. Now that the pieces had fallen into place, we needed to act.

The next morning, I went into my office and placed the private note from Daisidian on my desk. *Hit me up soon. The Vrelth learned of your family on Umillion.* This timing was bad. I'd take care of this as soon as I had time to breathe.

I showed up early for the finals for my class. Nylien and Elovar looked shaken. The briefing looked too strenuous for teenagers.

The first fifty students in the class passed without a problem. Each cast at least one glamor. The highflyers, the flyers, and half of the try-hards had done well.

The next batch of students coming into the test surprised me. Elovar and Nylien escorted in twenty students. These were students on my worry list.

I had not seen them work in two weeks, and a dozen of them had only managed the correct form for the rune once or twice in a row.

Three of the try-hards in that group attempted the test first and succeeded. They made the same rune ten times in a row. One coaster, or I should say previous coaster, stepped up and made the rune for the light glamor ten times in a row.

"Excellent job. Pass." It was nice to pass people who had worked hard, even if they had no talent. Feelings of happiness became euphoria. Sixteen more students made the light glamor ten times in a row. The last twenty students were anti-climactic. All together, ninety students had passed. Elovar and Nylien stayed, so I showed them how to fill out the forms on their new university pads. I asked, "How did you get through to those students?"

"Many of them were away from their home for the first time and got lost trying to get to class," said Elovar.

"Osahil gave us all a course on the trek here," said Nylien. "So, we helped them get comfortable, and they formed a group and practiced together each night."

I shook both of their hands. "Good job. I'm ecstatic every person passed, and many have you to thank."

Of course, the other side of the coin showed that I had forgotten that these were kids away from home for the first time. Being a leader was the only path for me. Others were competent and needed my trust. If I tried to do everything, we had no shot.

After we submitted the grades, I strode to the store, set up an account as a professor, put six hundred gold in it, and allowed the two to make purchases with it. They watched me cast *Planar Helper* once, so they watched the box in action and learned how to interact with it. Afterward, I traveled back to the house to change and cast *Bring it Back*, putting it on the decanter in my desk drawer.

"Hurry," said Talindra. "You have things in your handkerchief we need to sell, and the five of us need to meet at the shop before we leave."

I almost took off the silk pants and put on my jeans from back on Earth, but I realized I needed to dress appropriately. At the market district, we sold the items from the fighters on the ship, except Daisidian took a dagger that the captain of the first ship had carried, and I put the spell book of the mage in one of my empty squares on my bandolier.

We stopped at a building on the far side of the market.

"Let's do the Tuatha first," said a man with tattoos.

"Do I get to find out what's going on?"

"Sorry," said Kitara. "It's been a frantic day. We are getting our ears pierced because I infused earrings for everyone. You're getting three."

"Can you put them all in my left ear?"

The man backed up and looked at me to see if I had joked.

"It's how I wore them back in the eighties."

He shrugged and felt around my ear. "Yep, I can put the stud up top and the two danglers on the bottom."

He made the first hole.

Kitara handed him a sapphire. "This will let you and I communicate. It's good for a dozen to two dozen words. It gets unreliable after a dozen though. The diamond is for you and Talindra to communicate—same restrictions. The stud is so we can track each other."

Kitara wore six dangle earrings and a stud.

The five of us got earrings Kitara had made, and we were ready. We picked up Kelgolor, Grehn, and Thralk, dropped off our horses and my guard, and last, dropped Grehn and Thralk off at Schlobir Wap.

"Guys, we're heading to a place where enemies may wait for us," I said. "Don't draw your weapons yet, but we may be in a fight in a few seconds." I focused on the circle coordinates and brought our team with Kelgolor to Half Men Inn.

"This is new," said Talindra. "Is this where you go drinking when I'm not around?"

Chairs were overturned, drinks spilled and half eaten food were on the tables. The sounds of battle raged outside. The door crashed open.

"We'll have to run for it," cried the innkeeper, who'd originally given me the map.

"No, we won't." I pointed the team out the door, past the shocked innkeeper.

Kitara pushed by me and yelled, "Going right!"

Daisidian yelled, "I'm going left!"

Marick and Talindra followed up the middle, and I followed. "Nice to see you again," I said to the half orc innkeeper's who jaw had dropped so far his tusks did not touch his upper lip.

"Incoming," shouted two half-orcs and pointed to the sky where two wyverns bore down on the inn.

With my staff, I levitated. "They're mine," I yelled.

Without Geoe's powers and my bracers on, I cast *Increased Material* at each of them.

The two wyverns were on the ground. I cast two master extended *Ice Balls,* doubled and split, then examined the rest of the battlefield. The party looked to be fighting bears. They were far away but appeared to be doing well.

Instead of wasting more spells, I used the full power of my bracers and *Two-Handed Spell Casting* and spammed *Argrenn's Acid Attack* at the two grounded wyverns.

"Wave two," shouted the half-elves, who ran to the front of the inn with bows before taking up shooting positions.

I cast two more master extended *Ice Balls,* doubled and split, at the grounded wyverns to finish them. Two more wyverns flew toward the inn, so I cast *Aumentor Masa* on the wyvern the half-elves were shooting at and watched him crash to the ground. Then, with the power of my staff, I gave myself mounted flying skills.

When I cast *Planar Pull* at the wyvern, as I'd thought, it had too much mass and it flung me to him, where I grabbed him and rode. Using my new diamond earring, I sent, *I'm fine. Focus on your fight.* The wyvern screeched, twisted in the air, and swung its stinger at me in erratic motions. I stayed back, out of reach of its stinger.

You better be. Only you know where we are.

The wyvern flew too fast to keep track of my location. On the bright side, the earrings worked. I needed to save a conjuration to have a spell to get back to the inn. My head kicked off a soundtrack. It was Lemmy! <u>The Chase is Better than the Catch</u> ripped through my mind and the ride became fun. The wyvern straightened before its next move, so I cast an extended *Ice Ball* at it. It flew with jerking, haphazard turns and moves, then flew up high and dove into a barrel roll. I hung on with everything I had. My vomit didn't hurt him, but he got a liberal coating.

I cast another extended *Ice Ball* at the wyvern, which caused it to tree bash. He skimmed trunks and scraped trees as he twisted through the wooded area. I got flat as branches whipped at me, hitting me with force. The wyvern hurt itself trying to get me off his back. But I hung on until it miscalculated the thickness of a branch and caught his tail on it.

The Wyvern came to an abrupt halt, but I kept going and needed to cast levitate from my staff. In midair, I turned and cast an extended *Ice Ball. Five incantations, zero formulas, one conjuration, and three of my six extra spells left.*

The wyvern crashed to the ground, breaking tree limbs as he plummeted. It lumbered on the ground and clawed its way to a standing position, bleeding from dozens of locations and missing feathers and scales. Its tail had broken, and a leg looked broken as well.

I lowered to close and finish it.

It raised its wing and spoke in Aossi. "I submit." The screech affected the dialect but not the meaning.

I pulled back my spell and approached cautiously.

"On my word. Spare me. I will leave and give you a whistle where you may call me once in your time of need."

The mage in me wanted to blast him, the humanity in me wanted to believe him, and the leader in me knew we needed allies. "I will trust you and allow you to leave."

The wyvern ripped off a bone from a broken wing with its beak and tossed it to me. "Clean that, and when you blow through it, I will be on my way. Realize I only fly so fast." It took to the air and clumsily flew south.

A town bell rang nearby.

I grabbed the bone, stuffed it into my belt pouch, and ran to the bell.

There were a dozen wattle and daub houses around small farms near a stream. Civilians with spears were fighting three bears—thrall bears. I ran forward and cast an extended *Ice Ball* at one to judge its toughness. It staggered and fell.

Villagers fought on a road cut between two cliffs. I picked out loose dirt and collapsed it on the bear-thrall in the back, then threw rocks from the cliff tops at the backs of the bears.

Two more extended *Ice Balls* at the last two of these undead bears left me with three incantations, zero formulas, one conjuration, and three of my six extra spells left. With *Duplicate Me*, I crossed the stream over to the farmers, who were finishing the bear thralls with spears.

"What are these things?"

"No time." He pointed to wagons and more of these undead bears charging them.

I ran with the farmers and ripped the ground underneath the charging bears, throwing them to the ground. On the other side of the loaded wagons, a few guards wearing strange helmets with brims fought against the beasts. They wore bright red tabards with black on them. I got close enough to help with *Planar Reflection* on the ones they were fighting.

One bear must have gotten up fast, because he clubbed me with one paw and raked his claws across my Danaan-steel shirt, throwing me ten feet. Four of them charged me.

I cast *Duplicate Me*.

Two incantations, zero formulas, one conjuration, and one of my six extra spells left.

My materials' power ripped up the ground underneath the bears. With a large rock, I crushed one, the crunch of bones a satisfactory sound.

I threw a master extended *Ice Ball,* doubled and split, at two of the bears. Then *Duplicate Me* got me out of the way of the last bear.

The farmers stabbed it as it ripped into my duplicate.

I turned to where the guards were fighting and cast my last two incantations into the last two of these undead bears and walked over to meet a guard. Blood, branches, and dirt covered me. He looked better. "*Merci étranger — êtes-vous un ami?*" he asked.

Formian. I gave them my best bad high school French. "*Je m'appelle* Argrenn. *Oui, je suis ami.*"

More guards strolled over, laughing. "We speak Navarre better than you speak Formian."

"You recognize him, right?" asked one guard on a stretcher. "He is an adventurer of the Guardian Knights."

They gave me a curious glance. "He is correct. But, tell me, what were those creatures?"

"Brand new," said the farmer.

"Would you know how far the Half Men Inn is from here?"

"We've got two who will die without better healing," yelled another guard.

"Twenty miles up this road," said the farmer.

"I'm going to create a circle and go to the Half Men Inn. I'll take anyone who needs to go." A few minutes later, two guards on stretchers, the guard who healed, and myself were at the Half Men Inn.

Talindra stood up from where she sat at a table, tending to others, and healed me, laying a heal on both guards in stretchers.

"Hey, guys, I made new friends on the road."

She shook her head at me.

One of the three guards stood up and spoke to the other two. "I'm getting you two a room for the next couple of days. Rest and rejoin the caravan. I'm going to report to Caemlynn."

"One second," I said. "Can you tell me who the point of contact is for this circle in Caemlynn?" I drew the symbol on a napkin.

He shook his head. "I will let the court mages know you are asking, and someone will reach out to you."

The half-orc innkeeper stumbled over and gave me a hug. "Your team are heroes to the Half Men Inn. You are always welcome here. Not a single person died because of your team's arrival."

Seeing a half orc tear up took away any inclination to mention that the attack that would have destroyed the inn was only to slow the Guardian Knights down. But, had we known they were in trouble, we would have responded and saved them.

He helped me sit down where I almost fell asleep against Talindra.

"Kitara already got us rooms," said Talindra propping me up.

"Argrenn, you need to level. You might as well do it while we rest. We will head out tomorrow with everyone at tier three."

"Can we find out where we are now?" asked Talindra.

"Yep. I didn't want to be on camera studying the path." I felt my eyes waver and shut for a second.

"Well, we are on camera now. How does this change?" asked Marick.

"Let him finish. He is about to drop," said Talindra.

"I didn't want to let enemies know we were coming here. Now that we are here, all our enemies know exactly where we are going, and it's okay to let you know."

We pulled up a map, centered it on Half Men Inn, made the circumference one hundred miles, and projected it on the wall by our table. I put a marker on the coordinates Daisidian had given me back in the classroom and shrunk the map. We had sixteen miles to travel through the mountains.

The innkeeper called over a half-orc woman. "Falanchu, come here." He pointed to the dot. "You've traveled those parts. Is this the old magic research institute?"

She looked. "Can ya lemme see the trails?"

I zoomed in and found a stone outcropping with braces supporting it and a stone door. It obviously hid something from the top, but it may have looked better disguised at ground level.

"Yap," she said. "Iffen, you take it out. We'd no longer see these creatures."

I glanced at Kelgolor. "Your thing is in there?"

He pointed at Daisidian.

"That's the best intelligence from an intelligence group."

"I'ma draw you-en a map with rocks for trail markers," said Falanchu.

The innkeeper shook his head. "Hundreds of years ago, before the game and before mages died, mages did dangerous research away from population centers. They had created this one only for wizards for long-term research. Only a wizard could talk their way in past the door."

"OG, you've outsmarted doors."

"Oh my, geez, you put this together all at the meeting," said Kitara. "The amplifier is in that facility."

"The amplifier and one piece of the rod for Kelgolor," I said. "But it's not the only amplifier."

"We weaken them and strengthen our allies," said Marick. "This is a must complete dungeon before we go after Feston."

"Crud."

"What is it, OG?"

"I should have told you before, but Feston has studied us because of how, when we first met, I kept insulting him and his team."

"Yeh, so?"

I shook my head. "I believe his threats that he has done nothing except study and prepare to beat us. He has all the preparation and all the intelligence about us while we know one thing about him."

"Let's look at the thing in front of our face instead of becoming distracted with possibilities. Why is this place creating thralls from bears?" asked Talindra.

Marick put his arm around my shoulder but didn't say a word.

I felt Talindra scoop me in her arms. "Two in the afternoon and you're going to bed. You're like a toddler when you cast all your magic."

"It's only when I cast extensions," I said as my last waking action.

I woke up a little before the rest of the party and got to do what I've been doing best. I ignored the future and focused on the immediate actions to get us through the next day with the team.

Chapter 19

I only needed about fourteen hours of sleep and woke up before the rest of the party and did all the tasks the rest of the team did last night. Leveling to three-point-two gave me an additional power, but no powers remained to speed up spell casting. I chose *Ice Master* to help against enemies who had cold defense. The new spells were *Argrenn's Remove Presence*, *Timeonne's Spirit Entrapment*, *Argrenn's Explosive Cloud*, *Ball of Air*, and a spell called *Other World Viewing*. Once leveled to three-point-two, I was able to cast nine incantations, seven formulas, and three conjurations. Following Dean Mehli's advice, I extended *Argrenn's Explosive Cloud* and added a reactionary component to *Material Jump*, saving my additive extension.

I took the time to review the team's powers. The most interesting of them was Talindra could follow her shield anywhere. The key word was 'anywhere.' I think this was a miss in the game. Her earlier power allowed her to throw her shield anywhere, including across planes.

With time before bed, I went through the spell books I found. The mage on the boat had used an unreadable type of magic, so that belonged to Kitara.

The rest of the team had leveled to tier three and had new titles. Talindra had improved from Defender of Light to Angel of Light. Kitara progressed from loremaster to warmaster. Daisidian graduated from Shadow Stalker to Assassin, and Marick progressed from Murshid to Mawlawi.

When the rest of the team joined me after eating, we took Falunchu's map, sent Naomi and Scruffles ahead to scout, and took off for the Research Institute.

We walked throughout the morning and sat on a stone to eat. The hills were less strenuous than the mountains.

Marick finished praying and walked over to the rest of us. "Kelgolor, how did we get a full company of Yuennui chasing us?"

"That's a good question. Before that, they had a few dozen."

"How does he gather them?" I asked.

"If a Yuennui dies on Evros, he can move it and create a thrall by the use of undead connections to the pyramid back in Ardvente. If the Yuennui thrall dies, he can recover it and give it life back through the same magic that allows adventurers from other worlds to take on bodies."

Another piece of the puzzle. "Those are Vrelth inside those bodies."

Marick agreed. "Vrelth trained with firearms before they arrived."

Kelgolor shrugged. "I don't know how he grew from a few dozen to over a hundred without a landing, though."

"You each fought about twenty-five thralls. I killed a dozen and a half in the first invasion. Dean Mehli and I killed eight defending the Planar Mage Guild. I buried another twelve in the tunnels."

"That would explain it," said Kelgolor.

"Another twenty-four at the feint landing, so he has one hundred twenty-five, and I witnessed two armies, so he has one thousand Yuennui troops marching to Schlobir Wap."

Kelgolor brightened. "I know you need to defend that gnome town, but if Urnovher has moved that many troops to this continent, it is good news. We can take the pyramid back much quicker after I get dropped off."

"OG, that would solve a ton of problems, because then Urnovher's troops would stay dead."

"Why is he taking Schlobir Wap if he needs Sardyna?" asked Kitara.

I focused on the diamond earring. *Remember our math the other week and keep it on the down-low.*

"We will figure it out," said Marick.

I felt bad to keep the team in the dark, but couldn't let out the information on camera.

An hour further into the trip, we arrived at a cliff. Kitara put away his pad. "We need to climb this. The map says the other way, around it, adds a week to the schedule."

I could make quick work of this. "Guys,"

"Don't worry, honey, we'll carry you."

"I can do the climbing," said Daisidian. He grasped the rock to make sure it didn't crumble.

"Let me get a hook for your safety," said Kitara.

He threw the rope and anchor thing up high. It caught between a few outcrops of rocks.

I wanted to make a joke to lower the tension. "Let me check." I used levitation from my staff, picked up the clamp, brought it back down, and said, "I don't think it's safe. Here, take my hand, and I'll show you a good anchor spot."

I levitated Talindra.

She was not amused when we levitated up the cliff. "You're being a smart-butt."

"I want to be safe when you carry me."

"Put me on the top and bring the others."

After dropping her off, I levitated to the bottom. "Talindra didn't believe it looked safe to climb, so she stayed. Does anyone else want to adjust your rope solution?"

Marick shook his head. "Dude, that is so wrong."

"It is funny, OG, but, yeah, wrong."

"Okay," I said. "Let's get to the top, and we'll keep going."

We walked an hour, and Kitara held up his hand. "Guys, have you seen a bird or a squirrel all day?"

"Nope, I wanted to see an ibex up close," said Marick, "but there's been nothing."

"Me too. Lynxes are what I searched for, but, yeah, I've seen nothing," said Daisidian.

With a puffed-out chest, I played announcer. "For those of you tuning in, the Guardian Knights have picked up a trap and were about to teach those involved that Earthers are not to be messed with."

"What are you doing?" said Talindra.

With my best attempt at an innocent face, I said, "Keeping things light?"

"We care about our fans." Daisidian looked in the same direction as me. "Everyone, get in your votes in for sexiest member whose name begins with a D."

Marick laughed with us.

"Are you two done?" asked Kitara.

We walked more cautiously, which allowed us to see a trap the bear thralls were setting for us. Kitara held up a fist and spread us out. Talindra backed up, Daisidian went left, and Marick went right.

Before the bears sprung the trap, Kitara and Daisidian charged two of them. Three more of them charged from the right flank, toward Kitara and Daisidian. We fought in a semi -clearing with three tree stumps and limited underbrush. Neither undead of bears could have planned this fight that favored the larger creatures.

With my staff spinning in front of me, I cast *Manos Planas* to hold the three charging Kitara and Daisidian.

Nine incantations, seven formulas, three conjurations, and six of my extra spells left.

Two more would hit the other flank. I cast *Ice Ball* with no extensions. Marick's bell floated overhead and Talindra's sword bit into a bear behind me. I took a quick peek. She fought three and Marick fought two.

I cast *Planar Winter* on the ones trapped in the hands, and another *Ice Ball* with no extensions at the flankers from the other side. *Especially since my brain didn't think I needed a soundtrack.*

I did not know what lay in front of us and the team was right. Exhaustion was too big a risk to throw extensions around without a plan.

I turned to help Talindra and focused two extended *Ice Balls* on the wounded ones. One of them dropped with a crushed chest and bleeding from its neck. A second bear thrall had the side of his head caved in and a wicked slash across its shoulder from Talindra. It flopped to the ground, dead.

Talindra now fought one wounded bear thrall. Someone coated the remaining bear thralls with a thin coat of frost. "An enemy mage is near," I shouted.

I cast two formula strength extended *Fistful of Fires* at the ones on Marick. One of his bear thralls died in flames. Three of them were still in the *Manos Planas* and getting pummeled by hail. Kitara and Daisidian were fighting three thralls, but Daisidian looked hurt.

I cast two more of the big fire spells at the most wounded. One collapsed in flames, and the other died with Daisidian's daggers in its side.

"Drop the spells," shouted Talindra.

I dropped the *Manos Planas* and *Planar Winter* and joined Talindra and Marick, heading to the three until a wicked paw swiped at my back and sent me flying. I landed with a thud, my back screaming at me, but my mind was working fast as I rolled to my feet.

The mage needed to be found. I threw a *Planar Destruction* at this new bear thrall and pulled myself up. It still moved until two *Argrenn's Acid Attacks* hit it and it gurgled to the ground.

A lightning bolt shot toward me. My Scion of Hy Brasil absorbed it and put it into the rock that floated above it. I cast *Duplicate Me* and put myself in the direction where I'd seen the spell.

A body jumped and ran, so I threw a *Manos Planas* in that direction. There was no need to run, as the spell caught a human in midstride. This male wore half-plate covered in frost and a thin coat of fire.

"Please," he shouted. "I'm from Earth. They make me do this."

His accent was unmistakable, but this mage wore armor. I reached out with my materials power, but couldn't touch his breastplate or cuirass. Those pieces must have strong magical infusions. But the problem with piecemeal armor is just that. He may have had more magic items, but they were separate items. "If you lie to me once, I will make you pay. Were you part of the team from Caemlynn the mage backstabbed?"

His face contorted but he answered. "They left me. I was too good for them and they couldn't handle me."

Oh great, one of these guys.

"Who makes you attack people with the bear thralls?"

"The, uh, necromancers."

The accent alone told me not to give this guy any benefit of the doubt, but this guy sounded grade a jerk. With my materials' power, I crushed one of his iron greaves, and his left foot crimped off, then crushed the iron so that it staunched the blood.

He screamed and slumped. The hands held him upright.

I sat on a rock because the sounds of battle had stopped. "One more time. Who makes you?"

"I don't know. Please heal me. You have a paladin. The game requires you to heal me."

This guy worked with undead thralls and planned an ambush to kill us, and now he made up rules. I crushed the vambrace, and his right hand popped off. I let it bleed a little before I crushed it enough to staunch the flow of blood.

He whimpered and fell to the ground when I dispelled the magical hands, rolling in pain.

I shook my head and got more comfortable on the rock. "You tried to kill us. Do you have a reason?"

"Flick you. I'm crippled now."

"I lived eight stops south of Boylston as a kid before I moved to Georgia, so I recognize your accent."

"Perfect, we're like family. Heal me, and we go our separate ways. No harm, no foul."

"It seems to me you're out killing for fun. A mage with armor for protection."

He raised his good hand, tossed some dirt at me, and started a spell.

I crushed his iron helm and walked over to remove the armor from the corpse and put it into the handkerchief. He had a spell book and a blood-red crystal dagger. I added the spell book to the handkerchief.

I undid his belt, and the dagger drained of the blood-red color. It became clear, crystal—like Dean Mehli's sword.

"Kitara, do we want to pick up this dagger?"

Kitara walked over, touched the weapon, and said, "Yes, Argrenn, wear it. It's Khudarin's Dagger of Life. When you get injured, it will hold the damage until healed. It effectively doubles your health when it's empty."

I lifted my robe, undid the belt on my silk pants, and put the dagger on it.

Kitara looked at Talindra. "Make sure you check his dagger now and then, because he'll forget."

"That's for sure." She looked at the stripped corpse. "What's his story?"

"He wouldn't give it up. He setup the ambush, so he had control over the bears."

Talindra shook her head, and we gathered our bearings, turning to leave.

Back on the path, the area had cleared except for blood. None of the bodies of the twelve enemies remained.

We continued on in our normal order until we walked out into a cleared-out area with a pleasant feeling in the warm but quiet evening. The walk was pleasant through thinning trees until we came upon a rock outcropping in an open area. The rocky outcropping certainly hid something below it, but the disguise worked from this angle.

"Halt," said a door in the middle of the boulders. "Mage, step forward."

Why the mages went through the trouble to hide this facility as a rocky outcropping but put a metal door with magic in it eluded me. I put on my confident demeanor and stepped forward, fast and confident, and hoped my plan worked.

"Acceptable. Explain the ones you travel with."

"My wife, my doctor, my apprentice, and my manservant."

"Apprentice, step forward."

"Kitara," I ordered. "Come forward.

Kitara stepped forward.

"Acceptable," said the door. It slid up and allowed us in.

"Talindra," I said and held out my elbow. I wanted to put on the full show for this thing, just in case.

She took my arm, and we walked in, the other three followed.

We walked into more than a rough-cut warren. They'd mined the walls, ceiling, and floor from rock. These were markings left by picks and other devices. *Why didn't mages use magic?* Condensation lined the walls, but not enough to drip or cause mold. At least not yet.

I used my staff for light, and we walked down a hallway. Muffled animal cries and growls echoed throughout the entranceway. After walking in silence, the sound of animals in distress and anger disconcerted me.

The stairs brought us twenty more feet downward, into an oddly shaped room. It had four inlets at the four compass points. South were the stairs; north, east, and west had doors. The points between the doors contained levers. In the middle of the room, we found a button and a hook with three pieces of metal in the shapes of a circle, square, and triangle.

"Everyone step inside the room, do not risk getting separated."

"As your assistant, I should listen," teased Kitara.

"As your physician, you should not get excited."

"Guys, I wanted to get us through the door and had to think fast about how a mage who would live like a hermit would answer."

"OG. Manservant doesn't feel like a good fit for me," joked Daisidian.

"I promote you to assassin."

Daisidian gave me a fist bump. "One thing is for sure; you are the number one mage at outsmarting doors."

"No more of this Master of the Prime Material nonsense," joked Talindra. "You are Baron Argrenn Dawnstrike, Outsmarter of Doors."

Talindra turned her lights on to finish lighting up the room, and I studied each door. The west door had a square with a half circle. The north door had the word *sides* on it, and the east door had a tick mark with two arrows pointed downward with a tick mark and two arrows pointed up. Each had a place to lay a shape and were labeled *1, 2, 3,* or *4.*

"Which way do we want to go? Only one of these leads from the entry warren into the actual facility."

"Let's figure all this out first," said Marick.

"Kitara, will you?" I asked. "Marick doesn't believe the Outsmarter of Doors title."

"Argrenn already has it. None of you want to hear how his mind works."

"It can't be that bad," said Marick.

"Yeah, OG, lay it out."

"First the easy one. West has a square attached to a D, so the answer means squared. We put the circle on the one and the square on the two. That will open the west door."

"But of course," said Talindra with an eye roll.

"North has *sides* written on it. So, the circle goes on one, the triangle on three, and the square on four. That will open the north door."

"I had that one," said Marick.

"The last caught me off guard. Once you recognize the tick mark means prime, it wants the lowest prime on the lowest even and the highest prime on the highest even. It appeared tricky because the first arrow does double-duty in delineating the order and the quantity to calculate the landing spot."

"I had that one," said Kitara and Daisidian together. They laughed.

"North," said Talindra.

I put the circle on one, the square on four, and the triangle on three. The north door opened, and the door to the outside closed when I pushed the button.

"We were right, OG." Daisidian laughed, then got quiet as he slunk into the shadows of the hallway.

Daisidian snuck forward first, followed by Kitara and Marick. I kept my staff lit, and Talindra brought up the rear with more light.

Daisidian crept back and whispered to us, "That is a dead end with a small hallway. Wide enough for two doors heading north. I found no traps or locks on the doors, so I bet if we open one, we're fighting in both."

The sound of muffled animal cries had gotten louder.

"Talindra and Argrenn, you take the room in front of us, and the other three of us will take the second."

Kitara and Talindra kicked open both doors. Enthralled Ibexes lay in cages. Every so often, they got an electrical charge from a metal rod that jutted out from the wall.

"These are beautiful creatures. Why are they treating them like this?"

"Do you have lynxes in cages, too?" called out Kitara.

"Ibexes," I called back.

We walked back into the hallway. "They've killed them, turned them into thralls, and now they're medical experiments."

"We can't leave them like this, but we can't kill them," said Talindra.

I'd have to step up and end this misery. Leaders did not ask a person to do something they were not prepared to perform themselves. "Guys, it's too risky to do anything but from a distance. You all go hang by the door, but stay on this side of it. You don't have to watch."

Talindra, Kitara, and Marick headed over.

"You don't have to do this alone, OG."

I lit up the lynxes with *Fistful of Fires* as fast as possible, casting spells with the bracers, *Quickness*, and *Two-Handed Casting*. We walked out, and Daisidian shut the door. I did the same thing with the ibexes, and again Daisidian shut the door behind me, though it didn't stop the smell of burning fur.

Muffled growls were the only sounds in the dungeon now. The entire team met up in the room with the doors.

I put the circle on the first lever, the square on the second, and pushed the button. The door to the north closed, and a door leading down a long, dark hallway opened.

"The inner sanctum," said Kitara.

Our feet landed on a clear floor of sanded wood with a thick coat of varnish, while the walls had planed softwood. Tiles on the ceiling reflected the light and made it less dreary.

At a T-intersection, we took a left. The quiet contrasted to the earlier section of the dungeon. These cleaned halls had no dust or moisture, and the planks looked freshly laid.

The hallway veered to the right and led to five doors; one straight ahead, two to the left, and two to the right.

We surrounded the first door on the left and opened it. The room had a bed with folded white sheets, a wooden wardrobe, and a small table and chair. No belongings were in the room.

The other three side rooms were the same, and through the door straight ahead we discovered a privacy. No one looked down the hole.

"It looks like someone went through a lot of trouble for wizards to live here," said Kitara.

"Creepy people live under rock," said Talindra.

"If a few wizards lived here, the halls were lit, and we heard sounds, this wouldn't be so creepy," I said.

Talindra shrugged.

"Maybe if they cut in a skylight for sun," said Marick. "I'm going to go with Talindra on this one."

"Did you hear that?" asked Daisidian.

"That sounded like a wyvern," whispered Kelgolor.

We stopped. A loud breath snorted.

"Something with a long snout," agreed Marick.

Back in our marching order, we moved again, traveling back to the first T-junction and continuing until we hit another T-junction.

The breathing got stronger and louder after we turned right. A loud snort sounded, followed by a couple of loud clumping footsteps.

Kitara and Talindra surrounded a door to the left. Daisidian looked in, and we opened it. Kitara charged left, Talindra right. "Hold up," said Kitara. "It's only books."

I walked past them and looked. Magical books and research material filled the shelves. "Let's take these and look at them later," I said.

Everyone shrugged, but soon we had three dozen books in my handkerchief. We continued on, and lights turned on in the hallway. The hallway dead-ended, but to the left a large archway opened into a dark room. Daisidian snuck, peered in, and returned.

"There's a large wingless wyvern in the room," he said.

"Scordron."

"We all got a chuckle that you didn't recognize a wyvern," said Kitara.

"I still like scordron."

"If it's like a wyvern but has no wings, we'll call it a scordron," said Marick. "But if they cut its wings off, it's still a wyvern."

We walked to the end. Kitara wanted Talindra and Marick to go right, and he charged left. Daisidian and I charged up the middle.

The beast roared and belched fire at the door. I dove to the right, and the heat passed by me.

Talindra and Kitara had flanked its sides and slashed at it.

It tried to bite at Marick, but he got out of the way and swung his mace.

I cast *Fistful of Fires* at it and looked for other threats. When I turned back around, Daisidian pulled two daggers out of the top of its head.

"It's a scordron, OG. No wings or muscles for wings.

"This is a strange dungeon. Why have such wimpy battles?" asked Talindra.

"We weren't supposed to make it here, and this is how the lair would be without an ambush from the Vrelth," I said.

"Do you all fight life-and-death battles so often that this is nothing to you?" asked Kelgolor.

We were silent.

"Well, they called it a Wizard Research Center, not something cool like Lair of the Mad Mage," said Kitara.

"But you went through a door, then a puzzle room, then torture rooms, and then you found the actual facility and you shrug this off as one lair. You only have one tough fight and you're disappointed. Are you all crazy?"

We walked to the end of the original hallway. Kitara walked to the left of the door, Talindra to the right. Daisidian checked for traps. We opened the door and searched a large empty lab with multiple desks scattered around.

Kelgolor said, "There it is, way up on the ledge next to a chest."

This seemed suspicious. "Everyone, get a good view of that ledge. I'm going to bring Kelgolor up there. We'll grab the items and come back down."

Everyone got in position, and Daisidian and Kitara pulled out bows. I grabbed Kelgolor and cast *Material Jump*.

We grabbed the chest and put it into the handkerchief. Kelgolor grabbed the piece, pulled out a longer piece of wood, which fused with the final section and became a staff. I cast *Material Jump* and brought us back with the chest.

We walked back to the room selector.

"One direction left," said Talindra.

Once everyone had walked inside, I pointed to the east door. I put the circle shape on the second lever and the triangle on the fourth level and pushed the button.

The west door closed, and the east door opened. We found a ten-foot-long hallway that ended in a normal door. Daisidian checked it for traps, and Kitara moved down the hall opened, the door and turned left, Marick following and turning right. "More bear thralls."

The rest of us charged.

Two devices similar to the one we'd destroyed in Avaris' lair sat on opposite sides of the room. Only the supported balls were black, and instead of quartz, they'd used onyx. Four bear thralls stood in the room near the device at the far end of the room.

We'd killed twelve who had the support of a mage yesterday, so they posed no problem. I supplemented the team with *Fistful of Fires* until the bears were dead. Then, using my materials power, I pulled the four onyxes from the smaller of the two black orbs.

The room measured forty feet wide and a hundred feet long. A large hole opened to the outside on the south wall next to the device. Someone had exposed the large orb to the outside.

"This has to be one of the three amplifiers. Back in the hallway."

Everyone backed behind me, and I cast my first extended *Argrenn's Explosive Cloud* on the small device. It left nothing but tiny pieces.

"Maybe a test device they left running," said Daisidian.

"They tested the device on bears and let them run back into the open," said Kitara.

I pulled the onyx out of the large device and the large orb fell, broke, and let out black smoke.

I cast a second *Argrenn's Explosive Cloud,* and only pieces of the second device fell to the floor.

"We've already done good work," said Kelgolor. "Stopped suffering and at least slowed the recreation of the armies."

"Still work to do," said Marick.

"We need to bind up and catch our breaths," said Kitara.

"Guys, this is the end. How does this plan sound? I create a circle. I drop off Kelgolor, pop back here, and all of us go to Schlobir Wap."

"Wait, did you get a soundtrack in your head today?" joked Kitara?

While I laughed and shook my head, everyone else sat to catch their breath.

Kelgolor handed me a piece of paper with circle coordinates on it. I created a circle, focused on the symbols, and brought him to a circle inside of a building. They'd made the walls of white rock, and sand covered the floor. The room looked similar to the building I had destroyed when I'd rescued Daisidian, but Kelgolor seemed happy and took off, shouting orders to others.

After focusing on the symbols to my temporary circle, I was back in the dungeon, but trapped in a cloudy white ball.

A fuzzy image applauded my arrival with a slow clap. Blue bars surrounded the party.

"Your smart-ass attitude has annoyed me for months," said Feston. "I swallowed my pride and retreated more than once, but I watched."

I cast *Material Jump* to get to the floor, but the spell failed.

"Interesting that you let me get out a full sentence before you tried to kill me, but today it is futile. This is months of planning to hurt you—just as I promised. "

"Feston, you are the only one who will hurt."

"Good, stay angry. You make so many wonderful decisions when you are angry. But this barrier prevents you and your powers from passing. Plus, attacking a tier three party does me no harm. Congratulations on the leveling."

I had to listen and needed to stay calm. Feston had the upper hand.

"Magic is so finicky. I created a cage that prevented most powers. The cage could not stop all powers nor cause damage to the trapped. But I made a cage that blocks your wife's and friends' powers, even if I left it susceptible to yours."

Susceptible to mine. My first hint.

"But I needed more. I had to trap you in a spell that only blocked your powers so you would know who caused your suffering. That stupid spell does nothing except stop planar material magic and your silly little other power. I like what Talindra calls it—your gardening power." He smiled while he narrowed his eyes.

He must have spent an obscene amount of time watching us.

"Imagine my surprise for you to announce your location by breaking my spare amplifier and separating from your team long enough for me to arrive and cast both spells."

Why didn't I bring everyone?

"I know you found my lair, but previous adventurers lost the key. Fifty years now, and I learned it is not on Geoe. I have searched."

Did the Groove Train have the key? Had they stored it off-world? How?

"So, I will bring this cage and watch your friends die. They will lose hope and lose the will to live over the upcoming decades. I will watch you suffer, as you cannot rescue them from a place only I can reach."

"What do you want from this?" I tried to keep him talking.

"Don't you remember our talk on the ship? Nothing but your suffering. This is payback for you acting like a jerk. My plans will go off, regardless. Bye now. I'll watch you struggle on the big screen."

The ball blurred my sight too much to see the party's condition.

He prepared a spell to leave. "One more thing, sweetheart." He emphasized the insult I'd used on him before I gained control of my mouth. "An off-world alloy made of non-metals surrounds my crypt. Your powers cannot break through it." He laughed. It wasn't an evil laugh. It was a joyful laugh at my suffering.

My materials' power couldn't reach through the bubble. I wanted to keep him talking. There had to be more information. "How about we fight one-on-one?"

"I don't have your ego problems or your over confidence problems. By the way, a genuine leader wouldn't have left his team vulnerable. Look at them struggle, trying to use the little earrings. I wish I could share the panic on your wife's face with you."

He grabbed the cage, finished his spell, and left.

I dropped out of his bubble to the floor. He'd taken Talindra. I needed to get to Schlobir Wap and get help. Saving my use of extensions proved the correct decision. I had to save them until I found my team.

I would rescue my team. And my wife. I cannot fail the team again.

Chapter 20

In Schlobir Wap, I ran out of the extension house and to the front entrance. The gnomes, their morale broken and shoulders slumped, were falling back. Mayor Whizzburr walked in a circle, muttering, his wide eyes darting about.

"Whizzburr," I shouted.

It's time to lift Whizzburr.

He grabbed his horse's reins and turned him. "Most unusual. Most unusual."

"Friends help friends, and I arrived to help you."

With my staff, I broadcast my voice. "Schlobir Wap. Rally on the mayor!"

"Ma—me?"

"Whizzburr." I examined his eyes, waited for them to calm, and held his shoulders. "I believe in you. Light your beacon."

He smiled, held his scepter up, and yelled, "You found me! Now others need to find me." He held the scepter and lit the beacon, yelling, "Rally on me!" The beacon lit up high into the air and gnomes stopped retreating and regrouped around the mayor.

Yuennui broke through and I ripped up the earth under the invaders with my materials' power.

I want them to win, but I cannot do it for them.

Gnomes repeated the call, "Rally on the mayor."

I ripped up the ground in front of the organizing gnomes and threw it at the invaders. It didn't do much damage. It was a diversion, as I couldn't exhaust myself with extensions yet.

Halflings with slings formed up behind the mayor and me and sent a slew of bullets at the invaders.

Gnomes formed a line with their shields.

The boom of gunfire rang out, and I reached out and sensed the lead coming toward me. Now that I was a Master of the Prime Material, the enemy better not bring metalloids near me either.

"Incoming!" yelled the gnomes as they hit the ground behind the shields.

My materials' power caught the bullets and stacked them near the halflings. The gnomes and halflings formed up lines and moved forward in practiced military precision. Slings softening up the enemy for the gnomes to move into melee.

A bunch of light bullets very close. No extension needed. I asked my brain for a soundtrack to keep me focused. Run-DMC's <u>It's Tricky</u> started playing. *I'll take it.*

The Yuennui turned and fled. It was a pullback to the rest of the army. They ran to the eastern entrance to reform. There, another battle took place where the gnomes had constructed their airships. Engines sputtered to life, and the whirrs of propellors overwhelmed the battlefield.

The troops I followed led me there. I ripped up the ground underneath the Yuennui army to shake their confidence. Gnomes cheered. A gnome on horseback rode by me with a flag of Schlobir Wap. With my staff, I levitated over the battlefield. The gnome army on the eastern side, led by Zyronk, Grehn, Thralk, and Brigham, charged the enemy.

I projected my voice and called out, "Brigham, lead your troops onto the east flank!"

The canyon left the enemy one place to retreat, and they setup a retreat location in the back, where I found Feston standing with the largest Yuennui Teuer I had ever seen.

An idea came to mind with my brain's soundtrack, taking advantage of his constant viewing of me. I ripped up a bunch of earth and sent it toward him. Feston grabbed the large Yuennui and a squad of Yuennui soldiers and disappeared before the ground covered them.

It worked! He thought I would throw a whole extended pile of earth at him instead of a distraction, and he left the battlefield. Chalk one up for too much information.

The gnome army behind Whizzburr charged the flank of the army.

Guns fired again.

I reached out and caught the lead bullets and stacked them under me. The halflings picked them up if they needed them, using them in their slings.

Brigham's troops faced a large group, and once again I tore the earth up under their feet. The Yuennui fell to the ground as an airship flew over the battle and dropped an explosive into the middle of the army.

Boom.

Yuennui flew in all directions. Another spurt of shots rang out, and I grabbed the lead from the air and pulled the bullets back into my pile.

A loud horn sounded and we watched as the Yuennui retreated.

I projected my voice and ordered over the battlefield, "Stay in formation. Form on the Mayor's beacon." I ripped up the earth behind the invaders. The gnome armies caught the Yuennui on the ground and laid into them. Whizzburr aligned the gnomes into makeshift squads and led them to harangue the retreating troops, then called back. Good call. The gnomes ran out of energy and no longer maintained squad positions. They risked becoming strung out.

I projected my voice again: "Regroup on the mayor."

After lowering myself, I summoned Starlight and rode to Brigham and the guards.

He and the Persevering team were binding each other's wounds.

"Brigham, status?"

"I left a token force, but no forces attacked the Salas Keep."

"You did excellent. Return to the keep when you are ready. We have held Schlobir Wap."

I glanced around, taking stock of the fighters, and caught sight of Dean Mehli discussing something with Fergus. I dispelled Starlight and ran up to them.

"Feston captured Talindra and the rest of the team." I knew my voice sounded desperate, but I didn't care. They had won the battle here. Now, I focused all my attention on getting back what I had lost.

Fergus looked at Dean Mehli. "That's the answer—today. Grab Jealder and tell Lighttouch it's today. I'll grab Zyronk."

The dean looked at me and said, "Let's go to the temple."

Joined by Braun, we walked into the temple. Braun said, "It's an immediate attack. Fergus and Zyronk will be back soon."

Lighttouch stared at me. "Oh, dear. He has her, doesn't he?"

I tried to answer, but the words caught in my throat.

"Well, a good night's sleep and full strength didn't work. Gather around the statue, and I'll make preparations."

I followed Braun and the dean and sat next to them.

"Where is Jealder?"

"You mean General Jealder Braun Gr'Gra?" asked Timeonne.

"You didn't have everything figured out," said Braun.

"That was the last piece. I made sense of the bread crumbs. You joined an off-planet military to take the key off-world and returned with a new identity."

He laughed. "By the way, I like the term *cool beans*."

"You're the man from the note. You didn't slip up once with the lingo from your generation."

He winked. "Forty years in the military will change one's vernacular."

Fergus and Zyronk ambled in. A sweat covered Zyronk, but he smiled. "Fifty years, man."

Dean Mehli tapped me. "One more thing. This is my last chance to tell you. When we win, I have to start the calming."

"I haven't figured out one thing. Once mages retire, they are no threat to the Vrelth. Why are mages hunted?"

"I'm not privy to that information, but I think Dean Jarlenteria suspects something."

Lighttouch walked over. "We will take the temple's blessing and enter."

Two clerics strode over and initiated a magical ritual around the statue. Lighttouch sat next to Braun. I knew he was Jealder, but I'd always think of him as Braun.

A warm golden light surrounded us, and I felt my body absorb it.

I cast *Timeonne's Spirit Entrapment*, and a small birdcage hung from my bandolier. My spell-absorption stone contained a bunch of power I used to recharge my spells. *Nine incantations, seven formulas, three conjurations, and six of my extra spells left.*

Lord Fergus handed pads out to every member of the Groove Train. Feston had made a rule over fifty years ago to stop us, and today we use that rule for a second chance.

We stood.

"I accept the second-chance quest as leader of the Groove Train," said Braun.

"I unretire to accept the second chance of a failed quest and reform the Groove Train," said Dean Mehli.

Lord Fergus stood at the front. "I unretire to accept the second chance of a failed quest and reform the Groove Train."

Lighttouch wiped tears from her eyes. "I unretire to accept the second chance of a failed quest and reform the Groove Train to avenge my husband."

"I unretire to accept the second chance of a failed quest and re-form the Groove Train to prove love conquers all," said Zyronk.

"The Groove Train is back in action," said Braun.

Zyronk roared.

The two clerics pulled the statue back and revealed a set of stairs.

"Guys, Feston is stronger and smarter. If we see the Guardian Knights, set a strategy for a long fight to allow for both teams to engage," I said.

We walked into a small chamber with a giant stone door with a pattern carved into it.

"Good idea, Argrenn. Get them released and come back," said Braun. "Remember, we need a battlefield leader. It's the key to succeeding."

Braun held out his hands and cast *Bring it Back*. A large piece of metal in the inset's shape in the door appeared in his hands.

Fergus held out his hand and cast something on me. "You can't tell, but you are invisible until you attack."

He put the metal in the inset, and the door slid open.

We walked in to an enormous cavern.

Two stood in front of ten Yuennui Teuer, Feston, and the largest Yuennui Teuer I have ever seen.

"A Vrelth," said Braun.

Sheer walls surrounded us, but I landed on the level above us.

"I told you fifty years ago, Feston, the Groove Train would run you down," shouted Zyronk, and he charged.

Feston levitated and shouted. "Urnovher, meet them with your troops. Isilring, take your archers and provide cover."

Urnovher stood up and shook his Yuennui form off. Vrelth were like Yuennui Teuers without the snake features. He had a salamander complexion now. His bladed weapon matched the Vrelth weapons from the jail, with inputs for tentacles from his head and arm.

"He's a Vrelth. We only see three quarters of him with our eyes and the Scythreaver he wields will poison you," shouted Braun.

We had given Kelgolor his best opportunity, since the Vrelth, Urnovher, stood in the crypt.

I levitated to the left cliff as the Groove Train rushed to meet Urnovher and the Yuennui. On the ledge, I ran for the cage. Using my sapphire earring. *On my way. Get ready to fight.*

I focused on my diamond earring. *On my way. Get ready to fight.*

Talindra and Kitara stood. They helped up Marick and Daisidian. The four of them drew weapons. Across on the right cliff, Lord Isilring of Sardyna's noble court had elite archers lined up to provide support. More intelligence we missed.

Feston laughed at them. "You worms can relax. These has-beens have lost once already. None of them have the power to break the bars. Your precious Argrenn is getting run over by an army without you to protect him. I believe he may already be dead, because he tried to make a hero of that little mayor."

The Yuennui by Urnovher darted around rocks and stalagmites in front of the giant crypt in the huge cavern where the crypts sloped down to the floor. They had a planned defense to engage the Groove Train.

I heard Lighttouch scream at Feston's mention of her son and celestial flames came down on Feston. Feston burned, tried to swear, and ran towards his crypt while shouting orders to Urnovher and Isilring.

I heard a thumping beat and a guitar in my head. *Sorry, brain, I'm here to lead, not kill.* I recognized Sabaton's <u>Carolus Rex</u> and knew my brain was one step ahead of me. Music to lead an army into battle. First, I needed my half of the army. I levitated and reached out to the bars. They weren't iron or copper. I knew that metal from my navy days: hafnium. It had six stable isotopes. Nuclear reactors used them as control rods. No wonder Feston had made such a strong cage of protection from it.

I lifted the cage, crumpled it, threw it at Feston, casting *Aumentor Masa*. He plummeted to the floor to duck out of the way. He couldn't stop my spell. With my staff, I projected my voice and called out, "Kitara and Marick, join the Groove Train. Talindra, take on Feston. Braun, you have reinforcements. You can send two up to the archers."

The Yuennui charged directly into the Groove Train, and Braun could not spare two people to the archers. All the arrows were poison tipped and wood. They were ready for me and I could do nothing with wooden arrows. The arrows rained down and Lighttouch could barely keep her team healed.

I cast *Duplicate Me* and went to Dean Mehli. I grabbed him and levitated the two of us up the right cliff. "Take out the archers."

Daisidian hid to backstab Feston as I cast *Remove Presence* on the vampire. There was a risk since it was an untested spell, but now was not the time for worry. I stayed in the air and watched the battle unfold. The Groove Train needed an advantage, so I cast *Manos Planas* onto the Yuennui, fighting the Groove Train to give them an advantage.

Daisidian successfully stabbed Feston, so I focused on Urnovher, who hid behind a rock, flicking his tentacles toward anyone who got close. I cast my extended *Argrenn's Explosive Cloud* on the rock he hid behind. Marick helped Lighttouch heal, and I saw bright blue arcs of lightning from Dean Mehli and the screams of the archers haunted me, especially when they re-animated into undead archer thralls. I levitated over the middle of the battlefield to keep a good watch.

"That's the second spell you have not cast before. When you lose, you will only make it harder for the mages that follow you."

I didn't care what he had to say. I would unload on him and turn into a full Tuathan and sleep for a week if I needed to kill him.

I didn't take the bait and focused on Urnovher. Talindra and Daisidian kept them covered. I cast *Jagula Segura* and fashioned the cloud to catch Urnovher and as many of his soldiers as possible. *That should pull him out.*

A quick check on Feston showed he'd faded and become solid. When he faded, Talindra did more damage to him. This is why I needed to be above the battlefield. Something happened, and I needed to collect intelligence.

"Kitara and Marick, focus on Urnovher. He's about to run out of cover. Pay attention to his blade."

Marick's bell appeared, and Kitara threw a giant ball of fire into my *Jagula Segura.*

I cast two extended *Ice Balls* into Urnovher. *Nine incantations, four formulas, one conjuration, and three of my six extra spells left.*

Kitara sliced Urnovher and two of his tentacles fell off, then Marick bashed him. I cast two more extended *Ice Balls* into him.

Suddenly, the ceiling rose, and a giant red dragon appeared. He flew toward me, knocking stalactites off the ceiling in a frenzy, trying to fit his giant wingspan in the top of the tapered cavern, and breathing flaming magma. I cast my latest of the master extension, *Material Jump,* with no preparation, and jumped behind the dragon before it hit me. I cast *Aumentor Masa* on the beast, and it plummeted to the ground. What a bad summons. Feston was in a full panic. This dragon needed room to fly to bring its breath weapon to bear.

From this vantage point, I got a good look at the necromantic portal which amplified the pyramid's abilities. They hid it behind a group of rocks that jutted out from the right cliff at the cavern wall. I ripped the four onyx that supported the ball with my materials' power, and the black ball crashed to the ground.

A boom resonated but was nothing like the signal blocker in Avarais' crypt. The emanating black smoke didn't come close to the battlefield.

"There go your resurrections," I shouted with an amplified voice.

"The archers are down!" shouted Dean Mehli.

"So are the Yuennui soldiers," shouted Braun.

The sound of the battle had changed. Gone were the cries of my teams and instead I head confident calls to each other.

I took a rock from the top of the cliff and crashed it on the dragon's head, trapping it so it couldn't bite or breathe magma. The dragon's body thrashed, but with its wings trapped between the cliff walls, too heavy to stand, and its head caught, the poor beast's attempts were futile.

"That's how you cheated before, Feston," shouted Zyronk as he charged the dragon in a frenzy. His giant sword moved as fast as a dagger. I didn't know Zyronk's fascination with killing the dragon, but there was no stopping a barbarian in relentless charge.

I suddenly realized why Feston had faded. He had a second body. "Feston has two bodies!" I warned and quickly cast Planar Reflection on the second body, watching it light up with primal power. I caught Daisidian's eye and watched him hide to run to Feston safely.

Urnovher kept the others at bay with the reach of his poisoned blade, but the many wounds all over his slithery body showed how wounded he was. Kitara cast green spells, Marick hit him with celestial bolts and the Groove Train pummeled and sliced him. I added a *Planar Destruction* at him and an extended *Ice Ball*.

I had missed most of the attacks on Urnovher, but Kitara and Braun did a dance around the Vrelth and his Scythreaver. Marick jumped from behind a pile of rocks and took Urnovher's distraction with me, jumped up, and brought the full power of his bell with a mace slam, while Kitara stepped in and pierced his chest with his blade.

Urnovher collapsed in a pile of green blood and died. Lord Isil-ring teleported out under a lightning barrage from Dean Mehli. Lighttouch healed arrow wounds and poison whip marks on the team. The arrows had almost turned the battle, but Lighttouch could heal even faster than Marick.

"Kitara and Marick, focus on Feston, but surround him to avoid his balls of fire. Dean, help Zyronk finish the dragon. Braun and Fergus, help surround Feston, but don't give enough room for his balls of fire to hit more than two of us."

"I'll fight you one-on-one, Argrenn," shouted Feston. "It's what you wanted."

That made me smile. Feston got desperate and now jumped to the other body, where Talindra was ineffective, but Daisidian put a kill shot on that body and Feston barely made it back to his main body in time.

Daisidian limped over to help the team. Everyone had blood on them and rent armor. But they all stood and no one needed to be pulled away. We had this battle if we did not make a mistake.

"You had that chance." I paused and added, "enemy of Earth."

"I'm the one that kidnapped your wife."

"Sorry, Feston. I'm a leader, not a killer." I spammed *Argrenn's Acid Attack* onto the back of the dragon while avoiding Zyronk.

Feston jumped over to near Urnovher's body but I could tell he was hurt from his crooked stance.

"Spread out before you follow. Don't let him get the upper hand with his area of effect spells."

Both my teams coordinated and spread out. I surveyed the field. Feston in one body was all that was left, and we had him cornered. He would lash out like any trapped animal now. They knocked the stalagmites over and they circled him in an area devoid of rocks.

He popped back under me and said, "Then you can eat my spells."

He cast two balls of fire at me. My cast of *Duplicate Me* came too late. Both balls of fire hit me. I didn't have any damage, though. My duplicate disappeared before it formed, and I levitated sixty feet away.

My dagger felt warm, and I only had a few first-degree burns on me. They stung, but nothing hurt and my skin did not sizzle like on the boat. Test of the new dagger completed satisfactorily. *Five incantations, two formulas, zero conjurations, and one of my extra spells left.* With my diamond earring, I sent, *we need butt kicking Talindra now. No defense.* I threw an extended formula-strength *Fistful of Fire* before the party arrived, followed by a second. They both hit and he caught on fire.

The teams had closed in and surrounded Feston.

"When I say go, everyone unloads on Feston. We must do damage quickly."

I waited for Marick's bell to appear and shouted, "Go!"

Without the help of Geoe, I cast my last six incantations as *Ice Balls* at him and followed with *Fistful of Fires*.

Feston screamed and sent two more area of affect fireballs at me.

A shield from Talindra surrounded me, and the fireballs never hit me. They engulfed the shield and perverted it, and the entire mess blew up around me.

I looked up and saw Lighttouch. The noise had quieted and at my waist, a birdcage contained a little Feston. There was no sound, but he looked mad. Captured, defeated, after his many decades of planning, of killing, of running amok, cheating his way through the game. It was finally over.

I handed the bird cage to Dean Mehli. The teams lay on the rock ground or leaned against the left cliff. I was next to the scales of the red dragon's tail.

Relief washed through me as I looked around at those who had come together for this. No casualties, each one of them brave, heroic, Friends.

"Did you make my boy a hero?" Lighttouch looked at me wistfully. Blood covered her immaculate robes even though I saw no wounds on her. Her healing kits lay splayed on the ground and were nearly empty.

I shook off my confusion and held Lighttouch's hand. "He was already a hero. I helped him to realize who he was."

The Groove Train had taken the bulk of the early damage. Zyronk collapsed under the weight of his wounds. He lost his sandals and blood covered his feet. Fergus and Braun lay on their backs, covered in blood. Lighttouch and Dean Mehli staggered over and sat next to their friends and held them.

Talindra kneeled and cried next to me. "I failed. You told me to go all offense and my failure almost killed you."

"No, like leadership was a process for me. Aggression will be a process for you."

Kitara hugged Talindra. "I missed the intelligence from the nobles about the Isilring deception. People must have noticed the elite archers missing."

Marick walked over and healed Zyronk. Then he patted Kitara's and Talindra's shoulder. "Last I heard, the Vrelth still attacked Earth. These weren't failures, just setbacks."

Braun came over and sat with his teammates. "Last I checked, you defeated the Vrelth agent with the help of the Groove Train, and for the first time in a century a team from Earth has a chance to compete in the game and you have a real chance to grab the hearts and minds of the galaxy."

"Darn right." I embraced my wife, kissed her brow and took another look around at the effort spent here. Then I borrowed a dagger from Daisidian, sliced through Feston's robes, and cut out his heart.

When I did, spirits left that undead body. The fifth spirit to float out appeared as a half-elven woman with flowers in her hair and a flowing lace dress. "I love you always," her spirit said as it floated away.

Braun collapsed and cried and laughed.

Another spirit, a gnome man, rose. "Love conquered all, and I'm proud of how you raised our son," before that spirit disappeared, too.

The whole Groove Train collapsed onto the ground.

"Fifty years, man. It's over."

"It's over," said Lord Fergus.

"Kelgolor has the staff and said he would march his troops on the pyramid. We want to make sure we destroy the armies of Yuen-nui, and I need to blow up this crypt."

"Man, blow it up. Love has triumphed, and I'm tired," said Zyronk. "Living is not important now."

No one corrected him. "Living is the silver lining," I said. I winked at Talindra, who smiled in spite of herself.

"I don't know why," said Zyronk.

"You all heard of the Grateful Dead, right?" I knew they did, but I wanted to set them up for the values that set them on a fifty-year mission.

They looked at me but didn't seem to want to answer. After an awkward minute, Dean Mehli said, "On our last night on Earth, that was our last concert together."

"Truckin' is in the Library of Congress as a natural treasure."

They didn't believe me.

"It's true," added Talindra. She wiped away her tears.

"They did a couple more studio albums, but one in my generation. Listen to one song before you decide."

Lord Fergus chuckled. "One song to change our mind after fifty years of planning and a success?"

"Kitara, can you search for and project the video of a Grateful Dead song called *Touch of Gray*?"

Kitara looked at me like a grew a second head, but wiped away his tears and pulled out his pad. Soon, the video played against the cliff, and when it finished, Zyronk said, "That's not fair, man." Their eyes gave them away. They were coming back with us.

I brought the explosive from my office with the *Bring it Back* spell.

"I wondered what you had in that sack," said Braun. I'd never think of him as Jealder.

"Avaris had carried this. The necromancer should have buried us on our second day on Geoe. Only he tried to kill us instead. When we killed that party, Avaris had to retrieve another explosive. That's why he showed up too late to kill us. I've had this ever since."

"He bought the wax and decanter with a story of how he wanted to mix a fancy drink from home," said Kitara, and he laughed.

Talindra finished her prayer, and a golden light appeared over us and healed most of everyone's wounds.

Kitara offered his hand to Lord Fergus, and he stood. Dean Mehli stood up and said, "I'll be in the calming when you see me next."

Lighttouch kissed me on the cheek. "Thank you for this, and helping my son reach his potential."

Zyronk and Talindra helped me place the explosives under the crypt.

"Are we ready?"

We were the last three in there. I set the timer for two minutes, and we ran out. They closed the door behind us, and we sprinted up to the temple, where they put the statue back in place.

I hugged Talindra, and she hugged me back, then I sat back in a blue chair in the temple. The confidence that I knew everything that had happened, why it had happened, and that we had a direct path to save Earth in front of us was comforting.

The muffled explosion shook the floor. But today, nothing else mattered.

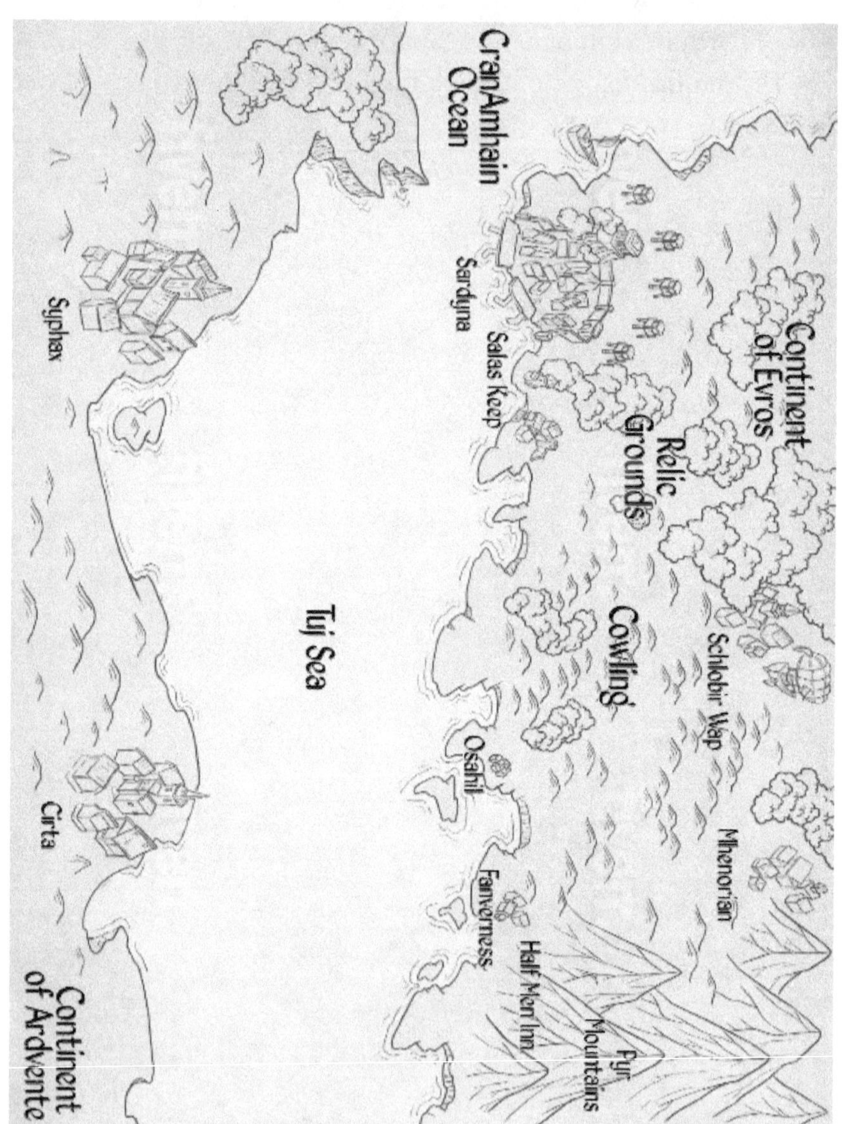
CranAmhain Ocean
Continent of Evros
Sardyna
Salas Keep
Relic Grounds
Cowling
Schlobir Wap
Mhenorian
Tuj Sea
Osahil
Fanvertress
Half Men Inn
Pyr Mountains
Syphax
Cirta
Continent of Ardvente

Argrenn's Spell Book

	Spell Name	**Power**
0	Fistful of Fire	Glamor
	Planar Pull	Glamor
Tier 1		
1.2	Planar Reflection	Incantation
	Magical Friend	Incantation
	Duplicate Me	Incantation
	Planar Platform	Ritual
	Planar Butler	Ritual
1.3	Body Extension	Glamor
	Ice Ball **Extended**	Incantation
	Espuma Inflam	Glamor
	Duplicate Me and Body Extension *	Additive Extension*
1.4	Shards of Glass	Incantation
	Planar Obscurement	Incantation
	Planar Winter	Incantation
	Planar Protection	
Tier 2		
2.1	Aumentor Masa	Formula
	Manipulate Own Material	Formula
	Fistful of Fire **Extended**	Incantation or Formula
	Planar Escape **Extended**	Incantation
	Planar Pull and Planar Escape*	Additive Extension*
2.2	Rotten Material	Formula
	Torre Mirador	Formula
	Manos Planas	Formula
2.3	Planar helper	Formula

	Trailing Pain	Formula
	Argrenn's Acid Attack	Glamor
	Manos Planos and Jagula Segura*	Additive Extension*
2.4	Material Jump	Conjuration
	Planar Destruction	Conjuration
	Jagula Segura	Conjuration
2.5	Create Circle	Conjuration
	Planar Swords	Conjuration
	Caja Fuerte	Conjuration
	Planar Stair Case	Incantation
	Material Abundance	Formula
	Duplicate Me by thought only**	Master Extension**
	Extended Ice Ball double and Split**	Master Extension**
Tier 3		
3.1	Timeonne's Spirit Entrapment	Conjuration
	Create Spring	Conjuration
	Create Air	Conjuration
	Bring it Back	Ritual
	Create Presence	Ritual
	Create Room	Ritual
3.2	Other World Viewing	Conjuration
	Argrenn's Explosive Cloud **extended**	Conjuration
	Ball of Air	Conjuration
	Remove Presence	Conjuration
	Material Jump by Reaction**	Master Extension**
3.3	Bubble of Life	Conjuration
	Planar Anchor	Conjuration
	Iron Guardian	Conjuration

Extended Ice Ball and Extended Ice Ball* Additive Extension*

* Additive extensions Count as one spell.

Don't miss out!

Visit the website below and you can sign up to receive emails whenever Shawn McGee publishes a new book. There's no charge and no obligation.

https://books2read.com/r/B-A-MTXT-AYTZB

BOOKS 2 READ

Connecting independent readers to independent writers.

Did you love *The Regnant*? Then you should read *TheVanquisher* by Shawn McGee!

Paladins filled the Knights of Honor Guild Hall. Every eye watched the Argrenn Dawnstrike on the screen struggle against barbed bindings. The room fell silent; the demons cut Argrenn off from his source of power and the archmage was a ninety-eight-pound weakling trapped in hell.

"You will die here today and your team will know foolishness caused you to abandon them." The demon kneeled on his hooves to taunt Argrenn face to face.

"Open the door!" Talindra Dawnstrike screamed and unhooked her shield.

"A lone paladin in hell against five demons?" Her elven friend Shelley tried to get Talindra's attention.

"That is my husband. Open the door!"

"Make a path." Cassiel held the door open and his order parted the room.

Argrenn laughed. "You're in trouble now. When I hear music, I'm about to dominate."

"What do you hear?" taunted the demon.

"I hear..." Argrenn frowned. "Chick music?"

A magma javelin flew.

Talindra screamed and threw her shield across the planes. The magic lit up the guild hall and all shielded their eyes. They knew Talindra blocked that javelin, and Talindra followed her shield.

Read more at https://WorldofGeoe.com.